deep in providence

PRAISE FOR *DEEP IN PROVIDENCE*

"Haunting, intimate, and beautifully told:
a magical debut novel from a writer to watch."
—EMILY M. DANFORTH, bestselling author of
The Miseducation of Cameron Post and *Plain Bad Heroines*

"Magic runs like a glittering thread through this densely
woven tale of friendship, grief, and identity, and what begins
as a backbeat of creeping dread deftly builds into a landscape of
supernatural terrors. Neilson balances her page-turning fantasy
narrative against the coming of age of a trio of bereaved best
friends with grace, delicacy, and startling humanity."
—MELISSA ALBERT, *New York Times*–bestselling author
of *The Hazel Wood* and *Our Crooked Hearts*

"A spellbinding tale of friendship and grief told with
startling tenderness and emotional truth."
—RYAN DOUGLASS, *New York Times*–bestselling author
of *The Taking of Jake Livingston*

"A beautiful exploration of friendship, grief, and love that
transcends everything—even death—*Deep in Providence* is a
searing debut novel. It is the perfect combination of terror
and tenderness."
—LILLIE LAINOFF, author of *One for All*

"With intricately woven storytelling that blends hurt and
hope, magic and secrets, *Deep in Providence* follows three teen

girls as they journey through love and loss, exploring the complexities of grief with raw, heartfelt honesty. Riss M. Neilson has crafted an absorbing debut that will hold readers spellbound."
—LYNDALL CLIPSTONE, author of *Lakesedge*

"Equal parts haunting and healing, *Deep in Providence* takes an intricate look at grief, family, spirituality, and love through the lenses of three magical girls on the edge of adulthood. A bittersweet story that's sure to linger in readers' hearts."
—RACQUEL MARIE, author of *Ophelia After All*

"Neilson harnesses the electric power of young female friendship, grief, and magic, in spooky and spellbinding ways. *Deep in Providence* will have you mesmerized from the first page."
—GOLDY MOLDAVSKY, *New York Times*–bestselling author of *The Mary Shelley Club*

"Reader beware: This book will enthrall you. Once I opened it, I could not put it down! By braiding together the perspectives of three bold and nuanced best friends who are grieving the loss of their fourth, Neilson casts a powerful spell that will haunt readers long after the final page. The friendships feel so tangibly real that I miss these girls already—and that's the best kind of magic."
—ROMINA GARBER, bestselling author of *Lobizona*

"Neilson's explorations of grief, love, and friendship are mesmerizing, gut-wrenching, and magical. It's refreshing to see characters who are allowed to make mistakes, who are allowed to grow and learn from their experiences. A spectacularly haunting debut that doesn't shy away from heavy hitting topics, all handled with the kind of tender storytelling that leaves an indelible mark."

—KALYNN BAYRON, bestselling author of
Cinderella Is Dead

"Riss M. Neilson's debut, *Deep in Providence*, is an unmissable read—a haunting and moving story about three girls who turn in desperation to magic after their friend dies in a car accident. This is a beautiful exploration of grief, love, friendship, and family. And Miliani, Inez, and Natalie have an intense depth that will make readers fall in love with them all."

—VANESSA LEN, author of
Only a Monster

"*Deep in Providence* is a searing, beautiful portrait of love and pain. With spellbinding characters and masterfully constructed scenes, this is a book that you can't put down, even when it's breaking your heart."

—KYLIE LEE BAKER, author of
The Keeper of Night

"Mesmerizing, spellbinding, and absolutely entrancing, this book had me wrapped into its magic from the first sentence."

—BELLE ELLRICH, B&N Bookseller,
follow @pagesofbellerose

deep in providence

RISS M. NEILSON

HENRY HOLT AND COMPANY

NEW YORK

Henry Holt and Company, *Publishers since 1866*
Henry Holt® is a registered trademark of
Macmillan Publishing Group, LLC
120 Broadway, New York, NY 10271 • fiercereads.com

Our books may be purchased in bulk for promotional, educational,
or business use. Please contact your local bookseller or the Macmillan
Corporate and Premium Sales Department at (800) 221-7945 ext. 5442
or by email at MacmillanSpecialMarkets@macmillan.com.

Library of Congress Cataloging-in-Publication Data

Names: Neilson, Riss M., author.
Title: Deep in Providence / Riss M. Neilson.
Description: First edition. | New York : Henry Holt Books for
Young Readers, 2022. | Audience: Ages 14-18. | Audience: Grades
10-12. | Summary: After Jasmine is killed in a car accident, her
remaining best friends Miliani, Inez, and Natalie plan to resurrect
her using magic learned from Miliani's Filipino aunt, but their
actions have dangerous consequences that threaten themselves and
those they care about.
Identifiers: LCCN 2021046303 | ISBN 9781250788528 (hardcover) |
ISBN 9781250788511 (ebook)
Subjects: CYAC: Magic—Fiction. | Grief—Fiction. | Death—Fiction. |
Friendship—Fiction. | Providence (R.I.)—Fiction. | LCGFT:
Novels.
Classification: LCC PZ7.1.N417 De 2022 | DDC [Fic]—dc23
LC record available at https://lccn.loc.gov/2021046303

First edition, 2022
Book design by Aurora Parlagreco
Printed in the United States of America

ISBN 978-1-250-78852-8 (hardcover)

1 3 5 7 9 10 8 6 4 2

For my children, My'ah and Jada,
who bring me the moon and the sun
on days I struggle to see magic for myself.

deep in providence

part one

《 ((

THESE LATENT THINGS

providence (noun):

- The protective care of God or of nature as a spiritual power.
- God or nature as providing protective or spiritual care.
- Timely preparation for future eventualities.

Providence (proper noun):

- The capital of Rhode Island, a port near the mouth of the Providence River, on the Atlantic coast; population 171,557 (est. 2008). It was founded in 1636 by Roger Williams (1604–83) as a haven for religious dissenters.

—*Lexico.com, http://www.lexico.com/definition/providence*

1

MILIANI

This isn't the first time I've touched a dead body.

When I was thirteen, I reached into the casket to feel death on my father's skin. We didn't know each other well, and gambling kept him busy. In the end, a heart attack caught him while he was playing keno at a gas station. Mom didn't want to go to his funeral. *He's your father*, she told me. *Maybe you should.* She sent her dad, my papa, along with me instead. As Papa and I peered down into the casket, I thought it was such a pretty body. My father had smooth brown skin, lengthy limbs, and long lashes. I wondered how his spirit felt after being disconnected, since only the body truly dies. Usually when the spirit moves on, it will leave energy behind in a place or an object.

A year later, Papa died, and I touched his body and knew his spirit was elsewhere. Moving. Finding space, like my father's spirit before his.

This feels different. Jasmine's body doesn't feel spiritless. It's firm but not hard—as if I could press against her skin with my finger and remove it to watch the blood circulate. There must have been magic in the embalming to make her feel warm. I reach to stroke her hair, run my thumb across her bottom lip, appreciate how rich with melanin her skin still is and how it contrasts with her white gown, the way it seems to glisten because she's wearing it.

I bite my lip in search of blood. My eyes burn. My stomach feels sick. I can't believe they put her in this dress. This isn't why she was supposed to wear it.

Behind me, someone coughs to signal I've spent my turn at the casket. I don't want to move from this spot. I don't want to leave her. When the person groans, I remind myself there's time to come up again, but I'm already winded when I notice Darleny standing near the entrance of the showing room. She's staring at me, and seeing her after laying eyes on Jasmine's body makes me dizzy. She looks more like her sister than ever before.

Jas and Darleny were identical twins, but they had distinctly different styles, and I could always tell them apart by the dark beauty mark above Jasmine's lip or the light-green specks in her sister's eyes. Darleny's hair falls below her shoulder blades and covers half the bruising on the side of her face from the accident. Her eyes lock with mine across the room. They hold until I blink away, and I swear they are the color of soil instead of bay leaf.

Papa used to say twins can harness more energy than any single born on earth. This is what I told Jas when we tried to get Darleny to practice with us years ago, but even back then, Darleny would call us freaks and threaten to snitch on us for doing dark magic. She had heard terrible things from her vovo who grew up around magic in Cape Verde: stories of witchcraft that could turn its users into monsters. *But no magic is inherently dark,* I'd say.

I wonder if she'll come up to the casket, slide by me, get too close, if I'll have to hear a voice like Jasmine's when I'm not ready.

But she goes to talk to people at the back of the room, and I'm able to slip away.

(☾ (

The cold weather has finally left Rhode Island, but when I step onto the patio, the bare skin below my skirt pricks with goosebumps. A little girl with chocolate on her mouth and two sleek buns at either side of her head walks over and taps my arm. "Pick a number," she says, holding out an origami fortune-teller. I point to the number two, and she opens the flap to tell me I'll always be ugly. I laugh and try to pick another, but she runs to tell someone else's fortune. I'm wishing I had thanked her for mine when I pass a group of students from school and overhear a girl in a yellow beanie say, "I went to all her soccer games last season. Told her she'd be in the major leagues someday."

My feet stop, and even though I tell myself to keep walking, to ignore it, that this happens at funerals, I turn and say, "Jasmine never played sports. You're talking about her sister. The next time you pretend to be a dead person's friend, make sure they're actually dead first."

She stares at me with a round mouth and a tucked jaw. The boy to her left inches closer to her, but everyone's quiet until I turn away. Then, they laugh. I press my tongue against the roof of my mouth, craving the power to make them shut up, but all I have is the urge to leave Bell's and never come back. I shouldn't have to be here. I should be at Jasmine's house, eating half of her couscous, even though I told her I didn't want any, while we watch reruns of *Dragon Ball Z* and cuss about all the commercials. But I can't leave without seeing her body again, without saying goodbye. And I need to see my friends.

❨ ❨ ❨

I find Inez next to the stairs, gripping the patio rail, her knuckles white, her breathing loud. "What happened back there?"

"Nothing important," I tell her because she's already rubbing the bridge of her nose the way she does when she's trying not to panic. I push hair out of her face, watch the tears make trails between the freckles on her cheeks. "Hey, you okay?"

"Of course not," she says. "Jasmine's dead. How are you okay?"

"I'm not," I whisper, and turn to rest against the rail, remembering the warmth in Jasmine's body and wondering if it was there because I wanted it to be. Because with some part of her to hold on to, it might be easier to avoid the facts: Jasmine and Darleny were in a car accident a few days ago. A drunk driver swerved into their lane and hit Darleny's car.

Darleny is still breathing. Jasmine is not.

Inez says sorry, over and over. "I can't believe I said that to you of all people. You're probably in shock." Her words don't make it better. They make it more real. *Take it back*, I want to say. I almost say. She shoves her hands in her coat and looks around. "Where's Natalie? She's late."

And like she manifested our best friend, Nat says, "Right here," in that soft voice of hers.

"Where have you been?" Inez moves past me to fling herself at Natalie, whose eyes go wide before she settles into the hug. Inez's shoulders slack, and she sobs.

Relief makes its way to me. Jasmine's the only one who always knew how to comfort Inez. Without saying a word, she'd know how to move, when to hold her. It seemed like Jas could stop a panic attack with her presence alone. She had a similar effect on all of us. Papa used to call her a "little moon." Controlling movements and emotions with her energy.

I don't think I could've calmed Inez, but Natalie rubs her back and they bury themselves in each other, and as grateful as I am for her—for Inez too—no one can be Jasmine.

"I'm here now. I'm not going anywhere," Nat says, and her words nick pieces of my heart, causing visions of Jas hours before her accident to flood my mind, until I force my focus on my fingers, on the fallen sign on the bodega window across the street, on my friends as Inez's long hair rises in the wind and sweeps across them both.

I fight the urge pulling me to them, the involuntary way my body aches to be hugged too, and find myself watching Natalie as she grips Inez's shoulder blades like she's not sure she should let go. I know why she's late. She's always been more frightened of death than the rest of us, or at least than me. Once, she took a failing grade so she wouldn't have to dissect a frog. Twice, she didn't show up to funerals of people in her own family. Jasmine's will be her first.

((((

Back inside Bell's, we say our condolences. People share memories of Jasmine; they cry a lot. I hope no one asks me to tell them a story because my brain will recount details of the last time I was with her and I can't tell anyone about it. I've been trying to forget it myself. But thankfully, everyone's so swept up in sharing I only have to listen. Her grandfather tells me that a few years ago, "in sweet summer of '98," Jas jumped from a tree onto his parked

Camaro and dented it. He pulls me aside to tell me the same story twenty minutes later. And maybe I'm listening too hard, because I swear Jas laughs. As I watch a kid count to ten on the staircase while others sneak off to find hiding spots behind the chairs their parents are sitting in, I think I hear her again.

I walk back to my friends, sweating and searching their faces, wondering why they don't seem to notice Jas whispering like she's trying to reach through the veil and tell us she's here. When Darleny walks out of the showing room, the whispers stop.

Nat unwinds the shoelace holding her hair in a puff until it falls in a protective circle around her head. "Darleny looks lost. We should go check on her."

Inez agrees, but I quickly shake my head. Darleny and I fought the morning Jasmine died. I'm probably the only person she doesn't want to see here. Inez doesn't argue with me, but I can tell she wants to before they walk off.

I try to look occupied by the floral arrangements, but when Darleny steps back inside the showing room with my friends trailing behind her, I'm so anxious I consider going in after them. I wonder who's at the casket right now, if anyone else felt Jasmine the way I felt her.

I dig my nails into my thigh until it burns, tell myself I'm being delusional. If I go back to Jasmine's body now, it'll be cold, it'll confirm her spirit has gone.

I sit on a chair and try to remember which calming spell works best for Inez because with nothing else to distract me, the memories of Jasmine with a flush in her cheeks and a little rasp in her voice and a beating heart surface again. Three weeks ago, she danced on a platform at her prom-dress fitting, shaking hips that shouldn't belong to a seventeen-year-old girl and teasing, "You see how good this hugs me?"

Now, someone decided it would be beautiful to bury her in that prom dress, but it just makes my skin crawl.

A few days ago, right before death crept up and stole her, we mapped out what would've been the summer of our lives: bouncing from one cookout to the next, dancing on parked cars in random neighborhoods, doing séances in darkened rooms.

My throat feels thick with a cry that may kill me.

Then I hear a scream. Faint, but clear enough it has me running.

I'm out of breath when I make it to the showing room, just in time to see Natalie clinging to the casket, her curls covering her face as she cries.

"Jasmine. Wake up, baby. Open your eyes. You're not dead."

Natalie's voice seems like it's the only sound in the room as everyone stares at her, stunned. But then she shakes Jasmine's body and it all goes to chaos.

Jasmine's mom shrieks, and her husband wraps both arms around her while Darleny hurries to console them. People gasp and curse and pray in Creole. A man I don't recognize is up out of his chair, rushing toward Natalie. I walk as fast as I can, cut him off with my hands in the air. The tattoo on his neck moves when he swallows.

"I'm sorry," I say. "I'll handle this."

He nods but doesn't sit back down.

Natalie's still bent over the casket, her shoulders trembling. I touch her back, try to coax her away, saying things like "C'mon, we have to go," and "We can come up again soon."

She swats at me. "No. They'll bury her alive."

Her fingers shake as she places them on Jasmine's wrist, then her neck. She does this again, and once more before she says, "No pulse. She has no pulse. It doesn't make sense."

"Help me," I whisper to Inez, who's standing stiffly a few feet away. She snaps out of it and shields us from onlookers as I pull a crystal from my pocket. I turn Nat toward me and place the hand holding the crystal on her chest, say her name once, twice, before she finally looks at my face. And then she steps into my arms, her body slumped while she cries.

"Shh. It's okay. I know, I know," I say over and over, so many times I don't sound like myself anymore. I chant a calming spell in her ear. The one Papa would say in Tagalog when I tripped playing hopscotch and scraped my knees, or when he'd pack for his trips to the Philippines. "Let it move through you, let it fill you up, let it go. Let it move through you, let it fill you up, let it go."

I'm not sure it'll work because it's harder to influence others with magic than it is to influence the self. When Natalie's breathing slows, I wonder if it's natural or if it's me.

Her cry goes silent. The residual is a soft, "She's not dead. She can't be dead."

I pull back and place my amethyst in her palm. "You hold this, and it'll help. You remember this one? How powerful it is?"

"I remember," she says, but tilts her head. "She's warm. How is she so warm, Mili?"

It hits me then. Makes my own body temperature rise and brings goosebumps with it. Natalie sees the same thing I saw. She feels it. A spark. A soul. Jasmine's spirit clinging to her body. Not ready to find space and move on.

I open my mouth, my heart beating fast, my body buzzing, then close it when Jasmine's mom's cry breaks through the room again. Here is not the place to speak about this.

I turn back to Nat, but she's scanning our surroundings. "Oh God. What'd I do?"

"It's fine," I tell her. "Get some air outside with Inez, okay?"

Nat tries to make herself smaller as Inez begins to pull her along, but I don't budge.

Inez's eyes flick to me nervously. "You coming?"

"I need more time with Jas," I say, and she hesitates before they leave me.

☾ ☾ ☾

I stay until the crowd in the showing room is sparse, right before they're about to close Jasmine's casket for burial. My voice trembles when I tell her, "We're going to fix this." I linger when I bend to kiss her forehead because my lips tingle against her skin. She's still so warm. I allow the remembering to take hold of me: the look in her eyes the last time I saw them, the way it felt like someone pried open my ribs and ripped my heart from my body when I found out it was the last time she'd look at me. I've told myself for days it couldn't end that way, and I was right.

I straighten out. Breathe. And then look over my shoulder before pulling out my Swiss Army knife and clipping her fingernails one by one.

2

MILIANI

The burial happens in front of me, but I am not here. I'm somewhere outside the cemetery gates with Jas. We are twelve years old, counting the number of penny candies we can buy at the corner store. We are fourteen and hoping our cloaking spell works so the cashier won't notice when we steal Starburst at 7-Eleven. We are seventeen, and we come to the cemetery to talk to the dead, but we are not the dead. I'm alive, and she's alive. We walk, laugh, count graves, share the blunt she rolled up this morning, and read names from tombstones. And all of this happens until the burial is a blur of something that isn't real. It's a haze, foggy and thickened by smoke, my heart hammering the whole time because weed and me don't mesh. And my ex-boyfriend isn't trying to catch my eye while he rubs Darleny's shoulder as she sobs, and Natalie isn't whispering about how ashamed she is when people stare at her, and Inez isn't hyperventilating when they lower the casket.

None of it is happening until I thumb the bag with Jasmine's fingernails in my coat pocket and realize this is real. But maybe it doesn't have to be.

When it's over, Inez thinks I'm going with them to her house. They'll say prayers with her mother. They'll cry and try to eat and talk about how overwhelming it is that Jasmine isn't here.

They look confused when I pull them in for a hug and say there's something I have to do.

Nat clings to me as I try to leave. "What's going on? We could come with you."

I grit my teeth, force myself to linger for another second, wanting to tell them my plan. But not yet. "Make sure to stop at a store before going home, okay?" I say to them. "I promise I'll call tonight."

❲ ❨ ❲

Auntie Lindy's doorbell isn't lit up. It might not work, but I ring it once and a few more times. I'm not sure she even still lives here until she parts the curtains of one of her windows and peers at me through the screen. "Miliani, is that you ringing me wild?"

"It's me, Auntie," I call back. "Sorry." She disappears behind the curtains. Then I wait for a long time on her stoop in the dark. Maybe she's deciding whether to let me up or not.

It's been a year since Mom and I bumped into her at the Filipino market in Cranston. Mom tried for a smile, which Auntie called a good fake one, and while Mom was cashing out, Auntie slipped a piece of paper with her address on it in the palm of my hand. *Shh,* she said. But Mom must have had a feeling because she made sure to remind me why we were keeping our distance from her sister on the ride home. *Your tita has been wrapped up with the dark stuff ever since we lost your lolo. You are not to get involved.*

But the "dark stuff" Mom spoke about was partly derived from the same stuff Papa, my lolo, had taught us. He'd carried his family's practices with him from the Philippines, where he had grown up Catholic while also believing in the spiritual realm. Most particularly, that it was all around us, existing in the soil and the trees and the rocks and the ocean. These are the most common places part of the energy from a person's spirit will rest to watch over their loved ones on earth.

Sometimes, the spirit of a person isn't able to move on to the afterlife. It gets stuck in the purgatory between realms. Papa called those who were stuck wandering spirits. And in rare cases, the luckiest wandering spirits will cling to a person and be free to roam. This is the unluckiest scenario for the person, Papa told me many years ago while we pruned his pear tree in our backyard. *A haunting?* I asked. *The worst kind*, he said, and didn't want to say any more. When he died, I was young and foolish. Had no idea what it meant for a spirit that couldn't move on. I would have welcomed a haunting if it had meant Papa would never leave me, but instead the energy of his spirit rested with the pear tree in our backyard, causing the pears to ripen quicker and taste sweeter. It's in the soil of his garden, preparing the tomatoes for growth. It's turning the grapes on the vines lining our fence a deeper shade of red.

Auntie isn't the only person in our family who believes in the spiritual realm and uses what she learns as fuel for practicing magic, but for some reason, Mom shuns her because of it.

I stand here, wondering if maybe Auntie Lindy's invitation had an expiration date, thinking it probably would've been smart to call from a pay phone before I took two buses to get here. But as soon as she opens the downstairs door and gives me a once-over, she folds me into her arms.

"Good to see you, kid. I knew you'd make it."

☾ ☾ ☾

Her apartment is brightened by floor lamps and yellow walls, which are covered in picture frames and collages and gorgeous paintings of flowers and trees. Auntie is an artist; I wonder if she painted them herself. There are plants on various stands and on windowsills, but nothing wildly exotic or outrageously long. And the books aren't stacked on the floor; they're neatly placed on small white bookshelves. She tells me to sit on one of her leather couches—instead of the nonexistent floor pillow I'd cooked up in my mind—and offers me soda. Everything seems normal until it happens, the thing she does that makes you feel your mind isn't safe.

"You expected the bones and innards of my enemies to be hanging from my ceilings as decoration?" I choke on my soda, and she smiles with one side of her mouth. "Maybe you can tell your mother it's safe to visit. If you decide to tell her you came at all."

Anything I say might be twisted—it's better I say nothing—but my silence seems to drain the coolness from her face.

"Ease up, and tell me why you're here."

"Don't you already know?" I reach my hand in my pocket and play with the cloth bag there. "Didn't you see it before I came?"

"That's not how it works." She laughs, waves her hand as if to say *Silly child*. "I can't see the future."

"But you can see my mind?"

"Not exactly."

I mean to push, to ask how it works. Those psychic abilities Mom claims aren't anything more than a quick mind. *A trickster* is what she calls Auntie when I try asking for stories of her sister. Stories I know will be buried with the rest of the ones she seems fixed on never sharing about our family. But Papa used to say *his* Lindy was just more in tune than most of us.

"I came from a funeral," I say, then quickly, "but I stopped at a gas station first."

There is a Filipino superstition that Papa told me about after my father died: if you go straight home after a funeral, you might bring a spirit home with you.

The corners of Auntie's lips twitch like she wants to smile. "Go on," she says.

"I need to ask for your help with something."

"With what, Miliani? Spit it out." She leans forward. A spark lights her eyes and lets me know she's interested, even though she plays at impatience. "What are you hiding over there?"

I take out the bag and dump the contents onto her coffee table. She reaches out to gently touch one of the fingernails.

While her head's low, I tell her, "I want to bring my friend back from the dead."

Auntie sits back, sinking into the pillows, and beats a rhythm into the arm of the couch with her fingers. Then she tilts her head to the side and watches me awhile. "No wonder your mother has kept you from me."

3

INEZ

Jasmine's been buried for eighteen hours. She's not far from where we sit under the hot sun at Roger Williams Park, and we should go visit her grave, but Mili is trying to convince me and Nat we can resurrect her instead. Or something like that. And there are only so many ways you can tell a person something's not possible, or right, before you have to give up or give in.

When Miliani's grandpa died, she stole some ashes from the urn to bring him back from the dead. Me and Natalie agreed to meet her at Oakland Cemetery in Washington Park, the one with the rusty metal gates that squeak like something out of a horror movie when you walk in. When I asked why it needed to happen there, Miliani said, *There's no place more sacred than a cemetery,* even though at Oakland you have to walk on top of five graves in order to get to the one you're looking for. But when Miliani had a plan, there was no arguing with her.

While we'd waited for her and Jasmine, Natalie took pictures of the beer cans and cigarette butts decorating the headstones to use in a portfolio she was building for future college applications. I kept busy complaining I wasn't down to play ghost hunter, it was already dark out, and Mami would have my ass if she knew I wasn't home. I used my palm to remove a thin layer of dirt from one of the headstones, and Natalie shuddered, watching me before saying that—even though we both knew it wouldn't work—we should be there for Miliani because she was always there for us. *Saint Miliani, in all her goodness*, I joked, but kept my mouth shut later when she stirred up a concoction and pricked her finger with a pocketknife to add blood to the mix. I even bit my tongue when she made the four of us sit in a sloppy diamond shape, cross-legged on the dirt, smacking away mosquitoes while chanting something in Latin she'd found on the internet. And when her papa's ashes never formed a skeleton and the flesh didn't start growing back, when he wasn't waiting for her in the kitchen with fried fish and open arms, I never told her only God should have that type of power and maybe we'd be judged for trying.

But here we are, three years smarter, three years more practiced, and Mili isn't backing down when I tell her she's avoiding her grief. I'm upset we're spending time talking about this when I can hardly think of Jasmine without wanting to cry.

"Say it were possible, what makes you think she'd want to come back?" I pluck a few blades of grass and toss them. "Say she does and it works, what makes you think she won't be some type of undead-like zombie?"

I can tell this pisses Miliani off because she stares straight at me, unblinking, and says, "You're not even listening. She won't be alive, not fully anyway. But we'll be able to talk to her, touch her." Mili hesitates. Then, "She wants this. She was sending us signs. Tell her, Nat."

Natalie has long, straight lashes to match her slender limbs. She blinks them rapidly, then brings her knees toward her chest to hug herself. None of us have spoken about the incident at the wake. I can't imagine how this conversation is affecting her.

"Don't forget what you told me," Mili challenges.

"Even if I did feel something," Nat says, "is communicating with the dead even possible?"

Mili tilts her head. I know she's fuming.

I'm still trying to figure out how magic can coexist with the rules of my religion, but I know it's real. Natalie has stayed skeptical over the years, though. When we're alone, I joke she goes along with it because she's scared of getting kicked out of the group. She'll tell me to shut up, she'll laugh, but she never denies it.

I clear my throat, try to cut the tension. "Isn't it dark magic?"

It doesn't work. Mili sounds irritated and insulted when she says, "Of course it's possible. My papa said he'd show me one day." Her voice trembles toward the end, and my eyes sting again, thinking of how many people she's lost. "And we wouldn't just communicate with her. We'd anchor her spirit here. Besides, there's no such thing as light and dark magic. It's all about intention."

"So, we'd be helping her find space?" Nat's voice is undemanding, soothing, as she stretches back out and her dark skin catches the sun just right, glinting against the green grass she's sitting on.

The heaviness comes down around us, thinning the air, and Miliani visibly relaxes before explaining how finding space is for spirits ready to move on. They only leave energy behind. This is different. Listening to Mili makes the earth start to spin. I look up at the sky. The movement there makes me dizzy too. Mili is telling us Jas will be a ghost we can interact with.

A few boys ride by us on bikes, smirking and making comments. One whistles and calls out that his back pegs are free if we want a ride. They wouldn't want us on their pegs if they knew what we were talking about. Natalie doesn't look their way. She presses her fingers to her temples, the tips disappearing beneath her hair. She sounds like she's doing everything she can to keep from crying. "This is too much. Don't we want her to move on?"

"She'll be with us again," Miliani says. "Don't you want that? If she's not ready to move on, why not help her stay? My auntie Lindy says she'll tell me how we can make it happen."

Nat's face screws up. "Your dangerous aunt gave you this idea?"

"She's not dangerous. And she said Jasmine's body will be too far decomposed to bring her back from the dead when we're ready. But this . . . this will work."

"Wait." I lean forward. "She told you it's actually possible to bring someone back from the dead? She's seen it happen?"

Miliani shakes her head. "I should've known you two would be like this."

"We don't know what to think right now," I say, "but you dropped this on us and we're trying to understand why you think it's possible. We tried with your grandfather. It didn't work."

"We were kids," Mili says. "We didn't have my auntie's help."

"I just . . . I don't know if it's something I should do."

Miliani plants her palms flat against the ground like she's trying to shift the earth. Her deep-set brown eyes burn. "Because of a religion you pick and choose when to follow?"

"That's not fair," I say, but try to remind myself she's speaking through her pain. "Just because I'm okay with some forms of magic doesn't mean I'm okay with this type of magic."

"I'm sorry," Mili mutters, then pushes herself to a standing position. It's bright out and hard to see her round chin, the dimple that sits there and her full bottom lip, but I can hear the tears in her throat. Her long curls sway as she speaks. "It's just . . . Jas would do it for any of us, and you both know it. She'd at least try."

Miliani hasn't cried in front of us since Jasmine died, and I have a feeling she hasn't cried on her own, either. I want to beg her to let it out so she can start to heal, but she picks her backpack off the grass. "Fine. I'll do it myself."

Natalie exhales, grabs hold of Miliani's hand, and pulls her back down. "If you think we should try, then maybe we can try."

I look at Nat in shock, but she looks back expectantly.

"No. It's fine," Miliani says. "I'll figure it out."

I want to tell her go on and do that while I visit Jasmine's grave and grieve and imagine she's in heaven cracking up at wild stories I'm telling her. Then I think the possibility of it working is slim: There are many miracles in the Bible, but they're God-granted, and I doubt God will grant a few seventeen-year-old girls that type of power. But maybe, along the way, it'll help Miliani realize Jas is gone, and it'll allow her to move on. Maybe it'll help us all.

I pray I don't regret saying, "What do we have to do?"

She squints for a moment, then tells us we have to do spells to make us stronger and to thin the walls between this realm and the other side. There's no hard time limit, but the longer it takes us, the harder it might be to anchor Jasmine's spirit here. And the longer Jas waits on the other side, the more likely her spirit will become angry and change. "It's a matter of weeks, not months."

Mili doesn't let us digest this information. She flicks open her pocketknife, and I can't pay attention to how my heart pounds thinking of Jasmine being a spirit, an angry one.

"Let's make a blood pact."

I'm nervous she feels the need to bind us. "For what?"

"A promise to try to help Jasmine, even if it gets hard or scary."

I look down at the old scar on my left hand. We all have one. The night after Miliani's grandfather didn't come back from the dead, Jasmine cut all of our palms and made us promise we'd be there for one another. *No matter what*, she said.

While Mili cried, we held hands, our blood intermingling, and I remember thinking, *We'll get through anything if we have each other.*

My eyes swell as they dart back and forth from the light gleaming off Mili's knife to the promise on my palm. She's about to cut herself when I hold out my hand. She looks surprised before she smiles and slices my scar open in a swift three seconds.

4

NATALIE

Ma's been gone almost two weeks now. She doesn't even know Jasmine died. If she were here, she'd worry over the cut on my palm, she'd hug me and sing Bob Marley's "Every little thing gonna be alright." I keep hoping she'll pull up in her two-door Corolla, reach to roll the passenger window down by hand, and say, "Get in so we can go spend the gold card." On the first of the month, she lets me and my brother, Devin, pick out snacks and makes us four-cheese lasagna. Sometimes, she invites the elderly couple across the street to come eat. We'll play a few games of bingo with them, and when they leave, we'll switch to spades. The house will smell like Devin's handmade cinna-buns and we'll stay up late, crouched over the coffee table, betting on who will win the next round with change we found under couch cushions. I suppose when Ma's doing bad, she still gets excited on the first, but we aren't around to see it. When she finally does come home, the EBT card balance will be on zero because she's sold the food stamps to buy cocaine.

I wait for my sister on the front steps outside my house so she doesn't rush me down three flights with her car horn, give my neighbor Harriet something to complain about. Harriet watched a man get stabbed on our street seven years ago and now she's the self-proclaimed neighborhood watch. She's on her porch in the morning when me and Dev walk up the street to catch the city bus, and she's still on it when the streetlights kick on.

Harriet was one of the first people to mention Jasmine's death. Said she heard from word on the street. I've been on edge wondering when she'll get wind of what I did at Jasmine's wake and come preaching at my door. But she doesn't know how helpless I felt seeing Jas in a casket, knowing there was no time left to fix our friendship.

I move those thoughts aside to make room for remembering that Harriet also drove my mom to the hospital when she was in labor with me. A fact she doesn't fail to mention every chance she gets but one setting her apart from other nosy neighbors in the area. She's watching me now. I have love for her but pretend not to notice. Until she leans over the rail a little and asks, "Leanna running late again?"

I lie, say she isn't, and pull out my camera to flip through clips I took last weekend for my portfolio: Mr. Rojas selling his sweet limbers on the corner of Broad and Sackett, kids throwing rocks into the man-made lakes running through Roger Williams Park, the crows perched on the cable wires outside my window. More in the sky, flying overhead, on my walk to the corner store. *Something seems off about these shots*, I imagine Mili saying if I show her.

Harriet swats the rail with a rolled-up newspaper and makes me jump. "Natalie, grow some backbone. That girl always got you out here waiting on her," she says. "Leanna's been a bougie brat since she learned to roll those oversized eyes. God gave your momma you and Devin to apologize. But Leanna needs to be apologizing to you."

Harriet has a lot of proclamations about God's intentions. She probably voices them in church on Sundays. But I just laugh at her knock on Leanna because saying something will keep her going, and if I keep her going, she'll ask me to pray with her for my mom.

Leanna pulls up in her blue Acura ILX with its tinted windows and shiny rims. When the passenger window slides down, she smiles and says to Harriet, "How you doing, ma'am?" And Harriet replies by sucking her teeth and fanning herself with her newspaper.

When I hop in the car, Leanna waves goodbye to her and presses down on her horn once, then once more. "You're the worst. Always provoking her," I say, and we crack up.

We have moments like this occasionally, but usually she's switching through radio stations and I'm messing with the lens on my camera. It's mostly just us, alone, in a small space, for a drive that takes ten minutes but feels like forty. There's only so long talking about Rhode Island's weather makes sense. If it's not that, it's: *Do you know about scabies? You and your friends still messing with those silly Ouija boards? When are you putting in those college apps? Have to get you out this neighborhood.* And even though she's the one who bought me my first Nikon, she never asks to see my photos. She gives one-word answers whenever I ask about her job in sales or her girlfriend, Ava, but the worst is when I mention Ma. It's like talking to a stranger on a city bus; I almost expect her to say *Ma who?*

I don't get paid from Ortega's Bodega until Friday, and there's nothing except the ends of bread loaf, a box of ramen noodles, and slimy deli turkey in our fridge. If it was just me, I'd suck it up, but Devin shouldn't have to starve or endure another day of me failing to make a gourmet meal out of ramen because I don't want to shop with Leanna. Besides, I offered to pick up herbs for spells on this pre-planned shopping trip because I want Mili to be able to count on me.

Leanna turns down the radio, and Taylor Swift goes silent. I'd be thankful, but I know it means a talk about college is coming. "I'm sorry, again. About your friend. How are you?"

I try to hide my surprise by answering quickly. "Feels hard to believe still." What I don't tell her is: I don't want her sympathy because I'm not sure I deserve it. What I couldn't tell her if I wanted to: even though I don't believe I'll really get to talk to Jas again, I wish it were possible.

Leanna nods, maybe frowns, and that's the end of that. "I think you and Dev should stay with me for a while."

I turn to look at her, wanting to ask her to repeat herself to make sure I've heard right. She's said it to Ma before, but it's never gone further than me listening in, never reached my ears on purpose until now. "What about when Ma comes back?"

"What about it?" Leanna says as we pull into the Whole Foods parking lot. It's pretty empty for the first of the month, especially compared to Price Rite, where Ma has to drive around the parking lot three times, beeping her horn for people to get out of the way. When we finally find a spot, Ma will tell me to be on the lookout for a spare carriage and to prepare for the elbow shoving at the bagging counter after we cash out.

When Leanna takes me shopping, we always come here.

"You're serious?" I ask. "Just pin Ma a note up on the fridge? 'Peace out. Went to live with Leanna.'"

Her big eyes look tired, more swollen. "She's a grown woman."

"Is she really? I didn't notice."

She sighs. "Save your sarcasm for someone else."

"I can't leave her," I say.

She chews on her bottom lip. It's thin like her father's, and reminds me of how different we are. "But she can leave you and Devin all the time?"

"Well, we're not kids," I say.

Her fingers tense around the wheel. "You're not a kid any-more, but Devin's only fourteen, in case you forget."

"He'll be fifteen in a month, and we've been at this awhile." I look away. A woman across the lot from us helps her child into the car while the man she's with puts the groceries in the trunk. "Who will be there for her when she comes home?"

"One day, she might not come back," Leanna says.

It's like she's surprised herself by saying it. Watching her open and close her mouth makes the words feel like they are floating above me. When the hurt settles in, it's somewhere below my breastbone. The dashboard starts to blur from the swell in my eyes, and I need air. It's not like I haven't thought it once or twice, prayed it'd never happen, berated myself for possibly thinking it into exis-tence, but this is different.

"Wait," she says when my hand goes to the door. Her voice is gentler. This is the voice reserved for our brother, for Ava, never for me. "I'm worried about you two."

"We're good," I say, then say it again in my head.

☾ ☾ ☾

Leanna doesn't look at price tags. I think she picks the most expensive options to prove a point. When she turned seventeen, she packed a bag and said she'd be better on her own. I was barely eleven, but I remember all the questions she had for Ma when she lived with us: *Where are you going? Who were you with? Are you doing drugs again?*

Ma never asked Leanna to come home after she left. I think she liked it better when she didn't have to lie. Once, though, I heard her call Leanna late at night to ask where she was staying. Said she missed her. The conversation only lasted a few minutes, but whatever was said made Ma stay with Devin and me all night. We watched movies on her bed until daylight cracked through the broken blinds, and when Ma's hand started shaking, I held it.

Whole Foods is a one-stop shop for my sister. She loads the cart with organic lipsticks and eye shadows, facial creams and go-green T-shirts. Last month she bought two bonsai trees to add "prosperity" to the growing jungle in her living room.

When we get to the fruit aisle, Leanna throws a bag of peaches into the cart and points at a carton of blueberries for me to hand her.

I look at the yellow price tag. "These are five dollars," I say. "You can get two big-ass cartons for five dollars at Price Rite."

She takes the blueberries from me. "The price for the trash they want to feed us."

I don't respond because I know it'll end with me listening to one of her speeches on GMOs and government tactics and the corn industry. It's not like I don't read, but Price Rite sells their *modified* avocados for $0.99 and Whole Foods sells the *real* ones for $1.99. Sometimes science can't outweigh math.

We get to the aisle with the natural herbs, and I push the carriage up against a wall to examine freehanded. I've never done this before. But Jasmine loved doing it. She'd come to us with a weird herb not on the list and say, *We can use this one for something special.* Between work, worrying over Ma, and going to Dev's games, I don't have time for this part of the spell work. Now, I have to make time, especially after accidentally encouraging Mili to believe she really felt Jas's spirit at the wake, when I'm positive I was only desperate for my friend to be alive and imagined she was.

Maybe by making an effort to commit to this ritual, it'll also ease the guilt I feel knowing I wanted distance from Jasmine when she was alive. And if by some wild chance, some movie-type miracle, the ritual does work, she'll know I fought for her too. She'll know our friendship was special, despite me acting like it wasn't.

Leanna is busy fussing over the cilantro when I take Miliani's list from my pocket. She writes in sloppy-looking scrawl, but I've mastered deciphering it.

Lots of Chicory
Bay Leaf
Check for Club Moss (Really check)
Echinacea Angustifolia
Devil's Shoestring (Don't freak out)
DON'T FORGET THE CHICORY!
PS: I love you as much as lumpia

I find a couple of the herbs and slip them in the carriage. Leanna continues loading it up too. When we get to the natural hair section, she pulls a bottle of conditioner from the shelf and asks if I've tried it. I say no because an eight-ounce bottle is $14.99. "My hair doesn't like it much, but yours might," she says, and adds two bottles to the cart. Her hair falls in waves down her back and she wears the front in layers, which frame her face. I tell her to put the products back, that I don't need them, but on the inside, I hope she'll ignore me.

She does.

Ma shopped here once before. *They take EBT cards. No excuse for why you can't eat healthy*, Leanna had said. We stuck to the grocery aisles, but my eyes wandered over to the natural hair section and Ma said, "We can go to Walmart after this and buy you conditioner."

When we loaded up the conveyor belt with fruits and veggies and organic pasta, Ma was smiling. I think she was proud, *I did good for my babies*, until the man at the register told her the total and Ma pulled out the EBT card with a shaky hand. I knew the amount was double we'd usually spend. For mostly fresh food that would only last a week. When we left Whole Foods, Ma didn't sing to the radio and I never reminded her about Walmart.

Leanna loads up the conveyor belt, and the girl at the register doesn't crack a smile. When the total comes through, I try to find something to focus on, a magazine reporting a scandal, but all I get is an organic granola bar to examine. At least checking out at Price Rite never feels uncomfortable. I swear the workers here look at Leanna like she's made a mistake, maybe wondering how she can afford it, but my sister never says a word when she reaches for her wallet and hands over her cash.

☾ ☽ ☾

When we get home, she gets out of the truck to help me carry bags, but Devin opens the downstairs door and heads straight for her. She smiles real big and throws her arms out. Someone might think he's a grown man, the way he towers over her, but he only has a sprinkle of chin hairs and hasn't grown into his ears. I start unloading the bags so I don't stare at the two of them.

Leanna never hugs me like that anymore. She used to, back when her dad picked her up to spend weekends with him. She'd come home and hug me and Dev before bragging about the in-ground pool in her dad's backyard and her flowery bed set with the matching pillowcase. She'd sneak us treasures she slipped into her backpack: packets of hot chocolate with marshmallows, comic books from her dad's stash, a cassette tape she hoped he wouldn't notice was missing.

Still, when she was gone, Dev would cry, ask Ma why he couldn't go, why we didn't know *our* dad. The only thing Ma ever told us is he's Black. *From off the coast of Africa,* she'd say sometimes. Other times it was, *Smack in the middle of Africa.* I have a feeling that, whoever he is, Ma never even told him Dev and I are his. But I'd sneak one of her photo albums and sit with Dev while we tried to match our brown skin with the deeper tones of random Black men we found in it, pretending this one or that one was *the one.*

Ma's white, and Leanna's got her freckles, but her dad was Puerto Rican with high cheekbones, and she's got those from him. He died of a heart attack right before Leanna's fifteenth birthday. I remember listening out in the hallway while she cried to her friend: *Before the quinceañera he promised me. Before I could tell him I like girls.*

While Leanna and Dev talk now, I take the herbs we just bought and head to my room. They have no name tags on them and they all look like noodle garnish to me, but Mili will know what they are. Jas would've been able to tell them apart too.

5

INEZ

The problem with sex is I can't stop having it, even though Mami wants me to be a virgin so bad there's nothing else I am to her. She used to send me to an after-school program at the Catholic church in my neighborhood Monday through Friday, but now she lets me stay after school twice a week for the math club that doesn't really exist. On weekends, we sit through hours of services, listening to the same passages we've heard dozens of times. So many times I can recite them without a glance at the Bible, just for her to talk about *fast-ass niñas that don't fear God* on the drive home.

Over the phone, she tells Papi how smart I am, how innocent, how proud he'll be when I sponsor him for citizenship and he's with us again, and then they pray. But I love my boyfriend, Aaron, and when Mami goes to work for the night shift, he sneaks in through my window so my brother won't notice. I turn up the volume on my radio, lock my door, even use a pillow to muffle my moans, hoping the bed won't squeak too loud when Aaron rocks his body over mine. It's harder to keep quiet today because it feels different, and I let myself get lost because I need to feel something other than sad about Jas and scared about the blood pact and the constant pressure to be perfect.

When it's over, he cleans us both with a T-shirt from my

"I love you, Aaron," I tell him. Saying it to each other is still new. It makes me nervous.

He leans his head against the wall, hand over his heart. "She finally said it first."

I throw a pillow at him. "Go."

He's got one foot out the window when he turns back to look at me. "The cut on your palm," he says, causing me to look at my bandaged hand, "you'd tell me if it wasn't an accident?"

I grind my teeth, try not to hold on to the sting of his words because it'll spread through my bones and stay there. "Are you asking if I hurt myself?"

He's careful when he says, "No, just saying you can talk to me about anything."

Not anything. I can't tell him about the blood pact because he might think I'm being wild. He blows me another kiss before he goes, but I'm still sore knowing he asked. Was this the first time he's wondered if I hurt myself? Does he make assumptions about me based on how bad my anxiety is?

With little time to dwell on it, I pick myself up off the bed and grab my towel. My little brother's door is open, and he's sitting on the carpet with a video-game controller in his lap. I clear my throat. "Better find a book to read before Mami comes home and beats you."

Victor talks without turning toward me. "She'll be home in an hour. You know that."

Something about his tone has me waiting at his door a moment before I slip into the bathroom to fill the tub. The mirror behind the bathroom door is my favorite to study my body.

When I was younger, Papi used to call me his celery stick.

Skinny and long, with a big head and frizzy hair. He loved my freckles, said they made me look innocent, said he hoped I'd stay looking that way forever. But my body has changed. Filled out and curved in places I didn't expect. I'm thick now. There is no more bra shopping at Walmart, which means Mami has to save to buy me the good bras, made for large breasts. And even though she makes comments about *expensive* things, she'd never want me hanging or sloppy, especially not in church, where we should be modest and dressed like ladies.

I unwrap the bandage on my palm and touch my thigh. It stings, but I chant a spell Mili taught me, over and over, running my hand over my breasts, my inner thighs, up the lips of my vagina. A spell to help take away the redness, the possible bruising, to make me look more innocent to Mami. Then I sink into the water while telling myself I'm fluid, light, dense, free. For a few minutes, I feel exactly that, but the feeling fades quicker than it came.

I grab a washcloth to scrub away the smell of sex, and find myself wishing I could call Jasmine to ask her if the feeling she was trying to describe to me was regret.

6

MILIANI

There are dozens of birds surrounding Auntie Lindy: Some of them perch on the fence between her apartment building and the next. Others walk close to her on the concrete. There are four on the bird feeder she just filled. They are different colors and sizes— breeds I've never seen together before. I slow my step and listen to the song of a mourning dove, but I'm not sure which bird it's coming from. She has her back turned to me as she fills another feeder with seed, and startles me when she says, "Thought you'd change your mind after the shock of the funeral wore off."

I shake my head, still distracted by the sight in front of me.

I'm careful moving closer, but the birds on her stoop seem to catch my scent and alert the rest that it's time to scatter and fly off. "How . . . do you get them to stay calm around you?"

Auntie looks at me with a strange expression and picks the bag of birdseed off the ground. "How do you manage to frighten them so easily?"

I feel a warm flash of embarrassment cut across my face while she heads up her stoop and into the hall, leaving the door open for me to follow.

In the kitchen, she slices oranges and slides a plate of them onto the table for me. I take a seat and tell her my friends agreed to help anchor Jasmine. We're ready to start. She drops the knife into the sink, says there's a lot to discuss first, but then goes to work caring for her plants.

She examines string of pearl roots while I eat and examine her. She is ethereal as she moves through the room. She looks like she can float. She hums a song Papa used to sing when working in his garden. It feels as if he's here with us. I try not to let her catch me peeking, or thinking, but she does. "You weren't his first favorite," she says.

"Stop doing that. Get out of my head."

She shrugs and continues to hum. She's calmer than I remember. More reserved and serious, instead of fiery like before we lost Papa. It's been three years, but the details surrounding his death stick in my mind. Papa's death wasn't sudden like Jasmine's. He died of cancer. Slow and painful and with stages of sadness, but at least he said goodbye. Which wasn't enough for his youngest daughter, Lindy, who'd guarded his bedside hours after he died in it.

I sat in the corner of his small room with the faintest smell of decay wafting through it, unable to take my eyes off Auntie as she crouched over Papa, digging her nails into his bedsheets with a feral look on her face. Mom got close to her younger sister. *Can't you smell that? We need to call for someone to take the body.* The body. Not Papa's body or Dad's body. *The* body. I wished Mom wouldn't speak of him like he hadn't taken care of everyone as a single father after Nana died from eclampsia. He was the most important man in our lives. But Auntie ignored her, so Mom opened the window to let the cold air inside because the stench of death got stronger as the minutes ticked by.

Hours later, my uncle Jonathan walked in after catching the first flight from where he was stationed in California. Auntie took a few startled breaths at the sight of him. A screechy cry erupted from her throat, loud enough to startle me. *Come here, little sister*, Uncle Jonathan said. He had tears streaming from his eyes as he pulled Auntie up from where she was kneeling.

Relief parted Mom's lips. She told me to dial the number for the hospice. The phone was ringing in my ear when Auntie gripped the arms of both of her siblings and said, *We're all here now. We can fix this. We can save him.*

Mom sent me out of the room after that, and later came to tell me not to entertain myself with Auntie's hysteria, and not to mention it to anyone, ever. But after hearing the heat behind Auntie's words, I knew it was possible and had tried to save him myself.

I'd ask Auntie now what happened when Mom sent me away, what went wrong if they had tried, but I'm nervous she'll change her mind about training me if I bring up Papa's death.

She points her chin at my hand. "Had to do a blood pact to get your friends on board?"

Her smile seems suggestive. I try not to be embarrassed and swallow the last bit of orange in my mouth. "Do you think it was stupid?"

She clips off a yellowing vine from an arrowhead plant. "Whatever works for you."

I think of the way Inez held out her hand, how good it felt when Natalie joined in and we mixed blood and promises. The night of the funeral, Auntie told me I'd have to have the stomach for the spell work that was to come because there would be risks. She said I'd have a better chance at obtaining more energy and widening the realms if my friends helped. The pact was my way of being sure they'll have the stomach to go through it too.

She sets her pruning shears down on the table and pulls out a chair to take a seat across from me. "I'll need to train you with some of the elements." My heart speeds up. Papa used to say cultivating nature was better than trying to control it. Auntie says, "No form of magic is inherently evil, Miliani. You know that."

I do, and still I ask, "But is it dangerous?"

"It can be."

If she wanted to say more, she would. "Okay. Well, how often do my friends need to be here? Inez has a hard time getting out of the house, and Natalie works, and—"

"Stop." Auntie knocks on the table. "I agreed to train *you*. You'll act like a conductor for the magic you obtain. Only one of you needs to be strong enough in elemental magic to channel the moon and complete the spell. I'm not training anyone else." Auntie presses a thumb to a pressure point at the side of her wrist. "I am not a babysitter, Miliani."

"I didn't mean to disrespect you," I say.

Her face softens at this. "I know, but part of the magic I'll be teaching you was taught to me by our family. You should be aware right now how sacred that is to me. There needs to be boundaries."

I think of how Papa hardly had any friends in his home. He said time with family and the spaces we inhabited were like sanctuaries, and he never talked about magic in mixed company. "How do my friends help, then?"

"They need to get stronger—through manifestation, by practicing substantial-sized spells to assist you when the time comes for the anchoring. Their energy will help open the doors from this realm to the spiritual one in order to pull your friend through."

I attempt to soak all of it in, but the questions don't stop popping up in my mind. "Will you tell me what spells we need to do?"

"I can give you some ideas," Auntie says, shifting the plant pot on her table. "But these spells should be brought out by your individual desires. Not silly love potions, spells to transform lives. Your desire will make tangible things you've never thought possible."

This throws me. I try to concentrate on the smell of oranges on my fingers, play with the seeds on my plate, hoping Auntie can't hear me panic. I thought she'd have all the answers for us. How do I keep Nat and Inez invested when I'm not sure what we're doing myself?

"Now, we should talk about the most important part," Auntie says, touching her elbow with three fingers. "You said you'll do anything it takes."

I wet my lips. Out of reflex, I touch my elbow too. "I did."

"Listen closely, because I'm not going to overexplain this. For a spell this significant, the anchor for your friend's spirit cannot be a place or an object," she says. "It needs to be a person."

I have to replay the revelation in my head more than once, and still the shock makes my brain a jumble of too many thoughts. "What are you saying?"

"The anchor and your friend's spirit will share a body."

"But how . . . ? Why?" I lean forward and the table presses against me, but her words have already stolen my breath.

Auntie's jaw ticks. "I can leave you to your grieving. We can forget you ever asked."

I think of what Papa told me all of those years ago by the pear tree. I am back there, under the skinny branches and the thick green leaves, hoping the pears don't fall on us when the wind makes them sway. My eyes flick to Auntie's face. "A haunting?"

"If that's what you wish to call it."

I feel sick, confused. I didn't know this was what I was asking for. "That's . . . It's wrong. How do you expect me to do that? And why would I if I'll only get to talk to Jas sometimes?"

"Is sometimes better than never?" Auntie Lindy leans closer too. We are almost a shared body, the way she touches her thumb to my wrist and presses down. The way it feels like I can hear her thinking it before she says, "Are you willing to lose your friend forever? If so, I don't know why I'm wasting my time with you."

She can hear me too. She knows a tightness forms in my chest at the thought of losing Jas forever. She knows it hurts to hear her measuring her time with me and calling it wasteful. I fight off chills and pull away slowly. "How do you expect me to find someone who will agree? Who would want to share their body?"

"You won't," she says, and something flashes across her face. "No one would do it willingly unless they were desperate."

My stomach clenches. My own body is suddenly shaky and cold. "I'll be . . . I'll have to steal someone's body against their will?"

Auntie doesn't even blink. "More like borrowing."

My eyes burn as I reach for a memory of Jas, try to hold on to it.

"We will talk details later," Auntie says. "For now, I need to know how bad you want this." My mind tries to untangle thoughts until I'm left with one. Auntie lets out a small gasp. She stands up. "No, it cannot be you, Miliani. It needs to be someone else."

"Why?" I'm desperate to keep the solution, but it's already falling from my grasp. "I'll have control and be able—"

"That's enough," she says. "It's not possible. Let it go."

"I don't think I can do that to someone else."

"Very well." She pushes in her chair to put on a pot of tea. "I had a feeling once you learned the truth, the little scar on your hand wouldn't be enough."

Auntie leans up against the stove while I stare at the cut on my palm. Jasmine's face is all angles and cheeks. Two single braids hang in front of it, and she pushes them back when she needs to let out a laugh, when she needs it to be big. She looks at me and opens her mouth, but the spell breaks as soon as the whistle of the teakettle rings through the room. Then Jas is gone.

Auntie lets the water overboil. After a while she says, "Please don't waste my time." The tenderness to her tone has me searching her face. She sounds tired.

I don't want to cry in front of her, but I can't stop the tears. "I need her back," I whisper.

"The guilt is radiating off you, Miliani. I can hear it. I don't know why, but you feel responsible for her death. Maybe this will help fix it. But you must decide now. In a few weeks it might not be possible."

My head drops to the table. It's cool and hard and easier to breathe here. I haven't told anyone about blaming myself for Jasmine's death. Auntie shouldn't have gone into my mind. She shouldn't have . . . But a sense of relief washes over me. I didn't have to say it out loud; she just knows. I lift my head to look at her.

"Will the person suffer when it happens?"

"Not much physically, but these things never go without sacrifices," she says, and the same faraway look from earlier flashes on her face. She turns to the window, doesn't seem to shy away from the sun in her eyes. "The person will live, and with them so will your friend. That has to be your bottom line. If it is not, we end this now."

Nat and Inez agreed to do this without knowing how serious the consequences are. If I tell them the truth about the anchoring, they'll never go for it. It's good they're not here with me.

I dig my teeth into my lips. My voice is unfamiliar when it comes. "I have no choice."

Auntie nods and finally shuts the burner off. She moves to stand at my side, reaches out to take my hand. "Perfect cut. It's going to heal up nicely."

My bones hurt, my head too, but Auntie's touch is soothing. "Who do I anchor Jas to?"

"A blood tie is best. Sometimes, it's the only viable option."

A name passes from my lips before I can stop it: "Darleny."

7

INEZ

Forty-two hours after the blood pact, I tell Dr. Baker I needed this appointment. She's been my psychologist for a year. I had two others before her, but neither were very friendly people. Mami said it's because we used to have Medicaid through the state, but now that she's been cut from the program for working overtime and has medical through her job, doctors might treat us better.

Dr. Baker is a nice enough woman, and I think maybe she wouldn't treat me differently with welfare medical. She has unjudging eyes and some really pretty teeth, which must have been straightened with braces and whitened with treatments because she smiles more than someone should in these sessions. But she also looks for reasons for the panic attacks and the inability to sleep at night. She's always worried that maybe it's the pressure of knowing in three years I need to sponsor my father so he can return to the States. Today, her push is a little softer after we talk at length about Jasmine's funeral and she comments on how fidgety I still am.

"Can you dig and tell me what else is going on in your life?"

Dr. Baker always says I can tell her whatever I'd like as long as it's not harmful to me or anyone else (doctor-patient confidentiality with a side note). But as comfortable as it is talking to her, I can't tell her about the magic, unless I want to end up in Butler with Mami throwing holy water at me on her visits. So there's no way to explain how I've been trying to figure out what kind of spells Miliani wants to do, with her only saying, "They have to have substantial outcomes." Which doesn't explain much but does have me evaluating everything we've been successful at so far: finding spells for lost things, and memory-enhancing ones before big tests, which always feels like cheating. And the vainer spells to make our skin clear and our hair thicker. We even attempted to make people fall in love with us when we were sophomores and silly, but Mili guessed it never worked because we didn't have the power to influence others.

None of these feel darker than having sex when my religion calls the way I do it sinning. None of them scare me more than I'm already scared I'm fucking up by following my gut instead of every scripture in the Bible. But the idea of binding Jas's spirit to earth, knowing God might've taken her for a reason, is terrifying, and even if I could tell Dr. Baker that all of this is on my mind, it's not the only thing bothering me right now.

"There's a lot of shit going on. But it's not just that."

"Then what is it?"

"Everyone always comes at me like 'Inez, why do you feel like this? There has to be a reason. Let's fix it.' But how do I let anyone help fix me if I don't know what's wrong with me?"

"Maybe you don't need to be fixed, Inez."

Jasmine used to say the same thing. *Your spirit just wants to wander, Inez. It feels trapped by all the earthly rules you give yourself.* I'd insist they were Mami's rules, the Bible's rules, but she'd say, *I never hear you standing up for yourself.*

I tried to believe her then, I want to now, but it's harder knowing she's gone and wondering what will happen to me when I die. How do I stand up for myself without knowing what's worth fighting for? What if, in my final moments, I regret not following the rules laid out for me?

My mouth opens before I can stop it. "Do you ever feel like it's exhausting to exist?"

Dr. Baker tenses, turns her pen cap and crosses her legs.

"I'm not going to hurt myself, but existing is exhausting. Sometimes, speaking to people wears me down." I make waves into the corduroy fabric of the chair I'm sitting in. "I don't know if you'll ever get the reason you're looking for, Dr. Baker. I didn't have a bad childhood. I'm not bullied in school. My parents are alive and love me. I have to sponsor my father and sometimes that weighs on me, yes. But there's nothing I want more than for him to be with us again. My friend just died and it hurts so much, but the heaviness in my chest is older than her death. You know that, right?"

I wait for Dr. Baker to reveal she hasn't been listening in these sessions, but instead she says, "I do know, Inez."

This makes me take a deep breath and close my eyes. "Sometimes I feel so tired of carrying it, which makes me feel guilty. I'm happy to be alive. But is it enough for God?"

Dr. Baker closes her notebook. "I think this is the most honest you've been with me." She leans forward in her chair. "I don't have answers, but I do understand. Sometimes existing is exhausting, and there's nothing we can do about it but keep existing."

"It's fucked-up," I say.

"More than a little." She nods. "But you'll tell me if it gets too hard?"

"Okay," I say. "I'll tell you."

(((

When I get home, Mami is waiting for me at the kitchen table. She's wearing jeans and a T-shirt. Her hair is thrown into a bun. It's such an unfamiliar sight; she's usually in work scrubs or church dresses. She doesn't look at me when I stand in front of her, but she sends my brother upstairs and orders me to take a seat.

"What's wrong, Mami? Why aren't you at work?"

She points her finger in my face. "Don't speak until I tell you to speak, ¿tú entiendes?"

I nod, but I'm nervous trying to imagine what I could've done to make her upset. She rarely talks to me this way.

"I work hard for you and your brother to live a good life." She starts to cry, swears in Spanish under her breath. "I am always tired. And all I ask is for you to respect me and my house. Most of all, respect God."

My spell box. She must've found it. She must know. "Mami, it's not what you—"

But she smacks me across my cheek before I can get the rest of the words out.

"I said not to talk unless I tell you to," she says, and when the shock fades, I touch my face where it stings. "Your brother told me everything." Now my heart stings too. "This is how you repay me? By sneaking boys into the house when I'm out working to take care of you?" All at once, my airway feels constricted, my heart beats hard and fast, I'm dizzy. "By defiling yourself and betraying God?"

She's sobbing now. "Did you open your legs for him?" she asks, but I'm still trying to grasp what's happening. My silence makes her shout, "Are you a virgin? Answer me."

I place my shaky hands on the table. "I am, Mami," I lie. It comes so easy, so smooth, it bothers me. "I'm sorry. We were just kissing."

She turns and takes my chin between her fingers, squeezes hard. "Mentirosa."

"I'm a virgin, Mami. I promise."

She pushes my face away. "If I find out that boy is anywhere near my house or you again, I'm calling the police, and you can go live out on the streets like your cousin Glenda."

No one wants to be like my cousin Glenda. Last I checked, she was sleeping under a bridge near Hope Street. But I know Mami wouldn't call the police or throw me out because that would risk my chances of being a sponsor. Still, I say, "It won't happen again. I promise," because I don't want to sneak around anymore. I never wanted to. I just felt like I had no choice.

After a few deep breaths, she says, "Bueno. Go get your Bible."

We pray until my knees bruise. In between passages, I chant to myself, *Forgive me, Mami. Please understand. Look at me.* And then I pray on it too. But she doesn't look at me, not even when she says a prayer for God to watch out for Jasmine's parents. When we're done, she doesn't speak another word to me. She unplugs the phone from the kitchen wall and takes it with her, sending a message in burning silence: I won't be creeping to call Aaron or get to call my friends to tell them what happened tonight.

She'll probably call Papi, though. Tell him I'm one of the nasty ones. Tell him I need to be saved, that they should pray for my soul.

My nerves fire, and my legs tingle with each step up the

stairs. I knock on Victor's door, but he doesn't open up. What would I say to him anyway? I want to be mad he ratted on me, but my stomach turns, wondering what he's heard. He's not the type of thirteen-year-old you see riding his bike up and down Broad Street, smoking a blunt, maybe even selling drugs on the corner. He does his homework after church, and his only guilty pleasure is sneaking a PlayStation 2 out of his bag until Mami gets home. I'm almost an adult, but that might not mean anything to him. Every time Father John preaches about people who listen to whispers of the devil and give their body before the right time, I pray the Bible got it fucked-up and God doesn't feel that way. But maybe my little brother thinks of me when Father John goes on about it.

The day Papi was deported, Mami and I were dancing salsa while she was cooking his favorite meal: arroz con habichuelas y chuleta. We always waited for Papi to come home to eat together. But that night, Mami looked up at the clock on the wall as she cleaned the same countertop again and again. Victor was too hungry and she finally let us eat, but she refused to eat without Papi. It was dark out by the time the house phone rang. She said maybe three words into it before sinking to the floor. The phone fell and swung by its cord near her head, and she screamed like someone was stabbing her. I tried to help her up, but she told me to take my brother and go upstairs.

We found out later the call was the news of Papi's deportation.

For weeks, I spent nights trying to console my brother, saying, *Victor, we have to be strong. And if you can't be strong, I'll be strong for the both of us. You can count on me.*

Maybe I didn't just fail Mami and Papi by sneaking Aaron in; maybe I failed Victor too.

(☾ (

I open my closet to take out my box. Years ago, Miliani filled the bottom of three boxes with crystals and rocks from the ocean floor to give to the rest of us. I was scared to touch any of it. If the things she had shown me were real, did that mean I'd be doing "the devil's work"? But after a rough night with Victor, I touched one of the crystals, and it felt like it touched me back. Jas explained it was a blue lace agate, one of the strongest calming crystals, especially used for people who suffer from nerves. The only thing I knew then was the spark was real and it was *for* me.

Now, my box is also filled with candles, oils, and spell books.

Mami grew up believing in the Bible, and I believe in God, but there's nothing else for her besides the rules of religion. She'd never understand the pull I feel to learn and explore. To not feel trapped. Jasmine was the only person in my life who understood how it feels when religion presses up against desire. For the first time since the blood pact, I let myself hope Mili's plan works because maybe I'll get to talk things out with Jas again.

Before I tuck my box away, deeper this time, I realize it's better Mami thinks I'm a hoe than finds out I use spells in her own house to help me sleep, and that soon I'll be involved in ones that make it possible to talk to the dead.

8

NATALIE

Dev and I barely made the bus this morning and the bell's about to ring, but that doesn't stop the universe from throwing a distraction our way. At school, some kids are standing outside the front doors laughing and pointing. We crane our necks and see pigeons hovering around a woman as she walks. She throws a piece of her sandwich into the street, and one goes after it while the rest pester her. The kids clown her. "She should know Providence pigeons are built different," one says. "They're about to follow her home."

I roll my eyes, but the woman throws her whole sandwich in the street this time, and she's still being stalked. I hope they don't peck at her ankles and she's got money for another meal.

☾ ☾ ☾

During lunch, Inez forks the shepherd's pie on her plate before pushing it away, probably stressing over what happened with her mom yesterday while Mili throws out ideas for spells. None of us have eaten around one another much since we lost Jas, but we snuck our lunch trays into an empty hall upstairs to finish our food, the way we used to when she was here.

"We can make your mom forgive you," Mili offers.

Inez presses her back into the locker. "With my luck, she'll receive a message from heaven warning her I'm trying brujería on her."

"True," Mili says, but her mind is turning, leg all jittery as she pulls on a curl till it reaches down to her belly button and springs up to her breasts when she lets it go. Then she fixes her sights on me. Her mouth is wide open like I've helped her discover the solutions to our problems. "Your mom's been gone awhile." Mili actually sounds excited. "Let's try a locator spell." Inez looks at me from under her lashes, rubs her nose till its red, but Mili keeps going. "We can alter a version of the spell we use for finding objects, and—"

"We're not doing a locator spell on my mom." I grind down on my teeth as heat finds a home in my chest. "She's going to come back because she wants to. She always does."

Mili raises her hoodie above her ears. With tawny-brown skin, she's not as light as Inez, but it's still easy to see the flush on her face.

"I didn't mean to imply she wouldn't."

I let my feelings simmer while Inez pipes in, "We'll think of something else."

No one offers up anything. I try to finish my food, but my appetite has left me. Inez breaks the silence, asking if we've heard from any schools. She's waiting on Rhode Island College and Johnson & Wales: colleges her mom forced her to apply to because they're close to home. But I know she's anxious to hear from the University of Rhode Island. She gushes about the beautiful campus, and I'm sure she fantasizes about the freedom. URI is only forty minutes from here, but that's forty minutes from church and forty minutes from her mom.

Mili sighs. "Do we really have to talk about this now?" She applied early action to every college in Rhode Island and gets to have her pick of them. With her 1500 SAT score, scholarship foundations are practically tossing money her way. She doesn't have to worry about a thing. Except starting somewhere in the fall without Jasmine.

The decisions I have to make aren't the same ones my friends have to make. They can worry about which college would suit them best; I have to worry about whether I can attend at all.

"Let's do the ritual before the bell rings," Mili says, and I'm happy to avoid talking about college for the foreseeable future, but I'm surprised she wants to do the water ritual. It's something the four of us did together every Friday. Jas used to call it a homework assignment for the weekend. This is our first Friday sitting in these halls since she died.

"Everything we do will help us prepare for the anchoring spell," Mili says. "But we have to take it seriously. You know? Actually believe it'll happen."

I feel called out for never believing in the ritual. It's a game to me. We all take turns looking inside a bowl of water, trying to predict strange things we'd see over the weekend. Jas would come back with a serious face to report her findings. Mili claimed her predictions came true a few times, Inez wondered why hers didn't, and I never had anything to say. But I loved to listen to Jasmine's elaborate stories, which always felt like entertaining lies.

Mili uses a styrofoam bowl she took from the cafeteria and dumps the rest of her water into it. Inez scooches close and rests her elbow against my knee while Mili leans over the bowl. She concentrates hard, and I wonder what craziness she'll pretend to see.

"It'll be . . . uh . . . pigeons attacking a woman," she says.

Inez's top lip curls. "Where do you come up with this stuff?"

I laugh at Mili. "She saw it this morning."

"What are you talking about?" Mili's eyes flick up to me.

"You saw the woman across the street. Stop playing."

Inez and Mili share a confused look, then Mili leans forward. The dimple in her chin deepens. "I don't know what you mean."

I smile while telling them about the woman and the pigeons, watch Mili sit back, playing innocent as I call her bluff. Inez shakes her head, says, "Well, guess Mili's a psychic now," but her joke doesn't catch laughs. Mili's quiet, and I wonder what other things she lies about.

Inez pulls the bowl toward her. A few seconds later, she looks at us with a smirk. "I'll see sweet Baby Jesus."

"Nah." Mili's tone is already a little lighter. "You're going to church this weekend. Of course you're going to see Baby Jesus."

Inez shrugs. "There are no rules to the water ritual."

I swat at Inez's leg and take the bowl, catching Mili's eyes. She's checking if I'll take it seriously. It makes my palms start to sweat. I look into the bowl and see the same thing I always see: a whole lot of nothing. But then my guilt about Jas grows deeper, and the water starts to change. With it, my heart changes its rhythm.

The water reflects rich colors, lines, pieces of me, and I think of Inez and Mili too. I hold my breath while it ripples, let it out when the water becomes cloudy. "What the . . . ?" I don't know what to think. How to feel. I don't know what's happening, but something is—for the first time.

I can feel Mili get closer. "What is it?" she says.

Before I can answer, an image forms out of the water's haze. It's as detailed as one of my photos. It sends a shiver up my spine. I dip my head lower, and the image is still there. All these years doing "magic" with my friends, there hasn't been anything I can't find an explanation for. I think back to touching Jasmine's skin at the wake and wonder if she really did feel warm, if it wasn't just my grief.

But when I blink and check again, the image is gone. The water is clear, and now I'm not sure if my mind was playing tricks on me.

"What was it?" Mili asks. "You saw something, didn't you?"

I sit back, touch my hand to my forehead, wet my lips.

"Nat." Mili's more forceful this time.

I wish there was a way to know if it was real before opening my mouth, but Mili will expect an answer anyway. "I saw a man in an oversized coat, bleeding from a cut on his head."

Inez's brows shoot up as Mili opens her mouth to speak, but then Darleny and her friend Cassie cut through the hall and walk toward us.

"Told you Miliani's a freak," Darleny says as they get close. "Over here thinking she's a witch." They laugh, but Mili just stares at Darleny, looking stunned and confused.

Before they pass us, Darleny says to her, "Why are you looking at me like that, weirdo?"

I'm about to cuss Darleny out, but Inez places a hand on my knee. So instead, I raise my camera from where it hangs on my chest and snap a few shots of them. This always messes people up good. Cassie straightens her slouch, suddenly self-conscious. Her open Gatorade rests against her forearm when she crosses her arms.

Darleny scowls at me. "Let's go," she says to Cassie.

When they're out of earshot, Mili doesn't seem shaken up anymore. She grabs both of our hands. "Let's make her trip."

Seems like a typical wish, except if a *star athlete* tripped in front of us, she'd never forget it. We've tried stuff like this a hundred times and always failed, but I'll do anything to make Mili feel better. The three of us squeeze our hands together, and I concentrate on Darleny's feet and try to imagine it happening, because I really, really want it to.

For a second, it doesn't seem like anything's going to happen. Then, as they're about to turn the hall corner out of our sight, Cassie trips—right over a snag in the rug—and stumbles into Darleny's side. Cassie's Gatorade spills all over Darleny's white soccer uniform.

"What the hell," Darleny hisses, pushing Cassie and causing her to stumble backward and fall on her ass.

We all bust out laughing, and they both turn to look at us.

"Wooooo, witchcraft," Inez mocks, raising her hands and fanning her fingers.

Darleny ignores Cassie's request to pull her up by a hand and disappears down the hall, leaving her friend looking at us in horror before she scrambles to her feet and follows.

"Did you see that?" Mili says. "We made that happen."

"We tried tripping Darleny, not Cassie. Just a coincidence," I say. But my stomach is tight, and a voice in my head isn't so sure.

Inez smiles. "Or a blessing."

"Neither of you will deny it when we can make her sneeze uncontrollably," Mili says.

Inez snorts so damn loud. "You're an awful human."

"I try," Mili says, and then the fun seems to fade out all at once. Maybe they're feeling the same thing I am: Cassie tripping may have been a coincidence, but we shared something without Jasmine. This is the first time we've really laughed together since she's been gone.

Mili shifts her focus to me. "Tell us more about the man. Why was he bleeding?"

I tell her it was only a couple of seconds, but she keeps asking questions about him. I don't want to make the same mistake of amping her up like at the wake. For all I know, wanting Jas back could be making me see things that don't exist. "If there was something else, I'd tell you."

"Would you, really?" Mili shakes her head before I can respond. "Are you sure you're not able to do a spell with us tonight?"

Inez's basement has decent lighting and plenty of floor space. But the best part is that on Fridays her mom works a double. And when most kids from school head to the mall to eat Chinese food and watch a movie, my friends and I usually try to do séances in Inez's basement. She seems hesitant now. I can tell she's worried after her brother snitched on her about Aaron, but there's no way her mom would miss another day of work. She'd probably install cameras on the front porch and metal bars on Inez's bedroom windows first.

But I can't go to Inez's tonight. Dev and I made plans to pick up my pay from the bodega (my boss pays me cash under the table so Ma doesn't have to report my income to Section 8), buy toiletries for the house, and stay up late watching rental movies. It's been too long since we've spent time together. I think Jas would tell me to put Dev first . . . if she wanted to talk to me at all. I press on the center of my chest, but it can't ease the way my heart starts to ache.

Mili doesn't argue with me, but she probably wants to. "As long as you're there to do a spell this weekend. It's important, Nat. We can't keep Jas waiting long."

"I'll be there," I say. "I promise."

❨ ❨ ❨

When the last bell rings, I find Dev at his locker, chatting up a freshman with a bad attitude and a body fit for a twenty-year-old. The girl and I have gym together, but she sits out on the bleachers in high heels and tight jeans. My brother catches sight of me and says something to make her leave.

"Flirting with trouble again?" I ask, and lean against the locker next to his.

He throws his backpack over one shoulder. "She's cute."

"Cute will catch you a case."

"You sound corny like Ma," he says, and when he shuts his locker, I see something glisten on the side of his neck.

"What the heck is this, Dev?" I reach forward to pick the chain up.

"Ciara wants me to wear it. Think she's trying to lay claim to me or something," he says, turning toward me with a sly smirk on his face. "But whatever. The chain is fly, right?"

"You're bugging. It's real gold. Give it back. I can't afford for you to lose it or break it."

"Don't trip. I'll give it back tomorrow." He touches the pendant dangling from the chain.

That's when I see, staring back at me, the gleaming gold eyes of Baby Jesus.

❨ ❨ ❨

Kennedy Plaza is packed. Different groups of kids from Providence schools move in waves on the walk over to their bus stops. Some fight to sit on the bench under the shelter to escape the heat, but Dev and

I stand as we talk about the cold chicken patties and watered-down chocolate milk we had at lunch. Each time the conversation lags, I think of Mili's prediction, and of Inez and Baby Jesus. The universe is definitely messing with me today. Even if the ritual were real, I'm not supposed to see *their* predictions; I'm supposed to see *mine*.

I'm distracted when Devin asks me a question. "Yo, you listening, elephant ears? I need Ma to sign off on a paper."

"Stop calling me that," I say. "Let me get it. I'll sign it."

He runs his fingers over his high-top fade. "Not in the mood to hear your mouth."

"Shut up and hand it over."

"I'll give it to you when I get home tonight."

"You're going out?" I frown. "Thought we had plans."

He cracks an apologetic smile. Tells me he forgot and has practice. Devin's played basketball at the Boys and Girls Club since elementary, and now he's the only freshman on our school's team. He nudges me with his arm. "I'm going home now to change, but I won't be back late. Maybe I'll even suffer through *Deep Blue Sea* again tonight. Okay?"

He hates watching movies we've already seen, but I hate being home alone. It'll be worse today, remembering Jas in a casket and feeling rattled over the water ritual. Someone calls Dev's name from a few bus stops down, and he throws a hand in the air like he's dunking a ball. When he leaves to say hi to his friend, I pick his backpack off the ground and hug it to my body.

☾ ☾ ☾

On the bus, Dev listens to music on his iPod while I look out the big windows, watching the world blur by. Days when my brother was too busy and Ma was gone, Jas would offer to run errands with me. We'd walk Broad Street to pick up my check, avoiding guys who pulled over their cars to holla at us, running from the ones who offered money for blow jobs, and laughing at the ones who would say things like *You pretty little babies shouldn't be out here alone.* Jasmine always knew what to say to make those men feel ridiculous and perverted. Sometimes, she'd even cuss them out in Creole, or we'd make up a fake chant on the spot to scare them away. Then we'd take the bus to Dollar Tree, making sure to buy a four-pack of Slim Jims to eat two and two on the way to Compare Foods, where we'd buy fresh baked bread and lunch meat for Devin to eat.

But this was before she started chilling with college kids who gave her pills to pop at their parties. Mili and Inez seemed excited to hear the stories, but my mom's an addict and Jas's stories worried me. I tried to warn her, and she brushed me off until eventually it was easier to stop listening to her altogether. But distance feeds on itself, and a hole too big to cross with a simple phone call had grown between us before I realized our friendship was at stake. It was hard to close the distance with my feelings still there. Too strong to ignore. Then Jas was gone. Now, I'm about to run these errands by myself.

The bus jerks to a stop and lets two people on before starting up again. I look out the window and see a man running toward us. His long black peacoat flares out as he holds up a hand and screams for the bus to wait.

My breath gets caught in my throat. It looks like the man from the water ritual. I wait for him to fall and cut his head, but he doesn't. The bus driver stops to let him on. As he walks down the aisle, touching the tops of seats, people shrink away. He sits across from Dev, and I force myself to face forward. *Another coincidence.*

But then my peripherals catch him fidgeting. I glance as he peels and picks at the scabs on his fingers. I play with the diamond ring on my necklace and watch as he scratches his face. It starts slow but becomes frantic as he itches his cheek, his nose, scrapes and picks his eyelids. Blood begins to trickle down his face when he strikes a sensitive spot on his forehead. He touches it and looks down at his red-tinged fingers. My stomach lurches.

At the last second, I pull on the stop cord and stand up. Devin pops off one of his headphones to question me. "Forgot I had something to do," I say, because everything else could wait for another day. "I'll be home later. Love you."

I take off running as soon as my feet hit the concrete. Even though we live less than a mile from each other, Inez and I take two different buses because her house is closer to Elmwood Ave and mine is closer to Broad. My bus leaves me much farther than hers would've left me, and when I get to her house, I'm out of breath and my hair is raggedy, but I didn't miss a beat. They're arguing over which spell to do when I throw my backpack to the floor.

"Where'd you come from?" Inez asks, snatching a purple candle from Mili's hand and tossing it on a pile of colored candles.

"I saw the man from the ritual," I manage to say, chest still heaving. "I saw all of it. Baby Jesus. The pigeons."

"What? How?" Mili asks.

Instead of answering, I bend to pick up a blue candle. "Let's find my mom."

Mili's expression switches from shocked to hopeful in two seconds. "A locator spell?"

I shake my head. "You think we can do one better and make her want to come home?"

9

MILIANI

The basement is warmer than it usually is, and sweat builds at the back of my neck. Influencing people with spells has never seemed to work, but after our desire to embarrass Darleny in the hall manifested before our eyes, and after Natalie, who won't say it but always has one foot out of the circle, saw all of our predictions, I know something is changing.

Our intention to fight for Jas is giving us more magic already.

This time, an influencing spell needs to work because we've spent six days without Jas, and I keep imagining small fibers of her spirit splitting apart, the color of her soul diluting until it's a shade of gray. I feel anxious until Natalie's hand connects with mine and, for the first time, her energy surges through me. Inez's energy feels stronger today too. We all want to do the calling spell. It pushes adrenaline through me, excitement mixing with nerves and heightening my need to get this right.

In the center of our circle, there are candles lit: orange for attraction, dark blue to enhance psychic abilities, white to balance it all. We burn the bay leaf and chicory root Natalie picked up from Whole Foods to help facilitate psychic connections. A picture of her mom sits on a mirror, along with a silver diamond ring she gave Natalie years ago. Nat keeps it around her neck on a chain she rarely takes off. As we hold hands, we chant her mom's name over and over.

"Donna Williams, Donna Williams, Donna Williams."

Natalie says, "Follow my voice. Come home." The candles flicker, and a strange scent starts to fill the room. My body tenses. I inhale greedily, hoping to catch lilac and lavender in the air, praying Jas is here with us, watching, leaning close. But the scent is unmistakably vanilla, potent enough to mask the burning bay leaf, and rich with a hint of smoke.

"Do you smell that?" Natalie asks, her voice wavering. I have to swallow my disappointment in order to speak up with Inez and let her know we both do. "It smells like my mom's perfume," Nat says. She closes her eyes, and her body trembles as she chants by herself, "Come home. You want to be home. Come to me, Ma."

We lock in on one another's faces, and a thickness to the air makes it hard to swallow. Then we bend down, one by one, to blow out the candles in front of us. But as Inez leans over to blow her last candle, a rat scuttles across the floor between us, knocking the candle to the ground. The fire goes out at the same time that Inez screams. She swerves her body to the side as the rat runs by, squeaking until it's out of sight under the staircase.

"A rat's gotta be a good sign, right?" Natalie asks.

There's a moment of silence before we crack up laughing.

☾ ☾ ☾

I'm still wired when I make it home. My body always buzzes a little after a spell, but never this intense. My vision is sharp enough to notice the tiniest fragments in our wooden door, and it's like there are sparks coming out of my fingertips when I turn the knob. I know Mom cooked today; the scent of garlic and soy sauce from the adobo fills my nose before I walk into the house. It feels as if I'm gliding through the living room, the lamps dimming and brightening as I pass them, my energy crackling and growing.

There's a plate waiting for me on the counter, and Mom's feeding her two cockatiels. Octavia has darker feathers than Petey, but Petey's cheeks are a brighter orange than hers. Octavia sits on Mom's shoulder as she wraps lumpia and fries it on the stove, and when Mom takes her outside, Octavia digs her claw feet into Mom's shirt and stays put. Petey is partial to the cage, plays a lot in their water bath, but will eat out of my hand if I'm gentle enough. Mom's had these birds since I was a girl. Sometimes, I tease she pays more attention to them than she does to me, and she never denies it.

I sit to eat, and she doesn't ask me about school or where I've been while she checks Octavia's feathers and pets Petey. We don't speak until I finish eating and put my plate in the sink. She turns to look at me. "Is that sage I smell on you?"

"Uh. No," I lie, knowing I burned it after the ritual.

"You smell like bay leaf and cedarwood and burn."

"I'm not sure how," I say.

"And witchcraft and lies," she adds.

She turns back around, and I feel even more guilty when she washes my dish and shuts off the water, but I hold my breath until she leaves the kitchen. Mom never wants to talk about magic. Says it's something silly that died with her dad. But I remember her teaching me about the power of herbs, the way Papa taught her when she was young.

Petey and Octavia start up again, but the sweet songs quickly turn to shrieking. I cover my ears—the piercing sounds make my eardrums pulse—and walk over to them. They're going wild, climbing on top of each other. Petey's pecking the feathers at the back of Octavia's head hard enough to pull them out.

I almost yell for Mom, but Petey attacks Octavia again, and I panic. "Shh," I say, and uncover my ears to place both hands against the metal cage. Quickly, my skin grows warm and the birds grow quiet. Black beaded eyes stare straight into mine.

I put a foot behind me and begin walking backward. They don't make a sound until I'm out of the kitchen and into the dark hall. But when I turn, there's a shadow waiting for me near the staircase. I flinch back, heart stammering, until I realize it's Mom, standing perfectly still.

I walk over to her and notice her face is scrunched in on itself. "You okay, Mom?"

She reaches for me like she might cup my cheeks, then lets her hands fall to her side. "Did you do something to make them scream?"

I shake my head, stunned by her question. She watches me for a while, but her eyes keep flickering to the walls before she walks past me into the kitchen.

☾ ☾ ☾

The call comes the way it does in the movies: in the middle of REM sleep, when I can hardly find my sight and I'm stumbling out of bed to answer before it wakes Mom.

"Mili, it's me."

I slip into a sitting position on the floor, with the cord tangled around me. The cold of the wood helps wake me. His voice is steady on the line, soft and slow, luring me out like it used to with these late-night calls when he couldn't sleep.

It's hasn't even been a week since we broke up, but it's the longest we've gone without speaking in years. Still, I say, "Jayson, why are you calling?"

He hesitates. "I . . . wanted to make sure you were okay. I'm here if you need someone."

I swallow. "Thank you, but why would you want to talk to me anyway?"

"I care about you. That didn't change when we broke up. You and Jasmine were best friends, and seeing you at the funeral, I just . . ." He stops, sighs. "Because I still love you."

The silence that follows gives me too much time to think of the way my stomach dropped at his mention of me and Jasmine. The night Jayson and I broke up was the same night she died. Those thoughts tumble into memories of when he'd call and we'd talk for hours—about comic books and moon phases and his dad's delicious mofongo. There was rarely silence then, always something else, and one more thing, and don't hang up yet. I tug on the telephone cord. If I tug hard enough, maybe it'll come right out of the wall.

"Don't do this," I say. "Not right now."

"I'm sorry," he starts. "Mili, don't you love me?"

I wasn't ready for this. "I do, but I can't be with you."

"Why?" His voice wavers. "I'm sorry for what happened. I promise I wasn't trying to pressure you. We don't even have to talk about sex until you're ready."

"You never pressured me," I say, "but I need space. And Jas just died, and . . ."

"But you don't have to go through it alone. Don't you miss us?"

Us. I haven't even had time to worry about us. I tell him I have to go and I hang up because I know if I give it any more time, I may never get there. If I gave it time, he'd say something else, and I'd think of how much I missed these calls, his voice. I might tell him how it felt to watch him comfort Darleny and not me at Jasmine's wake.

But there's no *us.* There can't be an *us.*

I just hate him thinking our relationship ended because he pressured me to lose my virginity when he didn't. I almost lost it to him in more places than I like to remember: on a black futon at a friend of a friend's house party when everyone else was downstairs, in a borrowed red Jeep with feathers dangling from the rearview mirror. After too many failed attempts, we made a plan to wait until senior year. We'd make it special.

But once we became seniors, things didn't change. Every time we'd get close, I'd scramble for my panties. *Here isn't the right place. What's that noise? I think the universe is saying we should wait.* The last time was a catalyst for the worst night of my life. His parents were out of town, and we were in his room. I remember his sheets smelling like fabric softener, how good it felt when he kissed my thigh, how wet I was. *This is it,* I thought. But when he pressed against me, Jasmine's face came to mind, and I pushed myself up off the bed and out of my two-year relationship.

I push myself off the floor now, my body swaying toward the bed for sleep, almost reaching it, until a dial tone rings out. It gets louder and louder. I turn and look down at the phone on the floor. It's tipped on its side and off the cradle. I bend to fix it, but the dial tone doesn't die. I pick up the phone again and slam it down. This time, the tone does die, but when I stand I feel a crackle against my cheek. A static shock that has me stumbling back until my legs hit the bed. It happens so fast I don't notice my door swing open until Mom steps into the room and switches on the light.

"What's going on? Why are you awake? Were you talking to someone?"

I felt something, I want to say. I almost say. But I tell her I had a nightmare. She scans the room like she knows it's not the truth. Her eyes linger in the corner near my closet for so long it gives me chills.

"I'll fix you some tea," she says, and disappears down the hall.

I climb into bed and pull my knees to my chest. "Hello?" I call out. Then softly I say, "Jas?"

I wait, but all I hear are the faint sounds of Petey and Octavia shrieking from the kitchen.

10

INEZ

My body feels doped up on adrenaline after the calling spell, and the calming ones don't work for sleep. I pop a Benadryl and pray the grogginess doesn't follow me through the day tomorrow. When sleep finally comes, I dream of Jasmine for the first time. She picks me up in her sister's hooptie. We blast Brandy's "Sittin' Up in My Room" and speed down I-95. We open the sunroof and stick our hands through it, and we scream silly shit to people passing by. It starts to rain, the road suddenly slippery, the music skipping until there's only radio static. Jas turns to me, face serious, as both of her hands come off the wheel.

My eyes go wide. I reach for the wheel, but she stops me.

We are swerving on the slick road, and she touches my shoulder.

"You're changing, Inez. But we'll work it out. We'll change together."

I shoot up in bed, clinging to my sheets, with a racing pulse and sweat up my back as I search the dark for her. My shoulder tingles as I touch it the way she did. I will myself to go back to sleep, chant for so long it sounds like a lullaby, cry because I'm desperate to see her face and hear her voice again. What did she mean when she said I'm changing? I need to know. But as soon as my eyes feel heavy, the suncatcher dangling from my wall begins to sway. I reach to steady it, but when I let go it sways harder.

There's an uneasiness in the pit of my stomach as I sit up and shrink away.

The suncatcher moves in a circle until it clanks against the window and comes to a stop.

I watch to see if it stirs again. Until daylight makes it burst colors around my room.

11

MILIANI

"Gimme the Light" by Sean Paul is blasting from Isobel's boom box when I walk into the botanica. I know her father stepped out if she has it turned up this loud. Hector owns this sweet basement botanica, with its stone walls and its piping running overhead and its musty smell when the sandalwood incense isn't burning. Isobel works the register and homeschools herself between customers. She has long brown hair which she keeps back in a loose braid. Sometimes, I walk by her and tug on it, and the dimples in her cheeks deepen when she realizes it's me. Today, she doesn't look up from her book while I browse.

"Don't you know it's rude not to greet your customers?" I call out. "Plus, this music is definitely not fitting for a botanica."

She sucks her teeth and puts her book down, but those dimples give her away. "And what do you feel is fitting for a botanica?"

I walk over, tap the boom box on the counter. "Anything but this."

"Always have something to say." Her voice is smooth, with a Dominican accent that picks up when she's being sassy. "But it's been a while. Thought you blessed me and found a new shop."

I don't tell her I haven't been by because of Jasmine. I lift a brown candle to my nose, then place it on the counter. "And miss out on bothering you?"

She gets shy when I say this. Takes her bottom lip into her mouth and doesn't meet my eyes. "You're only a bother when you come in here talking shit about my music."

We laugh, but there's a hint of nerves buzzing between us. Then I think of Jas, and I want the buzzing to stop. "Will your father be in soon? I'm looking for an oil I can't find on the shelf. Was hoping he had it in the back."

She says she can help me, and I hand her the list Auntie Lindy gave me. She scans it, then gives me a confused look. "Are you trying to conjure a demon? We don't sell half of this stuff."

"I only need the oil today," I say, suddenly irritated.

She leaves for the back room and returns with a small glass bottle. It's square-shaped with a black lid. The label is in Spanish, and I think of asking Isobel to tell me what it says, but she turns up the music before ringing me out. I brush it off. No need to be distracted with Isobel.

Jas needs me. I can't fail her again. It's my fault she's dead.

When we were younger, Jas used to sleep over and we'd kiss each other after Mom went to bed. We never called it practice because Jas was already an experienced kisser (I'd only ever tapped Kevin Rocha in the eighth grade). She'd massage my tongue with hers and suck on my lips gently, and her hands would travel up my shirt to trace my nipples over the fabric of my bra. I'd open my legs when her fingers would dance up my thigh. But when we were done, she'd fall asleep effortlessly, and I'd stay up most of the night with a racing heart and the urge to touch her the way she'd touched me. The kissing didn't stop between us when our friends found out about it, or when she started to have sex with other people. But I put a stop to it when I got into a relationship with Jayson—even though it was hard to do. And the reason I broke up with him wasn't because I didn't love him; it was because I realized I was in love with Jasmine too.

Jayson was pulling his boxers back on, confused and emotional, when I left him to walk three miles in the dark to ring her doorbell. She popped her head out of the third-floor window to throw me down her key. My hands were shaking while opening the downstairs door. Her family was watching TV in the living room, unaffected by the familiar sight of me walking in.

Jasmine was sitting on her bed in an oversized black T-shirt. I locked the door and began stripping off my clothes to stand naked in front of her.

"Milz, what are you doing?" she asked, her voice shaking.

But as she examined me, her breathing sharpened, her thick thighs parted slightly. She looked good with her bottom lip drooping and the hunger growing in her eyes.

I walked over to touch her face, and she closed her eyes.

"Oh," she said, rubbing her cheek against my palm.

I was careful climbing in her bed, slowly straddling her hips. I asked to kiss her, and she said, "Please."

"I want you," I told her. "Do you still want me?"

She didn't question my relationship status, and she answered by cupping my butt to pull me in deeper. "I've missed you," she said.

My heart was beating so hard I thought she might feel it on her own chest. To balance myself, I placed my arms on either side of her and let my fingers dip and dip, and then, "I love you," I said. "I broke up with Jayson. I want to be with you." It slipped out, I think. Or maybe I planned to say it on the walk over. Either way, it was too late to take it back.

Jas narrowed her eyes, a small smile forming on her lips. "Aw," she said, and my stomach dropped. "I love you, too."

Even though I could hear the reservation in her tone, I told myself all I needed was for her to tell me she loved me. My hands slipped under her shirt, but before I could pull it over her head, she gently pushed me off her. Flashes of Jayson's stunned expression came to mind. This time, I was in his place.

"I do love you. I always will," Jasmine said, sitting up, her hand reaching for mine, squeezing softly. "But we're too young to be tied to any one soul. I'm not ready to be in a relationship with anyone." She pulled her hand from mine and placed it on my cheek. "I can't be with you the way you want me to."

The sting of her words made her fingers feel rough against my face. When I pulled away, she reached for me again, but I was already up and getting dressed, trying to fight back my tears.

"Mili, wait. Let's talk. This was all so sudden, and . . . maybe I can explain better. Stay, okay?" She stood to get closer, but I backed up and threw my hands out. I didn't want her close to me. "Mili, please."

I could hear the desperation straining her voice, her tears coming, but my own were too. "I'm not mad," I said, "I just—"

I never finished that sentence. I left with her calling out for me.

If I would've stayed, she'd still be here.

12

MILIANI

Auntie wasn't expecting me to be so quick at the botanica. "Did you fly here?"

Before we start training, I use her phone to call Nat and ask if she's heard from her mom. She sounds miserable, tells me she hasn't, and rushes off the phone. I take my disappointment and join Auntie on her shag rug, where she sits with two pots filled midway with soil.

"Spells can take a while to manifest," she says, and hands me one of the pots. She points to a napkin. I unfold it to find small white seeds, cracked and sprouting. "Plant those half an inch apart, dig your nails into the soil, feel for the placement. Be careful with your intentions. Will the seeds to grow."

I tell myself to *feel* the soil, don't tell her when I don't feel anything. I take my time, try my best, copy her when she leans over the pot and blows her breath into it. We stay here a minute, hunched over, hands on either side of the pot. The wet soil smells sweet beneath my nose. When I look up, Auntie is studying me. With her eyebrows scrunched together and her head tilted, she says, "You look so much like him when you're focused."

"Who? My father?"

She clears her throat and touches the side of her pot. "No one."

"Papa?"

"Forget it, Miliani." She gets up from the floor. "If you did the work right, we'll be able to tell soon. I know this seems small, but elemental magic takes patience. We start with earth."

My leg shakes while she takes our pots to the window. She's asking me to be patient but telling me Jas's spirit can't wait long.

She sits back down. "Did you get the oil?"

I open my bag to take out the glass bottle from the botanica. She seems surprised I was able to get it. She opens it and smells it, takes a dab of the liquid between two fingers and rolls it around. It's the real deal, she decides. She looks pleased.

"Is it for the anchoring?" I say.

She shifts the bottle. The light from the window makes it look luminescent. "No."

"For a spell we'll do?"

"Yes. It's for the only spell we'll do together to ensure you've learned enough elemental magic when it's time for the anchoring. We won't be practicing spells in the interim. I've had enough of the shift from spell work to last me lifetimes." I quirk an eyebrow, and she sighs like I should know. "Opening the door to the spirit world with large requests like the ones you and your friends will make requires an exchange of something here." She taps the wooden floor, leans forward, and taps the side of my head. "Sometimes, even here."

"An energy exchange," I say.

"Yes. There's always a balance. You tap into their world, they want to tap into ours."

Nerves make knots in my stomach. "Is the rest of the list for me and my friends?"

She laughs. My neck burns. "I'm not a psychic. I don't know

what spells you'll decide to go with. The list is for me, but I'll tell you when I need items from it."

"Wait, you're sending me to run your errands now?"

She shrugs, smiles slowly. "Energy exchange. You help me, I help you." She sits back, arms at either side, palms pressed into the floor. "Unless you don't find my help valuable."

"I need it," I say. My mind flashes to the image of Jas crying out to me, and I work hard to pick another image: sitting between her legs while she works cornrows into my hair.

"But are you and your friends ready for the shift?"

"We have to be," I say, but cringe at the thought of asking them to deal with an energy exchange, after I already asked them to help me get Jas back. Especially when they don't even know the whole plan for how we're going to do it yet.

"I should remind you to think twice before telling them about the anchoring. They may not help you if they know."

She doesn't have to warn me. I want to argue, but how could I tell my friends the plan isn't just to give Jas a foothold on this side, but to use Darleny's body as the anchor for it? I feel queasy and ready to get it done with. "Maybe we'll be strong enough if the calling spell works."

Auntie shakes the bottle of oil before putting it in her pocket. "Like I said before, you only have one shot at this, and if you do it wrong, your friend's spirit will be trapped." She frowns at me. "There's no way one spell will give you the power or open the realms enough . . . even though I wish it could."

"But you said her spirit might get angry. You said she——"

She sighs, and it feels like the room temp drops 20 degrees. "You have to trust me."

I wrap my arms around myself. If she had a definite timeline for me to follow until I can see Jas again, a date to check boxes off my calendar until, this would be easier.

"How will we know when the realms are ready?"

"As they widen, the spirits will interact more. You and your friends will feel them; they may even be able to influence objects around you. The wider the realms, the bigger foothold the spirits get on this side. We will know the shift is complete when the spirits can appear fully corporeal, when they're able to look like you and me."

The hairs on my arms rise with goosebumps. Suddenly, what happened last night feels more real. I touch my cheek. Auntie narrows her eyes. "You felt something already, didn't you?"

"I think . . . I think there was a spirit in my room last night, but I'm not sure. It was late and I was tired, but I . . . felt something. I thought for a second it might be Jasmine, but the energy was . . . angry?" Her back straightens. "You said to trust you and . . ."

"It's not her," she says, and looks away. "I mean . . . there's no way she's changing this soon." She holds a finger out, signaling me to wait, and stands to hurry out of the room.

Imagining the ways Jas might be different makes my mouth dry, gives the room a claustrophobic feeling. I pick at the skin on my fingers, clench my fists, close my eyes, get up to take a step toward the door. I call to Auntie, but she returns a few seconds later with a shard of glass in her hand. I back away as she approaches.

"Be easy, girl." She pulls me close to the window, opening the shade as wide as it can go, and makes me sit on a stool.

When the shard of glass is close to my face, I notice it's actually a mirror. "What are—"

"Shh." She moves the mirror in different angles, examining

me while reflecting the light from the sun to the wall nearest me. "Hmm . . ." She takes a few steps back.

My heart is still racing when she wraps the mirror in a thick cloth she pulls from her pocket. "You're not being haunted," she says, but her eyes linger on my face like she's still unconvinced. "Must have been a wanderer passing through."

I'm shaken by what just happened, but I don't want to be. I want to be brave. Auntie can probably hear the fear inside me anyway. "And what about Jasmine? Will she pass through?"

"Usually, when new spirits aren't able to move on, they wander for a while, lost in the spaces on the other side. You might not make contact with her until the anchoring," she says, and I try to focus on the color in her cheeks, on the way her voice ticks up with excitement, so I don't focus on how devastating hearing that is right now. "Don't feel sad, Miliani. The calling spell must be opening the doors already." She hands me the piece of mirror. "Take this with you. Keep it somewhere dark and cool. It must be wrapped in the cloth when it's not in use. If you feel a spirit reaching out, use it to *see*. You need a source of light to reflect the shadow."

"How will I know? What will I see?"

She laughs. "Oh, you'll know."

Most times, Auntie sounds like a riddle. She speaks in puzzle pieces and half sentences. I want to ask her where she got it, how she knows it works, but I don't have the patience today. I need to tell Inez and Natalie about the energy exchange and help prepare them for it. I rub the fabric between my fingers. "Dark and cool."

"And definitely somewhere your mother won't find."

13

NATALIE

I keep jumping every time a phone rings, hoping it'll be Ma.

Mili called the bodega earlier to tell me about the talk she had with her aunt and reassure me the calling spell will work because she felt a spirit last night. But now I'm spooked and hoping I don't sweat through my shirt restocking these shelves. If Mili's call wasn't enough, it's so damn hot in the bodega today. There's already a lack of ventilation in here, but Rhode Island's weather doesn't help. It's only 65 degrees in Providence, but the humidity makes it feel like 80. Last week, I hung up my winter coat to wear a windbreaker; this week, I'm carrying around a frozen water bottle to cool my neck and thighs while I work.

Ortega's Bodega straddles the corner of Warrington and Broad, with its metal bars over the windows and graffiti art decorating the brick of the building. Worked here since I was fourteen, when I was still too young to get my permit and Mr. Ortega took a chance on a non-Spanish-speaking cashier in a predominately Hispanic community. Ma heard from a friend that he was hiring, and when she told me she was going to get me a job, I didn't complain about being too young to work because I knew we needed the money, but I did point out the fact.

"I got this," she said, and turned the volume up on the radio.

We sang out loud to Mariah Carey's "Fantasy," with Ma trying to hit the high notes and me telling her to stop.

Mr. Ortega sat at the register that night and didn't look up from counting the drawer until she spoke. "Well, if it isn't Luis Ortega, my high school sweetheart," she said as he adjusted his glasses. "What, you don't remember this face?"

"Face might've taken me a bit, but I'll never forget that voice."

I laughed because Ma has a raspy voice that sounds like she just came out of a dead sleep to puff on a hundred cigarettes, and she talks real loud all the time.

Mr. Ortega came out from behind the desk to wrap her in a hug. "It's good to see you, Donna," he said, and after reminiscing, he turned up the radio sitting on the counter, and they danced bachata. I sat on his office chair, spinning while I watched them.

That night, Ma helped close up shop and landed me the job.

Experiences like this *with* her used to outweigh the experiences *without* her, but now I feel an undercurrent of anger because she's making me worry about her when one of my friends just died.

I stack the canned beans, pulling at the back of my shirt to keep it from sticking to my skin. Trying to remember if I have to pay the electric or the cable bill to avoid thinking about Ma or Jas or ghosts, when the bell on the door rings and makes me jump.

"Be right there," I call out, and tiptoe it to place the last two cans on the high shelf.

"Need help?" someone asks from behind, making me damn near lose my balance. "Ah, sorry," he says, and I bite my top lip, embarrassed because I know that voice.

I climb down the stool to turn toward Ray Garrick.

One side of his mouth shoots up. "Didn't know you still work here, Williams."

I shrink to pass him in the small aisle. He follows me to the front but doesn't say anything. Nerves bubble in my gut as he studies me. *Maybe I have something in my teeth. Maybe he thinks I'm ugly now. Maybe he'll ask why I stopped talking to him.* "Can I help you, Ray?"

He smiles again, his teeth straight, even with the gap in the top middle, and so white against the dark brown of his skin. "Mr. Ortega didn't tell you? I'll be working here with you."

I'm about to call Ray's bullshit when Mr. Ortega opens his office door, peeks out, and calls Ray over. They shut the door, and I stare at it until a customer walks in.

When I'm at the register, I always imagine following customers around with my camera to see what their life is like. There's the woman with three kids, who comes here to spend her WIC checks because Mr. Ortega gives her fresh cheese and lets her pick any cereal she wants. She doesn't have to get the no-name-brand beans; she can get Goya. I wonder if her kids ask her for the fresh cheese at the big-name markets when we're not open so they can watch the butcher work and offer them a slice, but since she can only get the prepared block of cheese there, she tries to think of something to say other than *It's because we are poor, babies. Poor people don't deserve fresh cheese.*

But right now, even though the woman in front of me digs her hand in her butt to fix her undies and can't decide which scratch ticket she wants so she places those same hands on the glass and looks real close, I can't imagine her outside this store. I can't think of anything besides Ray, the guy who *needed* to show me up the summer our school funded a debate team but would kiss me on the lips after, tell me he was sorry he knew more about foreign policies. The guy who critiqued my photographs in class but would volunteer to edit them. What I hated most about seeing Ray in school was how bothered I was by it coming to an end once he graduated, but it also made it easier to quit seeing him when the time came.

When he comes out of Mr. Ortega's office, he does so alone, tossing a pack of Winterfresh on the counter, and whipping out his wallet. "Do you smile at any of your customers?"

I meet his eyes. "All the time," I say, and ring him out.

"You haven't smiled at me once." He places a hand over his heart. "Thought you'd be happy to see me. It's been months. Actually, it's going on a year since you went ghost on me."

"Why are you really here, Ray?"

He chuckles. "If you think I came to try to win back your affection or stalk you, that's only part of the reason."

I laugh, then try not to look on the outside how nervous he's making me feel on the inside. We never made things official back then, but I always wondered if he wanted to the way I did.

"Fine, I'll stop driving you wild with suspense," he says. "I'm here to install an air-conditioning system and set up real security cameras. Then you can go back to hating me."

I don't hate him, but letting him think what he wants saves me from explaining the reason I stopped seeing him. "Well, we don't have to talk at all then, do we?"

He blinks, looks wounded for a second, before he unwraps a stick of gum and pops it into his mouth. "If that's the way you want it, Williams."

"It is, Garrick."

He nods but doesn't listen. "Where's your camera?"

"I'm not allowed to use it inside the store."

"That's too bad. I'm sure you'd get sick shots of people in here." I feel like he's searched through my thoughts and pulled them from me. "Could've put them in art school apps, but I'm sure you have a strong portfolio already. Which schools did you apply to?"

"I don't want to talk about it," I say, but find myself fantasizing about a college classroom with camera lenses I've never been able to get my hands on, learning more about digital technology and new ways to work with lighting.

He leans over the counter a little. "Well, I'm sure you'll get into all of them, but if you need any help with late edits to your portfolio, I got you. Call it a belated parting gift."

My cheeks burn. I fix my mouth to say something, but the bell on the bodega door jingles.

Except . . . the door hasn't opened.

Ray looks at me, then around the store. "You see something?"

"You didn't hear that?"

Before he can answer, the telephone rings behind the counter and sends me out of my skin.

"Yo, you okay over there?" Ray says.

I nod and turn to pick up the phone, my heart pounding, my mind running back to Mili telling me about ghosts, and a shift, and other things I didn't want to know.

My voice is thick. "Ortega's Bodega."

"Hi, Natty Fatty."

I push the phone closer to my ear, heart thrumming faster. "Ma? Ma, where are you?"

"It's good to hear your voice, baby." But her own sounds smaller, slower. "I need help. I'm not feeling good, Natty."

The spell. It worked. My head spins and my throat feels like it's going to close up, and I can't think or hear Ma as she goes on about whatever she's saying.

I grip the phone. "Ma, where are you?"

"I'm in Newport with your godmother, Betty."

I've never heard of a Betty, but Ma does this. I ask her for the address and she tells me, asks if I have a pen, repeats the address for a second time. When I tell her to stop, that I'll be there soon, she tells me to hurry. I tremble putting the phone back on the cradle.

Ray quietly asks, "You all right?" and my stomach does a flip. I was wrapped up in talking to Ma and forgot he was even there.

"I'm fine," I say, and begin packing my bag.

He presses his body against the counter. "It sounded serious."

I look up at him. He's too close. "You wouldn't know if you weren't listening."

He holds his hands in the air, steps back once, twice. "You're right. I'm sorry."

As soon as Ray's gone, I call my sister, who tells me she'll be by to get me soon. And then it all hits me again: Ray working here, Ma calling. After leaving Inez's the other night, the adrenaline from the water ritual had worn off, and I doubted the calling spell would work. I push out a breath of air, close my eyes for a second because suddenly the thought of getting to talk to Jasmine doesn't feel like such a dream. And that's exciting, and scary, and makes me want to cry.

I call Mili. She answers on the third ring. "What's wrong?"

"You were right. My mom called. We're going to get her now."

"Oh my God." Her voice falters, then it sings: "We did it."

"Yeah," I say. "I really think we did."

14

NATALIE

Mr. Ortega says he'll finish my shift, and tells me to call with an update. I stand outside under the awning of the bodega to avoid the sun's heat and watch the steam rise from the grills in the food truck across the street. The cooks are getting ready for the long lines of people that'll be waiting for their weekend fix. Some will be posted up against their cars, blasting music. People will form groups and dance, crack jokes, and smoke weed. This is all before the club. After is when the nightlife really starts, when girls start tripping over their heels until they take them off and leave them on curbs, when the chimi trucks run out of meat and people start cussing, and the police show up to tell everybody it's time to go home.

I'm about to go back inside to call Leanna again, but her car rounds the corner and pulls in front of me. Ava rolls down the passenger window. I'm surprised she's here. Normally, I don't see her unless I go to their house, but I'm not complaining. She smells like brown-sugar perfume when we hug through the open window.

"What took so long?" I ask my sister. "Ma might change her mind and take off."

Leanna rolls her eyes. "Stop fussing and get in. I'll drop Ava home, then we'll go."

"We don't have time for—"

"She's right," Ava cuts in, her blunt purple-colored bob swaying as she shakes her head. "I'm coming."

"I'd rather you not," my sister replies, voice low.

Ava grabs Leanna's hand. "You're my family, so she's my family."

Leanna usually hides these private moments. Sometimes when I visit them, if I'm quiet and sneaky enough, I'll see Leanna come up from behind Ava while she cooks to wrap an arm around her stomach. But now, Leanna lifts Ava's hand and turns it to kiss her palm. She doesn't let go of it even though she knows I'm watching.

☾ ☾ ☾

The Newport Bridge is a rusty green beauty. To calm myself, I take out my camera to record the workers hooked near the top of it. My stomach does a flip watching them. One time, I cried on a Ferris wheel and Ma had to wave at the worker to get us off earlier. She climbed this bridge *many times* as a teenager when she needed some fun. I told her someone couldn't pay me a million dollars cash to climb a bridge. She said, "You'll forever be no fun."

Newport air is like a concentrated version of the way it smells in Warwick, where Leanna and Ava live, which is only three minutes' drive from the beach, close enough to smell salt water and wet sand when the wind blows.

But here there are so many docks, seagulls flying. There are cottages with rock walls, canoes hooked to the top of trucks, and the ocean is everywhere. I love paying attention to the people walking with huge surfboards, but I lean forward, gripping Ava's headrest.

"Can't you drive a little above the limit?"

Leanna sighs, speeds up some, but it doesn't feel fast enough.

❨ ❪ ❨

When we arrive at the projects, we park in the corner lot of the complex, and I think of when we played jump rope in this spot. We'd run around here with all the other kids while Ma sniffed lines of coke somewhere out of sight. One day, Dev brought home a used needle he'd found by the blue dumpsters. Ma never brought us along with her after that, said we'd be safer at home, where we could lock the door and dial her up when we needed her.

Leanna turns to me. "Stay in the car."

"You're bugging."

"I'll be right back," she says, getting out. "Wait with Ava."

I want to protest, but Ava shifts in her seat to smile at me.

I look out the window, watch the children who run through the clotheslines, playing games with the hanging laundry, tripping over broken concrete as they chase one another. I build a scene for them in my head: massive trees to climb, enough grass for them to roll in, clean walkways and a park with monkey bars. They look happy just like this, but what if they had more?

Ava taps the dashboard and says to me, "Your sister's taking too long. You coming?"

❨ ❪ ❨

Betty's door is cracked open, and Ava pushes it the rest of the way. Ma's lying on a couch with Leanna leaned over her. My "god-mother" Betty is throwing her arms open to hug us.

Leanna sucks her teeth. "We should call an ambulance," she says.

Ma tells Leanna she's fine, but she sits up to vomit in a big bowl. I freeze at the sight of her, and Ava is busy trying to get

Betty to shut up. Leanna says to me, "Get over here and help Ma stand."

Ma gets up on her own, swaying but on two feet. She looks at me and smiles. "Natty Fatty, my baby."

My eyes water, and I move my feet to hug my momma. Her skin is sticky. She smells like body odor and alcohol. She keeps saying she wants to go home. But we're together now.

Leanna looks through Betty's trash, with Betty protesting behind her. "Fuck," my sister says, then she shoves the garbage can and it falls on its side. "Let's go."

When we get in the car, she wastes no time. "You shooting up heroin now?"

Ma's holding her head in the back seat beside me. I'm stroking her arm till I stop and turn it over. The marks don't lie, and she's not trying to, either. "My head hurts, Leanna. Please."

Leanna grips the steering wheel and drives fast while she goes in on Ma: *That's what happens when you do heroin. Do you want to catch HIV? Have an overdose? Crack's not bad enough?*

My throat hurts. I look out the window, but the world outside the car gets hazy. Ma tells me she's sorry, and her sweaty hand grips mine. It's shaking as I try to push her away. But when we're almost on the highway home, she starts breathing heavy, gasping for air.

Leanna's still cussing in the front seat. "Shut up," I yell, then pull Ma against me. I tilt her head, try to remember CPR from health class. "Ma, can you breathe?"

Her eyes close, and her heart's beating fast. I can feel it going in and out against my fingertips, until I can't feel it at all. "We need to get her to a hospital. Now."

Ava's already opening a map she took from the glove

compartment to give my sister directions, and I'm stroking Ma's wet hair. "It's going to be okay, Momma." I lean to whisper in her ear, trying to chant healing spells I can't remember, wishing I paid more attention to Mili when she talked about the way her Papa would use spells to ease his own pain. If I'd believed sooner, if I was stronger, maybe I could fix this somehow. But all I can do is pray.

Somewhere between the docks and the hospital, Ma stops breathing.

☾ ☾ ☾

The doctors rush her in on a gurney. It's all beeps and clangs and so bright I'm dizzy. We follow them but get stuck outside the room, watching through glass as they use the paddles to shock Ma's heart. After a few seconds, it starts beating on the monitor, and I rush to heave into a wastebasket. Ava makes me sit on a chair, rubs my back, and a nurse hands me a wet rag. Leanna won't look at anyone; her back is still to us, her hand pressed against the emergency room window as she looks in on Ma. She's stiff when nurses rush by her with clipboards, pushing patients in wheelchairs, wanting her to move out of the way. One of them leads us to the waiting room, where we call Devin and Mr. Ortega and wait. Five minutes, ten minutes, maybe forty.

Leanna sits up straight as the doctor comes out and sits across from her. "How is she?" she says. "How's my mom?"

"Your mom is in a coma," he says. Bits of explanation and medical jargon get lost between the parts my brain is able to pay attention to: "I think she's suffered severe brain damage . . . I'm not sure she'll wake up . . . I'm so sorry."

His sorry makes the world splinter, but it's Leanna's cry that wrenches mine from me.

15

INEZ

My stomach lurches before the house phone rings, and Victor passes it to me without a word. I don't know how, but I know it's her before pressing my ear to the phone. "Natalie?"

A pained croak comes from the other side of the line.

"What's wrong?" She sucks in a breath and sobs some more. "Is it your mom?"

"She's . . . ," Natalie starts, her voice cracking like I've never heard before. "She can't die. I need you to come. I need you to come here right now. Mili's on her way to get you."

"But, Nat, what happened? Where are you?"

She tells me her mom is in a coma. "Please come. I need you." The line goes dead.

I'm stuck in shock, still gripping the phone, the dial tone blaring out, my anxiety creeping in, when the doorbell rings. Miliani is waiting on the other side of the door, with her arms wrapped around herself and her curly hair in a messy ponytail.

"We need to head up to Newport," she tells me.

I spot Jayson's parked car and raise both brows.

"Don't ask," she says.

"It's Sunday," I say, and it sounds ridiculous. Natalie's mom is in a coma. Our Nat.

But Miliani puts on her best sympathetic face. The one that says she's choosing to be more understanding than judgmental. "Maybe your mom will understand."

❨ ☾ ❩

Mami's facing the mirror, working curls into the ends of her hair with a big round brush. She notices me behind her but keeps going. Then I see something creep behind us both. The hairs on my arms prick, and everything suddenly stops, including my breathing. Time slows, right before a few shadows shoot by us. Mami doesn't even blink. I tremble and turn to look around the room, but they're gone. Am I seeing shit because Mili mentioned spirits earlier?

"What is it, Inez? Need something?"

I grab my left elbow with my right hand to still the shakes. For more reasons than one, I can't tell Mami why I'm spooked. This is the first time she's spoken directly to me since confronting me about Aaron. Victor learned the silent treatment from her.

While watching the mirror for shadows, I tell her about Nat's mom. It takes her a few seconds, it takes me a prayer, but she says, "Ay dios mío. That poor family," and puts down her brush.

I try to study her face while I say, "Nat wants me to go pray for her mom."

"I don't like you missing church, but"—Mami sighs and turns to grab both of my hands—"go show her the power of God."

❨ ☾ ❩

On the ride up to Newport, Jayson tries to make small talk with Mili. I haven't had to be around the two of them since the breakup, and it's not as awkward as I expected, but I wish he wasn't here.

Me and Mili need to talk about what I saw in Mami's room. My wishes usually never amount to much, though, and after the small talk, I have to suffer through them filling each other in about which comic books they've read lately.

When we arrive, I think about the whir of hospital ventilation and the probing lights and the squeaky floors, and become even more anxious. I like to avoid hospitals after spending too much time in them years ago.

My first panic attack was "only heartburn, mija." Mami gave me Tums and a pat on the back, but the chest pain became more constant, the dizziness kicked in. She didn't take me seriously until my vision went black and I fell to the floor. Abuelo had had a heart attack that year, and I remember wondering if the doctors would confirm that I was dying too. But when they suggested anxiety, Mami refused the diagnosis. I was thirteen. What could I possibly have anxiety about?

They promised Mami they'd run tests: an EKG, an MRI with contrast, so not only was my chest burning, it felt like I'd peed myself too. But the ultrasound of my heart was comforting. The tech had the silkiest voice. She turned the screen. "See that? Those are the chambers. And that flutter? It's working well." She leaned in and whispered, "I'm not supposed to tell you, but your heart looks normal to me. When I'm scared or stressed, sometimes for no reason I can think of at all, I feel the same way you feel." And in that darkened room, with her rolling jelly over my chest with an ultrasound probe, it was the calmest I'd felt all week.

☽ ☾ ☽

The antiseptic smell sticks in my nose as we walk the halls, but at least Leanna looks relieved when she sees us. "Natalie hasn't left my mom's side. Maybe you guys can get her to eat something. Dev's been trying."

Mili pats her messenger bag. "Brought her favorite snacks."

Leanna smiles, exhausted. "I'm going to step out for a while with Ava, but I'll be right outside if you need me." She takes her girlfriend by the hand and goes. Miliani asks Jayson if he can give us some time with Natalie, and he takes a seat by the window.

☾ ☾ ☾

When we walk in, Dev taps Nat on the shoulder.

She's hunched over her mom's bed, unmoving. "Finally," she says without looking up.

Miliani rubs Devin's back. "You look so tired," she tells him. "You should go get rest."

He doesn't have to be told twice. Once we're alone with Nat, I wrap my arms around her from behind. "We should get you out of this room," I say to her. "Get you changed, some food."

But she stiffens and says, "Please shut the door and put down the privacy screen."

"Are we allowed to do that here?"

Miliani doesn't wait for an answer—she rushes to do it—and props a chair up under the door to keep it from opening.

I let go of Nat to look at her closely. I remember this look from Jasmine's funeral. Her eyes are dark and open, red-rimmed.

She stands, and the chair makes a screeching noise against the marble floor. "We probably don't have a lot of time. The nurses pop in and out." She turns to Mili. "Did you bring it?"

Miliani opens her messenger bag—and it's not filled with snacks, not one damn snack—then starts taking out supplies for a spell. My gaze bounces between them. "What's going on?"

Natalie grabs my arms. "If the calling worked, maybe we can help heal my mom."

16

INEZ

I'm speechless before it settles in. I was thinking we came up here to love and support Natalie. To try our best to do friendship the normal way. But I should've known.

"You can't think we can wake her from a coma," I say.

Miliani hands Natalie a bottle and shouts out some instructions before she starts to pour salt around the hospital bed, but neither of them bothers to answer me. Natalie shakes the bottle, which seems to be filled with oil and crushed herbs, and dumps some into her hands. She rubs it into her mom's forehead, over her neck and the bones protruding out of her chest, around her ankles, and, with fidgeting fingers, she tilts her mom's head back and pops a thumb into her mouth.

I try not to panic.

"Are either of you listening to me? We've only pulled off one other spell, and this is different. It's huge." I try to catch Natalie's eye. Does she truly believe we have power now, or is she desperate? What if we make things worse than they are?

Mili looks up at me. "If you don't believe we can, then we can't."

"It's not a matter of believing." I tug on my hair. "I just . . . Do you think we should?"

"What are you talking about?" Natalie's face contorts. "This is my mom."

"I know, but what if magic did this?" I gesture to her mom's hospital bed with my hands. "What if the calling spell messed something up? Changed her fate? What if we try to help her from the coma and something bad happens?"

What if God punishes us? I think. *What if God punishes me?* I don't say out loud.

Mili pauses pouring the salt, hesitation on her face. "My auntie said we're shifting energy with each spell. We don't know what the repercussions will be."

"I'm willing to do whatever it takes," Natalie snaps. "Just like I'm willing to help the ghost of Jasmine literally do things ghosts shouldn't be able to do."

And that's that. Mili nods, and I don't argue. I can't. This is Natalie. If she thinks the risk is worth it, I can't say no. She's had my back since the third grade, when someone snatched my Bible from me and she cussed them out at recess before I got the chance to do it myself.

I look down at her mom. Donna is a skinny woman with long legs and skin two shades paler than mine. I expected her to look sickly, but she just looks like Donna. I imagine if she were awake, she would be ringing her call light every hour to gossip about hospital drama with the nurses. She would probably embarrass Natalie by hitting on the doctors and by asking for another drip of morphine. And she would definitely not be wearing this hospital gown.

I shut the blinds, turn off the lights, and stand at the foot of the hospital bed. Miliani asks if we're ready and places her hands on either side of Natalie's mom's head. I grab Donna's ankles, and

Natalie slides her hands under her mom's gown and places them on her stomach. We're ready. Miliani starts to chant in a low voice, and I close my eyes.

There's a dip when what we're doing starts to feel more real. It's like going up on a roller coaster—up, up, up—and even though you might know when the drop is supposed to happen, you're still not ready for it. It takes my breath when we drop. I've only ever felt like this once before, with the calling spell. Slowly, the dip fades away. We never practice what to say and usually struggle to follow along, but not this time. Miliani believes that true magic doesn't sound like poetry, that we all just have to want the same thing. And she's right. Soon, we're repeating one another as if we'd practiced for days: "We ask you to bring this woman on the side of the living. We ask you to bring this woman on the side of the living."

We say this until the words stir together and I can't distinguish their voices from my own.

Donna's skin gets warm, but not warmer than my body. The sensation starts in my hands, tingles up and down my arms, from my knees to my toes and my back. I pull away and open my eyes. Natalie and Miliani are both staring down at their hands too.

But Donna doesn't startle awake. There isn't a moment where her fingers twitch and her eyes open. Natalie shakes her a couple of times—"Please, please"—and then there's a knock on the door and we all stare at one another before Miliani moves to fix Donna's gown and throw a blanket over her. I open the blinds and turn on the light.

Natalie doesn't act like we're about to be caught. She leans forward, kisses her mom's forehead, and strokes her hair. "Wake up, Ma. Don't you dare leave me."

Leanna tells us to open up. "What the hell is blocking this door?" But I rub Natalie's back while Miliani finishes packing her bag of tricks before going to move the chair.

Leanna bursts in. "What was going on in here?"

"We were praying and we didn't want to be interrupted," I rush to say. "My mom sends prayers as well."

"Oh." Leanna blinks. I think she's going to say the excuse sounds foolish, but she seems caught off guard. "That's nice, Inez. Thank you very much. Thank your mom too." She looks down at her mom, then over at the machines reading her vitals. "I've never seen her sleep this peacefully," she says. It takes me by surprise. Not her words, but to hear gentleness in them. To hear pain there too. She never has anything nice to say about Donna when I'm around.

"We're going to get some food," Natalie says, and smooths over her mom's blanket.

Leanna looks pleased. She walks over to the window to sit on the ledge. We almost make it out of the room, but her voice stops us. "What is this?" I turn to see her bent near the bed. She brings her fingers to her face. "Is this salt?"

"Probably some sort of dust." Natalie's voice is flat. "I think it's been there all day."

Leanna sends a suspicious look from Nat to Mili to me before she walks to the sink to scrub at her hands. "I'll call housekeeping. This is ridiculous."

Outside the room, people pass us with carts toting machines. The call lights ding. We just did something unbelieveable in a hospital. I need to get out of here. But Nat leans up against the wall, holds the diamond ring on her neck, and cries about her mom not waking up.

Mili strokes her hair. "Don't put doubt into the universe. It was a big spell. The calling spell had lag time; this one will too. Give it a chance."

For a moment, I'm grateful for Mili because Natalie wipes her eyes with her shirt and straightens out. But after, I'm pissed she may have given Nat hope for nothing.

☾ ☾ ☾

We leave Natalie at the hospital, and Jayson drops me off at home. When I walk in the door, Mami fixes me a plate of food, then fries me some fresh tostones. She's being gentle with me still, and I hope it lasts. She asks how Donna looked. "Like she was asleep," I tell her, thinking of Leanna's words. Mami sighs. She tried to recruit Donna for church years ago, but Donna refused. Mami was convinced the devil was responsible. *It's easier to make bad decisions and do drugs when you don't have to think about God*, she said. But I think about God every day, and Mami might say the same thing about me if she knew all the things I really do.

17

MILIANI

It's always hard to go back to school after a weekend, but it's even harder after leaving Nat at the hospital. I sit on the bench at my bus stop, but Jayson pulls up in his car and offers me a ride. When Natalie called to ask me for help with her mom, he was already sitting on my couch. He'd shown up with a plate of his dad's pastelón and a handful of notes he'd written me. I told him I could borrow my mom's car to get there, but he insisted on driving me to the hospital, with the promise of no strings attached. Now, I feel the weight of his favor.

"What?" he says. "We can't be friends, either?"

I squint at him, suspicious. "We can be friends."

"I hope so."

"Large chai from Dunkin' on the way there?"

"And a sprinkled donut," he says.

It feels good to be around Jayson. Especially sipping chai in a happy silence. He reaches over and laces our fingers, and his are big but fit so well with mine. It might be easy to go back to doing this while waiting on news about Nat's mom. I'm feeling a crushing guilt because I worry about what it means for widening the realms if Donna doesn't wake up. The worry weighs me down, makes me feel selfish, makes me want to push that selfishness a bit further and find comfort in Jayson the way I used to. But I remind myself how unfair it'd be to him once Jasmine's here, telling me about her adventures, screaming ridiculous things out the car window, and asking me what I want out of life—with me thinking, *Her.*

Jayson rubs my fingers with his thumb. I become distracted, thinking of what will happen when Jas is in Darleny's body and I want her to hold my hand like this. Will Darleny allow it to happen? Will Jas ask her if it's okay? My stomach flips. There's so much I don't know about the anchoring spell and what it looks like. Will Jas want any kind of intimacy with me after the way I reacted that night in her room? There's so much I shouldn't be thinking about right now.

"I hope there's still a chance for us," Jayson says. "Friends is good for now, but I'm not giving up on you."

I let go of his hand and hope it doesn't hurt his heart too much. Jasmine may not want to be with me when she's here. Darleny . . . it might not be possible.

But I can't go back to being Jayson's girlfriend, either.

"Let's feed the pigeons our leftovers before the bell rings," I say. "Bet they love donuts."

"You're strange." He laughs, but there's sadness coming off his aura that I have to ignore.

☾ ☾ ☾

After school, I ring Jasmine's doorbell because Auntie said I should start collecting things for the anchoring spell, but this time Jas isn't alive to throw down the key. Upstairs, her mom sits across from me. The house doesn't smell of food, and the dishes are piled in the sink. She speaks to me mostly in English, but she'll slip Creole in because she knows I understand some. She tells me how quiet it's been without Jasmine's music and her whining for a bowl of cachupa every day. I hold her hand while she cries. It's been hard on Jasmine's father, too, who returned to work but can't sleep at night.

"Would you mind if I sat in her room awhile?"

"Of course not." She pats my hand. "I'm happy you came."

She gives me privacy in Jasmine's room, and I'm reminded of how Jas never tried to hide her love of magic. Her room isn't a place you'd go to look for her hidden treasures; it was a place you'd come to appreciate her spirituality. On her desk, I flip through two spell books. I kneel next to her altar and fill the dish with candy from my pockets for her ancestors. She'd kneel here, smile as she said sweet things, laugh as she offered them funny stories. I lie on her bed, roll over, and try to remember the way she'd rub her face against mine like a cat, stare at my mouth, and massage circles into my hairline with her fingers when we were younger.

I could stay all day like this, but there's no time to waste. I fix myself, and pocket one of her hairbrushes before leaving the room. Jasmine's mom is singing in the kitchen, and the sink water is running. Maybe having me here is comforting. Maybe it allows her to pretend I'm in the room with her daughter.

I creep down the hall as quietly as I can. Darleny's door isn't locked, so I slip inside. Her room is different than Jasmine's: Soccer trophies sit on cabinets. All her clothes are put away. Her walls are bare of tapestry and pictures.

Darleny and I used to be friends. Back in middle school, we would all play double dutch during recess and walk to the corner store after school. I'd buy Jasmine and Darleny bags of chips with the allowance money Papa gave me. And even though their mom bought them matching outfits and tried to do their hair in similar styles, it was easy for me to tell them apart. Jasmine was always wanting to hear about my papa and his magical garden. Darleny got quieter and quieter until she no longer spoke at all.

I find brushes in her desk and pull a clump of hair to take with me. Then I notice a brown journal in the corner of the drawer. I can't help but flip it open to a bookmarked page that reads *I love you, Jasmine.* I've turned back a page, ready to read the note in full, when someone says, *Psst*, from behind me. I drop the journal and look around, but no one's there.

"Jas?" I whisper. I wait. I panic. Then comes the faintest sound: a laugh. Far away but close enough. *Psst.*

I stand and shut the drawer, taking the whisper as a warning to leave. But the door opens before I can, and Jasmine walks into the room, sending my heart through my throat.

It's not Jasmine, I tell myself. *Stop. It's not Jasmine.*

Look at the eyes. The eyes.

Darleny's green ones narrow at me. "What the hell are you doing in my room?"

I glance around again, still feeling the adrenaline of the spirit speaking to me. It was Jasmine. It had to be Jasmine. Who else would care to warn me?

"I asked you a question," Darleny says.

"I, uh . . . ," I start, giving her a side smile and gesturing to her forehead. "Wanted to check to see how you were doing. Looks like the swelling's going down and the scars are healing."

"So you knock on my door, and when I don't answer you decide it's okay to let yourself in? What kind of bullshit is that?"

"I'm sorry. I just—"

"Listen," she says, "my mom might allow you to pull that crap, but don't ever think it's okay with me. Don't ever think I'll forget you making my sister chase you around all night. You're the reason she's dead."

Her words cut me up, make it hard to stand. I remember Jas calling for me to come back after I told her I loved her. Darleny's right: If I would've put my pride and hurt away, Jasmine wouldn't have been in the car the night she died.

Darleny swallows, and her voice wavers when she says, "Leave us alone."

But I don't want to leave. Maybe if I linger a little, I'll feel Jasmine's energy here. And there's a part of me that wants to keep Darleny talking because even though Jasmine would never talk to me *this* way, having Darleny close feels like pressing on a bruise. It hurts in a good way. It makes me feel alive. It makes the thought of Jasmine becoming part of Darleny feel more tangible too. Then I see their differences again: Darleny's blemish-free face, the way her eyebrows are arched high, how her lips curl up at me in disgust.

The deep breaths she takes mirror mine for a second, reminding me she's human too. She's a person, same as me. We are eleven again, with crooked teeth, and betting on who can blow the biggest bubble from Big League Chew gum. She holds her hand out to help me not step on a crack and I avoid breaking my momma's back. Some days, she doesn't hug me goodbye.

Each day, she does whatever the hell she wants.

Now we are seventeen, and she's able to hold hate for me on her face. Jasmine never looked at me like this.

Darleny opens her mouth, tells me, "Get out," but I am already turning away from her.

18

INEZ

Father John comes up to me before Bible study to tell me he's heard of my dirty doings from Mami. I'm not bothered because I expected it, but I think his focus on me is over, until he moves to the front of the room—full of others my age—and opens his sermon with: "Sex before marriage is a sin." We talked about this two weeks ago, but he gives the same references to waiting for the sweetest fruit, he warns about teen pregnancy, and he says AIDS more times than I can count. At the end, he asks if anyone has confessions or questions, then looks my way. "Inez, do you have anything you want to say?" Everyone else looks at me too.

Yes, John, I do. Mind your business.

"No, Father. I don't think so," I say.

Once a week, the teens of the congregation are assigned work around the church. Normally, I rearrange the Bibles or stuff envelopes to be mailed, but today I'm assigned the job no one ever wants. It's not a coincidence I have to wash the windows; it's a punishment. But if I hadn't been assigned this job, I wouldn't see Aaron sitting on the steps across the lot. Nothing is coincidence. I look around to make sure no one sees me before slipping outside. I follow after him when he walks up some steps.

"I told you we needed to lay low," I say.

He wraps an arm around my waist. "I had to see you."

"Not here. Not like this," I say, but I'm happy to see his face. I've been caught up with worry over Nat's mom, over the spell; I didn't know how bad I needed to feel him close.

He kisses my neck, trails up my ear, is awarded with a moan. "Are you sure?"

Somehow, we end up against the building. I forgot how good of a distraction he is. How skilled he is with his mouth. The brick is hard against my back until he swaps our positions, and then it's him hard against my stomach. My whole body is tingling. My nipples are hard. There's a warmth between my thighs. His tongue tastes like spearmint gum, and there's a residual of weed smoke on his lips. His hands are greedy for my skin, rubbing on the more modest places they rarely find and making even that feel like sex. Except I wasn't prepared for the memory of the last time we had sex to spring into my mind and make me feel that regret again.

And then, someone calls, "Inez? Inez, where are you?" and we both freeze.

I put distance between us, even though it's so damn hard. "You have to go," I whisper.

"I miss you, baby," he says, and when the calling stops, he tries to pull me back to him.

I push him against the wall. "I miss you too. But we have to give it time."

He looks resigned, grabs himself through his pants, and says, "Not too much time."

C (C

When I sneak back into the church, I'm right in time to climb the ladder with shaky legs and start to wash the window. Priscilla and Father John walk up behind me. I should've known it was her. She sits in the front row of the pews with her mother and has a high-pitched laugh I'd be happy never hearing again in my life.

"Inez. Where were you? I looked everywhere," she says.

I climb down the ladder, hang my cloth on one of the rungs, fake-wipe the sweat from my forehead with the back of my hand, and tell them I was in the bathroom. Priscilla shakes her head and says she checked there for me. "I use the one upstairs," I say. "Much cleaner."

Her eyes widen. Oops. Got her. She tries to smile. "Maybe I was too worried to think about checking that one. I thought something bad happened to you."

I tilt my head. "At church? Nothing bad ever happens here."

Father John smiles. "Well, we're glad you're okay, Inez. Keep up the good work on the windows." He turns to leave, and after an astounded minute, Priscilla tries to follow.

She should be washing these windows. If only Father John would turn around and . . .

And then he does. "Priscilla, weren't you looking for Inez to offer her some help?"

My heart does sprints. I touch my fingers to my temple and watch her cheeks redden.

"I, uh," she says. "She seems to be doing okay."

I gather myself to grin. "Oh, Priscilla, you're such a great friend. And actually, these windows are really big. I'd love the help."

Priscilla bestows on us a small nervous laugh. It's ugly even at a low octave.

Father John nods, using this as an opportunity for Bible verse. "Two are better off than one because together they can work more effectively."

"If one of them falls down," I continue, "the other can help him up."

Father John seems pleased with me. Priscilla looks pissed.

He leaves, and she steps closer. All the fury of a Sunday school mom with a badass kid radiates off her. "God sees you're slick like a snake, and soon so will Father John."

I'm not even pissed at the audacity she has for hinting she'll be hunting me at church because I keep replaying the moment I wished for Father John to make her help and then he did. Did I make that happen? Miliani said we'd be able to pull on the energy around us after each big spell, but she never said anything about manifesting our wishes. I'm nervous. I'm excited. Does this mean we actually helped Natalie's mom?

I place my hands over my chest and let out a low laugh.

"What's so funny?" Priscilla crosses her arms. I shake my head, toss a dirty rag at her. It hits her shirtsleeves. "Oh my God," she cries.

"You can wash those windows." I point. "And try not to use the Lord's name in vain."

19

MILIANI

Two things catch my attention when I get home from Jasmine's house. The first is that there isn't a home-cooked meal on the stove; there's a box of pizza. The second is how dark the house is. I flip on light switches as I pass them. The bathroom door is shut but not locked. When I open it, I see Mom standing by the sink, staring into the mirror, with thick brown paste coating her bare arms. She doesn't notice me, or hear me when I apologize for intruding.

Her lips move like she's speaking, but no sound is coming out. My breathing quickens.

"Mom," I call again, and use my free hand to knock on the open door.

She flinches and curses in Tagalog before running the sink water. "You're supposed to knock *before* you come in. Not *after*." She washes the paste off in a hurry. "Hand me a towel."

"What is that stuff, Mom? It smells awful."

She catches my eyes in the mirror, then looks away. "It's an old remedy," she tells me. "One of your grandfather's."

Hearing Mom speak of Papa and remedies makes me feel warm. Hearing her tell me anything at all surprises me. "What's it for?"

She uses the towel to wipe the sink, then throws it in the hamper. "Dry skin . . . ," she says. "I'm going up to my room."

When she's through the door, but not far, I ask, "Do you miss him?"

Mom turns quick. The look in her eyes unsettles me. Especially when her gaze lands beside me on the bathtub. She opens her mouth, closes it. Gnaws her lip. "Who?"

"Papa?"

"Oh." She wraps her arms around herself. "I do."

"Who did you think I was talking about?"

"I don't know, Miliani," she says. "That's why I asked you."

When she turns and leaves, I open the shower curtain to be sure nothing's there.

☾ ☾ ☾

Upstairs, I lock my bedroom door and sit on the floor. Papa used to joke that old wooden floors are a good place to talk to the dead. I place the strands of Darleny's hair in a glass bottle and start working through Jasmine's brush to do the same. I stuff them in a separate bottle and label it with her initials. These are supposed to be for the anchoring spell, but I light candles and drop a single strand of Jasmine's hair into a glass of water in front of me.

Auntie said Jasmine's spirit might be lost, but these hair strands might say something different after what happened in Darleny's room.

I need them to say something different.

"Jasmine, if you're here, show me." I try to concentrate on remembering her face, her touch, her voice. I call to her a few times, but my call goes unanswered. It had to be her laughing, the way she used to do when we'd almost get caught sneaking around. It had to be. I know how her energy feels. I remember.

"Jas, I'm going to fix this," I say. "I promise."

One of the candles pools on the holder quicker than it should have and goes out. My senses pick up when the rest sway. I carefully unfold the cloth on the mirror Auntie gave me.

"Jas. Is that you?" I'm on my feet, tilting the light of my lamp toward the wall and lifting the shard of mirror to my face.

Someone whispers my name and sends a shiver up my spine. I tilt the mirror around. Nothing.

"Hello?" I try again. "Jasmine?"

A shadow materializes behind me. My hand is shaky as the shape becomes more defined. I inhale. Tell myself I'm just excited when goosebumps rise on my flesh, but my body wants me to move and my mind tells me to run. This isn't the way I felt in Darleny's room.

A knock comes on my door, and the mirror slips from my grasp and hits the floor. The shadow disappears. I pick up the mirror, scared it's shattered, but it's not.

"No burning candles up here," Mom calls. "Miliani, do you hear me?"

"Yes," I call back before tucking the mirror away and blowing the candles out.

My breathing is rapid when I open the door, but she's already down the hall, shutting hers behind her. Sometimes, I wish she'd ask what I'm doing instead of just telling me to stop. She wasn't this way when I was a girl. She'd tell me about the time she traveled to the Philippines with Papa. "I'll bring you some day," she'd say. We'd sit in the yard with a telescope, counting constellations and talking horoscopes. But it changed when she got sick with blackouts and body shakes. No one explained what caused her illness, but we moved in with Papa because of it. He took care of her and gave me the attention she couldn't. We never left when she got better, and she never gave me that kind of attention again.

I pick up the mirror and try and try, but the spirit doesn't want to be seen anymore.

20

INEZ

"It's been two days," Natalie says over the phone. "How much time will it take?"

It hurts to hear her like this. Her life seems to always be caving in around her, but she hardly cries. What can I do for her? Guilt bubbles in my body, realizing my friends are usually the ones comforting me. What would Jas say? I tell Nat about what happened with Priscilla, praying it helps her hold on to hope.

She's quiet while she processes what I said. I'm not sure she even believes me. "What if the spell doesn't work? Then what?" She sighs. "I've got to go."

Mili's words resurface in my head, but they sound forced coming out of my mouth. "It won't work if we don't believe." I cringe. "Call me if anything happens. Even if it doesn't."

"I'll call," she says.

When the line goes dead, I agonize over the conversation. Was she was looking for me to say something else? What if she has to call Mili because I couldn't ease her pain? Then I agonize over feeling relieved I didn't have to answer any more of her questions.

But I raise my hands in prayer, and when I'm done, I wish the way I wished for Priscilla's payback. Hoping God or magic or both will answer and wake Donna up.

I walk past my stand-up mirror on the way out of the room. A gleam from it catches my attention. I hold my breath, remembering the shadows in Mami's mirror. But there are no shadows this time.

Instead, a long crack runs down it, splintering out and distorting my body in places. It doesn't look shattered; it looks smooth. I reach out to run my finger down it, expecting an illusion. But I cry out when a shard pierces my skin, then jerk my finger back.

My blood trickles to the rug.

❨ ❨ ❨

The next day, I convince Mili we need something to do besides wait for news from Nat. We hop on a bus to the botanica because the crystals I have aren't working for my anxiety.

"We could also get more salt, in case we need to try the spell for Nat's mom again," Mili says. I ignore her. If it didn't work the first time, if it possibly made Nat's mom worse, then what would happen if we try again?

"Maybe we'll be able to see if Isobel's still weirded out by your shopping choices," I say.

Mili throws her feet up on the bus seat in front of her and leans back. She is the definition of someone who tries hard to look unbothered when they are.

"Why should I care what Isobel thinks?"

"Because then you can't flirt with her anymore."

Mili rolls her eyes, but Jas used to tease, "Isobel looks cute today, huh, Milz?" One time, she said, "You like Isobel. Why are you scared of it?" and Mili's cheeks had colored when she said, "I'm with Jayson."

I'd wonder what Jas was doing. It was clear that she still had feelings for Mili. There's no way I'd push Aaron into someone else's arms. But Jas also constantly flaunted her lovers. Maybe she wondered how Mili would feel about an open relationship.

When we get to the botanica, Isobel isn't working the register today, and Mili pretends she doesn't notice as we restock on candles and she picks up more sea salt. I buy a black tourmaline crystal and hope it helps protect me from spirits. But on the way out, we run into Isobel while we're walking up the steps. She notices us, tugs on her backpack straps, and averts her eyes as she heads down the steps.

I swat at Mili. "Stop being ridiculous. Say something to her."

"You're so damn loud," Mili says, pushing me a little, but Isobel had already heard.

She looks back and up at us. "Did you say something, Miliani?"

Mili shakes her head, and I elbow her. She shoots me a look before asking Isobel, "Maybe we can hang out sometime? Outside of the shop."

I hold my breath as Isobel tries to remain hard and unaffected, but her deep-ass dimples get deeper. "I'm free Friday night."

Mili hesitates, and I almost faint from lack of oxygen until she solidifies the plans.

When Isobel goes into the shop, I tease, "Mili got game. I wasn't expecting all of that. You ready for a date?"

She shakes out her limbs like they've caught the jitters. "You peer-pressured me."

"I did not," I say. "I simply nudged you toward your blessings."

"I should cancel. We don't have time for this. We've already wasted a week. What about Jas? Nat?"

I sling an arm around her shoulder. "No canceling. You're going to take a night off. We'll call it resting to rejuvenate your magical energy. And besides, Jas would want this for you."

(((

When we get to my house, I swing open my bedroom door, and the sight makes me dizzy. My antique jewelry box is upended on the floor. I move into the room and see my gold jewelry scattered around the rug like someone took the box and shook it violently. I feel shaky picking up the broken-off ballerina, and turning toward Mili. "Do you see this?"

We sit on my bed, trying to untangle my collection of rope necklaces and Cuban link bracelets that are twined together. Mili's not really religious, but even she seems extra shaken up as she examines the rosary beads. I feel sick from noticing the chain holding my larimar gemstone is twisted up around it. This necklace has been passed down in my family for generations, the stone so rare Mami hesitated to give it to me. It's been three days since Newport, and each one brings a new surprise. Yesterday, I woke up surrounded by crystals, the suncatcher string hanging bare above my head. I've been dreaming of Jasmine too.

"Feels like she's sending me messages from wherever she is," I tell Mili. "Are we sure she hasn't found space and gone to heaven?"

Mili looks up at me. "I'm sure, Inez."

I avoid her eyes. "But why wake up to chaos, then?" And if Jas isn't doing it, is she trying to warn me about it? My insides feel as tangled as the bracelet in my hand, but I don't want to go on about it because Mili looks hurt and wonders out loud why she hasn't been dreaming of Jas too. "Lindy said this will all get worse, right?" I say.

"She did, and Auntie said just because the spell didn't do what we wanted it to doesn't mean it didn't do something. But I don't really understand why Nat's mom is still in a coma." Mili fiddles with a knot and groans. "I'm hoping it's just slow to take. We followed her instructions exactly. It has to work."

I'm not as convinced, but hearing her faith makes me feel better. She looks over her shoulder like a spirit is listening. It puts my own body on alert. "I feel your pain, though," Mili says. "I'm hardly sleeping. With the birds going wild all night, I'm surprised my mom is."

I toss the bracelet back in the box. There's no fixing it. "Maybe we're taking too long, and Jas is trying to tell us."

Mili's face twists up as she leans back on her hands. "No, I trust my auntie. And Jasmine wouldn't do angry like this."

"I hope not." I look down at the pile of jewelry, gifts from family members throughout the years. "Mami's going to kill me."

"We'll fix it," Mili tells me, even though some of the necklaces are too delicate for the knots they're holding. "Let's fix it." She grabs my hands, and we form a circle with our arms around the jewelry. "Imagine it all loose, flowing, untangled, like new."

We close our eyes and say it out loud. *Loose, flowing, untangled, like new.* We say it until my throat burns. When I open my eyes, I can't help but laugh at the tangled heap. Mili laughs too. But then she picks one up, twists it, and the knots come undone.

My face goes slack. "What the . . . ?" I pick another one up, twist it in my fingers. The tangles in the bracelet fall away with ease.

We're too amazed to speak for a second. But suddenly, we're pushing each other and fighting over who gets to unravel the most pieces.

❨ ❨ ❨

We head to the kitchen to make sandwiches, decked out in too much of my jewelry, spreading peanut butter and jelly on toast with chunky rings on our fingers, and smiling like fools. But after the high wears off, I grow quiet and admit to feeling guilty for having fun without Natalie. Mili says, "We'll fix that too," and picks up the phone in the kitchen to call the hospital. Nat tells us that the more time goes by, the surer the doctors are her mother will have lasting brain damage if she wakes at all. They've been talking about pulling the plug, but Natalie has been guarding her mother's bedside, keeping Leanna and the doctors at bay.

None of us want to talk about the spell and how it hasn't worked, so none of us do. I try not to be stuck wondering if the calling spell caused the coma and if maybe we made the coma worse by attempting to pull Donna from it, even though Lindy told Mili not to worry about that as a consequence. I tell Nat I've been collecting work from her teachers so she won't fall far behind, but Nat only offers a quick "Thanks. I'll call with an update soon." I can't blame her for not caring about school right now, but I feel the pit in my stomach grow.

When we're off the call, I sit at the kitchen table, peeling the crust off my sandwich but not wanting to eat it. "Don't you feel helpless? I don't know how to comfort her."

Mili sits across from me and steals my sandwich for a bite. "Pretty sure we can bang out her homework before your mom gets home. What do you think?"

I smile. "I'll do the math. You can handle the essay."

21

MILIANI

I'm never prepared for guilt. I pick the phone up three times to cancel with Isobel. Instead of calling her, I call Nat. She doesn't seem upset that I'm going out when she's chained to the side of her mom's hospital bed. Her voice perks up. "Please tell me about the movie trailers they play."

But after talking to her, I'm still nervous to see Isobel. We never said it was a date, but we never said it wasn't one, and Jas might be watching from the other side. I tell myself Inez is right—Jas would encourage me to go—and I change my outfit three times, trying to imagine what she'd help me pick. I settle on a jean jacket and black jeans, and even put on mascara because she'd make me do that.

On my way down the stairs, I hear noises toward the back of the house, where Papa's room sits. After Mom boxed up his belongings, took his tapestries off the walls, and gave his furniture to Goodwill, she warned he was feeling disrespected by her invading his special living space. I complained about how unfair it was she got to go through his things and I didn't, but she said, "You don't want to disappoint your lolo, do you?" And as much as I ache to investigate his room, I worry about breaking some kind of spell.

The doorknob sparks with static and shocks me. The only

thing that hasn't changed inside is the faint staleness in the air. Mom's back is turned to me, and she's crouched in flip-flops, going through one of the boxes. I call out to her, and she startles so hard she almost trips. "Miliani. What are you doing in here?"

"I was looking for you."

She nods, closes the box back up, and beckons me out of the room with her hand.

In the kitchen, I ask what she was looking for, then wait for her to shoot me a look, tell me I should know better than to be rude and ask questions when if she wanted me to know she'd offer the information herself. She and Auntie have this in common.

"Nothing," she says. "Are you okay, Miliani?"

I laugh a little. "Why wouldn't I be?"

She scans me, then her gaze slips past me like she sees something over my shoulder. It makes me shudder and look back, too, until she gets my attention by saying: "Be safe at the movies, and please don't come home late."

She never clocks me or tells me to be safe. Her words sit with me on the bus to the mall.

☾ ☾ ☾

Isobel wears a yellow dress, which hits above her knees, and brown sandals to show off her pink toenails. She's sitting on the steps outside the mall, reading a book when I walk over. "You know," she says, "I've been asking myself, 'Is she habitually late? Will she show up? Will she never come back to the botanica?'"

Her tone tells me she's teasing, but her word choices make my face warm. She's already wondering if this is something she should expect from me. Maybe this *is* a date. "Or maybe," I say, trying to ignore the urge I feel to leave, "she takes public transport and rarely has much control in these situations."

Isobel scrunches her nose. "I guess she's forgiven."

((((

We eat Chinese food, and she orders an extra pork egg roll and double the sesame chicken. She even asks for one of my shrimps and chews while talking. It seems like a date when she pays for my movie ticket, but there's a normalcy to our banter that has me thinking maybe I was wrong about the connection. Maybe she doesn't like girls. Or maybe she does and she doesn't like me. Regardless, it makes me feel more at ease for doing this when I probably should be practicing elemental magic. When I'm not sure if Jasmine can see me with Isobel.

The theater is relatively empty. We get good seats in the back row, right in the middle, and kick up our feet. "Looking at my pretty toes?" she says when she catches me.

I tilt my head to get a better view. "Maybe I am," I say, but regret it as soon as Isobel grins and moves closer to me.

After the movie, we pass by a photo booth and she pulls me inside. We take six pictures, and my head looks big and Isobel says her smile's too gummy. I bend it and rip it down the middle to give her half. She says, "This is the kind of thing you put in a box to look back at years later and say, 'We were so innocent.'"

Her hinting at our possible future strikes me. It scares me. Suddenly, I'm aware of how close she is. I remember the last time I was this close to Jasmine. For a moment, I can smell the tea tree and lavender oil on her skin, can feel the soft of her belly below mine, can see the face she made when she told me she loved me but didn't want to be with me. I wonder what she'll say when we're able to talk again. I don't even know what I'll say. I've hoped so much for some kind of future for us that I haven't thought past needing to tell her I'm sorry.

Isobel clears her throat and nudges me with her elbow. "You all right over there?"

I smile at her while shoving the photo strip into my pocket. "Yeah. Let's get out of here."

On the way out of the mall, there's nothing we don't talk about. She tells me her father's annoying, puffs out her chest, and plasters on a deep Dominican accent. "Me tiene harta. The candles go on the counter, not on the shelf. Ven aquí, let me show you."

"You sound nothing like him," I say. "I'm upset for my boy Hector."

I ask if I should wait with her, but she shakes her head. "My brother should be here any minute. Are you sure you don't want a ride home?"

"I'm sure," I say. "But this was nice. I'll see you at the shop soon?"

The streetlights don't do much for this dark night, and there aren't many cars on the road, either. It feels like it's just me and Isobel. She chews on her bottom lip. "Yeah, it was nice."

"Get home sa—"

She closes the gap between us and presses her lips against mine before I can finish. Her lips are plump and soft. She leans to deepen the kiss without pulling away for a breath. When the surprise fades, my body reacts to hers. I grasp her waist, and she passes her tongue over mine. It tastes like blue raspberry slush.

A car horn beeps, and she pulls away but presses her forehead to mine. "My brother," she breathes. My face gets hot. What is he thinking right now? Is she going to get in trouble?

But she leans in and kisses me one last time. "Yeah, this was definitely nice."

☾ ☾ ☾

I make it to Kennedy Plaza, half-dazed from Isobel's kisses and half a wreck from comparing them to Jasmine's. I flash my bus pass to the driver and sit in the way back, replaying the date in my head. I'm the only one left on the bus when I'm done reminiscing. I close my eyes and open them, and the lights flicker. Once. Then again. The bus driver doesn't seem to notice. He taps his hand on the steering wheel, as if willing the light to turn green.

I sit up, my stomach twisting for some reason. From the corner of my eye, a single light to my left flickers before a sensation slinks up the side of my arm, like a spider climbing me. I stand and shake myself off. The bus driver comes to another stop, and my body jerks. He's looking at me through the rearview. "Everything okay back there?"

All the lights flicker now. "Don't you see that? The lights keep flickering."

"Didn't see anything, but it's probably the bulbs dying."

I pull the cord and get off three stops early to walk home. If the knots in my stomach grow any wider, they'll swallow me.

☾ ☾ ☾

In bed, I try to measure how good it felt to kiss Isobel against how bad it made me feel after, but something tickles my legs. This isn't the same crawling feeling I experienced on the bus. This feels like an unwanted brush of fingertips. My hypothalamus tells different parts of my body to prepare. I grip the bedsheets, my heart rate rising.

"Jasmine?" I call out.

Jasmine, a voice echoes back.

I sit up and pull the cord on my bedside lamp, my body still bracing for something to happen. For Jas to speak to me again. The room is bright but thick with energy.

Jasmine, Jasmine, the voice whispers.

My excitement fades as I listen. They're saying her name, but it doesn't sound like her. And, like the other night, it doesn't feel like her, either. The curtains on my window sway up in the air. They're catching wind, cooling my bones, but the window isn't open.

22

NATALIE

Ma wakes six days after the spell.

The doctors call it a miracle. Maybe this was God's doing, but my mind keeps fluttering to me and my friends chanting over Ma's body. The doctors take the tubes out, and she's loopy and weak, complains her eyelids are heavy when her voice comes through. She looks bad, but she's alive. Devin crawls in bed with her, rests his head on her shoulder, and she jokes about his head being big enough to put her back into a coma. We all laugh, but we shouldn't. The sun starts to rise at this point, the dullness of the room giving way to a slight glow. Leanna takes out her flip phone and calls the family, then I borrow it to tell Mili and Inez. They sob, same as me.

Throughout the day, there's a myriad of visitors, including Ma's brother, Uncle Robb, who I haven't seen since a cousin's birthday party a few months ago. He sees me leaning against the wall outside Ma's hospital room and snakes an arm around my back. My skin crawls everywhere his body touches mine. "Your mom makes friends with anyone," he says.

He's right. I've never met half the people who've come to the hospital. None of them are around when she's doing bad or gone. Still, I shrug him off me. "At least she has friends."

Uncle Robb puts a hand up and laughs dryly. "You're no fun,

kid," he says, and the liquor is like lacquer on his breath. According to Uncle Robb, who gravitates toward the kids at family parties, I've never been fun. He usually passes me up to get too close to Adina or Eve because whenever he asks for another beer out of the cooler, they'll listen "like a good niece should." But none of my cousins are here. I'm the only choice today. I came out to the hall because Ma's room is cramped, but it'll feel claustrophobic wherever Uncle Robb is.

He reaches over to fiddle with the camera strap around my neck, and my breath catches. "Wonder what kind of pictures you got in there." I wish he would leave. I wish it so hard that when my next-door neighbor Harriet calls out my name, I am too dazed to answer her.

But I've never been happier to hear her voice.

"Where you going, Robert?" she asks, hobbling down the hospital corridor with her cane. Uncle Robb grunts and takes this as his cue to slip away. Harriet's been up here three times since Ma's overdose, with a Bible in hand. Normally, I'd try to think of an excuse to leave, too, but Harriet's eyes brighten when I smile, and Ma's voice is carrying several feet so some gratefulness might be nice. Especially because her presence made Uncle Robb scurry off. But it wasn't only her presence. I think it was magic. I felt it radiating in my bones. I wanted Uncle Robb to go away, and he did. A brief thought crosses my mind: If it was magic, maybe I'll never have to feel helpless around him again. Maybe I'll never have to feel helpless at all.

Harriet says, "Robert needs Jesus," and brings me back. "I'll find him later."

The sun is seeping through the big windows and bouncing off her white shirt, the dark brown of her skin even more radiant under the light. I step back and start to take pictures of her before she reads, but Leanna heads over and asks if she can talk to me for a second.

Harriet grunts, closes her Bible, and tucks it under her arm. "Go on, child. Your sister doesn't want you to have a relationship with God because she doesn't have one."

Leanna's eyes roll. "Don't start. It's been a good day."

"It's a miraculous day. You shouldn't keep your sister away from showing gratitude for God's power because you don't want to face him."

"Harriet," I hiss. "What's up with you?"

Her face relaxes, but Leanna walks away. "I'm sorry, Natalie. It's been an awful week."

I nod and leave Harriet standing there so I can find my sister. She's by the elevator with Ava, and they get quiet when they see me near. "What was that about?"

Leanna says, "Nothing new." But my mind circles. I've always suspected Harriet had a problem with Leanna being gay. Even though she's the same woman who'd make us Easter baskets when we were kids and tend to us when we were sick. She even covered, said she was staying with us, when someone called CPS on Ma because me and Dev were home alone.

"She was hostile," I say. "Is it because Ava is here with you?"

Ava averts her eyes, and Leanna presses the elevator button.

"Leave it alone," Leanna says.

I don't want to, but Ava looks uncomfortable now. I play with the hem of my dress and ask Leanna what she needed me for.

She gets into the open elevator. "Looked like you needed saving."

((((

Visiting hours are over, and Mr. Ortega gives Ma kisses on her forehead before he says goodbye. Leanna and Ava go home to shower,
and they take Devin with them. I'm alone with Ma for the first
time all day, but she's exhausted. I hold a cup up to her mouth, and
she sips slow.

"I know you want to talk about what I did," she says after she's
finished drinking, "but can we talk tomorrow? I'm so tired."

"Of course, Ma." I brush her hair out of her face and watch the
machines to make sure her breathing is steady as she closes her eyes.

But then she says, "I don't remember much from when I was
under, but I do remember you, baby. Miliani and Inez too. Your
voices were on repeat in my head, whispering to me, something
like a song, telling me to get better. I'm warm thinking 'bout it."

She falls asleep at that last bit, and it all courses through me.
She remembers the chant. She heard us. The spell brought her back
to me. I use the hospital phone to make a quick three-way call to
my friends. Mili says, "I can't believe you doubted it for a second,"
and they're both excited. It makes my eyes sting with tears, thinking of what else magic could make possible.

After we hang up, I lift my camera to flip through old pictures,
landing on one of Jasmine standing on a table in the lunchroom, insisting everyone fight against being subjected to cardboard-tasting pizza
and funky-smelling sloppy joe. Her eyes gleam with light and life.

((((

Throughout the night, the nurses do two-hour round checks on Ma,
but she sleeps through most of them. I sit by the window with my

laptop, uploading pictures I've taken this week. The shots are few but beautiful: the machines monitoring Ma's vitals, Devin sleeping beside her in the hospital bed, Ava and Leanna holding hands, the sun setting into a pink-and-purple sky. I click on a picture from today of a nurse walking down the hall, and blink before bringing the laptop closer to stare at it. I click out of it, then open it back up. I offer myself explanations for what I'm seeing—overexposure, poor lighting, dirty lens—but my body goes rigid. I compare the picture on my camera, and it looks exactly the same. There are five solid black shadow lines, small and spread a half inch apart.

They look like fingers cupping the back of the nurse's head.

I zoom in to get a better look but stop dead as my body goes on alert. I can feel something hovering behind me. Then the slightest pressure of fingers slow-walking from the back of my neck to my throat. I hold my breath, still my body as best as I can. But my camera slips from my grasp, lands on the ledge with a thud, and the feeling disappears. I grip the ledge, turn to look behind me and around the room, over at Ma who's still asleep. My hands tremble, reaching to touch the spots on my neck still tingling.

I pick up my camera and delete the picture as fast as I can, still breathing heavy when my eyes land on the next one. It's of Harriet. There are shadows creating cascading lines across her face and blocking some of the sun that was bouncing off her. I delete it too. And the next one and the next one, without even checking them. But I stop on a picture of Ma midlaugh, propped up in bed, machine cords dangling around her. There's nothing wrong with it. No shadows, no fingers, no spirits. Is there something wrong with me?

I get up to wash my face in the bathroom and spend time searching for marks on my skin that aren't there.

part two

(((

EMISSION OF LIGHT

On place: Neutaconkanut Hill in the Silver Lake neighborhood of Providence. Commonly called Uni Park.

The Hill is a public wildlife park consisting of eighty-eight acres of woodland. It marks the highest point of Providence, with an elevation of 296 feet above sea level.

"The Rhode Island Native American Indian, the mighty Narragansett Tribe, lived on the Hill centuries before the white man arrived, and continued to hold ceremonies on the Hill into the 1920s. In 1636, Roger Williams obtained land from Narragansett Sachems Canonicus and Miantonomi and named his settlement Providence in thanks to God. The northwest boundary of this land, set forth by Williams and the Sachems, was the Great Hill of Neutaconkanut . . ."

In 1892, the Public Park Commission wrote, *"Nature has made a natural park more perfect than the hand of man could devise."*

—*Neutaconkanut Hill Conservancy, http://www.nhill.org*

23

MILIANI

You're doing it wrong, Papa said to me. I was only eleven, twitchy and with one curious eye, which would not stay shut. We were meditating in the woods of Uni Park, right near the paved trail that turns into a dirt path. The grass was high, and scratchy against my skin. My cousins and I'd spend summers searching for garter and rat snakes here, but there was something different about sitting in the grass, trying not to think of it at all.

Focus, Miliani. Listen to the sounds around us, and only the sounds.

But I don't hear anything.

You wanted to learn. Here I am to teach you, and you won't try.

I do want to learn, Papa. What will it sound like?

Close your eyes. Everything has a sound. Even the rocks.

I dug my nails into the grass and dirt, and shut everything else out. Soon after, my fingers went slack, and I heard the birds in the trees, the leaves moving softly in the wind, the ticking of the bugs, the grass growing beneath us. And then even the rocks. When we were done, I thought it'd be easier to catch snakes if I could hear them as they slither. *Could we catch some now?*

Papa had a belly laugh, completely unrestrained and contagious. *In the Philippines*, he said, *my sisters and I'd catch snakes too.*

He was the last born of five children. Two of his sisters died when the house was ravished by a virus Papa said was probably the common cold. His mother, too poor to know for sure, *stricken* she couldn't save them without the help of modern medicine, stopped practicing and meditating and believing in natural cures.

Did something happen to Mommy too? I asked while we hiked up to the clearing at the top of the hill so we could look out at Providence as the sun started to go down and the sky changed colors. Transfer time, Papa used to call it. *Is that why she doesn't meditate anymore?*

But Papa never answered these questions.

$$\math161{C} \;\mathbb{(}\!\!\mathbb{C} \;\mathbb{C}$$

We woke Nat's mom from a coma yesterday, and it feels like my mom can sense it or hear my thoughts the way Auntie can, but she looks away whenever my own senses alert me to her staring. She watches me do homework from the kitchen.

"I'm not having sex," I say.

Her eyebrows dip like she's surprised, but I don't want her catching on to me doing magic. Maybe reminding her I'm a teenager will help. Even though we've never even spoken about kissing. When my period came for the first time, pads appeared under the sink like she'd known it would come before I did, but we didn't talk about how to apply them. By my bed, she left *Viburnum opulus*, better known as cramp bark, for the pain, and that's it.

"I didn't think you were," she says. "I hope you'll tell me when you do."

"I will," I say. Then the thought makes me uncomfortable. Jasmine and I had a chance to have sex, but now it's gone. Soon, she'll be in Darleny's body. My stomach twists. Then it twists harder when the kiss with Isobel pops into my mind.

I put away my textbook and head to the table. Mom's going through old mail, sorting the necessary envelopes from the ones that need to be thrown. "So why do you keep looking at me?"

"I can't look at you?" Her lips curve up, revealing the wrinkles forming above her cheeks. She's only in her forties but predisposed because Papa had the same ones. Just like the streak of white that runs down the middle of her hair, the way it'd run in a skunk. I wonder if I'll develop more of her features as I age, but I'm only part Filipino. My father's genes have already given me rounder eyes and darker skin. I am bits and pieces of the both of them.

"Of course you can look at me," I say.

"Kind of you." She places an envelope in the trash pile. "I did give birth to you after all."

"You know what I mean." I laugh. "You'd tell me if I was growing ugly or something?"

She laughs, too, and pushes a stack toward me. "Be quiet and help me with this."

I pick up a random envelope. "Do you need this letter from"—I pause, squint at it—"Nardolillo Funeral Home?"

Mom snaps her head up and snatches the envelope from my hand. I watch, confused, while she examines it, exhales, shakes her head. Then her eyes dart back and forth between the kitchen walls. I feel the hair rise on my arms and wonder if she's seeing spirits. I crane my neck, but there aren't even shadows. Just a big silver cross that has been hanging on the wall forever. "Miliani," Mom says, snapping my eyes back to her and giving me a small smile. "Let's finish this up before dinner, eh?"

She puts the envelope into the trash pile, her fingers lingering there a second.

24

NATALIE

This morning makes two days since Ma woke up, which, according to my sister, is two too many of my "ass being out of school." She throws my backpack over her shoulder. "Ma's fine. You're going. Period." And she seems it; Ma's walking around with the physical therapist to gain more strength in her legs and complaining the two-hour round checks give her "no goddamn time to sleep." But I'm especially thankful for those checks because the longer she sleeps, the longer I spend worried she won't wake up.

At school, Mili and Inez are sitting in the hall with their backs against the lockers, and bagels and chocolate milk on their laps. We talked on the phone for a long time yesterday, but seeing them in the flesh hits different. Inez is sliding down the lockers like she's sinking in sand, and she looks exhausted. It surprises me when she stands to give me a hug with the quickness.

"You're choking me," I say.

She pulls back. "Let me look at you."

"What do you see?"

"You look tired."

"So do you."

"Being haunted is draining." Inez shrugs, but I catch her

trembling lip before she pulls me in again. "I'm happy your mom's okay. So damn happy."

Miliani gets up, too, and now they're both crushing me, each inching to get closer until they start play-shoving the other away. When we sit, Mili insists I take her bagel, says they're done serving breakfast in the caf. Inez always jokes, "Mother Mili," and I usually laugh, but I'll never forget that Mili and I became friends when Ma was off on a drug binge.

The week of freshman orientation, I slid on too-tight shoes and clothes I struggled to match. Some girl in our group called me a "flea-market baby" and had everybody but Mili laughing. Mili invited me for dinner and was blunt about her offerings. "Before you say no," she said, "I don't think you're a charity case." She handed me clothes picked from her closet. "I hope you'd do the same for me if I needed it." Mili is smaller up top and has wider hips, but because she loves baggy tees and sweatpants, her clothes fit me fine. We even wore the same size in shoes.

But what matters the most is she never again mentioned what she did for me.

She breaks the silence between us now. "I have to say it. We— as in the three of us—actually pulled your mom from a coma."

I smile, but Inez purses her lips and clasps her hands together. "Are we sure we did this? Are we sure it wasn't . . . ?"

"God?" I reach to squeeze her knee, wondering if she's struggling more with religion the deeper we dig into magic. It's probably easier for me and Mili, who believe in God but don't follow a religion. "If you believe it was, then maybe God gave us this power because one minute we were talking about pulling the plug, and the next she was breathing on her own, telling me she heard our *song*."

Mili gets up on her knees and raises her hands in the air, the way people do on TV when they've "caught the Holy Ghost" in church. "We can do anything," she screams into the corridor.

Kids from school stare as they pass. I tell Mili she's wild and yank her ass back down.

"I'm really happy," she says, her voice radiating with emotion.

Inez leans her head against the locker and exhales. After a few seconds, she says, "Wow. We're badass bitches, huh?" Me and Mili laugh hard. "You listening to this, Jas?" she calls out.

I guess if they're doing wild, I can do it too. "You see us out here getting stronger?" I yell. The hope seems like a force in front of me. I can almost hear Jas telling me stories, see her as she stands camera-ready, feel her arms around me after she tells me she forgives me. I let the hope envelop me in all of its wildness, and my eyes well up. "We'll be ready for you."

The exhilaration buzzes between us. It is a spark, a charge, a flash lighting the negative spaces. "And I knew we helped her deep down," Mili says. "With the spirits being able to interact more, it's clear the spell really put a dent in the realms."

That's when the flash of light goes out. Mili says it like it's good, but I can almost feel fingers on my skin again. I touch the back of my neck, swallow, try to tell myself that whatever happens is worth it if Ma's alive, if it means Jas and I can fix our relationship.

But I don't want spirits to be able to touch me or mess with my camera.

Inez bites her lip and starts braiding her waist-length hair. "This seems wide enough, no?" Then, "Just . . . if the spirits can break our things, what's stopping them from hurting us too?"

I watch Mili's face fall, but I ask, "Are you sure your aunt thinks we'll be safe?"

Mili's eyes dart from me to Inez, panic in them. "Well, she told me there are risks, but she wouldn't let me do this if the spirits could hurt me or either of you." She's quiet as she thinks of what to say next. We all are. "What if I get her to agree to a séance?" she finally says. "We can try to make direct contact, see if the spirits are here to hurt us. Maybe we'll even be able to talk to Jas."

"But didn't Lindy say she's not a babysitter? You directly quoted her."

"She did, but she knows how important this is to us," Mili says, and gives us a fake smile. "She'll make us feel better. I know it."

Inez sighs and stands. "If you can convince her, I guess it's okay. But I gotta pee before the bell rings."

When she leaves, Mili touches my wrist. "I know things are weird, but we did a good thing with magic, Nat. I'm happy for you."

She makes the worry subside for a second. I hope magic can make her happy too.

((((

Back at the hospital, the doctor and social worker say that something as severe as an overdose requires sending patients straight to a rehabilitation facility. Ma fights with them, saying it's the cleanest she's been in years. She can hold conversations better now and isn't as anxious. The IV fluids and rest have even put some color in her cheeks. But sometimes, there's this look on her face when she zones out—a look I've learned means she's wanting a fix.

Leanna uses a motherly tone to convince Ma going to rehab is best for all of us. Ma signs the paperwork after that, and I think it's partly because she's so happy Leanna is speaking to her after the overdose she doesn't want to ruin it. The deal goes like this: a week in a rehab center, and if that goes well, she can go home but must attend three months of meetings at the CODAC Center five days a week. When the doctors leave, so does Leanna.

Ma sits on a shower chair as I wash her hair.

"Why'd you do it?" I say.

"Do what, Natty?"

"Really?"

Her shoulders slump. "I told you I didn't want to talk about it."

"You told me we would, but we haven't." I wash the shampoo out of her hair. "What made you do heroin, Ma? You said you'd never."

"You know what they say: Never say never."

"This isn't a joke." I'm angry now. "You almost died."

"But I didn't." Ma gets up on wobbly legs, takes the shower hose from me. "I'll finish."

"No, please talk to me."

"I don't know why I did it, okay?" Ma holds the hose to her body. "I wanted to get high. The other stuff wasn't getting me as high anymore. Is that what you want to hear?"

My eyes burn. "You weren't thinking of me and Dev? How this would affect us?"

"No," Ma says, turning to adjust the shower water, her voice quieter. "I wasn't. But it's not like I'm proud of it, Natty."

"Are you happy to be alive?"

She looks back at me like I smacked her. "Excuse me?"

"Do you want to be alive?"

"Of course I do. What kind of a question is that?"

I take the hose from her, and she breathes in deep before she sits back on the chair. We're quiet while I finish, and I find myself wondering if magic saved her temporarily. If she'll get out and next time will be the last time because it'll end in her death.

But then she says, "I'll never do it again. I promise."

And with her back turned to me and the water running, I let the tears come.

25

INEZ

Jasmine looks back at me through the mirror when I'm brushing my teeth. She pulls the handle on the fridge, and *we* open it, *we* eat the cereal in my bowl, *we* don't like the taste of it, *we* pinch my stomach when I lean back in the kitchen chair. *We* laugh until it hurts.

I wake winded and sore all over. But nothing's missing from my room, nothing's broken, there isn't a ghost lying beside me. Not that the latter has happened, but every morning I expect it to. Sleep has been easier to come by, and I'm thankful I get to see Jasmine because it's getting harder to be awake and alone with the spirits. But when I go downstairs, I'm still jittery from the dream. I wonder if Mili convinced her aunt. Maybe we'll get to talk to Jas during the séance and I can ask what the dreams mean.

Victor passes me the phone without warning. "It's Papi." My stomach churns. I haven't spoken to him since Mami found out about Aaron. I was sure he'd heard about my indiscretions and disowned me, but he says he's happy he caught me while I was still home. We talk about his new job at an auto sales shop, and he goes on about my cousin Joselito's new car.

"I miss you," he says. "Mi niña, mi corazón, what've you been up to?"

Having sex and falling in love with a boy you wouldn't like, waking people up from comas, interacting with ghosts.

"Nothing, Papi," I say. Victor snorts from behind me, and my body tenses. "How about you?"

"I hope to be able to move out of Joselito's and buy land, get my own house soon."

My heart sinks. His own house? In DR?

"Te quiero, niña," he says. "I have to go. I'll call you later."

When we hang up, I pray Papi misspoke. The government told him he wouldn't be able to apply for another visa for twenty years after he was deported, but since then his immigration lawyer has been making headway in getting the waiting period lowered to only five years, which means he'd be able to reapply when I turn twenty-one. And Papi deserves it. My reasoning runs deeper than the fact he was deported to DR after spending twenty-eight years in the US, working hard jobs. When he finally got to hear our voices over the phone, from many miles away, across the ocean, he cried, telling us someone from work had snitched about him not being a citizen. The same someone he'd bring slices of Mami's flan to. Papi told me to only trust myself then. Afterward, Mami told me he was wrong. I couldn't even trust myself; the only one I could trust was God.

I want to ask Victor if he's heard anything about the visa from Papi, but he packs his bag for his church program in silence and I know trying to start a conversation with him might leave me annoyed. I don't understand why he's still mad when he's the one who sold me out to Mami. Papi should talk to him about snitches and trust too.

When Victor walks by me to catch his bus, something surges through me, and I wish, wish, wish he'd turn around and say something. Anything.

And then he does. "See you later, Inez."

That's all I needed to stand and follow him out. "Victor, can we talk tonight?"

He looks a little nervous, but he nods before he's off, walking up the street. I lean against the doorframe. Unlike in church with Father John and Priscilla, this time I know it was me using magic on Victor. We're growing. I'm growing, changing. I can feel it in my body. Maybe this is what Jas meant when she said it. I'm just not sure if it should feel this damn good.

26

NATALIE

"From one prison to the next," Ma says as she gets ready to be discharged, packing a small bag of trinkets she'd collected from the hospital: grippy socks, a stack of alcohol pads, three bottles of witch hazel. I'm nervous about her being away from me again, too, but I know this will help her. I think about how good things will be when she's out and clean, before resting my hand on her shoulder and whispering, "It's going to be okay," then watching the tension within her float away. She turns over her hand and holds mine like she always does. "I missed you, Natty Fatty," she says. "Your face is like sunshine. I'm so happy you're with me."

After she leaves, I wait for Mr. Ortega outside the hospital because Leanna took Devin to basketball practice. His coach said if he missed another one, he'd be off the team, and Leanna wasn't having it; she rushed him down to Providence before the sun came up.

But Mr. Ortega isn't the one who pulls up—Ray is.

My stomach does a flip, but I'm too tired to complain about Mr. Ortega sending him to get me because the bodega was busy, or argue once I'm in the car about Ray's choice in music. I'm just thankful he's not running his mouth like he usually does—until he turns down the volume on the radio and tells me he's sorry about the overdose. I look at him, tell him she's alive, but he adjusts his rearview mirror. "Thank God. I'm still sorry, though. No one should have to go through what you go through. You deserve better."

I shift in my seat so he can see my whole serious face. "You don't even know her."

"But I know you."

"Barely," I say. "You barely know me, Ray."

He chuckles. "All right, Natalie."

I fight the urge to tell him he doesn't know a thing about Ma. How big her heart is, how much she loves me. But what irritates me most is that when I was seeing Ray last year, I kept my homelife to myself so he'd never feel the need to pity me. Yet here we are.

The quiet between us is uncomfortable now, but when Ray turns up the music it's loud, crackling static. He doesn't try to mess with it or change the station, and when the static turns to a soft humming sound, he keeps his attention on the road. My skin tingles everywhere.

"Aren't you going to shut that off?" I ask, voice trembling.

Ray turns to me with narrowed eyes. "It's the only station picking up songs right now, but I guess."

He presses the power button on the radio, and it shuts off. Except we're not back in silence. The humming is softer, sweeter. Ray doesn't seem to notice at all. I close my eyes, scared as hell, but can't turn off the sound in my head.

❨ ❨ ❨

When we pull in front of my house, he gets out of the car, and I have to catch my breath before following him. "I got it," I say, but he takes my bags from the trunk and walks right past me. I'm already on edge, and Ray know how to piss me off.

Upstairs, he places them on the landing by my door. "Before you come for me, I know you could've carried them up yourself, but I wanted to help."

"I don't need your help." My voice cracks as I challenge him. "Quit bothering me. You're always forcing it."

My words hit. I can tell by the way he takes a breath in through his teeth. The landing before my door suddenly seems smaller with the both of us standing here and my words taking space between us. Part of me wishes I could rewind twenty seconds and just thank him. But I don't wish it hard enough because I'm not sure how I'd handle my wish coming true.

"Bet." He backs up but keeps his eyes on me. "Next time, I'll tell Mr. Ortega you know how to take a bus."

He walks down the stairs before I can get another word out, and I hurry after him, quick to lock the door like the spirits can't get me in here. Then I lean against it, mad at myself for thinking I should've tried to fix it and told Ray to stay.

27

INEZ

Nat's back at school, but she's just another ghost in the halls. She doesn't make eye contact with us in gym when Mili says Lindy agreed to the séance. I search for her eyes to tell her how scared I am, but Nat just nods and walks off to play dodgeball. Mili's not in the mood to get hit in the face today, and I'm too tired to run. But I wish I would've asked Nat to stay.

This séance isn't going to be like the rest of the ones we've attempted. This I know. But we're not going to feel safe unless we try. We walk the track, watching Natalie loosen up. For the first time in months, it looks like she's having fun. Without having to worry about where her mom is, Nat's free to look her age. I tell Mili this, and she agrees. The overdose may have been a blessing, I think, but decide not to say.

When class is halfway through, Nat falls into step beside us with a sore ankle, saying, "Those boys don't know how to act," and it's the first time in a long time we don't talk about spirits or our parents or death. We talk about kissing. Mili fills Nat in: "Isobel called my house the next day and didn't even mention her brother catching us."

For a moment, I feel like I am hovering outside my body. I see us glide along the track, stifling booms of laughter. Our eyes light up, catch the sun. Nat is smiling again. All I can see is the tiny circle of track we walk along, the edges of the space beyond us disappearing like watercolors running. There's nothing before or after us. No one else matters as I hover above us. We are a tiny scene of love.

"Maybe he didn't *catch* anything. Maybe Isobel's family knows." Nat snickers. "Just because you like to get freaky with boys *and* girls, but keep the latter closeted, doesn't mean she uses any discretion."

Miliani play-sulks. "I am not closeted."

"You ever going to tell Jayson about the history between you and Jasmine?" I pipe in. "Or maybe you can introduce him to your new girlfriend. That'll probably do the trick."

"She's not my girlfriend," Mili stresses, then sighs. "And it's weird. You know? I wish I would've told him sooner. Maybe he'll think it's some post-breakup crisis."

"You mean, maybe he'll figure out you left him for some pussy?" Natalie says.

I laugh so hard I almost choke on my gum. Mili sticks out her tongue. "Maybe that too."

"And he's trash if he thinks you liking girls is some post-breakup nonsense," I say.

"I'll fight him if he says anything that obnoxious," Nat adds.

Miliani laughs and leans her head against mine, and we walk as if our heads together are awkwardly attached. Natalie comes up between us. "I want some loving too." We trip over one another's feet, laugh, talk shit, and I imagine the three of us at the same college, sharing a dorm, fighting over the bathroom. Mili coming up with spells to help us ace our tests, Natalie not having to work hard. But my eyes water a little because for the first time,

I can't see Jas when I think about our future. And that doesn't seem right.

We saved Nat's mom, and we're going to save Jas too. Maybe one more big spell and we'll have her with us. She'll be playing pranks on us and telling us stories of all the things she sees when she sneaks around campus while we sleep and . . . And what will it physically look like? Will she have a corporeal body? Will other people be able to see her too? I've asked Mili these questions, and she never has answers. She just insists we need Jasmine here—in any form the ritual offers. And I want her back so bad it hurts, but I can't see it. I can't see her fitting into our future in another form that's not her living, breathing body, and it terrifies me.

But then I hear her voice. "Weirdos."

The chill travels up my spine and stays after I realize it's just Darleny.

She turns to Cassie as they jog by. "They're probably trying to think up spells to force people to love them." She fixes a look on Mili that I don't understand but makes my blood boil.

"Maybe you should run faster before we set our sights on you next," Nat says.

Darleny rolls her eyes, but she and Cassie speed up to put some distance between us.

We stop walking. I wrap my arms around myself. "It's weird she's here and Jas is not."

Nat agrees. "If only we could make her disappear." She laughs. "Kidding, kinda. She's worse without Jas here to shut her up."

"And hearing her voice, seeing her, freaks me out," I say, and put a hand on Mili's back. "It must freak you out too."

Mili seems dazed, still staring off at Darleny, until she focuses on her feet. "Sometimes it's nice. Sometimes I can——" She cuts herself off, shakes her head, then takes off jogging ahead of us like she never said a thing.

Natalie gives me a nervous look. Then we both watch Mili turn a corner on the track.

☾ ☾ ☾

When the last bell of the day rings, we walk down to Kennedy Plaza and hop on Bus 42. Lindy lives far from school, so after twenty minutes on one bus we hop off and wait for a different one. The second driver handles curves like he's playing a video game, and the cheeseburger I ate for lunch almost comes back up. My head begins to hurt, and all I can think about is having to do this again on the way home later. Miliani presses a hand to my forehead because I'm "not looking well." Maybe I'm a tad bit warm, she decides, and lets me use her as a pillow the rest of the ride.

☾ ☾ ☾

Lindy is pissed when we show up at her house. Her nostrils flare as she berates Mili. She only lets us inside to "do it privately," because her neighbors across the street are nosy. She points a finger at Mili. "I told you to stop being a baby. Spirits are around us even when you can't see them. I told you no, but you brought people to my house anyway."

"I'm sorry if I disrespected you, Auntie," Mili pleads. "But they're not just people—they're my friends. If being scared makes us babies, then we're babies. But we need your help."

"Well, they're not my friends, are they?" Lindy says, and it makes the almost ten years of age she has on us feel like two. She shakes her head and paces the living room. "You said you'd all be able to stomach this. Maybe we were both wrong. Maybe you can't handle it."

As Mili insists we can, I move closer to Natalie and tilt my head to motion we should head out. I'm pissed we're here. Natalie looks even more pissed. But then Lindy turns sharply and sets her eyes on me. The look rattles my bones. I'm not sure what I'm scared of, but I say a silent prayer before she says, "You. Sit."

My body is not mine. I sit without wanting to.

She doesn't move from where she stands but says, "Tell me about your last dream with Jasmine."

I wonder how she knows I had another dream. I didn't get a chance to tell Mili about it.

Lindy crosses the room, kneels on the floor in front of me. I push into the couch to put some distance between us, but her eyes call to me and I find myself moving back toward her.

"Jasmine was mimicking me. And it seemed like . . . like we were doing things as one?"

She purses her lips, says, "And the physical contact?"

I touch the side of my stomach. "She pinched me here. Well . . . we did it together in the dream. But she used to do it all the time when she was . . . alive."

Lindy gets so close I can feel her breath on my skin. It smells like peppermint. She turns my wrists over a few times, examines my neckline, takes two fingers and opens my eye really wide, then does the other. She asks permission to lift my shirt and puts a finger into my belly button. None of it makes me uncomfortable, even though it probably should.

She stands so abruptly I almost fall forward. "Be careful, clumsy one," she tells me, and leaves the room.

Natalie whispers, "What in the world was that? And why the hell did you lie to us, Mili?" but Miliani mouths, *Shh.*

I miss the smell of peppermint, and the headache returns. Or maybe it never went away. But it's pounding at my temples now.

28

MILIANI

Auntie's voice seems to float to us from the sky: a soft haze of unrecognizable words seeping through the ceiling and landing around us. I can hear it everywhere and nowhere. It pulls me to my feet and out of the room, where a door creaks open at the end of the hall. A door I've never noticed before. I rush to get to it, thinking it'll disappear, it'll be my imagination, it'll be something that isn't for me to see.

I don't realize my friends are following me until I stop short and one of them bumps into me. I don't look at them. I place one hand on the doorframe and look inside.

It's as if Auntie conjured a portal just for us.

"What is this?"

"Come in. All of you," she says from where she sits on the floor.

Moving into the room feels like moving through my childhood. A mist of memories drifts by me: eating foods I helped grow, burning candles until they pooled pretty colors on white ceramic plates, listening to Papa's stories of spirits, monsters, and haunted spaces under moonlight while he smoked tobacco. Wearing my shirt inside out and praying to God the kapre creatures he spoke about wouldn't come down from the treetops to get me.

The smell of wisteria fills the room and connects me with sitting under the purple flowers of a tree as a child.

Where Auntie's other rooms look ordinary, this one is magic.

The floor is old plank wood, which creaks on random steps. Wisteria plants and a mass of English ivy are draped along the walls, and there are huge potted Monstera on the floor. This room has one window, which lets in little sunlight, and I'm not sure how my auntie keeps this much greenery alive. The back wall holds an enormous bookshelf filled with worn-looking books, a bunch of small relics, and statues of gods from different religions. There's a glass cabinet with oils, crystals, and a collection of cotton and manila rope which is neatly stacked on the bottom shelf. Enough rope for Auntie to keep someone tied in the basement.

She lets us look around for a while to "get the curious over with" before telling us to join her on the floor. But my eyes are busy trying to soak up all the details around us.

"Why haven't you invited me back here before?"

"I am now," Auntie says. "To do the séance with you."

But she's not looking at me; she's too busy examining Inez. I feel a prick of jealousy, watching and wondering if Auntie's change of heart had something to do with her. Maybe she sees something in Inez that she doesn't see in me.

Auntie uses a box of matches to light the purple and yellow candles around us. There are so many, caging us in. I've never been surrounded by candles. Usually, we're surrounding them.

Inez scrubs at the bridge of her nose with her pointer finger. "Isn't this dangerous?"

After she says it, I imagine a scenario where we're deep in a trance and one of the candles tips and crashes into another: a domino effect, creating a circle of fire.

Auntie looks at me. She looks so much like Mom it gives me goosebumps. Something about her eyes and the way her lips curve on one side. But she says, "There's nothing to fear. I'm in control," which reminds me she's nothing like Mom at all.

"I don't know about this." Natalie eyes flick around the room. "Something feels off."

"That's because you're not used to doing magic with someone who knows what they're doing," Auntie says, choosing to embarrass me in front of my friends. "Never hesitate when going into a séance. The spirits will smell it all over you."

Papa always said he'd do a séance with me when I was old enough, but then he died. Despite Auntie's warning, my chest is tight when I hold my hands out for my friends to take. Natalie's hand trembles and Inez's palm starts to sweat in mine, but we're here together.

Then Auntie Lindy laughs. "I'm not sure how you do things in your kiddie circles, but there will be none of that this time."

We pull apart slowly, and it feels like there's a million miles between us as Auntie opens a red velvet bag, takes out crystals, and hands them to us. I don't recognize these. They are flat and ringed like the inside of a tree, each ring holding a different color, and they seem to glow. In this moment, there is an endless amount of magic I've never learned, but hope to.

"Whatever you do, don't let those go until I tell you all to," says Auntie.

I look at Nat and Inez, hoping they're as hungry and anxious to get this right, to maybe make contact with Jas before the anchoring. "Push through no matter what happens," I say. "Okay?"

"Yes," Auntie agrees. "You girls were right about needing a séance. Spiritual magic can act as a gateway to tap into other parts of you, and it'll help widen the doors to the other side so we can speed things up." This is the reason she gives us, but her eyes keep flicking to Inez, and it's obvious she's keeping something from us.

She pours sea salt into a wooden bowl and crushes in some herbs before dumping the contents of a glass bottle into it too. She hands the bowl to Natalie for mixing, then grabs my hand, turns it over, and—without warning—slices my thumb with a blade. I hiss at the sharp burn but lean forward to let a few drops of blood trickle into the bowl.

Inez's eyes are wide. Nat's too. They look horrified as I suck on my thumb.

"Who's next?" asks Auntie.

But then all I can see is Jasmine's face in front of me, and it's hard to breathe. I blink and the séance has already started, and my friends are bleeding from their thumbs, and Auntie is calling directly to the spirit world.

"Travelers, if you're with us now, give us a sign. Show me you can hear me."

There's a long stretch of silence, and the walls shrink as my breathing quickens. Suddenly, I think I can hear the thoughts of my friends, like Auntie's abilities have been given to me: Natalie wondering if she should get the hell out of here. Inez thinking, *Maybe the spirits won't like this. They'll trap us here or pull us into the other side. Maybe even God won't want to help me from there.*

Auntie closes her eyes, and I'm rocked back to a normal

equilibrium, where I don't hear any inner voices except for my own. And I'm wild with wondering how Jas will sound, what she'll say, how it'll feel to be in her presence.

Then something else starts to happen: The flames on the candles grow higher. Higher. Higher. Until they die down again.

"Travelers, tell me what you want. Tell me what you see." Auntie dips her fingers into the bowl and uses it to draw a circle on her forehead. Our blood drips down her face. She makes no sound. I can't even tell if she's breathing. But I am, fast and hard. My heart pounds so strong the spirits can probably hear it.

Auntie finally makes a noise, a deep growl from her throat, and the crystal in my hand starts to cool. Then Auntie lifts her head, eyes glossy, mouth smiling, and I shudder.

"Shaky children." She tilts her head. "Mmm. What a shame."

I lean in a little. "Auntie?"

"You," she says to me, voice higher, tone more playful. "You're a slick one, aren't you? Have you told your friends? Have you told your friends? Have you—"

My chest is on fire, but Auntie's teeth snap together, biting away her words with a force that makes Natalie gasp. Was she going to tell them about using Darleny for the anchoring? Her words reverberate in my mind until she turns away from me and uses a trembling chin to point toward Natalie.

"And you," she says. "Were you even her friend? Were you ever? We don't think so."

"What?" Natalie chokes out, forming a fist around the crystal.

"Were you ever? Did you love her?"

"Stop," Natalie cries.

"Leave her alone," Inez says, but then she winces and looks

down at the stone in her hand. Auntie's eyes are burnished copper, then bottomless black as they land on Inez.

Auntie opens her mouth to speak, but Inez flinches backward, nearly knocking into the candles. "It burns," she screams out. "The crystal . . ."

"Don't drop it," Auntie says. Or not Auntie. "Don't drop it, don't," a singsong voice repeats. "You're——" But she's cut off when the crystal tumbles out of Inez's hand and hits the floor.

All the candles go out at once. The room fades to darkness, and Inez stands, fumbling over our feet to find the door.

29

INEZ

Natalie knocks on the bathroom door repeatedly, fear in her voice, but I splash water on my face and stare down at my right hand. It's red and already bubbling like a blister. The shape of it mirrors the scars from our pacts on my left hand. I don't know why I'm here. I miss Jasmine, but this? I can't do this. I'll have to try to convince Mili to grieve and move on so we all can. None of us should ever have to sit through a séance again. I say a silent prayer to God, asking for forgiveness and to show me a way out of this. Then Lindy knocks on the door.

"We're leaving." Her voice sounds like her own again, but somehow that's scarier.

☾ ☾ ☾

No one questions where we're going. No one talks to Lindy. For most of the drive, she watches me through her rearview mirror, and the black rosary beads hanging from it catch my attention. I'm surprised to see them after the séance. Even though I know Mili's papa was raised Catholic, it's as if my brain can't make sense of his daughter Lindy following the religious traditions. I keep seeing her glossy eyes, hearing her haunting words in my head. She pulls in front of CVS and gets out.

Miliani turns in the passenger seat to study me. "What happened to you back there?" There's a slight edge in her tone. "Was it your anxiety?"

"No," I say, massaging my right palm with my cut thumb. "The crystal burned me."

"Well, it didn't burn the rest of us. You couldn't keep it together for Jas's sake? It's bad enough we're working slow. The days are disappearing. And now we can't even talk to her."

"Are you really questioning me after what we saw?" I hold up my hand.

Natalie takes it in her own. "Shit, Inez."

Miliani's mouth droops as she looks too. "Sorry," she mutters.

"You should be," Natalie says. "You ran bullshit on us, and your aunt wasn't even prepared for a séance. Maybe you're the reason she became possessed."

"She . . ." Mili stops, shakes her head. "She was letting them speak through her."

"Possessed," I say, repeating Nat's word. "This was a bad idea. We don't know what kind of dark spirits she may have unleashed on us in there. She probably made things worse."

Mili fixes a look on us. "I'm sorry for lying, but you both were hesitating—when Jasmine needs us. Auntie was trying to help with that. Don't be dramatic."

Natalie doesn't care. "Dramatic? She hasn't even wiped our blood from her forehead."

Right when she says it, Lindy comes out of CVS. What did the cashiers think when they saw her like this? She gets in and puts a brown paper bag on the console.

On the ride back, she does a vague job of telling us what

happened. "The spirits aren't here to harm you. They're trying to get a hold on this side without being anchored. I told them this was foolish, but that won't stop them from trying."

Natalie cuts her eyes at Lindy. "Was that before or after they took control of you?"

"I never lost control," Lindy says, but her voice falters. "How will you ever open the realms enough to anchor your friend if you can't handle a séance?"

"Séances require possession now, or . . . ?"

Lindy's voice tilts into something like amusement. "Are you upset the spirits were implying you weren't friends with Jasmine, or are you upset with me?"

This shuts Natalie up. I open my mouth to defend her, but Miliani turns around. "What was that about anyway?"

"I don't want to talk about it," Nat says, but Mili presses till she cracks. "Things were different before Jas died. I know you remember. Let's not act like Jas and I were good."

Mili looks confused. "But she was still your friend."

"I know that." Nat leans forward. "And what about you? What are you keeping from us?"

Miliani's eyebrows knit together. "Nothing. I don't know what that was about."

"Oh," I say, finally finding my voice but still not wanting to speak around Lindy. "So Nat has to answer right now, but you get to keep shut?"

Lindy throws a quick glance at Mili, who sinks in her seat. A whole minute must go by before Mili sighs. "I told Jas I was in love with her, and . . . she said it back, but she died that night."

My stomach drops hearing it. The tension leaves my body,

but Mili wraps her arms around herself. I wonder how it all went down. If they planned to be together. Suddenly, I feel guilty for pressing Mili to talk to Isobel. I want to pull her close, but not with creepy Lindy watching.

"Damn." Natalie runs a hand over her own face before she sits back.

Lindy clears her throat. "Now that you're all done with your sharing circle and I don't have to suffer through teen angst, you should all proceed with the spell work. Some of the spirits just like to have a bit of fun."

I gingerly flex my blistered hand. "How did they know things? About us?"

Lindy shrugs. "It must be a combination of them watching you, and . . ."

"And what?"

"And maybe they tapped into my mind."

"So they used your . . . your abilities to read our minds?" Natalie and I share a look, and then Nat inches closer to me. But Lindy doesn't answer. I hope she's ashamed. I open the window to let the air in. Maybe it'll make it easier for me to breathe with her sitting this close to me.

Mili doesn't seem shaken by her aunt's revelation, but her voice quavers asking if Jas made contact. When Lindy says the connection broke too soon to find out, Mili pulls her hoodie over her head and doesn't look at us for the rest of the ride. I know she blames me, but it's hard to feel guilty for being the one to break the séance connection when I'm worried we did it at all.

We pull up in front of Lindy's house, and she looks in her rearview at me and Nat. "Don't run scared."

What she doesn't know is that my mind is already miles from here, praying with Mami, even listening to Father John in church, but Mili speaks for all of us. "We won't."

I want to slap some sense into her. How does she expect us to be okay with knowing spirits are watching, and waiting for the opportunity to be able to come through? My hand still stings. I don't care what Lindy claims; they must want to hurt us.

"Let's go upstairs," Lindy says. I shake my head, but she uses her weird mind-reading tricks. "We won't even talk about spirits, Inez. I have something to do, then I'll drive you all home after." I don't believe her, but I remember the two buses it'll take to get to the South Side and feel queasy. Walking home from the bus stop alone after the séance wouldn't be fun, either.

Lindy's offer makes me uneasy, but maybe it's better than the latter.

☾ ☾ ☾

Upstairs, she makes us tea with a hint of peppermint, and we sit on her stools at the table. We sip the tea quietly. It doesn't taste bad, and soothes the ache in my stomach. I flinch when Lindy reaches for my hand, but her touch is soft. She opens up a small tin and rubs salve on the burn. I can feel it cooling while she stands to retrieve the CVS bag from the counter.

"I've never had to do this. I don't have any kids. My siblings are older than me. There aren't people in my life I'd care about telling if I knew. But with the confirmation from the séance, I think it's the responsible thing for me to do."

Miliani laughs a little. "Auntie, what are you talking about? Are you okay?"

"I'm perfectly fine," Lindy says, and slides the bag across the table toward me. "But I can't say the same for you, Inez."

Something churns in my stomach again, but this time a wave of nausea hits. Why is Lindy paying so much attention to me? Is this some kind of punishment for dropping the crystal? Goose bumps rise on my skin, but I open the bag carefully and look inside.

It's a pregnancy test.

30

INEZ

When the tears start, it's hard to get them to stop.

On the ride, Mili and Nat try to comfort me, but I can't even look at them. They drop me off at home, and Victor is in the living room, reading a book.

I look at the pictures on the wall. Victor was a cuter baby. He had really big eyes with huge lashes, a round face and thick hair. I had eczema on my cheeks and did the ugly cry in every picture. I wasn't one of those chubby babies everyone gushes over, and I had hair only at the sides of my head, so I looked like an old man who went bald in the middle. Mami always says she worried I'd never grow hair there and that I'd look like a viejo on my first birthday. So when my hair did start growing a little, she was so excited she gave me the smallest ponytail at the top of my head and made sure to take lots of pictures. She's proud of them, always telling me to be quiet when I complain about them being the first thing people see when they come over. "You were a pretty baby. Even when you looked like a viejo," she says. "You'll know how it feels when you get married and have kids."

Victor dog-ears the page he's reading and asks if I still want to talk. I'd forgotten I used magic to make a wish. If I could use another wish to go back in time and erase what happened with Aaron, I would.

"Not right now," I manage to say.

Right now, I need Mami.

I look for her in the kitchen, in her bedroom, in the bathroom. I open my bedroom door and find her standing near the wall beside my bed, three cans of paint and a roller at her feet. She's holding two paintbrushes in her hand, and the whites of her eyes look pink, but there's a smile for me on her face. It makes my shoulders slack in relief. She doesn't know I'm fresh out of a séance. She doesn't know I'm pregnant.

"I wasn't sure what color you'd like, but these were on sale," she says.

I'm in her arms before I can think about it. The tears come back, and Mami is crying too. "The lawyer called. It's not looking good for the five years," she says. "Who knows if Papi will be able to come back at all." She kisses my head, and we take turns brushing the hair out of each other's faces. "It's just us, baby. Me, you, and Victor. We'll be okay, I promise. Don't you worry. We will be okay. God"— her voice trembles—"is with us."

My heart breaks for her, and it breaks for me. The way it did the night Mami cried on the kitchen floor after getting the worst phone call of her life.

But at least this time, we're crying together.

When we pull apart, I wipe the tears from her face with my sleeve. There's no way either of us can handle any more pain tonight. I take a paintbrush from her hand. "Should we start?"

She bends over to take the lids off the cans and asks, "Which color do you like?"

The colors are a plum purple, a teal, and a crimson. "I like them all," I tell her, even though it's not the truth. "How about we do one on each wall? Is that suitable for someone my age?"

She laughs. "Yeah, baby. I think that'll look nice."

We spend the rest of the night listening to bachata and laying the first coats of paint.

31

MILIANI

The first symptom we notice is an aversion to chocolate milk. Inez takes small sips and complains it tastes sour, even though Natalie takes the carton from her and says it tastes just fine. We've known about her pregnancy only a few days, but she already throws up in her mouth off the smell of it. That's when we all stop drinking milk. Soda sits well in Inez's stomach, and when she's done she finishes my can too. Nat says we're already doing healthy pregnancy wrong. I tell her she sounds like Leanna. She makes a face and says she sounds like me. I'm not concerned about the soda. People do far worse while pregnant, but I am concerned Inez doesn't want to talk about it.

"Let's do the water ritual," she says every day at lunch, and when we tire of it, she insists we cut lunch altogether for me to practice elemental magic in the patchy area of grass across the street from our school. I pretend to know what I'm doing and she asks if I can teach them, but there's nothing to offer. I feel sick about it, especially when Inez says, "Jas really needs us. We can't leave her over there to become like those evil spirits."

I'm scared to ask her where this new determination is coming from because I don't want to break it, but right after the séance she looked like she never wanted to touch magic again.

☾ ☾ ☾

I've spent afternoons at Auntie's house, trying to connect with nature. She's shown me how she channels the energy of fire by stoking the flame of a candle, but it seems to me she's only intensely staring. She's tried to teach me how to relax my aura because the birds find me repulsive instead of magnetic, but I usually find myself holding back frustrated tears until I leave her house.

Today, I'm here alone. Auntie's gone on an artist retreat, even though I'm stressed Jasmine's still on the other side. "And she'll stay there if you don't get to learning," she said, and gave me a spare key to water her plants while she's away. The back room is off-limits. _Just_ water the plants reads a note she left on the kitchen table, along with fifteen dollars and three spring rolls.

I take special care to water the plants we started growing the day she began teaching me elemental magic. Her plant is overgrown and beautiful: green leaves trickling down in a vine of an impossible length for such a short time. Mine is smaller, but it's budding and branching off more than it probably should be as well. I marvel at the only proof that I'm learning something.

When I'm done, I pick up Auntie's note, crumble it into a ball, and throw it in the trash before heading to her room.

I don't come in here much because Auntie says bedrooms are for sleeping only. Her room is all white: the linen, comforter and curtains, the platform bed. There's a huge mirror on the wall and a desk with nothing on it but a blank notebook. Some moon water we collected last week sits in a jar on her nightstand. I open it up, swirl my finger around until the blue-calcite, amethyst, and orange-citrine crystals stir at the bottom of the jar. And finally, I throw myself onto her bed, turn on my side, and imagine Jasmine in my arms, stroking my hair, smelling my neck, asking me if when we touch it feels like lightning to me too. I can see her so clearly—until her eyes turn green and the beauty mark above her lip disappears and suddenly she's Darleny.

I inhale sharply and shake my head again and again, but then my senses pick up. My eyes flicker to the mirror hanging on Auntie's wall. I see me and see someone else too.

It's not Darleny or Jasmine.

My body goes rigid when the shadow moves closer to me on the bed. I try to control the erratic beating of my heart, but the shadow stands and disappears. I can't see it anymore, but I feel a brush of wind by my face and hear footsteps on the floor. I'm up and following the sounds before I can think. All the way to Auntie's back room. I hear her warning in my head before I turn the knob and push the door open.

There are no more sounds or shadows, but the room pulls me in like it has mastered magnetism. It feels different now than it did the night of the séance. The meld of potential energy buzzes as it comes off the collection of artifacts and books. I think I can see it. But what draws me closer are the few canvases lined up and facing a wall. My fingers are fast to find the edge of one, like it's calling out to me, but before I can turn it around, the house phone rings.

I flinch and hurry out of the room, steadying myself before answering the phone, hoping the distance blots some of Auntie's abilities.

"It's time for you to leave my house." Auntie seems a bit out of breath. "Hope you enjoyed the spring rolls, and my bed."

32

MILIANI

When Inez doesn't show up to school the next day, we worry. Nat wonders out loud if something is wrong with the pregnancy, if the spirits have hurt Inez somehow, if her anxiety is debilitating today. I reassure Nat everything is fine and insist it's not about the spirits, but during fifth period, I ask to use the bathroom and I go bother the admin Mrs. Julie. She's an older woman with short curly hair and a cackle like a movie character. She wears bright-red lipstick on her thin lips and has the nicest purses I've ever seen.

"Get out of here before I hit you with my ruler," she says when I take the seat beside her. But I beg her, and she takes a look around to make sure the principal is in his office before passing me the phone. "You have thirty seconds." I blow her a kiss. She rolls her eyes.

Inez claims she's trapped in bed with a vomit bucket. "Be there tomorrow, Mother Mili," she says and hangs up on me.

But as soon as the next bell rings, Nat and I, sneak out through the back of the building while the halls are packed and lockers are being opened, and hope no one notices. Darleny does. She's coming back into school when we hit the yard and run into her.

I've been feeling a rush whenever I see her now, and I've found myself peeking around corners to stare at her, trying to steal glimpses of Jasmine on her when she thinks I'm not watching. But right now, in her baggy clothes, with her hair pushed out of her face in a clean sleek bun and her face bare, I can't see Jasmine.

She smirks. "Off to bunk school and conjure some demons?"

I get ready to come up with some excuse, but Natalie puts a hand on my shoulder. "Darleny, if you tell anyone, you'll have to explain why you weren't here for fifth period. Why you're hardly here for fifth period lately."

Darleny shrugs. "Well, then, you creatures be safe."

When she walks inside, I grip my backpack strap. "She's been skipping fifth period?"

Nat looks at me like she's wondering why I care. "Yeah, but the teachers won't keep going easy on her 'cause of Jas. The sympathy card doesn't last forever. I probably can't even use it with Ma in rehab because I've used it too many times before."

(((

We ring Inez's doorbell, and she opens it fully clothed. Her hair is in a gelled-up ponytail. Her sneakers are on her feet. There's color in her cheeks and gloss on her lips.

"You don't look sick to me," I say.

"Not one bit of sick, Inez," says Nat. "You look better than you have all week."

Inez moves aside to let us in. "I have one mother, and neither of you is her."

I'm not sure how she could act so careless about all of this. "Okay, when are you going to tell her that you're about to be one and she can take care of you and her grandbaby?"

"I don't need you to take care of me, Miliani. Worry about your-self for once. Don't you need to be learning something to save the girl you love? How many more weeks do you think she can wait?"

Inez's words and tone catch me off guard, and they must have done the same for Natalie because we're both quiet for a moment before Nat sighs and sits down on the couch. "We're worried about you, Inez.'"

Inez sits next to Nat and lies back against the couch. "What do you want me to say?"

"Anything would be great, since you've been saying a whole lotta nothing lately," Natalie says. "You can start by telling us where you were today."

Inez pokes at her cheeks, causing red blotches between her freckles. "I was supposed to meet up with Aaron today. I was going to tell him I'm . . . I'm pregnant. But he never showed."

I want to talk shit about him, and I'm pretty sure Natalie does too, but we'd probably make Inez feel worse. She looks at us. "You guys cut sixth period for me? You *love* art."

☾ ☾ ☾

We lie on her couches for over an hour, eating snacks and watching Maury Povich. Jas got us hooked on *Maury*. She'd pretend to be him, mimicking his voice in the middle of class, and say, "You are *not* the father," and everyone would start laughing.

Today on *Maury*, a woman slept with her cousin's husband and got pregnant, but the baby isn't his. It's her fifth time on the show, and Maury still looks invested. The audience too. They holler and clap and say, "Ouuuuu."

Inez says, "At least we know who my baby daddy is," and we

laugh until it's not funny anymore. It's the first time we've joked about her pregnancy, but it doesn't feel right.

"I think the baby is the size of a pea right now," I say.

This also doesn't feel right. Inez never said she was keeping it.

Inez sighs. "Stay off the internet, Miliani. I was joking. It's hardly a fetus."

I want to ask her if she's considering an abortion or if she's being irresponsible and not thinking about it enough. I don't even know how I feel. I just want to be there for Inez, but she turns the volume up on the TV, probably using *Maury* to drown me out.

33

NATALIE

Mili's mom serves us bowls of beef sinigang and seems happy I want two servings. I'm happy she doesn't mind me sleeping over. Dev's spending the night at a friend's house, and I don't want to be alone with ghosts tonight. After dinner, she teaches me how to gut and clean the fish they'll be storing for the month. Once I get started, she says I slide the knife like a natural and passes me fish after fish. I let Mili use my camera to take pictures of me while I scale them. When we're done, we bag and freeze the batch, then clean the kitchen with vinegar and lemon water. Mili's mom doesn't talk much, but she does tell us she's going to bed, and that there's chai and crackers for snacking if we get hungry later.

"Did I mention how much I love your mom?" I ask Mili as we try to wash the smell off our hands for the third time. "She's too dope." *Completely different than Lindy*, I think. And as much as magic seems a part of Mili's life, the energy in her house feels normal.

"Sometimes," Mili says. "But so is yours."

"She's pretty cool in a wild kinda way." I give her a grin, but it doesn't last. "When she's around."

Mili wipes her hands on a towel. "Do you think she'll be okay when she gets out?"

I feel a lump in my throat while drying my own hands. "I want to say yes, but who knows. They won't let her have visitors yet. Leanna said it's cause she's not acclimating well. What does 'acclimating well' in rehab even look like?" I turn to sit on the counter. I miss my momma, and there's nothing I can do about it. "And doesn't she know the better she does in rehab, the quicker they'll let her out? It's almost been a week."

Mili bites her top lip. "Do they think she's having bad withdrawals?"

I hate the question, but I've been asking myself the same thing. "I think maybe she's struggling with the structure of it all. And what if . . ." I pause. "What if she's worse? Do you think that could be a consequence of using magic to wake her?"

Mili gets up on the counter too. "I don't think our spell had a negative effect on her at all. We gave her another chance at life. It's a good thing." She sighs. "I hate that the séance has made you skeptical after we finally got you to believe. What about Jasmine?"

I look down at my legs, let some silence pass between us. The bathroom vent drones above our heads, and the water drips a bit. With everything going on, I can't help but feel like Inez's warnings about the way we use magic were right. I hope we didn't do damage to Ma, but I keep telling myself at least she's alive. "I still believe. I'm just scared. Even for Jas."

Mili nods and puts her hair in a puff with a scrunchie. She looks in my eyes. "It won't be because of what we did, but will you be okay if your mom has a hard time when she gets out?"

The sadness comes for me. "I don't think so. I'm just so tired. You know?"

"Yeah," she says, resting her head against my shoulder, our legs dangling. "I know."

☾ ☾ ☾

Mili's room smells like lemons, and her bed is soft. It's nice with just the two of us, but she complains about spirits not communicating with her in here.

"One reached out to me at my auntie's the other day, but they've gone quiet when I'm home. I light candles and call to them, but there's only a dull whir of energy. I don't understand why things are getting more intense for you and Inez but not for me."

"Me neither, but I hate it," I say. "Never thought I'd be scared to take pictures."

Mili lets out a loud exhale and snatches my camera. She snaps a picture of me. We both bend to look at it. The previous summer comes to my mind. A supercut plays. I see Inez carefully painting Mili's nails a deep, iridescent purple. I see fireworks lighting up the late summer evening sky, and the four us sitting on the grass at Roger Williams, with my arm stretched high and my camera angled toward us. Jasmine is at the center. There's no smile on her face, but you can feel the warmth in her eyes. She was happy with us. Mili has her tongue between her teeth. And Inez is beaming, her face full of love, as I smash into her side, trying to fit into the frame, happy to capture the memory.

Mili sighs, pulling me out of the past. There aren't any shadows or signs of spirits in the photo she took. When she looks at the ones of me scaling the fish, there aren't any there, either. But the pictures I took this week all have signs: distorted faces, white light where there shouldn't be white light, darkness where there shouldn't be darkness. There's one picture of Leanna cooking with a shadow standing right beside her, like it's cooking too. It gives me chills.

"I don't know if it's this house or if I took it, but something is wrong." Mili tilts her head at me. "Maybe you should tell Devin to take some pictures. See what happens."

My stomach goes tight. I feel like flicking her in the forehead for mentioning Dev at all. "No way in hell I'm involving my brother in any of this. He'll touch my camera, and next thing I know they'll be out to get him too. When I took the picture of Leanna, I could feel the oil crackling against my skin." I run my finger along my forearm. "Like I was being burned."

"I'm sorry," Mili says, her lips turning down. "But are you sure it wasn't in your head? Psychosomatic? My auntie said the spirits aren't here to hurt us."

"You calling me a liar? I'm anxious but I'm not imagining shit."

Mili puts my camera down. "I shouldn't have said that, but I don't want to feel like I'm subjecting you to something you don't want. If you're feeling unsure, tell me now."

I feel myself soften at the look on her face. "You're not the only one who wants Jas back. Maybe I'll stop taking pictures till this is over."

"But what if they find another way to materialize?" When I groan, she says, "At least, they're trying to communicate with you."

"Are you serious?" I laugh. She can't be serious. "Listen, you can have all your ghost friends. I don't want them. Particularly, because none of them are Jasmine."

Mili pulls her knees to her chest. "We don't know that."

"Well, if one of them is Jas, then she's definitely pissed at me. We definitely aren't friends."

A few beats of silence, and then, "No, you're right." She gives me her best reassuring smile. "It can't be Jas. She's out there somewhere, making mischief where she shouldn't."

It takes me a moment, but I smile too. "Wreaking havoc on the innocent."

"That's right," she says. "Wild as ever."

"Can we hurry with all of this?"

Mili starts talking about how we'll need another substantial spell, and how she needs to learn elemental magic faster. She rolls over onto her stomach and puts her face in her hands. "I feel like I'm failing everyone. The longer we take, the longer the realms stay open. And the longer we take, the more likely it is Jasmine will come back to us changed."

I remember her confession in the car after the séance. I can't believe Jasmine died just as they were figuring out they loved each other. "We'll get her back in time."

"We need to. I don't even want to consider the possibility she'll be different," Mili says. Then her head shoots up the way it does when she's convinced she's thought of something good. "We don't want Jas to change, but we do want your mom to change her habits, right?"

"What do you mean?" I tug on my camera strap. "Where did that come from?"

She smiles real big. "We have to widen the realms. What if there's a way to do it and help your mom stay sober?"

"Like a spell?"

"More like a cure."

I slide my hand over her pillow. My nerves are kicking. "But we can't cure an addiction. And we've already used magic on my mom twice—what if there's a limit before it messes with her?"

"Don't think of magic that way," Mili says, and pinches my wrist gently. "And I've seen my papa do all kinds of things. I think we can try."

I lie flat on the bed, staring up at the ceiling. Magic has helped Ma so far. If the calling spell never happened, she might have died at Betty's house. If we hadn't used the spell for the coma, the doctors would've pulled the plug eventually. These are the things I do know, and maybe I have to believe they outweigh the things I don't.

"If you think it's safe . . ."

"I do," she says. "Let's speak it into existence, and I'll ask my auntie, to make sure."

I turn on my side. Mili's cool sheets feel good on my skin. "I don't want to give up on her."

"Then we won't." She gets up to open her window like she knew I was hot.

"We won't give up on Jasmine, either," I tell her.

She turns around. The wind whistles and her curls rise in the air. "I won't let us," she says.

I watch her standing there, her eyes lit up and her skin glowing in the dim light, looking like someone I know and someone I don't, and I wonder how far she would go to get what she wants.

34

INEZ

It felt good being around Mili and Nat, but I'm relieved they're gone. I take another pregnancy test and stash it in my box, hoping the crystals will fix this mess for me. But each test has two dark-pink lines. They only get darker. The money Mami gave me for the week is running low, but five bucks at Dollar Tree gets me five tests, and I need them to make sure this is real. Every time I open the box, the tests are there, telling me I'm still pregnant. I stare down at them, wondering how Aaron is going to react when he finds out. If he ever does. Unlike Nat, who keeps looking at me like I'm fragile, and Mili, who is convinced I need to think more about the pregnancy than I already am, Jas would steal Darleny's car and drive me around town looking for him if she were here. She'd know I need to tell him I don't want to be a mother, and I'd need him to tell me he doesn't want to be a father. He can't want to be one with his life set up the way it is.

My bedroom door creeps open. I freeze like it's a spirit.

It's worse. Mami comes in without knocking, without calling my name, with quiet feet.

My back is turned to her, and I shove the test in my box as quickly as I can.

"Inez? You were supposed to clean out the fridge, since you seem to be feeling just fine now." I tell her I'll be down in a second, but she doesn't leave. She moves closer. "What's in that box?"

I push it into my closet and stand. "Just a bunch of old pictures of my friends."

She doesn't believe me. I can tell by the way her mouth twitches and her eyes narrow. "Well, let me see them."

The panic starts. How can I refuse her? But then, God or magic or both makes Victor call her from downstairs. Papi is on the phone. She doesn't stop staring at me or move. My brother screams, "He said it's important." Mami groans and leaves.

I creep down the stairs, past Mami arguing on the phone, and out the front door with my box to walk down the street and sneak into my neighbor's driveway. I toss every pregnancy test in their trash. The wrappers too. My heart is pounding so fast. Should I throw out my crystals? I don't. I hurry home and slip into the basement to tuck the box under the stairs instead. Hopefully, Mami doesn't want to clean the basement too.

☾ ☾ ☾

At night now, the sleeping spells don't work and neither does my medicine. I roll on my side and shake the bottle, wondering if they can affect pregnancy. The label states to consult a doctor, but would it give me a miscarriage if I didn't? Would the baby be born sick? Thinking about it makes *me* feel sick, but I pop a couple and put on my headphones. The music doesn't help. I switch to reading the Bible until it brings on a sense of dread. Pregnancy before marriage, possible abortion, doing magic without knowing the consequences. Before I know it, my left arm is numb and my face feels hot and I have to stop myself from calling out to wake Mami. She'd ask me why I'm having a panic attack, maybe count my pills, want to take me to the doctor if it gets too bad.

So I get out of bed and take the stairs slowly, shutting my eyes halfway against the shadows following me as I go.

In the kitchen, I consider calling Miliani. She and Nat are probably together watching movies right now, laughing and catching up while I'm here. While I'm pregnant.

I dial Dr. Baker's number. When she picks up on the second ring, voice groggy from sleep, I start to cry. She tries to calm me by counting. "One. Two. Three. Deep breath. Four. Five. Six. Deep breath." This works some.

I sink to the floor and lay my head against the wall. "I'm sorry for calling so late. I didn't know what else to do."

She pauses for a second. "That's okay. I gave you this number for emergencies. Tell me what's wrong."

"I can't say it here."

"Are you in danger, Inez?"

"No. No, I'm not."

"Do you need to see me?"

"Please," I say. "I can't wait till next week."

"I can squeeze you in for a session tomorrow at three P.M. Can you hold off until then?"

The panic starts to cease, and now I feel bad for waking her.

"Yes. I'll be okay, but are you sure?"

"I'm positive," she says. "Try to get some rest."

"I'm sorry, Dr. Baker."

"It's perfectly fine, Inez. I promise."

35

MILIANI

Nat and I trash the game closet in my hallway and all the drawers in the kitchen, searching for a deck of cards because we're bored. I hop on the counter to check the cabinets, and feel something deep inside, but it's not what we're looking for. I pull down a burlap sack, and Nat leans over to look when I open it. "What is that?"

I'm stunned when I take out the board. My mind tries to recall things I've forgotten. I run my fingers along the wood. "It's a sungka board from the Philippines."

"Is it a game?" Natalie asks. "It looks a little like mancala."

"It is. Didn't even know we still had this. I haven't played since I was a kid." I look in the sack for the shells it's supposed to come with, but find none. "That's weird. It's missing the pieces, but we can use the mancala marbles from the closet to play."

❨ ❨ ❨

We sit on the floor in my room with the sungka board. Natalie turns it diagonally, but I fix it so it's lying horizontally between us. I teach Natalie as much as I can remember. I wing it some. I struggle to form the memories of playing with Papa, but the images of his hands circling the board make me remember to capture Nat's pieces when they land in an empty pit on my side of the board. At the end of the first game, we count the number of marbles, and I win by six. Natalie is very competitive; she beats me the second round.

"Come from a board-game family, baby," she says.

We line the board for the fifth game, but when I pick up the marbles something presses down on my hand, and I drop all but one marble into the next pit.

It overflows, and marbles spill to the floor.

"What're you doing?" Nat looks up at me.

"It wasn't . . . ," I start to say, but sound fills the room. A melodic humming, soothing, like a lullaby. Natalie stares at me, then her eyes go wide. She scoots back from the board and looks around the room. The humming grows louder and quicker, more frantic.

I still my body, my breathing. If I make any sudden movements, the spirit might disappear. But the last marble slips from my hand and falls into a pit with a clink, and the song cuts out the same time as the lights in my room do.

All I can see is the whites of Natalie's eyes while my own adjust to the darkness.

"Mili," she says. "I'm scared."

I move to grab her hand but miss. She exhales sharply, and I reach for her again, but someone else exhales too. Right beside my ear. The hair stands on my neck, and Nat whispers my name just as my door flings open.

We both back away, but it's only Mom with a flashlight. "Are you okay in here?" The hall behind her is dark. "Must be the wind. I'm going to report it to the . . ." She stops, her flashlight flitting to the floor. The light makes the mancala marbles shine. "What are you doing with that?"

I look down at the sungka and back up at her. "We found it in the cabinet."

"Give it to me," Mom says. "Give it to me right now."

"What? Mom. It's just a game."

"It's not a game," she snaps. "And don't you dare use it in the house."

"But why?"

"Hand me the board, Miliani."

I stand up and give it to her. She holds the flashlight in one hand and balances the sungka in the other. She looks at it closely. "What is this? Where are the shells?"

"I found it empty. There were no shells."

"Don't lie to me."

My eyes start to prick, not sure what I did wrong. "I'm not lying, Mom. I swear."

She shines the flashlight at Nat. "There were no pieces when we found it," Nat says.

Mom gives me a hard look, tilts the sungka board, and dumps all the mancala marbles. They clatter to the floor at my feet, then she leaves.

Nat freaks out about the spirit. Then she starts asking questions about why Mom got mad, but I have no answers for her. It's dark again, and I'm glad she's here. I crouch down, wanting to be close to her while my mind tries to make something. Form another memory I can't quite grasp. But the power kicks back on, and Natalie doesn't want to talk about any of it anymore. She picks up a marble from the floor and avoids my gaze. I don't get to tell her that even though it was scary, I'm relieved it happened. Maybe this means the blockage is gone and spirits will reach out again. Maybe *Jasmine* will reach out soon.

I help her pick up all the marbles, and we climb into my bed.

☾ ☾ ☾

Hours later, I wake in panic, but it's a bad dream lost to inertia. I turn over to face Nat and see someone behind her, standing by the window with their back to us. I gasp, move to shake Nat awake, but then realize it's my mom. She doesn't answer when I call out. I get up and walk over to her slowly, tapping her shoulder when she doesn't move.

She turns quick and grabs me by the shoulders. My breathing hitches, but she recoils like my body has burned her hands.

"Oh, I'm . . . I'm sorry, Miliani. You scared me."

"You scared me, Mom. What are you doing in here?"

She shakes her head. "Thought I heard something. I came in here to check on you two, then the moon caught my attention. That's all."

I nod, but my stomach is still churning. "Why were you so mad earlier?"

She looks in my eyes, her voice gentle. "Don't touch what doesn't belong to you."

When she leaves the room, her words sting me again and again. She'll never let me in.

I look out the window. The cloud cover is too dense tonight. There is no moon to be seen.

When I crawl back in bed, Natalie groans. "Was that your mom, or was I dreaming?"

"You weren't dreaming," I say, then hesitate. I never wanted to complain about my mom's illness to her because she hardly complains about her mom, but she shared with me today, so it feels safe to do the same. I tell her everything. How different things were back before Uncle Jonathan joined the military. When there was a storm outside, my cousins and I would run through the rain, and our parents would make us sit in our soaked clothes until we dried. We were always together. Sometimes we would all attend church with Papa on Sundays. We would sing karaoke and dance in the yard at night. We were happy.

I tell her that things began to change when Mom got really sick. Papa was debating on taking us to the beach when Mom got quiet and her face drooped some and she seemed to be staring off to one spot over the fence in the yard. Auntie Lindy told me it was the heat. Mom came down from the sickness that day, but a few days later, the shakes started. She'd be cooking, and all at once her whole body would begin to tremble. But we didn't move into Papa's until the blank spots. I tell Natalie about the days Mom would go away in her mind and leave me by myself for hours.

Until it all stopped. She was suddenly better, and didn't want to talk about any of it. But my family had already started to fracture. Auntie distanced herself. Uncle Jonathan moved away. My mom didn't even want to hear it when Papa mentioned church or God.

I don't realize Natalie's holding my hand until she laces our fingers.

"I'd worry she would get sick again, but Papa was here to reassure me she was fine. He's not here now." It's hard to keep the tears from coming. The way I miss him breaks my heart, makes me ache for things I'll never have again.

"Is she getting sick again?" Natalie rubs circles into the crevice between my thumb and pointer finger when I don't answer. "I'm sorry. I can't reassure you like your Papa did, but I'm here. And we have magic, right? Maybe we can help your mom too?"

"Maybe," I say. "But remember when Inez joked about heaven sending her mom a warning about brujería? Well, it seems like my mom has an actual radar for magic."

Natalie nods. "Hmm . . . so maybe not. But, Mili, why didn't you tell me sooner? Or Inez?"

"You both have been going through so much."

"And you're there for us," she says. "Every single time. You don't have to hide things." She purses her lips. "Like you being hurt because you told Jas you loved her before she died. That's special. That's important. You can tell us things."

My face burns because she doesn't know the whole truth about that, either.

"Do you even like Isobel?" she asks.

I hesitate at hearing her name because I haven't allowed myself to think of her much. "I mean . . . there are some sparks, but it's not the same. She's not Jasmine. You know?"

Nat moves closer to me. "But Jas will be a spirit when we get her back."

Grief tries to envelop me, but I refuse to think about all the ways my relationship with Jasmine might change right now. I've already spent too much time wondering how Jas will feel about me when she's in Darleny's body. What it'll mean for us if Darleny doesn't want me close to them. But Natalie doesn't know about that, either.

"You don't have to shut us out and handle everything alone," she says, "okay?"

I hug her, but the guilt settles in to stay because there are things I still have to hide. Auntie could be wrong—maybe telling them the truth about the anchoring is safe—but what if she's right and I jeopardize everything?

Nat smiles. "You should probably tell Isobel before you break the girl's heart."

"The way you broke Ray's heart after the ride from Newport? After," I stress, "going ghost on him last year? The boy is about to fall out of love with you."

"Shut up," she says, and smacks me upside the head with a pillow. "He doesn't love me."

36

INEZ

After school, Nat and Mili talk about what happened at the sleepover, and I wish I was there and I'm glad I wasn't. We all hold hands as we walk to Kennedy Plaza. Mili wants to practice what Lindy's been trying to teach her. "Elemental magic isn't hard," she says to herself, then, "You both can learn too."

The séance made me scared of doing magic for a second, but now I'm eager. Anything to forget about my pregnancy. Anything that'll help widen the realms so Jas can be in my life again. I concentrate on the way the wind feels on my face, try not to look away as the sun pierces my eyes, try to feel Nat and Mili's energy as we play a witchy version of I spy on our surroundings. This part of downtown Providence is gray and gritty, filled with pigeons and concrete, so we set out to see something we wouldn't normally see.

"A red robin," Nat offers, and it makes me excited.

We count the birds on one block: twenty-two, all black and gray, some spotted. We walk between two buildings. Mili closes her eyes and tells us to picture the robin with our mind. Closing our eyes in downtown seems like calling for trouble. I do it anyway. Nat sighs but does it too. We walk with no sight, holding hands and letting our senses lead. We stop after about twenty steps, and a tin-gling sensation moves from my toes to the top of my head. When we open our eyes, we see it. A red robin—perched on a black fence outside a parking lot.

I feel a rush of emotion. I'm sure it's not only mine. I feel less of it when Mili lets go of our hands and walks over to the bird.

"You're going to scare it away," Nat calls.

But it sits there, tilting its head at her. None of us move, none of us speak, while Mili reaches out a finger. The robin lets her touch it before it chirps and flies off into the sky.

Mili turns around, eyes big like her smile. "I finally did it. We did it together." Her curls bounce as she walks up to us. "Did you see me touch it? Did you?"

"All right, animal whisperer," Natalie says, but she's grinning too. "We get it."

We get it. While they're talking about how amazing it was, I'm realizing, in one of those weird moments to realize some-thing, another reason it's been hard to try to talk to them about the pregnancy is because I don't know if they'd get it. They didn't grow up with religion the way I did. Without Jas here, I feel a loss of having someone who understands. She'd know why I'm con-flicted about whether to get an abortion like no one else could. How many more times in life will I need her to talk the Bible, God, and magic too? I need her here, right now. Because not only do I have to consider my religion, my mother, my own wants and needs, there is also Papi's sponsorship. Three years from now is not looking good, but what if it does happen within the next few? Will being a young mother affect the decision and have me labeled as an unfit sponsor?

Jas's not here to talk to, and I don't know how much time I have to decide on an abortion. For now, I'll have to talk to Dr. Baker, the only other person who will listen without offering judgment.

37

MILIANI

The conversation with Natalie replays in my head as I walk into the botanica to meet Isobel for ice cream. Last night, Isobel called, and instead of telling her we can't link up anymore, I somehow agreed to this date, and to study advanced calculus over the weekend too.

But the botanica is empty. I think it's a sign to slip out and tell her it wasn't meant to be. Until she peeks her head out of the back room. "There you are," she says. "Come here."

I've never been in the back room. I had imagined old scrolls covering tabletops and candles lighting the space, but it's more of a storage unit, with boxes on the floor, and shelves with more boxes, and cobwebs above the shelves for decoration. Isobel sits at a folding table with her abuela and stands to kiss me on the mouth. Her abuela doesn't flinch like I do.

Isobel says, "Abuela's finishing up my reading now."

"Oh. Should I go?"

But her abuela fans the cards down on the table and gives Isobel the rest of her reading in Spanish. After, she tells me to sit. "You stay. She goes."

Isobel rolls her eyes. "Abuela, what if she doesn't want one?"

"She does. I can tell."

"Abuela."

I laugh. It smells like dust and my nose itches, but I say, "A reading will be good."

Isobel smiles and leaves us alone. I've never had a legit tarot reading before. Auntie has a few different decks in her room, but she never mentions them. Jasmine practiced for a while, but she grew bored of it. Isobel's abuela flips over three cards: Death, the Knight of Swords, the Four of Swords. She stares at me.

"You're making a mistake." She taps the Four of Swords. "You need to stop while you have the chance. You're being followed by Death, and it will become you if you let it."

"Abuelita," Isobel says, walking in the room. "Stop trying to scare her."

"You were listening? You're just like your father."

They argue back and forth for a while, and all I can think about is the reading, the warning, the dimensions I've been fine with opening. But soon, I'll be able to see the girl I love. Once she's in this realm, I'll worry about fixing the mess I've made.

"I'm sorry about that," Isobel says, and leads me out of the room. "Ready to go?"

"Actually, can we reschedule? My stomach is starting to hurt."

Her face falls. "But you came all this way. Is it because of what Abuela said?"

I lean in to kiss her on the lips. "It's not because of that," I say. It's only a half lie. It's not just because of the reading. It's realizing ice-cream dates aren't necessary but training is.

She smiles, but I know she's hurt when she says, "Okay. Feel better."

☾ ☾ ☾

The tarot reading replays in my head all day and prevents me from feeling better. At night, I'm strung up worrying Isobel's abuela saw something in the cards I haven't been able to predict. I light a candle for Jas and wait, itching for a sign from her, but it's gone back to no spiritual contact since the day Nat and I played sungka, and I have no idea why.

Mom's taking a bath when I creep down the hall and into Papa's room. I hit the switch, and the lightbulb flickers but doesn't fizzle out. The sungka board has to be here, and Papa will forgive me for searching. I start with a plastic container full of his clothing and slip on his old military jacket. It smells of must and a tinge of smoke from cigarettes but fits me just right. It's easy to forget how small of a person Papa was, given the weight of his presence. Inside one of the pockets is a handkerchief folded in a triangle and a pocketknife. I don't remember this knife, but it has the sun-and-moon symbol carved into the handle, and it feels light in my hand. It's also mine now. I smell and touch everything, my fingers and nose greedy for bits and pieces of Papa. I trace over my initials in the floorboards, remembering how he wasn't upset when he found them carved there.

The sungka board isn't here, but the small box Mom was going through catches my eye in the corner of the room. I pull it over to me. It has Papa's navy medals, a stale pack of cigarettes, notes with hearts and misspelled *I love you*s from me and Auntie when we were kids. I pocket one of her notes to tease her later, then dig through the bottom of the box where the good stuff usually hides. It's mostly old photographs, some black-and-white, from Papa's younger years. There's a single picture of him and his sisters in the Philippines, a few from when he was recruited for the navy at eighteen,

Uncle Jonathan and Mom fishing off a pier, so many pictures of me as a child.

And then, there's one of a young boy.

I pause, wondering if it's a visiting cousin. His back is turned to the camera, and he's riding a tricycle. I run my pointer finger over it like maybe I'll be able to see him more clearly, before flipping it over. There's a sun penned on the back, the ink runny. I'm tempted to pocket the picture, but shift my gaze to the rest of the pile. The next photo is the boy again, but this time he's smiling and looking directly into the camera. The same boy on the tricycle, I'm sure. There's no writing on the back of this one, and I search the rest of the pile but don't find any more of him.

☾ ☾ ☾

I make it out of Papa's room with Mom still in the bathroom, but a light knock at my front door startles me. No one comes over at night. Unless it's Nat and something bad has happened. But when I open the door, Isobel is standing on my porch, the small shroud of light making her skin a weird hue of yellow.

My heart stammers. "Wha-what are you doing here?"

I try to breathe while searching her face. Is it really her, or is this what Auntie meant by spirits shifting to look like us? I feel cold all over. "How did you know where I lived?"

Isobel frowns. "You gave me your address over the phone to study together this weekend." She shakes her head. "Oh, I knew this was a bad idea. I just . . . My dad made sancocho, and I thought it would help your stomach."

The fear leaves my body when I notice the container in her

hand, but it's replaced with disappointment because the realms aren't wider. I'm not the only one who looks disappointed.

I close the door behind me and step onto the porch. "No, no. Thank you for thinking of me." I say it to ease the awkwardness, but her shoulders are high as she passes me the container. The soup is warm like my chest.

I tell her I'm glad she came, and it takes a few seconds but she steps closer and hugs me. Her body feels soft, and her breath tickles my neck. "I'd kiss you on the lips, but I think your mom's watching from the window," she says, and plants her lips on my cheek instead.

But feeling them again doesn't just make me think of Mom; it makes me think of Jas. Waiting. Watching this. I push away. "Isobel, I can't . . ."

Her face contorts before she bites on her bottom lip. "I knew something was up." The sassiness changes her voice. "Listen, I don't want to play games. I've been in shady situations before, and I'm not doing it again. Maybe we can talk when you're ready."

Ready. The word strikes me, and I fear losing hours of the day to it. I know Isobel thinks it's because she's a girl. I wish I could say, *If you could see my heart, you'd know I need to make things right with this other girl I love, who's not quite alive but needs me very much.* A part of me nudges, whispers, *And I'm not ready to stop loving her and wanting it to be her for me, one day, somehow.*

I have to let Isobel believe what she believes, but Nat was right: I should've told her sooner. She doesn't look back at me when she speeds down the steps and off my porch.

After she's gone, my face burns where she kissed me, like there's an outline of her lips on my skin specifically for Mom to see. When

I walk in, she sits down on the couch and grabs the remote, pretending she wasn't spying, but she doesn't even watch TV.

"Who's the girl you were with? Is that the one who's been calling lately?"

This is two questions more than Mom usually asks about my friends.

"Yes. She works at a shop I go to. She brought me soup."

"Maybe you'll introduce her next time," Mom says, and it gives me this tingling sensation in my stomach. Maybe she knows Isobel isn't just a friend. *Wasn't* just a friend.

If there'd ever be a perfect moment to tell her I like women the same way I like men, it'd be now. And it's not like I'm unwilling to confide in her. I just feel like a mirror, giving her what she gives me, adapting to her rarely sharing with me or inviting me to share with her. I wouldn't even know where or how to start. And I always thought if I did start, it would be with Jasmine.

"I don't think she'll be coming around anymore," I finally say. "You can have the soup." I move to set it down on the coffee table and notice a small glass jar sitting on one of the windowsills. I walk over and pick it up. There are flakes of herbs and seeds floating inside liquid. I turn to ask Mom what it is and bump right into her.

She takes the jar from my hand, says, "Forgot to wash this," and hurries off into the kitchen with it.

I turn back to the windowsill and touch it. My fingers come back sticky, and they smell like lemon and something I can't quite place.

38

INEZ

The street in front of me has always been long, but I've never been pregnant until now. I walk halfway, and I'm out of breath when Aaron cuts the corner and walks up to me.

"I knew I'd catch you before you got on the bus," he says, and I'm dazed seeing him, dizzy from it and the hormones and the heat.

I lean against someone's fence. "You ridiculous? What if my mom or Victor saw you?"

He rubs the back of his neck. "She doesn't even know what I look like, and I watched Victor hop on his bus earlier. This street doesn't belong to her anyway. We're safe."

I cut my eyes at him. "Well, don't you have someplace else to be, since you can't show up for me?"

"I tried apologizing, but you hung up," Aaron says. "And I left a message with Victor, pretending to be one of your little church friends yesterday. You haven't called me."

"I'm not going to be late for school, Aaron. I'll call you later."

But he closes the distance between us by pulling me into a hug. I push him away. I'm mad, and we're out in the open in broad daylight.

"Why haven't you been around?" I say. "Are you in some kind of trouble?"

He shakes his head.

I give him a look, and he sighs. "I've been really busy making some runs."

"Runs?" I question, and then my stomach sinks. The dizziness doubles back and I feel like I'm going to faint. "Are you selling drugs?"

"It's only weed," he says. "My family really needs the money. Mom's out of a job."

Forget being a young mother, if the US finds out I have a drug-dealing boyfriend, I'll never be able to petition for Papi. "I can't be with a drug dealer, Aaron. I can't."

He opens his mouth to protest, but then nods. "Your father," he says after a few seconds.

I don't speak. He pulls me close, plays with my hair. I feel the anger in me dissolving to something quieter. I missed him. I want him around. I understand why he needs to make money, but he doesn't need to make it like this. "Not just that, but I can't be worried you're out on the streets risking your life when you shouldn't have to."

"Hey, hey." He keeps his arm around my waist but leans back to look me in the eyes. "I'll stop selling. Let me just get rid of what I picked up, then I promise I will."

Cars pass by us on the street. I turn my face from them. "You should be in school too."

"Not today."

My throat is dry, my stomach hurts, and tears well in my eyes. "Did you drop out?"

"No, but I keep thinking, who will pay the rent and keep my brothers off the streets if I'm worried about school? Especially if I'm not selling drugs. I'll need to work full time." He gets close again, says sweet things about missing me and loving me. "Let's hop on Bus 11, and I'll walk you the rest of the way. One of us needs a degree."

"I'm pregnant," I snap. "I'm pregnant; you're dealing drugs and might drop out of school."

He takes a deep breath against my neck. Then lets me go and backs away till he hits the fence. "What?" I can see in his face he's trying to work out which time it happened, but he asks, "How do you know?"

The distance between us brings a fresh wave of ache for him. My body begs for him to come back, but my mouth goes to work. "I took a test, and my period is MIA. Also, there's the morning sickness and deep naps."

He swings his arms and takes a breath. Then he sits on the sidewalk. "You're napping?"

"I have to nap."

"Wow, you really are pregnant."

"Is that all you have to say?" I roll my eyes. "Aaron, what are we going to do?"

He clasps his hand to his mouth, speaks through his fingers. My body is above him, blocking sunlight and dousing him in shadow. He looks different from up here. He is a face and body of hard lines and dark circles from sleepless nights. He is too old for his time, and even when I step out of his sunlight, he still looks tired.

"Shit, Inez. Give me time to process this, please?"

"I tried to tell you sooner."

His voice is low and desperate. "I know. I'm sorry. I'm sorry, okay?"

I drop down beside him. We watch people walk up the street, cars pass. I'm nervous but scoot over and lean my head against him.

Mili and Nat would probably judge me if they could see how soft I am with him, but I'm relieved he finally knows. It soothes something in me to be close to him. It feels like medicine when he tilts his head and kisses my forehead.

Until he says, "When's the baby due?"

My eyes snap up to meet his. "I never said I was having the baby."

He stares at me for a few seconds. I count five. "You talking about an abortion?"

"I'm too young to have a baby, Aaron."

"And you think it's okay to make this decision without me?" He stands up suddenly and steps into the street. Someone on a bike swerves to pass him. My hands reach for him out of instinct, but he's too far.

"I'm talking about it with you now, aren't I? Get out of the street. You're too young for a baby too," I say.

I stand up to grab his hand and pull him back onto the sidewalk. "Aaron, think of what you're saying. We haven't even graduated high school. My mom would kill us."

"I hear you, but doesn't mean we should kill our baby."

I can hear tires rolling up the street, birds chirping on the power lines, someone whistling somewhere, but I can't see anything except for him.

He steps forward and cups my face in his big hands, massages my cheeks with his thumb. "People our age have babies all the time. Your mom will get over it. Think about how happy she'll be with a grandchild to dress up for church."

"She won't ever show her face in church again," I say. "She'll never forgive me."

And she definitely won't ever forgive him. Unless I make her. Maybe there's a spell to make her more understanding. Maybe I can wish it on her. I haven't used that kind of magic on anyone since Victor. I take a breath, remembering the uneasiness in his face after he spoke to me that day. But what I also remember is how steady my heart was beating, how in control I felt.

I look into Aaron's eyes and sigh. I can't go around using magic on everyone. Natalie said if I believe in God, then maybe I should believe God gave me this power. But if that's the case, what if I'm being judged for the way I use it?

Aaron's adamant, not realizing Mami will think the devil sent him into our lives. "She *will* forgive you, and I'll figure this job situation out. Maybe stay in school or get my GED. Think about it? For me?"

I let him kiss me. But at school, while Nat talks shit about how Aaron won't be the one bearing most of the responsibility and while Mili wonders if maybe a baby will help him get on track to clean up his life, I can't stop wishing there was going to be no baby at all.

39

MILIANI

The candle goes out even with my hands cupped around it. I complain about the wind, but Auntie's candle stays lit while we snip overgrown vines in her yard and she sings to her tulips. I want her to tell me why Mom is keeping the sungka board from me, but her lips curve up on one side. "You're still concerned about that old thing?" She starts singing again. The heat is sweltering today, and sweat beads on her forehead as she works to water the tulips too. "When I was young, Dad would make me sing while we played sungka. I'd complain about how unfair it was. It was difficult to sing and play a decent hand. Until I realized he was teaching me how to think better, move smarter, listen to myself while being distracted."

"Did you start winning then?"

"Against him? Never. But I did get good enough to beat my sister here and there."

My stomach clenches. "Mom used to play sungka?"

"She was amazing. It was her favorite game." Auntie runs her finger along the edge of a tulip. "But it makes for more than a good game, Miliani. It can be used as a visionary board, to tell the outcome of a day. In the Philippines, it's sometimes used to see how many children a woman will have. To see when someone will die." She tilts her head toward the sun, and I wait.

But she doesn't say more. "So just another piece of magic to keep from me?" I say.

Auntie's aura has changed. I can't place it, but the energy around us grows sad. I watch as her candle flickers higher but then goes out. I don't want her to feel sad, so when she tells me, "Let's talk about this later, huh? Finish singing to the tulips," I sing the best I can. Even though I'm anxious to know more, I really try. Auntie laughs. "Listen to yourself, focus on your vocal range. I can't bear to find dead tulips tomorrow."

☾ ☾ ☾

We sit down to drink lemonade and chew on ginger, and Auntie tells me she's researched what I need to help Nat's mom, says it'll be safe with the right ingredients, but I couldn't go back to the best botanica in Providence if I needed to. I hate it, and hope Isobel doesn't hate me.

"Bringing Dad back from the dead wasn't ever going to work," Auntie randomly says. "He wouldn't have wanted to come back anyway, even if I could've gotten it right."

The ginger is peppery, but I swallow it, surprised. "You tried, though?"

"With your mom and Uncle Jonathan, the day he died." She puts down her lemonade. "All you get with necromancy is one shot while the body is still fresh."

"Why didn't you try to anchor him, like I'm doing with Jas?"

Her lips twitch. "Dad wouldn't have liked that."

"I don't understand why you're telling me this now. Are you changing your mind about training me?" The lemonade is stinging my throat. I push hair from my face. I sweat.

"Calm down. I'm telling you because he found space, but he's also here with us, laughing at the way you pretend to like the taste of ginger," she says. "Remember he used to say the afterlife with God is probably complex and more beautiful than this one?"

"I remember. And I do hate the taste of ginger, but you're worrying me."

She smiles. "The ritual for Jasmine is a good idea. She hasn't moved on. But Dad was a particular type of person with very specific desires for his afterlife. I was talking to you, that's all."

Relief floods through me, and appreciation makes me warm. Auntie likes to talk to me. "I've been meaning to ask . . . ," I say. I shake one leg out, look anywhere but at her. "Darleny . . . She doesn't like me. Will that affect the way Jas feels about me when they're tied together?"

Auntie smirks. "Jasmine will still have her own desires."

My cheeks burn. The spirits have been materializing more: I connected with the robin. Even my plant is growing. It isn't just budding and branching; it's beginning to bloom now. "But what if I'm not learning fast enough? I'm scared she'll change."

Auntie strokes the blades of grass underneath her for a minute too long. "I've been training you the way I was trained, but maybe you need a swifter approach," she says.

We sit in the brightest part of the yard after this. Side by side, but not touching. She holds her hand out and lets the sun catch it, and then she turns it so her palm is facing the sky. Soon it looks like she's holding a ray of light, bending it to a fine point in her palm.

Watching Papa heal people and do spell work was one thing, but I've never seen anything like this. The other day, Auntie told me that controlling the way sunlight is filtered is part of elemental magic, but I didn't know this is what she meant.

A kick of exhilaration flows through me. I blink to make sure I'm still seeing what I'm seeing. It feels like Auntie even brought the temperature down a few degrees.

"Why the sun and not the moon?"

"Most spells require the moon." Auntie makes a fist, and the ball of light still shines through the spaces of her fingers. She closes her eyes. "But there are some that need the sun."

We practice until the last of the light fades into a night sky.

40

NATALIE

Mili drops some of her mom's homegrown chamomile into a bowl and says it's essential for curing illness. Everything we need for an elixir is in her kitchen, including turmeric powder which colors the ginger and garlic in the bowl a rusty orange. "Your mom could give the botanica and the bodega on Elmwood Ave a run for their money," I joke. "And you could probably avoid Isobel if you shop for herbs here instead of the botanica."

Mili cuts a look at me, and Inez's laugh makes her have to pee.

When Inez is gone, I hope she's okay. Seems like her bladder is always on the brink of bursting. I cut echinacea at the root, *carefully*, per Mili's orders. "Inez called me three times this week," I say, "asking if I have family drama we can solve for a spell."

Mili stops chopping herbs to look up at me. "Do you?"

I shake my head, and she sighs, then stands on a chair to get some bottles down from a cabinet. The bottles are from the Philippines; each has a design so intricate I start taking pictures as soon as she hands them to me. "I see you're not worried about using the camera in my house."

"Only place taking pictures is safe these days," I say, getting the angle right for a shot.

She's a grump about it, mumbling that the house is scary quiet since the sungka board incident while reaching in the cabinet for another bottle. Inez creeps into the kitchen and grabs Mili's ankle. "Since you enjoy being scared," she says, ducking Mili's swatting hand.

Mili hops off the counter with the last bottle. "My auntie tipped me off to where Mom had these stashed. I wonder what else she has hiding in this kitchen."

I bring an open bottle to my nose. It smells sweet, but another makes me gag. "Is this from a sewer?"

Inez leans over to smell it and recoils. Mili laughs before she sees the horror on my face and says, "Of course not. Each one has oil mixed with water from hot springs in the Philippines. Auntie said people travel to drink from them in order to heal from disease. Some people believe drinking from certain hot springs can even delay death." Mili stares at the labels on the bottles for a while, trying to decipher which is which, then pushes three toward me. "These."

"Are you sure?" I ask. "Not trying to poison my mom with your half-hearted Tagalog."

Mili's annoyed look is ripe for a picture. I take it. "I'm sure," she says. "A tablespoon for each bowl."

When we're done, we clean up and bring the mixture outside. Mili sets the bowl out on the ground in front of her porch, and we sit around it. My thighs burn on the hot concrete, and the sunlight slices through Mili's mouth and bounces off her teeth as she reads a spell Lindy gave her in Tagalog I hope she understands.

I pray this works. For me and Ma. Maybe it'll help us with Jasmine too.

After we pour the mixture into vials, Mili tries but fails to manipulate sunlight like Lindy.

Inez says, "You'll get it soon. You have to," and I feel bad when Mili's face falls.

She changes the subject. "So, you excited to see Ray at work today, Nat?"

"Her boo," Inez teases.

"He is not my boo. Not anymore," I say.

"But you wish he was." Inez changes her voice to mimic me: "Oh, he's so annoying. But when he works hard, the muscles in his biceps flex, and the sweat rolls down his chest, and I—"

"Want to take him into Mr. Ortega's office," Mili adds, "and lay him out on the desk."

"Gross." I slap them both on their thighs. "Doesn't sound like me at all."

☾ ☾ ☾

But I'm mad as hell they're right. Ray works a few feet away on a ladder or right beside me behind the counter, messing with the computer system, winking at me, sometimes sticking his tongue out. And I know I'm warming up to him because if I could use my camera at the bodega to capture these moments of him, I would. But they'd probably come out all jacked up, and then I'd worry about how they'd affect me. I'd have to worry if, somehow, they'd affect him too.

He's switching from humming to singing now, and I forgot how beautiful his voice is. He catches me watching and smiles. He seems easy to forgive, but I know that what I said to him at the top of my stairs hurt him. Heat creeps up my neck when I remember Mili saying he loves me. I don't think it's love, but his feelings might be deeper than I thought.

Today, I don't complain about him taking his time to get the job done or tease him about how much he talks while I'm trying to do mine. I listen to him make music for us. When he offers to get us dinner, I don't say no.

He's out picking up the food while I examine the elixir for Ma. It's clumpy. Flakes of herbs float around it. The smell is rancid enough to take my appetite, even though my stomach still rumbles when Ray walks back in. Ma's not going to want to drink this.

I tuck the vial away and watch Ray flip the BE BACK IN 20 sign on the door.

"That might look suspicious with the both of us in here," I say.

He lays our Cubanos out on the counter and unwraps them both. "What do you think it looks like exactly?"

"I don't know. The two of us in here behind locked doors? What if Mr. Ortega drops in?"

"You watch too many movies." He laughs. It's cute. "But if that did happen, Ortega would be happy we've finally cut the sexual tension, and he'd give us a thumbs-up."

Ray looks off to the side like he's waiting for me to say something smart and ruin it, but I try something new. "Maybe he'll give us a raise."

"If that's the case, I hope he does come by."

☾ ☾ ☾

Ray doesn't think I notice he stays later than he has to so I don't have to lock up alone. "You going to let me take you home or whip out that handy-dandy bus pass of yours?"

"Don't hate on my bus pass now that you have a car. Remember where you came from."

He rolls his eyes. "I remember, but I don't miss it."

"I'll let you take me home," I say, "if you let me drive."

"You don't know how to drive. Is it a bad thing if I take you home?"

I shrug. "I don't want to get dramatic over taking the bus when you're done here."

His face gets serious. He motions for the door. "I won't let you get used to it. I promise."

41

NATALIE

Ray passes my street but says he'll take me home after he shows me something. We pull into Roger Williams. He parks, gets out, and walks around to open my door. "Come on," he says.

"What? Where?"

"I promised," he says. "Get in the driver's seat."

There are so many reasons to say no: I don't have a permit. It's dark. This isn't a parking lot. *Are you even old enough to teach me how to drive? What if I crash into a tree? Drive us both into the lake?* I could be on the phone with my friends brainstorming ways to speed things up for Jas. But Ma always talks about teaching me to drive. She'll jiggle her keys and say she can't wait till I can make runs to the market for her. She's just never around enough to follow through. I've imagined Leanna teaching me, but in every scenario she was racked with anxiety over me stepping on the brakes too hard or getting too close to curbs with her brand-new whip. Real Leanna would probably pay to send me to driver's school instead.

It was supposed to be Jas. She'd offered to teach me when she took Darleny's car on weekends. I was too nervous, always told her, *Next time.*

She'd shake her head, say to me, *You've gotta be brave.*

Ray raps his knuckles against the window. "I'm waiting, Williams."

We start slow, driving in a straight line, avoiding the curb, and I feel like I'm watching a simulation of myself. Ray puts his seat back and says, "You're good," and the simulation snaps. Real me shakes as he makes me drive down one of the hills and around a rotary. When I don't crash, he tells me to bang a left onto Broad Street as soon as the light turns green.

I swallow. I sweat. I go. *Be brave.*

☾ ☾ ☾

Parking behind another car is harder than it looks, and my attempts have Ray going, "Whoa, whoa, whoa," but I manage.

"I didn't kill us."

Ray exhales deeply. "You did not."

"That was . . . fun."

He squints his eyes at me, smiles. "The feeling doesn't last long, so enjoy it." He tilts his head and waves at Harriet through the window. She's staring at us from her porch. She cranes her neck for a better view but doesn't wave back. "I don't think she remembers me."

"Of course she does. Harriet remembers what she ate March sixth, 1979. She's probably checking to make sure we aren't sinning in this darkened vehicle."

He laughs. "Or maybe she's surprised you're driving."

I grin, still amazed, and imagine telling Jas when she's back. She'll be proud. Or will she be mad I didn't wait for her? Will it be another thing I've done without her?

"I'm proud of you," Ray says, surprising me. "You'll be a better driver than me soon."

A tingling sensation streams through me as I look at him. Jas will be happy when I tell her. She'll say Ray's incredible.

I bite down on my lips to try and contain my smile. "Yeah?"

"Yeah," he says. "And I like sitting on this side of the car."

"Don't get used to it," I tease.

(((

We meet at the back of Ray's car, and he leans against the trunk. "I'd ask to come up, but you might push me down the stairs once we reach the top."

"I'm sorry for being so damn awful that day." I reach up and touch my hair, look anywhere but at him. "You didn't deserve it. I was wound up about my mom, and—"

"You talk a lot for someone who told me on my first day at the shop we'll never have a reason to speak to each other," he says.

I narrow my eyes and nudge him with an elbow. "You're an ass."

"And you're forgiven, but don't let it happen again."

"Are you threatening me, Garrick?"

"Oh, definitely," he says, and his beautiful teeth flash in the dark.

I laugh and lean forward to kiss him on the cheek. He looks surprised but doesn't say it. Mili and Nat aren't going to believe what happened tonight. "I'll see you tomorrow?"

"Your workday wouldn't be the same without my pretty face."

I suck my teeth but thank him for trusting me with our lives, for helping me be brave.

When he leaves, Harriet calls my name and asks me to come sit with her, but it's late, I'm tired, and I've effectively avoided her since the hospital up until now. I lie about having homework, and she nods her head.

As soon as I put my bags down in my room, I sit at the chair by my window. It faces the side of the porch Harriet sits on. Even though the street is empty, even though there's no drama or entertainment for her to witness tonight, she waits. Maybe I'm still feeling high and brave after driving because I don't hesitate to grab my camera.

I open the screen on my window to get a clearer view of her waiting there, snap some shots. It feels good. I take a few more. She's waiting for something to happen, and I'm waiting for her to do something different. Harriet's husband died when I was a kid. I wonder if he'd be sitting opposite her on the porch, calling the police when something pops off on the street, or if she'd be a different person right now. Maybe she'd spend days with him drinking wine while watching movies and playing poker with Ma and the other old folks on the block.

When I look at the pictures on the viewer, there are no shadows or defects. Not even the company of Harriet's dead husband. Only Harriet, looking good for her age, but lonely too.

☾ ☾ ☾

I dream of Harriet, but she's not alone. She's with Ma. They're talking on Harriet's porch and I'm watching from the window, but Ma leaves with Harriet hobbling after her. She gets in a black car, and my heart speeds up. I didn't even have a chance to give Ma the elixir. I run down three flights of stairs with bare feet, swing the door open, but the car she's in disappears while I wave my hands.

I'm panting, and I realize my legs are trembling. My thighs are bare. I'm pulling down my T-shirt to hide my undies and trying to catch my breath.

Harriet's leaning over her porch rail. "Come over here, child. We can call on the Lord."

I shake my head and go upstairs. My feet stick to the unmopped floor. I check my wallet to find it empty. Ma stole from me again. I cry until my throat goes dry and it makes me choke.

That's how I wake up: choking and crying. My body is cold. I've lost my blanket to the floor. The window is cracked open, but Harriet's lights aren't on. Ma's not home. She's in rehab, getting better. This is what I tell myself to stop crying, only I'm not sure it's true. Not yet.

The elixir has to work. I need to get it to her.

☾ ☾ ☾

I drink a glass of water from the sink and head to Devin's room. He's got a movie from Blockbuster on, and he's doing push-ups on the blue carpet. I take pictures of him to try to still my shaky hands, then sit on his bed and look over at the cable box. It flashes 3:00 A.M. in fluorescent blue.

"Why are you awake?" I ask him.

"Thinking about Ma. I hope they're treating her okay in there."

"I'm sure they are," I say. "And at least she'll be better and won't slip up when she's home."

"Leanna said the exact same thing yesterday," he says. "You both are bugging. Ma wouldn't do drugs after the overdose."

I scrunch my nose up. This is the second time someone's told me I sound like Leanna. I want to tell him about my dream, but if

I do, I'm being a bad older sister. He needs to believe Ma is going to be all right so he can play basketball and laugh with his friends and go on dates with girls I don't approve of. I take a breath before flipping through my photo viewer. The pictures I took of him are out of focus and pretty dark, but they're normal like the ones of Harriet. I smile and skip the gap of time when I stopped taking pictures of Jas to look at one of her, Mili, and Inez sitting on top of their backpacks on the cement at KP, sticking their middle fingers up at me.

Dev finishes his push-ups, grabs one of his pillows, and makes a bed for himself on the floor. I lie on his bed like I always do on rough nights when Ma doesn't come home and it's hard to sleep without the sound of Devin breathing close by. On those nights, we tell each other stories or stay up watching unsolved murder mysteries until it's time to get ready for school, but tonight's different. There's a heaviness between us, too many unspoken wishes and feelings. And then he says, "I really hope Ma stays clean this time. I miss her."

His wavering voice is so small I wonder if he wanted me to hear. But then, "What's your friend Mili say? Put positive vibes out, and that's what you'll get back. With her cute-ass smile."

"Ew." I throw a pillow at him. "Stop crushing on my friends."

"Tell her to stop being cute, and bet I will."

When the laughter dies down, I scoot closer to the edge of the bed so my view of him is at a better angle. "I miss Ma too, Dev," I say, and watch him till he falls asleep.

☽ ☾ ☽

A clicking noise wakes me up three hours later. My skin feels damp from sweat and itchy all over. Dev's sleeping on his belly, squirming and probably more uncomfortable than I am. The clicking happens again, but this time the room lights up with a flash. My camera is on Dev's dresser, facing me. I sit up, and the camera takes another picture. Dev stirs in his sleep when the flash lights up the room six more times. My heart is racing when I stand, careful not to trip over Dev, and scoop it up—expecting to be burned, expecting static or something supernatural. But I feel nothing. It doesn't take any more pictures as I turn it over in my hand and play with the lens. Then I hear a click, and the flash goes off in my face, burning my eyes and blurring my vision. I hurry to take out the battery.

When I crawl back into Dev's bed, I pull the comforter to my chest and stare at it on the dresser. I wonder if maybe it was Jas and she's not happy I'm wasting time with Ray while she's slowly changing on the other side. I fuss over the thought until sleep finds me again.

42

INEZ

Jasmine and I dance in the street. We spin our arms and move our bodies. Cars pass on the side of us, beeping their horns, but we don't care. Jasmine steadies me after I swirl too hard and almost lose my balance. Around her neck, a gold chain shines in the sun. It has a black crystal caged and dangling from it. I reach out to touch it, and she asks if it feels warm. It does. "You can wear it if you want to," she tells me. "You should wear it. For the baby."

I wake up right then. My throat is too dry to swallow. I try to roll out of bed for some water but can't move, either. There's weight pressing down on my limbs and chest. I close my eyes and count to ten, the way Nat's been doing. When that doesn't work, I chant in my head, *You are weightless. You are safe. You are free.* But I'm still trapped. I open my eyes, my mouth, scream Mami's name, Victor's, but no sound comes out. Someone whispers above me, and then the whisper turns to a hiss, and the hiss gets closer until it's right up against my ear.

Inez, someone says.

I chant again, and this time my breathing levels out and, finally, my screams cut through the room. Mami comes rushing in, flicking on the lights and stumbling to get over to me. I grab my throat, touch my chest, press on my belly. "I'm right here, baby," Mami says, brushing hair out of my face. "Dios mío, you're soaked. What happened?" She helps me sit up. My shirt clings to my back, my head hurts. I hold it while telling her I had a bad dream. She clicks her tongue against the roof of her mouth. "Are you taking your medication?"

I say yes, but it's another lie. The pills started to make me nauseous, so I've been relying on spells. "This was a plain bad dream, Mami. I don't feel anxious."

"I get them too." She fixes a roller that falls from her bonnet and looks up at the clock on my wall. "Why don't you get cleaned up? I'll make you something warm to eat."

She stands, but I grab her nightgown. "Mami, wait." I want to tell her I'm pregnant and scared, about the dreams and the ghosts. Tears spill from my eyes. "Te quiero."

She looks taken aback, and it makes my heart heavy. When was the last time I told my mother I love her? But she leans in to kiss my forehead and says, "Te quiero también, mija."

When she leaves, Victor is standing in my doorway. "You okay, Inez?"

My legs shake when I stand. He watches as I pull fresh pajamas from my drawer. "I'm . . . scared to be alone." I touch my bare neck, thinking of the dream and the crystal and the demon on top of me. "Would you leave your bedroom door open while I shower?"

The corner of his mouth turns up on one side. "Scream out if you see the boogeyman."

☾ ☾ ☾

Mami fixes us bowls of farina and turns the TV on in the living room. She never allows food outside the kitchen, but she sits down and pats the spot beside her for me. Mami uses cinnamon sticks and condensed milk in her farina. It's thick and warm and doesn't make me want to throw up. We eat while watching a rerun of a telenovela, and I catch her snickering. Tomorrow, she'll go to bed after a Bible reading; tonight, she's someone else. When we're done, I wash our bowls. She tells me it's okay to let the pan soak overnight.

Back upstairs, she turns to me. "Why don't you sleep with me tonight?"

I'm scared I'll get nauseous or have to pee too many times, but I follow her, climb into bed beside her, and sleep through the night.

43

NATALIE

Leanna comes over to make breakfast, and Devin finishes his food with the quickness. When he puts his foot on a chair to lace his sneakers, Leanna swats it away and tells us Butler Hospital called. Ma can have visitors now. Two at a time, between the hours of 2 and 5 P.M., but to call ahead in case the privileges get revoked for the day. She chews her cheek while explaining how Ma's still being snippy with the nurses because of withdrawals.

"Maybe that's because they told her a week," says Dev. "She should be home by now."

I fork my egg yolk till the yellow runs beneath the home fries. "They know better than we do. More time in there will probably do her some good."

Leanna's head snaps in my direction. She wipes her face with a napkin.

Dev ignores me. "She needs some lovin'. When we go, they'll see she needs us."

I know Leanna wants to say being with us never helped Ma stay clean before because it comes to my mind too. She stands to empty her plate, pulls mine from me and empties it too. "I think we should give it a while before visiting," she says.

"What? Nah." Devin's brows scrunch. "She'll think we don't wanna see her."

"The nurses suggested—"

"Wait. They said she can have visitors, but you're listening to their suggestions?"

"She's allowed visitors per the rehab's rules," Leanna says. "Doesn't mean she should have them yet."

Dev doesn't look happy. "I got practice anyway, but I want to see her tomorrow."

"Okay," Leanna says, voice softer. "Promise I'll bring you."

He kisses her on her cheek, flashes me a smile, and he's out the door. Leanna comments on how loud his feet are on the staircase: "Like thunder crackling." My orange juice tastes sour so I don't care much when she snatches it up and runs the sink water.

I sit back. "Why don't you want to see Ma?"

"I do want to see her," she says, "but I think it's too soon. For all of us."

"It's not your decision to make. Think we can handle seeing her while she's actually sober and trying."

She turns to see me. "You agreed she should stay longer, but you've got something to say about this?"

"That's different. She needs to know we're here for her while she's in there. And Dev and I know what we're doing. You were hardly around before her overdose."

"Oh, I was hardly around?" She drops the cup in the sink. The sound startles me. "Okay. But that didn't stop you from calling me when you were hungry."

"Really?" I shake my head. "You're going to bring it there?"

Her back is to me again. She picks up the cup, scrubs at it with the sponge. "I didn't mean that, but you've got a mouth on you. Listen, I know you've had to help take care of Devin, but you really don't know what's best. You're still a child. You should be able to be a child without having to worry about any of this. That's what I'm here for."

Hearing this makes me furious. I stand. "A child who goes to school, works full-time, raises her little brother, and sticks by a mother who needs her." A child who can use magic to fix things. "I think I'm more adult than you. At least I don't run from my problems."

Her shoulders rise as she turns to me. "Don't assume you know anything about my life."

"You make sure of that," I say. "We're your seasonal charity case. When you feel bad for leaving us with an addict, you step in. Otherwise, you're a stranger. At least with me." The words leave my mouth in a rush, make my face hot. I don't know why they came now, how long I've been wanting to say them, but here they are, clouding the space between us.

"Shut up." She slams her hands flat against the table. "Shut the hell up, Natalie. You don't know a damn thing. You've never had to do half of what I've had to do to survive."

"I'm going to be late for work," I say, grabbing my coat off the rack and leaving Leanna propped against the table, her hands still wet from washing dishes, staring at my empty chair.

❨ ❨ ❨

Lying to Leanna about work doesn't make me feel guilty, but calling Ray from a pay phone to ask him for a ride makes me feel bad. Mili can't get her mom's car, and even if Inez could, she's feeling like shit. He doesn't mind but makes me drive some of the way.

When we get to Butler, he lifts my camera strap off my shoulder. "You bringing this?" The small touch makes me straighten my back and reminds me of the last time he touched me after he graduated. He pulled me in to cuddle then and talked about his plans for the future. "Maybe college in Georgia, or the military. It's hard to think about life after high school. But sometimes, I want to get out of Rhode Island and start over. Do you ever feel that way?"

Never. I couldn't see past being here for Devin. Being wherever Ma was so she'd always have a home to come back to. And now I can't imagine being far from my friends. It's hard enough that I've gone this long without seeing Jas.

That day, the thought of Ray up and leaving the state gave me a sinking feeling in my stomach. It made me think of Leanna leaving and Ma never staying, and the next day when he called, I told him I needed space. He never called again. I told myself what we had was nothing. That we hadn't even defined it. That the pain I was feeling by ending things was because I'd let myself get too close, too used to him being around. I'm scared of doing the same thing now, but I tell myself we're just friends. We can be friends.

I hide under my curls. "I bring my camera everywhere." I don't tell him I don't want to let it out of my sight after what happened in Dev's room last night. I need to keep it close until we anchor Jasmine here. "Besides, can't trust to leave it in the car with how nosy you are."

"I resent that." He smiles and takes *Sister, Sister* by Eric Jerome Dickey from his glove box to read. "But good luck making it through check-in with it."

☾ ☾ ☾

The shorter of two security guards tells me cameras aren't allowed inside the facility because of patient confidentiality. I decide I'm not telling Ray he was right. The guard gives me a key to a locker, and I check the lock twice to make sure my camera is safe.

I wait for Ma on a beige love seat in a small room with off-white walls that smells more sterile than the hospital. When the door opens, my heart rate picks up, but it's only a nurse. She smiles, introduces herself, says, "We're hoping she'll be ready for the out-patient facility in another week, but she's had some trouble with socialization and has shown some signs of self-harm and aggression toward others."

"Aggression? My mom's never been aggressive in her life." Unless it's the first of the month at Price Rite, which doesn't count. Not really.

The nurse puts her hands up. "Not to worry. It can happen in this stage of detox, and we're keeping an eye on it."

She goes on to tell me things to avoid saying, which might make Ma more eager to leave: *I can't wait till you come home. We're doing bad without you. The weather is beautiful.* And others I hardly hear because I'm thinking of Ma trying to hurt herself and, worse than that, trying to hurt others. Maybe this is what Lindy meant about spells having consequences. Did waking Ma up from a coma change her while she was so close to the other side? What does that mean for Jas? I've been telling Mili everything will be okay, but how much of Jas will be changed when we bring her back?

When the nurse leaves, Ma comes in and rushes over and we hug and hug. She swipes at the tears on her face. "Are you taking me home?"

I sit down on the couch and pat the seat beside me. "Soon, Ma."

She puts her hands in her hair. It's brushed and clean and smells faintly like flowers. "You don't know how bad it is in here," she says. "I can't even take a walk outside without someone following me around." I hold her hand; she squeezes mine. "And the food is . . . God, the food. It's terrible. They don't bother with seasoning—it's like they're feeding us cardboard and cat pee. All the rooms smell like feet." She squeezes tighter. "I don't belong here, Natty."

"But after what happened . . ."

"I want to go home," she says, and moves to shake me by the shoulders.

"Ma, you're hurting me."

She looks at her hands, lets go. "I'm sorry," she cries. "I'm sorry, Natty."

I'm stunned for a moment, but I hate watching her cry. "Hey, hey, listen, Ma." I cup her face. "Look at me. Everything is okay. You're okay. We are going to get you out of here. You're doing great." Ma takes a breath. Her shoulders fall.

I reach under my pant leg into my sock and pull out a small vial. The liquid in it looks muddier than it did earlier. "I have something for you. It's going to help you get better faster. It will help them see it too. And then they'll let you sign out of here and you can come home. Okay?"

"What is it?" She scrunches her nose like I'm trying to poison her. It doesn't look edible to me, either, but I try not to make the same face.

"It's a natural remedy from the Philippines. Miliani's mom sent it over."

Ma's brows loosen after knitting together. "You really think it'll help?"

"I know it will," I say. Even though I'm not sure anymore. As good and as clean as she looks on the outside, I've never seen her act this way. She's never grabbed me like that. And when I take a closer look, I see that her nails are bitten down to stubs, the skin a bit bloody.

Even if the elixir does work for her addiction, will it trickle down and hurt her some other way? Hurt someone else? Maybe I should have talked this over with Lindy myself to make sure it was a good idea. But then she wouldn't tell Mili it was safe if it wasn't, would she?

Ma's waiting for me to hand her the bottle, to change the pace of this interaction so she can go back to biting her nails.

I say to her, "You have to promise not to tell anyone about this. If anyone here finds out I gave you something to help, they won't let me come back."

She nods at me eagerly, and I wonder if this is how it feels being a drug dealer when I take the cap off before handing her the vial. She smells it, makes a face, and downs the whole thing in one shot. "Ugh," she says, then wipes her mouth. "That tasted almost as bad as the garbage they feed us and call soup." She licks her lips. "But if you think it can help me somehow . . . I'll try anything."

I slide the vial back in my sock. "It can and it will. You're going to get out of here soon, Ma. Then you can be home. Me and Devin will cook for you every night."

She straightens her back. "I'll be the one doing the cooking. It'll be a feast every day. We'll buy some crabs with the stamps. You want crabs, Natty? With butter and garlic?"

"Sounds amazing, Ma." My eyes sting. "And we can get a bird like you've been wanting."

"We'll name him Craig," she says, and smiles back. "Craig the Cock-a-tail." She sheds some tears and kisses me on the face. "I love you, baby. Will you come back soon?"

"I will, Ma," I tell her. "Every single time I can."

☾ ☾ ☾

Ray's napping when I bang on the window. "Don't scare me like that," he says when he unlocks the door and lets me in. I apologize for taking long. I tell him things like he should have left me here and I'm not sure why he cares. I say so many things that make no sense. I cry into my hands. He rubs circles into my back. "What the hell happened in there?"

"I wasn't ready to see her," I say. "My sister was right. I don't know a damn thing."

44

MILIANI

The smell of sage sneaks through the crack under my door as the sun rises. I peek into the hall and choke on the smoke. Mom doesn't hear me or see me. She whisks the sage stick into the air, singing as she goes. The song sounds familiar. I try to place it as she makes her way toward the staircase. She stops there and starts to twitch. I move to help her, scared she'll fall down the stairs, but she shakes it off and starts singing again.

She walks slowly, the sage smoke floating as she goes.

I three-way my friends to vent. Nat says she's still sick over the rehab visit. I tell them the sage is stuck in my lungs. Inez wins: "A demon was on top of me while I slept."

After the call, Auntie parks a street over from mine so Mom doesn't say anything, and we head up to Sandy Point Beach in Portsmouth. I ask her if the spirit that was in Inez's room could be the manananggal: a creature said to be able to separate its torso from its lower half, and prey on pregnant women while they sleep—using its tongue to suck the fetus from the womb.

"Your papa told you a lot of scary stories," Auntie says with a laugh. "Probably not, but who really knows? I wouldn't tell Inez that story, though. It'll just scare her more."

She offers up some things we can do for protection, just in

case, and then turns up the radio. She's in a good mood. We listen to music most of the way, and we dance in our seats. For the first time, I remember she's only twenty-six. When we arrive, she opens her trunk and hands me two fishing poles and a cooler. "Thought we were heading here for training. I know how to fish, and there's nothing magical about it."

"Clearly you weren't paying attention years ago. Your grandfather would be ashamed."

Her words don't sting. I smirk. "You always sound a bit jealous of me and Papa."

Auntie chooses to ignore me. She's carrying only the bag of bait and doesn't look back at me when I complain about her having two hands to help. She picks a spot she thinks is perfect, but people are walking their dogs by the water, and others are fishing close by, some taking pictures with their catch. The space doesn't feel as private as the navy base Papa fished at did. How are we going to practice elemental magic with all of these people around?

She grabs a pole from me and hands me a night crawler, which is longer than I've handled in the past and uglier than I remember. "Just bait your hook." She casts her line at the perfect angle, which lands in an amazing spot without having to readjust, while I struggle to cast mine. It takes me three tries, but she doesn't tease me about it like I expect her to. When I'm done, she gives me a can of soda and says, "What are you waiting for? Sit."

This is nice, but I don't see how it's helping. Inez is pushing to practice, Natalie is giving her mom magical elixirs, and I'm fishing. My heart beats faster to remind me it's in my chest. The more time ticks on, the farther Jas feels. Auntie slithers back into my mind, says, "You're an anxious little one. Listen to the water."

I take a sip of my soda, tug on my line. "Auntie, why do you think I'm having trouble making contact with spirits inside my house? Does Mom have something to do with it?"

She looks at me. "What exactly would she have to do with it?"

"I'm not sure," I say. "But she was burning sage this morning, and—" I cut myself off because Auntie is staring at me strangely. "Or maybe Papa's energy is scaring them away? Some kind of territorial spirit thing?"

"Could be," she says, shrugs. "Or maybe the spirits think you're boring."

I frown. "I'm not."

She stands up to check the tugging on her line. "Spirits are fickle. Same as humans. Just focus on what you're supposed to be doing."

"And what exactly am I supposed to be doing right now? Should I be filtering the sun?"

She takes her sunglasses off to look at it. "You've lost so much of what you were taught as a child." Her words seem to settle in my stomach. She turns toward me. "I brought you here because you should be able to filter it by now, but I think you're blocking yourself."

I try not to look ashamed. "How do I get past it?"

"You can find your deepest magic by meditating, drawing energy from the earth and the sun and the moon. That's what I've been trying to teach you in the yard with the plants. Even the one you potted in the house isn't growing as quick as it's supposed to be." She shifts her gaze to the water, closes her eyes when the wind hits. "Elemental magic is different, Miliani. You don't need spells. There's nothing to create. It's already there for you to shape. It's pure, and can make you stronger than anything else, but you've got to try to find your roots first."

"So that's why we're here? Because I used to fish with Papa?"

"Mmm," she says, and I remember that Papa would tend his garden, reading books to his plants and singing to the pear tree. He used plants and herbs from our own backyard to heal a wandering dog's leg when he was attacked by another dog. Papa didn't use candles or crystals, just chopped things from his garden, mixed them with mud, and the dog was healed within a day. He told me elemental magic can be dangerous, but maybe it's the magic he used.

Auntie takes her pole from where it was anchored and reins back a little. "If you don't learn soon, if you and your friends don't perform some spells, the anchoring won't work. I said it'd take time, but I thought you'd be ready by now."

Her words are like a knife scaling my skin. I've been trying so hard. I've even forced thoughts of Isobel from my mind to make sure I'm focused. The magic Auntie's described sounds counterproductive—slow and steady—a learning process with no time to spare. But if it's what's going to help me with the ritual, then I have to trust it.

I grab my pole, close my eyes, and let myself listen to the sounds of the water.

☾ ☾ ☾

We catch so many fish we have to throw some of them back because there aren't enough buckets. With the sun beating down on my skin, I bend between two rocks to splash water on my face. When I bend a second time, my left foot slips. I fall onto one of the rocks, and the barnacles cut open my bare leg, scrape the skin on my hands. My pact scar burns. Auntie's at my side the second I scream out and roll over on the rock.

"Looks bad," she says, examining me. "Let's take care of it."

She grabs her small bag, with all of its different compartments containing vials and crushed herbs, and sits down beside me. She cleans the cuts on my fingers with some salt water and runs her thumb along them. I flinch from how bad it stings, and she says something in Tagalog I can't understand. She works on my leg next. The gash separating the skin on my ankle is deep and ragged, and the blood won't stop flowing from it.

"Do I need stitches?" I ask, but she just mixes a few vials together in a shallow jar, adds in some wet sand, and places it on my cut. I wince from the burn, confused, watching sand sink into my wound. She speaks in Tagalog again while massaging the mixture until it looks dry, until my leg begins to tingle.

When she's done, she wraps it with gauze. "Let's get you home."

$$\text{(} \mathbb{C} \text{ (}$$

We don't drive to the hospital for stitches. Auntie pulls right in front of my house, parks, and turns off the car. "What are you doing? Mom will see you."

"How is she?" Auntie Lindy taps her fingers against the steering wheel. Her tapping is distracting, but she waves a hand in front of me so my eyes lock with hers. "You're worried about her. Tell me what's going on."

I rub the small cuts on my fingers. "She . . . It's like when she was sick years ago. You remember? The shaking, not eating, blacking out? And I think, maybe she's been seeing the spirits too."

"Hmm." Auntie nods and stares at my house. "You better get going, then."

When she pulls off, I stand on the sidewalk awhile, wondering why she asked about Mom only to leave right away.

Inside, Mom is standing by the window. I almost start explaining why I was with Auntie, but she doesn't even acknowledge me, just stares out in silence. I sit on the staircase and watch until she comes to, turns around without glancing my way, and walks into the kitchen.

She starts cutting vegetables on the chopping block. Both birds whistle from the cage, trying to mimic the sounds of mom's knife hitting the block in a rhythm.

I pray she doesn't cut her fingers instead of the food.

❨ ❨ ❨

In the bathroom, I unwrap the gauze on my ankle to soak the cut in tea tree oil, but there's only a pink mark on my skin, the cut nearly healed and the pain fading too. I probably won't even be able to show my friends what Auntie did because it'll be gone tomorrow.

45

INEZ

Back at school on Monday, I can't make it through class without running to the bathroom when the nausea hits. Both stalls are taken. I
swallow the bile in my throat. A toilet flushes, but it's too late. I throw
up in the sink. The stall door opens, and with my luck, it's Darleny.

She washes her hands and makes a face from the smell. "Are
you pregnant?"

"No," I say. "And if I was, I'm not sure why you'd think to
ask me."

She laughs. "What a polite way to tell me to mind my business,
Inez. Jas always said you were timid."

Her words sting. Darleny knows a side of Jas none of us do. I
wonder how much Jas used to talk about us. My feelings subside
when I realize Darleny might know if the crystal Jas gave me in
my dream is real. But then she pulls some paper towels from the
dispenser. "You might want to clean your shirt up. Before it starts
to stink like your breath."

☾ ☾ ☾

Wearing Miliani's hoodie is better than smelling like throw-up
all day, but she's small and it's snug around my neck. She worries

Darleny will tell someone. I joke about casting a memory-wipe spell, and Mili quietly considers it.

"I was thinking," she finally says, "we should go to the hospital soon. To get an ultrasound."

"Some people don't see a doctor their whole pregnancy, and they're perfectly fine," I say. But if I am going to continue this pregnancy, it would be smart to know how it's going. And if I'm not, then I'll definitely need to see a doctor soon.

Mili shakes her head and opens her mouth, but I interrupt because I want to talk about what happened the other night again. I've heard of sleep paralysis before, but this was something else. "A spirit was trying to enter my body. What if they're successful next time?" It's hard to still my voice. "And does that mean we'll be able to do the anchoring soon?"

"I hope so," she says. "I've barely made any contact lately. And we're running out of time."

This annoys me. Mili should be the one fending off the spirits while I try to sleep. "Well, we should find the necklace Jas was wearing then. She said it would protect me."

Mili's eyes narrow. "Real Jas didn't say anything; it was a dream."

I pretend she's not looking at me like she wants to take my head off, and open a notebook to draw the necklace the best I can. I've never been much of an artist—the crystal looks more like a blob—but Miliani doesn't insult me.

"Do you remember it? I think it was an obsidian."

"Hmm." She looks at my kindergarten-style drawing again. "Jasmine didn't take to obsidian crystals, said she liked to deal with drama as it came. They made her feel like she was in a bubble. And she liked to keep her crystals in a pouch in her pocket."

She's right. Obsidian is mostly used to block out negative energy, but it's also a truth-telling crystal. Jasmine was an honest person, but honest on her terms. She liked her anonymity in certain situations—only choosing to tell people what she wanted them to know, when she wanted them to know it. So she wouldn't wear an obsidian. She wouldn't give up her privacy by choice.

"It felt so real," I say. "I'm thinking she wanted me to have it to keep away whatever was in my room the other night."

"I talked to my auntie about that. She said we should make some salt jars for protection."

"We can do that, but I want the necklace, Mili. It's real. I can feel it. Maybe it's important for the ritual, and she's trying to send us a sign. Will you and Nat check her house soon?" Mili reminds me that last time she was there, Darleny looked like she wanted to beat her ass. I pout and beg some more. "Please. I'd do it, but after the bathroom incident, I should avoid Darleny at all costs before she starts spreading rumors."

Mili finally sighs.

"You're a good friend," I tell her.

"Suddenly."

"You're always a good friend." I bat my eyelashes. "Even when you're overbearing."

"I'm never overbearing," she says. "But if we do this, you need to go to a doctor."

I stare down at my drawing. "If you do this, we can discuss

how we'd go about getting me checked without my mom finding out."

"Fair enough."

☾ ☾ ☾

Most of the school day is spent with me avoiding eyes, trying not to assume every whisper is about me. Darleny and her friends are huddled outside the principal's office before lunch. When I walk by her, she asks, "How you doing, Inez?" in a sarcastic tone. A couple of her friend's cackle, and my stomach drops. They all must know. Soon, everyone will know. Will the principal be calling me into his office with the counselor? Will they want to speak with Mami? My chest starts to hurt, but then I feel a cool hand grab mine and I know it's Natalie's.

"Don't let her get to you. She doesn't know shit." She's right. Darleny doesn't know anything right now, but if I don't get an abortion, how soon will my stomach start to expand? How long will it take for everyone to find out that I'm going to be a teenage mother?

I cling to Natalie a little harder on the way to the cafeteria.

46

MILIANI

Darleny looks at me like I spit in her cachupa when she answers the door.

Nat smiles at her. "How you doing, D?"

Darleny doesn't smile back. "What the hell are you two doing here? I distinctly remember telling Mili to stay away."

In the past when Mom would freak out, I'd watch Papa as he spoke to her, his lips moving slow, telling her to calm down, to relax. I'd ask if he used his magic on her, and he'd tell me no. Now that I've done it myself, I know it's exactly what he was doing. Right now, I could use it to ask about the crystal. If Darleny were anyone else, I might be able to talk her into anything at all, whisper like a vampire, watch her eyes change. But she knows I practice. She wouldn't let me get close.

"We're making a shrine for Jasmine for graduation," Nat says. "We wanted to see if we could get a couple of her things."

Darleny rolls her eyes. "You're with Mili. Just do what she does, and creep in to take whatever you like." With that, she turns and goes upstairs, leaving the door open for us.

☾ ☾ ☾

Their mom isn't home, but the kitchen smells good. I look under the tinfoiled plate on the stove, and there are plenty of pastel for the taking, but Darleny mutters something under her breath and walks off to her room.

"Guess we don't have to worry about her watching us search, thanks to you," Nat says.

€ ☾ €

Jas wouldn't care, but it feels inappropriate to search inside her drawers, touch her panties and bras, when she's not here. I'm happy her mom still hasn't bagged her stuff up, though. My mom was quick to start disposing of Papa's things, but she never finished. Now, his room sits off-limits, like it's not part of the house. It's tangible evidence of letting go and holding on, half of Papa but not him at all. When Jasmine comes back, she'll want her room the way it was. My stomach dips as, suddenly, I wonder how it'll play out with their parents when Jas is half herself and half Darleny. Will she still have a room here? Will her parents find out what happened and call it dark magic, or think Darleny needs help and send her to Butler?

"You gonna help me find the necklace or nah?" Natalie asks, snapping me out of it, making me grateful. I can't think about logistics right now. Or feel guilt.

We don't find the necklace. I'm sure it doesn't exist. But we do find old pictures under a calendar in Jasmine's desk. We sit on her rug and go through them: the freshman ski trip, Sophomore Spring Fling, Spirit Week, Inez and Jasmine sharing a blunt at the back of the school. "I hated when they'd come in fourth period, smelling like weed, and sit real close to me," Natalie says. "Mrs. Banano's nosy self would always walk by and look at me funny."

We keep flipping through pictures, and Nat says, "Oh. Oh, wow. Look. There it is. Jasmine's wearing it." I lean over. It looks exactly how Inez described. The cage, the shape, the colors. Nat hands me the picture. "I'm upset this thing is real. It's so damn creepy."

"It is," I say. "Except that's Darleny wearing it, not Jasmine."

Natalie lets out a breath. "Wow. Why didn't I realize?"

"How could you? They look just alike here."

"But you noticed," she says, lips curving in a smile.

What I don't say: Only because I've felt those lips, touched that skin. I know there's a scar right on Jas's collarbone that's absent in this picture. "I wonder where Darleny keeps it," I say.

Nat's eyebrows scrunch together. "How important is this thing? Did we have to prove it existed? Or do we need it for something? I doubt Darleny's going to willingly give it up."

I give her a pointed look.

"We can't steal it," she warns.

"We can borrow it, though."

She sighs. "Let's get this over with."

(((

I call Darleny into the room to ask her what she feels like we can take for the shrine and what she doesn't want to give up while Natalie slips off to the "bathroom." At first, Darleny doesn't seem to want any part of it, but then she sits on the carpet beside me. To lessen suspicion, Nat and I had collected beads, an old deck of tarot cards, a T-shirt Jasmine liked to wear. Darleny sighs while looking through the pictures. "She was always making that face."

I lean over, nod. "Yeah, and the one with the—"

"Tongue between her teeth," Darleny finishes. We both laugh, and soon, like something has eased between us, we start passing pictures back and forth. She tells me stories about Jasmine. She mimics her manners. When she tilts her head back and chuckles, she sounds just like her. Even the silence becomes comfortable between us. She looks at my face when she passes me a picture and says, "Guess which one of us is which?"

I stare down. In it, they're both around five years old, wearing matching outfits. In it, I can't tell who is who. "Wow, this is tough. I'll have to take a wild guess."

"Do it," she insists, and I look up at her face. It's soft and close, and I wish her eyes were brown instead of green. And suddenly, they are. My heart thrums, my fingers grip the picture, and I want to lean closer so I can—

"You good?" Darleny cuts off my thoughts. I watch as she blinks back to green eyes.

I shake my head. Swallow. Close my own eyes to stop from crying. "You must miss her."

"Of course I do," she says, her voice sharp now. She snatches the picture from my hand, puts it back into the box. "I don't know why I'm bothering speaking to you." She stands up. "You think because we weren't as close when she died, you knew her better than I did."

I throw my hands up. "I never said I did. I wouldn't."

Darleny puts one hand on the dresser, steadying herself. "But it's what you think every time you look at me."

"I wasn't trying to offend you. I don't feel that way. I promise."

She watches me stand. "I don't care what you think. Not after what you did to her."

"Darleny, I'm really sorry. But you don't even know what happened between us that night. I didn't do anything to her." I walk closer. There are only a couple of steps between us now. "I was hurt, and I left. I never thought she'd try to follow me. I wanted to be alone."

Darleny's eyes widen, and tears start to escape. "She was out of her mind. We were driving around for hours, looking for you. You wanted to be alone? Well, how does it feel?"

My voice trembles some when I say, "I was in the woods. I . . ."

That night, I took the bus from Jasmine's to Uni Park to sit in the grass like Papa and I used to, trying to center myself, trying even harder not to freak out, imagining how much might change because I'd told Jas I wanted to be with her and she didn't feel the same.

"It doesn't matter," Darleny says. "None of it matters now."

Her words hit me. *It has to matter.*

Darleny shakes off a sob. I get close to her. Today is the first time I've felt her pain. I've been too focused on my own, but I feel it now: deep, a cut that won't heal with some sand and pretty words. She misses her sister and might always blame me for what happened.

I feel guilty for what I have to do to her, but then realize the ritual is for her too. If we put Jas in Darleny's body, they can be together. A stitch on the wound.

Darleny backs up again and turns for the door. If I can't keep her here, she'll find Natalie.

"Darleny, please wait," I say, and she turns back to me. "Just calm down."

Her face is hard at first, but I say it again, softer, and let the power swell inside me. "Calm down," Darleny repeats, and repeats it again. Soon her eyes are unblinking, her shoulders relax. Guilt makes me feel heavy, but my adrenaline starts to spike with it working.

Then she blinks and steps back so fast she hits the wall.

"What are you doing? What did you do to me? Stay away from me, you freak." She turns around and grabs the door handle and collides right into Natalie. She doesn't say sorry, just disappears down the hall.

Natalie gives me a wide-eyed look and mouths, *Let's go.*

☾ ☾ ☾

Nat doesn't feel comfortable holding the crystal after stealing it so I don't even have to ask for it. Inez was right. It's a black obsidian, with a sharp edge pointing downward in the cage. On the bus, I separate the coils of the cage and take out the crystal. It feels weighty in my palm. I want to concentrate on it, but Darleny's green eyes burn in my mind. For a second, I made them brown. For a second, she was Jasmine. I place the crystal back in its cage, put it around my neck. It settles nicely there. It feels cool against my chest. Darleny will notice it's missing soon, but I can't care right now. If Jasmine wants us to have it, we must need it for something.

47

NATALIE

I'm exhausted from being a thief with Mili, but I see Harriet lugging shopping bags up her porch stairs, leaning against the rail with each step so her bad leg has some support. Her car door is open when I cross into her driveway and take out the remaining bags. She doesn't crack a smile when I place them on the porch beside her. "Thank you, child, but if you have something to say"—her breathing is ragged, the stairs still taking their toll—"I ain't getting any younger."

"I don't know what you're talking about."

She swings her cane, and it smacks the side of her rocking chair. "Bullshit." The thwack alarms me, but then Harriet's face becomes gentle. "You haven't spoken to me since Newport. Is it because of what I said to that sister of yours?"

"Her name is Leanna."

"I know her name. Damn near raised the girl myself."

My breathing comes out in spurts. I can feel the tears coming. "Then why treat her bad?"

"I love that girl."

"You don't get to love her if you hate her for who she loves."

Harriet's face contorts. Her eyebrows come together, then loosen when her mouth slacks. "You think I hate Leanna because she's a lesbian?" She grunts and wobbles to sit in her chair. Her eyes lock me in place, and I can't stop the tears from sliding down my face. I cross my arms. Her chest rises and falls when she chuckles, the sound peppering my eardrums. She taps the seat beside her with her cane as an offering, but I shake my head.

"I'm not some silly old woman, Natalie," she says. "Just because I'm religious doesn't mean I don't know the Bible is man-made. A guide at best." Harriet begins crying, and I'm more confused than ever. "God brought you children into my life for a reason, and it wasn't so I could hate you for who you love."

"Then what is it?" My voice is tight. It doesn't sound like my own. "What the hell is it? What did she do to make you hate her?"

Harriet stands like she doesn't have two bad legs and tired lungs. "You watch your damn tone with me, little girl."

My resolve slips as I stand face-to-face with this woman who has known me my whole life. "Tell me," I say, quieter.

She looks out at the street. "Hate doesn't live here. And it's not my business to tell." This is coming from the same woman who has the scoop on all the shop owners on Broad Street, the cashiers who work at the dollar store. "Ask her yourself, and when the answer shakes you up, come knock on my door and apologize."

☾ ☽ ☾

My friends and I keep thinking of ways we can dig up family drama for a spell, but I didn't realize it's been in my face all along. The first time my sister came home after leaving, I thought it was forever. She was waiting on the couch with new toys and books for me and Dev. Her hair was highlighted, and her nails were manicured. She smelled like perfume, and I asked if she would spray some on me. Leanna said she'd help me get ready for a school dance, while Ma counted the money Leanna gave her. But I never made it to the dance. Ma took off the following day and left me and Dev with just enough money to buy takeout. And months went by until we saw Leanna again.

She's surprised when she sees me standing in her doorway. She's wearing dramatic gold-glittered lids, fake lashes, and cherry-red lipstick, much more makeup than her normal lip gloss and mascara. "Where you going?" I ask her.

"To have drinks with friends," she says. "I told you we'd talk soon. I didn't say today."

"You also told me you weren't doing anything. I'm sorry, but I really need to talk."

Leanna shakes her head and lets me in.

"That's not what you're wearing to go out, right?" I say. For all her makeup, she has oversized gray jogging pants on and a baggy white T-shirt that reads FREE THE NIPS. It must be Ava's because Leanna isn't cool enough to own a shirt like that.

She crosses her arms. "Of course not."

"Well, we could talk while you get ready?"

"We can talk first. Come on." Usually, Leanna makes me take my shoes off, complains about my mismatched socks, and hangs my coat on the wall rack. There is none of that now. She sits on one couch and I sit across from her on the other, and she looks at me expectantly.

"I went to see Ma."

She crosses her legs. "I'm not surprised."

"She looked bad. Real bad."

"Also not a surprise." Leanna looks up at the clock on the wall, so I look too.

But the hands of the clock aren't moving at all.

"Need some new batteries?" I ask, but my skin is already tingling before my sister squints at me, then back up at the clock.

"What are you talking about?"

I check again and the hands are moving now, and Leanna's eyes burn into me while I look around the room, turn and check to see if there's a ghost behind the couch I'm sitting on.

Leanna clears her throat. "Why are you really here, Natalie? I know you didn't come all this way for me to say I told you so."

I force myself to face her, but lean forward so my back isn't touching the couch. "What's the real reason you and Harriet don't talk? It's not because you're gay."

"I never said it was." I raise a brow, and she picks invisible lint off her couch cushion. "I don't know. She's always been that way with me. You know that woman's a little eccentric."

"But she's also one of the most caring people I know. She used to love having you around when we were young."

Leanna shrugs. "Maybe she's mad I left you guys."

This doesn't sting because it feels like a cheap way out of the conversation. And though this could be part of Harriet's reason, the Leanna I know would never willingly take the blame for leaving us, not in the way she did. "That's not it," I say.

"Because you're a psychic?"

"Because you're trying to push me away."

"I'm not." She frowns. "I don't know where this question is coming from and why it's suddenly important. I have no idea what goes on in Harriet's head. Do you?"

It's clear she's not going to tell me the truth, but I already knew that. I came here knowing there was another way to get it. "Okay. Whatever, then."

She watches me for a minute. "Is that all?"

"It is," I say, but then shake my head. It's so hard to form the words, but she needs to hear them. "Actually, I'm sorry for some of the things I said to you yesterday."

"Hmm," she says. "I accept your apology because I deserve it, but I want you to know you and Dev can rely on me. I've been working a ton of hours so I can pay off some bills in both houses. I planned to come by and take you shopping tomorrow, after you had time to cool off."

I try for a smile. "But no apology for me?"

She laughs. "How about money to take a cab back home?"

I tell her it's a start, and lie about having to pee.

"Clean the toilet seat with the Clorox wipes when you're done," she says.

I roll my eyes, shut and lock the bathroom door behind me. As soon as I do, it seems like a set of eyes locks me in here too. Something watches as I search for hair strands in the bathtub, on the tile wall, but even the brushes are cleaned out. I wonder if I'll have to pull hair out of her head to get what I need, but I take my chance stepping on the metal lever of her trash can.

The bag is almost empty, save for a floss stick and a small ball of Leanna's brown hair. I take it from the trash. Mili and Inez will be happy to know I finally figured out what spell we can do, and I'll be happy when it doesn't always feel like I'm being followed.

48

MILIANI

Borrowing Mom's car is usually only an issue when she's busy, but tonight she's worried about the moon. She finishes polishing one of her dress shoes and signals for me to give her the other. "I suppose I'd rather you drive than be out on foot or on the bus tonight. Just be careful."

Tonight is spring solstice. There's a supermoon in the sky to signal the start of spring. Even though Mom doesn't talk much of magic, she follows astrology, sun and moon signs, religiously. A supermoon can cause large shifts in human emotion, can make people feel physically ill or drained, and can heighten senses. It also reminds me Jasmine isn't here to see it.

"And watch out for the siyokoy," she says in a joking tone.

When we'd go swimming, Papa would say the siyokoy were in the water with us. He said the myth in the Philippines is that these scaled sea creatures liked to eat humans after drowning them. Hearing Mom mention it makes me happy. I reassure her I'll be careful, and she smiles. I want to kiss her on the cheek, but I'm not sure how to close the gap. She looks down at the shoe polish and starts to sing. The song from the hallway again. I stand to leave, but her voice fades until she's humming. I've heard the melody before. It's the same as the night Natalie and I played sungka. Suddenly, it sounds like she can vibrate the whole room. The hair raises on my arms. "Mom, what song is that?"

She looks up at me, confusion crinkling the lines on her forehead. "What song?"

"The one you were singing," I say.

Her brows dip. "I wasn't singing."

"You were." I take a few steps toward her. She scooches back in her chair and away from me. I stop moving. Tears gather in my throat, betray me when I say, "I'm not going to touch you. I just want to know if you're okay." I want to know if she's getting sick again. I want to know why she's humming the same song the spirit did. Maybe she still senses it here.

But she turns away from me. "I am. You be safe out there, Miliani."

Convincing Inez's mom that Inez needs a night out like a normal teenager doesn't take as much begging as we'd prepared for. She seems softer these days. Maybe it has something to do with the news about Inez's father. Either way, we rush to leave so she doesn't change her mind. On the ride to Conimicut Point Park, we open Mom's sunroof, and Inez unbuckles her seat belt and shoves her body through it. Natalie shakes her head and says, "You're so damn wild," and we let Inez be something other than pregnant.

I slow the car down a little but not too much because then she'd notice.

She says, "Nat, you next." But Natalie shakes her head.

At the beach, there's nothing but open space, and we pick a spot by the water, a dip in the sand, some rocks and shells under our feet. We lay a blanket down, and Natalie takes so many pictures of the moon Inez jokes the clicking hurts her ears. But it's nice to see Natalie using her camera. I try to think of how good it feels to be here with my friends and how the spell we'll do tonight can help ensure we don't have to see another supermoon without Jasmine, so I don't think of my mom and the song. I open my bag and take out mason jars.

"Wait." Inez plops down on the blanket. "Not yet."

We follow her, lying faceup with the tops of our heads pressed against one another, legs off the blanket and in the sand.

"Whoa, this is so fucking beautiful," Inez says.

The Worm Moon is probably the brightest supermoon. It got its name because it aligns with the spring equinox, a time when earthworms come out of the ground. Lying here with it looming above us—this glowing thing lighting up the beach—makes me think of Auntie telling me I have to find my roots. I reach my arm out, dig my fingernails in the sand, and breathe.

My body feels like it might levitate off the blanket, maybe bring my friends with me.

"Remember when magic was fun?" Natalie says. She sounds wistful, and I do remember. We'd sneak out here to create love potions with the seawater, drink the beer I stole from Mom's stash in the basement, dance with bare feet on the sand. Jasmine would give each of us braid crowns, and collect seashells and small stones for necklaces she'd string together later.

Inez laughs. "It could still be fun if Miliani didn't forget to bring the beer."

I don't mention she shouldn't drink because she's pregnant. I take Darleny's necklace off my neck and let it dangle between us. "There's something I didn't forget to bring."

She gasps and reaches for it, pulls back. "Should I be prepared for something intense?"

"Maybe."

When she takes it, she rolls the cage in her palm, then puts it around her neck. A few seconds later, she sulks. "Nothing. I feel nothing."

"You sure?" I ask. "Give it a second."

She does. Then she takes a breath so loud it makes Natalie flinch. "It's warm," Inez says. "It's almost hot against my skin."

"Really?" I turn on my side to touch it, but it feels cool to me.

"Yes. It's incredible." She balls the crystal in her fist. "Thank you for finding it."

"Stealing it," Natalie chimes in. "Mili says 'borrow,' but we committed a crime for you."

Inez grasps it and smiles. "I'm very loved."

❨ ❨ ❨

Before the spell, we get to work making protection jars. I fill four mason jars with water from the ocean, add sea salt, pink Himalayan salt, and raw rice. I give two to Natalie and two to Inez. Natalie adds juniper berries to her salt jars—lots of juniper berries—then peppermint oil, peppercorn herbs, and cloves. Inez does the same with her jars. They add in leaves from the bushes, then grass, and leave the lids off the jars so they can bake under the Worm Moon awhile. Inez mentions feeling lighter here. Like the spirits couldn't make it out onto the beach. I don't make a jar for myself, and Nat cracks jokes about me wanting spirit friends.

Inez laughs. "You can do as you please, but I'd rather not wake up with a ghost sitting on my chest again."

I ignore her comment and hold a jar to my own chest, chanting what Papa taught me. Mom used to leave these jars all around the house, but she'd chant to herself so low I could never make out the words. Papa said she was placing a trapping spell. If a spirit got close enough to the jar, it would get caught there, becoming mesmerized until it got sucked in. But trapping spells act more as a deterrent than anything else. A spirit can easily break free once the spell wears off.

"Place them in the corners of your bedroom," I say. "They should help protect you."

"Here's to hoping," Nat says before she pulls a Ziploc bag from her back pocket, opens it, and holds out a ball of hair. She hopes it's enough for the truth spell. I tell her it's plenty.

49

NATALIE

Dev and I used to watch this late-night show where a gang of witches would bleed people out as sacrifices to the gods. And to get the truth out of a person, all a witch had to do was twist a finger, and words would spill out of the person's mouth. Last year, when Miliani mentioned trying truth spells, a twist of a finger and blood extraction is what popped into my mind.

But she said, "That's silly, Nat. We only need a spell."

Then we tried three different spells, but nothing ever happened—until a few months ago, when Mili decided we'd need more than a picture of a person, an image in our minds; we'd need something from their body. So we tried again. This time, Jas brought a baggie filled with her father's shavings she collected from the bathroom sink because she wanted to know where he was sneaking off to at night. Two days later, she heard her parents arguing, found out he wasn't sneaking off for a woman like she'd suspected, but to gamble with his friends. Jas was relieved he wasn't cheating, but her mom was upset he was wasting their money. Her parents separated for a month, and Jas said she'd never do another truth spell.

That wasn't the worst of it, though. The next day, Inez told her mom she didn't want to read the Bible, and caught a slap across the face. Mili faked sick and barricaded herself in her room after almost slipping to Jayson about her sexuality. And I told Jas I needed space from her toxic stories and seeing her with hangovers. She said she wondered how far I'd make it in life before realizing I wasn't living at all.

Mili told us the truth spell must be bleeding, spilling over, though she hadn't known that could happen. I didn't really believe in magic, thought these things were already built up, ready to bust out, blended and exacerbated by knowing we did a spell, but when it wore off a few days later, everyone got real quiet, like we were practicing our right to keep a closed mouth.

Jas and I apologized to each other, but the distance was already in the making. I couldn't ignore the seesaw feeling of missing her while also being upset that she couldn't understand why I was so bothered with what she was doing. It's hard not to still feel that seesaw.

Mili warns us again now about what happened before, then follows that with, "But we've done harder things. We just have to do it perfectly. No self-centered thoughts."

I worry about Inez, remembering how she had to beg her mom and God for forgiveness, blame it on her anxiety, the last time. If something goes wrong with keeping Inez's pregnancy a secret, I won't forgive myself. And just as I think it, Inez says, "My mom can't find out about me."

"I agree," I say. "I think you should sit this one out."

Miliani shakes her head. "If we aren't all in on this, we risk not being strong enough to carry it out, and we need this spell. Jas needs us. We're not working fast enough. I can feel it."

Inez says, "Yeah. Let's just be really careful, please." But I can tell she's nervous because she's chewing on the skin around her fingers.

Mili leans forward and lights the candle closest to her.

I clear the clutter in my mind as soon as Inez positions the mirror so it's directly in the middle of the triangle we create with our bodies. Mili seems particular about the white and blue candles, which go in the center of the mirror but get rearranged a few times. This spell isn't one you wing. Miliani had told me exactly what to say: "Leanna Nunez, speak your truth. Reveal to me your truth." I pinch the ball of Leanna's hair between my thumb and pointer, and hold it over one candle until it sizzles and burns. Mili says Leanna's name, then Inez does the same. I close my eyes and think of my sister's face—picture it like a photo—then blow out the candles.

Inez coughs, and my eyes widen. Miliani leans over and rubs her back. I stand to kneel in front of Inez, but she pushes me away. "I'm fine. Damn. I had a tickle in my throat."

"You weren't thinking of it during the spell, were you?"

"I wasn't thinking of a damn thing. You can be sure of that," she says. "Now can we wrap this up and get some pizza before I'm back to the prison cell?"

Miliani tosses sand at her, and Inez tosses it back. Soon, we're pouring sand down one another's shirts, rolling in it. It's stuck in my hair, in my eyes. We wash our hands in the salt water. It's so cold I shiver. I remember nights with Ma here. Me and Dev would bury her neck-deep. She'd say the sand crabs were going to feast on her. After, she'd strip down to her bra and panties and jump in the water to wash off, insisting me and Dev get in with her. But even Devin would stay out of the water, too dark and too cold for his liking. Now, I worry about the bacteria count, pneumonia, and sharks, but I remember Ray handing me the keys to his car. And before I know it, I'm stripping down. I hear Miliani gasp, Inez call my name when I start to run.

It hurts. It pricks, it stings, it burns, but I'm here. In the ocean. In the dark. Under this bright moon, feeling like myself and like someone new all at once. I don't even have to ask. Miliani and Inez are screaming and laughing and running toward me. Their splashing feels freezing on my face, but they're here with me and it's more than I can ask. We wash one another off, dunk in the water to get the sand out of our hair, swim a little, but not too far in case there really are sharks. And then we float. We're probably on the verge of hypothermia as we hold hands while trembling, while our teeth chatter, and we stare up at the moon.

"This is better than pizza," Inez says.

My eyes water some. "So much better."

"We can still get pizza too," Miliani says. "Let's get out and dry off before we get sick, or the sea creatures come to eat us."

"Just one more minute," I say, looking to my left and imagining Jasmine there. Her hair floating around her, holding my hand and kicking her feet slowly as she floats too.

☾ ☾ ☾

Back home, I shower quick, throw on some deodorant, and I'm out the door. It only takes me one bus to get where I'm going, but buses stop running soon and the whole ride I'm thinking I'm wild. What if it doesn't work out and I have to walk back? My stomach is in knots when I get off the bus and run the rest of the way. Ray looks shocked when he opens his door.

"Why you breathing so heavy, Williams?"

I kiss him. He stumbles back. We both almost fall through his open door, but he catches us, balances by holding the rail, and slides his other arm around my waist. Now, we're both breathing heavy. He presses his forehead to mine, says, "Whoa. That was so good I'm dizzy. Um, have you been drinking?"

I laugh. "I'm under no influence."

"This is just you? Wanting to kiss me?"

I can feel the burn creep up my neck. "Just me. Wanting you."

He inhales, closes his eyes. "Do you want to come inside?"

"I do."

He pulls me by the hand. "Should I ask why your hair is soaking wet?"

"Yes, you should. It's a good story," I say.

50

MILIANI

Auntie gives me her books to borrow, says the truth spell might not be the big show of magic we need. I read up on manifestation, learn more about the way personal desire can change the outcome of spells, but it hits me while soaking in the information about elemental magic. I rush down the stairs in nothing but flip-flops and a big T-shirt to open the shed and pull out the lawn mower. Auntie keeps talking about finding roots, and I can't believe it's taken me this long to realize my love of magic started in this yard.

Right here with Papa.

I'm ashamed to see how neglected it is. Even though I come back here every day after school to pay respect at his pear tree, Ma and I let it get so bad. Jasmine used to offer to help me clean it up, but we'd sit on the porch and waste hours looking out into the yard instead. Sometimes, she'd walk through the high grass and try to find rocks and four-leaf clovers and twigs. Sophmore year, we'd climb trees at the way back and kiss under the leaves.

"You're lucky," she said once. "If I was the type to own a house, I'd want a yard like this."

"You could own one," I said. "Eventually."

"No." She laughed. "Houses are for people who like to stay in one place."

(((

The daylight is still with me when I put on some gloves to pull weeds. Some of them are too deep for my pulling, but at least the garden plot looks like one now. I work on cleaning stems off the overgrown grapevines, which died between the holes in the fence before we could taste grapes this year. When I'm finished, I sit against Papa's pear tree, where he used to sit, under a low-hanging branch. Even with the yard wild, I've spent summers since Papa's passing laid up under this tree, picking off bad leaves, gathering up fallen pears. I'd tell Papa stories and read to him. But sometime in the last year, I'd stopped because there was always something to do, somewhere else to be, someone to be loving.

And wouldn't Papa want that for me?

But the sun sets, and the guilt does too. If he's happy I'm here, he's not letting me know it. I stand and grab construction tape from inside the toolshed and use it to wrap one of the weak branches. Winter isn't all gone from the wood yet, but soon, this tree will be growing fruit for us. I put my hand against it, promise this summer I'll make sure it doesn't go to waste.

Mom comes from work and notices me fiddling with the branches. "Who cleaned up?"

"I did it myself."

"Hmm," she says, nodding her head. "What's my father think?"

"He hasn't said." I shrug. "Think he might feel abandoned."

Her bottom lip juts out. "Come help me start on dinner."

(((

The next morning, I notice a bowl with the remnants of last night's dinner under Papa's tree. There's a cup of water beside it and some fresh fruit spread over the trunk. Mom's feeding her father, and I swear his tree looks like it's about to give way to green already.

Maybe I'm not the only one who has roots right here.

I'm excited about it at school. I stay that way even after reminding Inez we have to make her an appointment at the clinic, and she rolls her eyes and asks Nat to go with her to the bathroom before we eat. My energy is at a peak from the truth spell, from taking care of Papa's yard, but I still don't feel like standing in this lunch line, especially alone.

When I get to the front, Darleny cuts a lot of people to slide in back of me. She grabs regular milk, even though there's strawberry milk for the picking, and says, "I know you took it."

I turn enough so she can see the dismay on my face. "Excuse me?"

"My necklace. I know you stole it from me."

"What are you talking about? I've never even seen you wear a necklace."

She frowns, bottom lip drooping. I stare at it. She leans in, her mouth close to my ear now. Her voice takes on a deeper tone and reminds me of her sister's. I shudder when she whispers, "Give it back, or I'm telling Jayson why you broke up with him."

I'm disoriented, trying to remember what her normal voice sounds like, and by the time her ultimatum hits, she's already out of the line and she's left her lunch behind.

I look over at Jayson from across the lunchroom. He notices me quickly but doesn't give me a smile right away. He makes me wait for it. I let my shoulders rest once it comes with a wink. If Darleny tells him, he might not ever look at me the same again.

51

INEZ

We pull up to Planned Parenthood, and Lindy tells us to keep our eyes forward. I'm scared to be here, but Mili wouldn't take no for an answer. Trying to get into the building reminds me of one of the video games Victor plays, where a riot slowly builds into chaos. Mili glares at the people holding signs with Dr. Seuss quotes like "A person's a person, no matter how small," and more creative slogans like "Give women love instead of abortions," and some people have posters with graphic pictures of dead, bloody fetuses. Lindy tells someone to "back the hell off" when they try to hand her a flyer. Natalie holds my hand.

Inside is a different level of the game. The first thing I notice is how quiet it is, how beige. The women behind the desk are fully covered in glass, but I tell myself it's not a hospital, I tell myself to breathe. We sit down while Lindy brings back paperwork from the counter. "You don't need medical, and I'll sign for you, so leave that part blank."

I realize I've never filled out one of these forms before. Mami always does it for me. It seems simple enough, but my hand shakes until Miliani takes the clipboard from me and fills it out herself. She marks everything, including my anxiety and minus my social security, which Lindy says isn't required right now. Miliani even knows the possible date of conception.

While we wait, Natalie reads a few brochures about birth control, and Miliani examines the basket labeled FREE CONDOMS. Lindy keeps her eyes closed most of the time. A nurse calls my name, and Natalie and Miliani both stand to follow. I look at Lindy, but she says, "Go ahead, kid. This is your thing." The nurse explains that only one person can go back with me anyway, and Mili bites her lip before sitting back down.

The nurse does all the stuff they do at my doctor's office, but when she weighs me she has no reference to say *You've gained another three pounds, Inez*, or, *You're still growing in the ninetieth percentile for your age*. She gives me a cup to pee in, then leads us to a room with a bed that has stirrups. I've seen women get Pap smears in movies, but these look scarier in person.

"It'll be okay," Nat reassures me, but looks horrified herself.

The doctor is nice. She's a tall lady with thick eyebrows and stick-straight hair. She introduces herself, but I don't retain it. "The in-office pregnancy test came back positive," she says, and I feel like saying, *Duh*, but I don't. "I'm going to give you a physical exam to see how everything is looking down there. Do you want your friend to step out of the room?"

"She can stay if she doesn't mind seeing my goods."

Natalie laughs. "Nothing new there."

The doctor smiles, helps me lift my feet onto the stirrups, and tells me to slide down. I wonder if the hair on my inner thighs is long. She tells me to relax my legs and walks me through it: the stickiness of the lube, the cold of the speculum, the pressure. It hurts more than I thought it would when she inserts it and opens me up.

I breathe deep, and Natalie grabs my hand and squeezes. The doctor asks if I want STD swabs done today, and I don't want to say no but I hate saying yes. She uses a giant Q-tip to swab my insides and then takes the speculum out to trade with her two fingers for a pelvic exam. I sit up when it's over, and Nat helps adjust the blanket over me like she knows I somehow feel more exposed now.

"Everything looks okay. Based on your last period, you're around six weeks. We can do an ultrasound today." She writes in her chart. "Are you planning to proceed with the pregnancy?"

Her tone gives off business-venture vibes, which makes me feel comfortable to say, "I'm not sure." But I think of Aaron, glance at Nat, and ask, "How long do I have to decide?"

"I'd say you have a couple of weeks to think it over. That way, we have time to schedule it if you decide on an abortion. Does that sound all right?" I tell her it does, even though two weeks sounds like too little time to make a decision that will change my life no matter what. The doctor finishes jotting notes, then looks up at me. "The ultrasound tech will keep the machine turned, in case you don't want to see, but do let her know if you would."

There should be a warning before these appointments: You're going to have a lot of stuff stuck up your vag. The ultrasound probe pain isn't as sharp as the speculum's, but the technician has to shift the probe in different directions, in crazy-ass angles, in order to see my ovaries. She keeps the screen turned, as promised, but Natalie cranes her neck to see. They both look concentrated. Natalie has the occasional frown, and I'm not sure if it's because something is wrong or because she's perplexed. It's probably the latter, but I begin counting the ceiling tiles and grasping the obsidian crystal in my palm until I can't help but ask to see too.

The tech turns the screen to me, points to a blob, and shows me where the head is. When she turns up the sound on the machine, my thrumming pulse is drowned out by the beating of the fetus's heart. She prints a few pictures and asks if I'd like one. I think about it but tell her no. Where would I hide the pictures from Mami even if I did want them?

The tech smiles politely and tucks the pictures in my chart.

☾ ☾ ☾

I can tell Mili has questions she's trying not to throw at me. I eye Lindy as she whips out her wallet up at the counter and ask Mili, "How much do you think this visit costs?"

"My auntie says they use a sliding scale sometimes."

"How am I going to pay her back?"

She furrows her brows. "I don't think she's worried about that right now."

"Hey." Natalie rubs my leg. "You wanna talk about what happened?"

I tug on my shirtsleeve. "It looks . . . It looks like something already, doesn't it?"

"It does." Natalie's smile is small but still a smile. "A little like an alien, though."

"Wish I was there," Mili says, leaning back in her chair. I feel bad because I know it must be different now that Jasmine's not here to balance our group out. But Mili turns toward Nat and says, "Tell me everything."

Natalie slaps the brochure she's holding against her thigh. "The tech clocked the heartbeat at one hundred forty bpm. Didn't it sound so damn fast, Inez?"

I can't match her enthusiasm, so I nod and let them talk about it—while I imagine we're back on the beach, playing in the water, floating and feeling free.

((((

On the way out, I grip the obsidian, bracing myself for the protestors, but they seem strangely less aggressive than earlier. As if they're weakened and decaying zombies in this level of the game. When we get in the car, someone stumbles over their feet with a flyer they were trying to shove under Lindy's windshield wiper. I watch people sway from the safety of the car, wondering if it's the heat making them seem tired or if it's something else. But as we pull out of the parking lot, Natalie says, "I swear I see shadows weaving through the crowd," and even though Mili agrees and Lindy looks back, I don't see anything.

On the road, I ask Lindy how much I'd have to come up with if I wanted to terminate. Miliani stares at me from the front seat, and Natalie scooches closer to me. Lindy pulls in front of Natalie's house. "They said it'll be five hundred dollars."

Natalie sucks in air. "Jesus, that's a whole lotta money."

"Yeah," I say. My stomach turns. "Yeah. Thank you for asking, Lindy. For everything."

The car is quiet until Nat picks her bags off the floor and kisses my cheek. "Love you."

((((

When we're on my street and I'm out of the car, Lindy rolls down her window. "Inez, I did this one thing, but if you decide motherhood isn't for you, you'll have to find someone else to sign off on it." I open my mouth, and she shakes her head. "It's not because I think you shouldn't have an abortion. Every person has a right to do whatever they feel is best for themselves. But it doesn't feel like my place. You're not my kid."

What do I even say to that? She's right. "I appreciate today."

Miliani mouths, "Call me," before Lindy drives away.

☾ ☾ ☾

Mami's sitting by the stove on a stool with the house phone against her ear and using her shirt to wipe her tears. She gives a deep, dramatic sigh and passes the phone to me. Papi's voice sounds strained too. Mami hasn't wanted to speak to him since the lawyer told her to prepare for a longer wait to apply for the visa. Papi asks me how I'm doing, but I can tell he wants to talk to her. When he tells me he misses me, tears spring to my eyes. I wonder if I'd feel differently about this pregnancy if Papi was here. I think he'd be easier on me than Mami and support whatever decision I make.

When we hang up, I wish Mami would've told him goodbye.

"Are you ever going to forgive Papi?"

Her shoulders stiffen. "There's nothing to forgive. It's not his fault. I'm not mad at him."

"So why don't you want to talk to him?"

"I do. More than anything. But I can't," Mami says, and she starts sobbing freely. "Mija, eat your dinner and do the dishes, please."

While watching her leave, I realize I was wrong for thinking she was punishing Papi. Maybe the reason Mami can't talk to him is because she's sad thinking of having to live without him, and she doesn't know how to say it. Talking to Papi forces her to face her loneliness, her disappointment, and sometimes that's scarier than acting like it's not happening at all.

She's living in an indefinite limbo, and I know that's hard.

Maybe Mami and I are more alike than I thought.

My plate of food goes in the garbage and gets covered with napkins so Mami won't notice. I don't want food right now; my stomach won't handle it well. While doing the dishes, I see a blob on a screen with a heart beating twice as fast as my own.

☾ ☾ ☾

When Mami is snoring at night, I walk by Victor's room and watch him plug in the PlayStation. He untangles and clicks things in place so quick he could probably do it blindfolded. He sits as close to the TV as possible and says, "Will you shut my door, please?"

I walk in, close the door behind me and sit on the floor beside him. "Can I play too?"

Victor doesn't groan like a typical younger brother might. He does look at me like I'm joking before passing me a controller, though. I forget which buttons are which as soon as we start playing, but Victor doesn't mind showing me again. Once I get the hang of it, I'm jumping over barrels and running fast and scoring points. Victor seems happy I'm here.

We play for two hours straight, but I have to pee. It makes me think of how little time I'll have for these types of things if I have a baby. Will I have any time for my brother? Will he love me like he does right now? Will the responsibility of petitioning for Papi in the future fall on him? I ruffle his hair and tell him I'm going to bed. He says good night, but when my hand is on his door, I turn around.

"Why did you tell Mami?"

Victor pauses the game. His shoulders slump. "I don't know."

I walk back over to him, tears in my throat that I wish would go away. "Why wouldn't you come to me first and say it was bothering you?"

Victor looks up at me. "You're always so busy with your friends and the weird stuff you do. You don't talk to me anymore."

The weird stuff. Does he know about the magic? "Oh, Victor. I'm not too busy for you."

"You are. And I see the way you look at Mami when it's time to say our prayers. I thought maybe you stopped believing in God."

"Of course not, Victor. Of course I still believe in God. I'm . . . I don't know. I'm getting older." I can't tell him it seems that magic and the version of God I was taught clash so much it's hard for me to fully believe in the Bible. But that doesn't mean I don't believe in God. "I know it doesn't make much sense to you right now," I say. "It doesn't make a lot of sense to me, either, but I promise I still believe in God, and I promise I'm here for you."

He flips the controller over in his hand. "I'm sorry, Inez."

"I'm sorry too," I say, because I am, even though I never meant to hurt him. I sit back down and take the controller from his hand. "One more game?"

He smiles and presses START and we play until my bladder feels like it's about to burst. But it's worth it to see the way he looks at me before I leave for the night.

52

NATALIE

Leanna's phone rings like someone's trying to collect debt: clock-work, no voicemails, repeat. Inez has avoided talking about Planned Parenthood every time I call her, and Leanna's avoiding something too. She rejects another call but stares down at her phone like maybe she should've answered. I wonder if the truth spell is about to take effect, but she says, "Let's go inside before we get bad seats."

Dev's team is facing Mount Pleasant High School, and the game is being held there. It's about three times bigger than our school, with a full-sized court and wooden bleachers. Leanna takes the seats closest to the court, like she usually does. Being here with her reminds me of how many games she comes to, which is most of them, and it makes me regret saying she's hardly around, when what I should've said is she's hardly around for *me*.

Dev plays it cool when he sees us, gives us a half-interested wave, but I know he's excited we're both here. He stops before taking his seat on the bench to talk to the girl who's always at his locker. She's wearing a leather skirt, which barely covers her butt cheeks, and a white shirt. "I swear that girl got no bra on," Leanna says. "Devin needs to stop playing before I walk over there and embarrass him."

❨ ❨ ❨

After Dev's team wins the game, they all go out to celebrate. Leanna is supposed to take me home, but her phone won't stop ringing. She takes a sharp left, pulls into a dark parking lot on Chalkstone Avenue behind a brick building. A flashing sign at the top of it reads FOXY LADY. "What are we doing here?"

It takes her a good minute, but she says, "This is where I work. Natalie, I'm a stripper."

I laugh. It's involuntary. Leanna's face turns red. Her mouth does the same twitchy thing Jasmine's did when we argued after the truth spell. I brace myself, but I'm not steady enough when Leanna says, "Come see for yourself."

❨ ❨ ❨

My head spins. A rush of sickness comes over me. I follow her slowly, like she's leading me into some kind of trap. She's talking to a bouncer at the entrance when I get there. He looks me over once before he lets us inside. Strobe lights streak the darkened room with color, and the music seems to move with them. I try not to get distracted, and rush to keep up with Leanna. The men pay me no mind, too busy throwing money and hollering, getting lap dances and shoving their faces in between uncovered breasts. Leanna leads us to a back room, full of outfits and women in front of mirrors, doing their makeup and fixing one another's wigs.

"You wanted to know why I'm not around. Well, I'm here fifty hours a week to make sure we're all good. You wanted to know why Harriet hates me, and now you do."

A redhead getting ready spots us in the mirror and gasps so

loud it puts my response on pause. "Lexy," she says to my sister, in a thick southern accent I'm sure is fake. "I thought I'd have to send Bubba out looking for you."

Lexy?

Leanna sucks her teeth. "Bridge, I told you I couldn't work tonight." She has the same edge in her voice that I always hear.

"You dying or something?" The redhead twirls in her seat, and I'm taken aback by her lashes. They're so long it seems to take an extra second for her to lift her lids after she blinks. Under these bright lights, her makeup looks meticulous, and she stands in the tallest heels I've ever seen. They're clear at the bottoms with shiny silver straps, and she has no problem walking over to us in them. "I really needed my lucky pin," she says, "and figured if you came by you'd join me on the stage tonight. You know they like it when we go on together."

"Not tonight, Bridge."

"C'mon, Peaches can get you ready in a snap."

I wonder which one is Peaches while Leanna opens her purse and hands over a small golden arrow, which the woman pins to her panties. "Not that it's any of your business," Leanna says, "but I had a family thing. Still do. Please don't leave your stuff in my car."

"It dropped," Bridge says, smiling. "You're more sensitive than usual." She gapes at me like she's just noticing I'm here. "Oh, is this . . . ?" She gasps again but this time with a squeal at the end. "Is this your little sister?"

Leanna doesn't glance my way but tells me to go wait in a chair in the far right corner of the room so she can speak to Bridge privately. The women getting ready smile at me when they see me staring.

One pulls a stack of money from her panties and starts counting it right in front of me. A bald guy with a pointy chin pokes his head through the door and says, "Roses, Tina's getting tired out there. You ready yet or what?"

"Be out in a bit," the one called Roses says, slabbing a thick layer of oil on her brown legs while another woman rubs it in.

They're all beautiful. My cheeks are burning by the time I force my eyes in front of me and focus on myself in a vanity mirror. My round mouth and uncolored lips, my breasts so small I still wear a sports bra, the length of my lashes. "So long," Leanna used to say, "you'll probably never need falsies."

I look back at her, but she's busy helping Bridge adjust her outfit. I open the top drawer of the vanity, and the inside is immaculate. Lipsticks are organized by color. Dozens of eyelash kits sit stacked against one another so neat it hurts to look at. Lace panties are folded up in triangles and placed inside a small white basket. This is definitely Leanna's drawer.

Leanna is Lexy, and Lexy is a stripper.

☾ ☾ ☾

On the ride home, Leanna's quietly gripping the steering wheel, while my brain tries to dissect clues to what she's been doing all along. There's not enough time to rewire the memories on the drive home, but I try anyway.

When I was younger, Leanna took me and Dev in for a while when she realized we had been home alone for two days with no food. I remember creeping through her closet. She had the shiniest dresses and leather pants I had ever seen. Tons and tons of high heels and wigs and makeup. While she was using the bathroom, I put one of her wigs on and danced in the mirror. She came in the room and she didn't yell; she put a wig on her head too. She did my makeup, let me wear her heels, showed me how to walk in them. "Just this once," she said.

Now, Leanna stares straight ahead. She'll take me grocery shopping tomorrow, but tonight she doesn't want to look at me. I can't tell if she's crying, but I think she is. I wonder if she's ashamed, or if she's crying because the spell forced her truth out. I leave the car, wanting to feel sorry, but how long would she have kept this from me if I hadn't? And why did she keep it in the first place?

My house is dark, but I'm too tired to be scared of spirits or wonder why Mili's trapping-spell jars haven't trapped them. I crawl into bed with day-old breath and an unwashed face, and my brain tries to rewire again, each memory of Leanna becoming layered and more complex than it was before. Each one making more sense. But the memory I see before I drift off is Leanna crying after confessing her secret because of what I did.

53

INEZ

We head to Roger Williams after school to do another spell because Lindy says we have to keep working. Nat is still in shock about Leanna, and I'm happy the truth spell didn't spill onto me. I lie on the grass. If I blink too many times, I'll fall asleep. Mili heads to collect water while Nat plops down beside me. I turn the obsidian crystal, watch the way the light shines on it at different angles. It's felt warm all day, and I pretend Jasmine's telling me she's with me.

I turn to look at Natalie. "You seem different. I know you're worried about your sister, but you seem happier too. Did something happen with Ray?"

She tries to hide her smile. "I sorta slept over his house after the beach."

"What?" I smack her on the arm. "You hoe! Why didn't you tell me?"

"Because I knew you'd make it a big deal, and I don't even know what to think of it yet."

"Blah, blah. You had sex, didn't you? Did you use a condom?"

She picks at the grass. "Both times, yes."

"Keep doing that so you don't get knocked up like me," I say, and she rolls her eyes. Then, "Do you think it'll hurt? If I decide on the abortion, you think it'll hurt?"

She lies on her side and faces me. She doesn't ask if I mean physically or mentally. She says, "Maybe. But if I'm thinking long-term hurt, I feel like not getting one will be worse." She shrugs. "I'll support you for whatever, but having to help raise Dev wasn't easy. And I didn't really have a choice."

I exhale. "But what about the money? Who will sign for me?"

Nat sucks on her top lip, releases it, and says, "We'll figure out the signing. And I'll work extra hours at the bodega for the money. See if Mr. Ortega will give me an advance too."

"I love you," I say. My eyes water, and I tilt my head to look up at the sky, not sure if I'm talking to her or God or myself. "What if God won't forgive me for an abortion?"

Natalie considers this for a few seconds, then says, "I can't tell you how to feel about God. But I think, most importantly, you'll forgive yourself."

I turn back to her. "And if I decide to keep it?"

"You'll be a mother."

"What if I'm not a good one?"

"I'd never allow that."

"What if Aaron isn't a good father? Will you be my baby daddy?"

"You watch too much Maury Povich. But, yes, you'll have me. And Miliani too."

I snort. "Miliani would be mom, dad, uncle, pastor, teacher, and hairstylist if I let her."

"If you let her, Mili would birth the baby in your bathroom."

We laugh so hard my stomach hurts—a small twinge, almost

a pulling feeling. The smell of grass is strong today. It's sweet, and something about it makes me nauseous. But it also feels nice against my skin. "If I keep it, I might be homeless and have to camp out here."

"You could always move in with me," Natalie says. "Devin makes good scrambled eggs, and we started a chore chart, thanks to my sister's constant bitching."

Before I can respond, Mili walks over with a jar of swamp-looking water. "You two should've been setting up."

Nat looks at me, says, "And we could add disciplinary figure of the family to said list."

Miliani ignores our giggling. She sits with that serious face of hers and tells me, "If you really want the abortion, I'll sell some of my comics so I can help come up with the money."

Nat smiles. I sit up and reach to squeeze Mili's hand. Even if we could come up with the money, get someone to sign, how would it feel to look at Mami, to go to church every week, knowing what I've done? I hear the fetus's heartbeat in my head again and think of how much I love Aaron. He wants this.

"I love you, both," I tell them. "I really wish Jasmine was here right now, but it almost feels like she is. And I know she'd be supportive of my choices too." I'm crying when I say, "But I think maybe I need to keep this pregnancy."

They lean their foreheads against mine. "Okay. We're here," Mili says.

"Always," says Nat. "No matter what."

I sob something awful, wipe my nose on the inside of my shirt, straighten myself the best I can. "If we do this spell to keep my baby daddy out of trouble, how long will it last?"

Mili says, "I think it'll last as long as he likes the way he changes from it."

But that's what I'm worried about. If I don't trust Aaron's word enough and have to use a spell to make sure he stops selling drugs, how will I ever know if he really wants to? How many times will I have to use magic on him while we raise a kid together?

Before we start, I pull his shirt from my bag. I haven't washed it, so it still smells like him. Mili rolls it up and puts it into the frothy water. We dip our hands in wrist-deep and make a wish that he'll keep his word and change the course of his life.

When we're done and his shirt is smelling like sewage, I pray we did the right thing.

☾ ☾ ☾

The next day, Aaron comes over to cuddle me while my house is empty. I told myself I wouldn't sneak him in anymore, but it's been too long since we've spent time together and I need his hugs right now. He apologizes for being busy but says he's been getting money "the legal way." He slow-kisses my lips and dips down to kiss my belly too. I squirm, pull him back up so quick he widens his eyes, but then he smiles sheepishly and rolls over to pull me to his side.

Everything after the belly kiss is fine—until I feel something cold against my back. I turn and see a new gold chain on Aaron's neck. A big, fat chain with diamonds on it. In this neighborhood, you can get snatched up for showing off. I sit up and scold him for wearing it.

He tries to turn away from me.

"Don't ignore me," I say. "Te pasaste. Out here on foot asking for trouble."

"Chill," he says, smoothing my sheet with his hand. "I'm 'bout to get a nice little whip too. For me, you, and the baby."

My stomach flips at being forced to picture us with a baby. "With what money, Aaron? Where'd you get the money for this chain? Dique. Some legal money job."

"Don't worry about that, babe," Aaron says. "Just know I'm going to take care of us."

I knew the spell couldn't have worked that fast. "You lied to me. You said no dealing."

Aaron pulls me back to his chest, careful to leave space for my belly, and puts his fingers in my hair. "I said I'd stop soon. I need one more week. My promise still stands."

"Your promises don't mean shit if you get locked up or end up dead off a diamond chain. And you won't be the only one who suffers, Aaron. If I'm dragged into it . . ."

"Inez"—he sits up on the bed and puts both hands in the air—"aren't you the one who's always talking about manifesting energy or whatever? Now you're speaking bad on me." He rubs his face, then sighs and reaches to rub my belly. "I'm not going to drag you into anything, okay?" When I nod, he gets out of bed for his backpack. He pulls out a tiny button-up shirt with a cute bow tie and the smallest vest I've ever seen. "Look. Aaron Junior is gonna stay fly."

He's a fool, but it makes me feel warm for a second. "What if it's a girl?"

"She can wear it too." He holds the shirt to his chest, and the thoughts trickle in: *What if I ask Aaron to come up with the money for the abortion? Would I be okay with him selling drugs if it meant he could help with the bill? Am I a hypocrite? Selfish? Probably both. But how much will our relationship change if we have a child? Will he look at me the way he does now? Will he still want me? Will I even want him? Will we need child-care money while I go to school? Can I even go at all? Will the spell make him do things differently but somehow change the dynamic between us?* When the worst thought hits, it leaves little room for me to remember I've already decided to keep the pregnancy: *If Aaron does whatever it takes to get money for his brothers, how far would he go for his own child? What if I have to raise the baby without him?*

Aaron puts the outfit in my lap, and my vision blurs and my chest gets tight and the space around us feels like a casket. I push him away when he reaches for me. "What's wrong, Inez?"

It feels like I might die, so I ignore his questions to take a sack of crystals and go to the bathroom. I lock the door and slide down into the empty tub, placing my crystals around me while holding the obsidian in the palm of my left hand—right above my pact scars. I can feel its vibration before I see its slight glow. Whatever magic is in this crystal is unlike any other I've found because the muscles in my chest loosen and my vision clears without a mantra.

I see Jasmine's face: not smiling, brows dipped. For a second, she is sitting opposite me in the tub. Our knees touching. She breathes. I breathe. Then she's gone.

I stay in the bathroom awhile because Aaron is still in my room with the baby outfit.

54

MILIANI

Every Tuesday, Mom and I go to the Filipino market to buy fresh crabs. It's the only time we spend outside the house together. But I forget it's Tuesday and bring my friends home after school. We all offer to go, but Mom insists we stay home and cook rice.

Inez and Natalie don't notice how shaky she seems when she leaves, but I do.

We sit on the couch while the rice boils and Inez reads a note Aaron managed to get to her through a friend of his that goes to our school. Natalie tries to keep her eyes straight ahead for privacy, but I peek over at the note. Aaron misses her. All the usual, except Inez sighs instead of smiles when she puts the letter in her back pocket. She hasn't talked about her decision to keep the baby. I wonder if she spoke too soon and is still deciding. If I had Auntie Lindy's gifts, I'd figure it out for myself to save from asking and possibly confusing her more.

"He's being sweet because he's still selling drugs. Our spell was a long shot," Inez says.

Natalie pops a grape from a bowl into her mouth. "Don't count it out with the way these spell lag times have been set up. Look at Leanna."

Inez shrugs, all miserable until Nat loops back to tease, "Maybe he stopped selling but wants to rub your belly again. Pick out baby names."

Inez snorts and shifts her gaze onto me. "Enough about this. Let's talk about why Mili's not telling Jayson about Jasmine before Darleny does."

I run my hand over the coffee table and listen to the birds sing. I don't have time to worry about Jayson being hurt after I tell him. "Maybe she's lying."

"Maybe she's not."

Natalie cuts in to say, "Would she really do something like that? I'll cuss her out."

"It'll be fine," I say.

"What about the way you never mention Isobel anymore? You fine with that too?"

I don't talk about Isobel because it makes me sad. We could have had something special in another lifetime, but I'd probably be in love with Jas in all of them. "There are more important things. Let's check the rice and go upstairs to study my auntie's spell books."

But Inez grabs Nat's bowl to throw up in.

"Guess I'm done eating." Natalie cringes. "This kid is going to be rude—watch."

And for the briefest moment, I try to imagine us with a child to teach magic to. But the door in the living room swings open and Mom walks through it with two big bags in her hand. She narrows her eyes at us then continues into the kitchen.

"Do you think she noticed?" Inez whispers. "Smelled it?"

"Even if she did, she'd never mention it."

"You're lucky. I wish my mom would give me some damn space," she says.

Natalie looks at me. I wonder if we're both remembering the night we played sungka.

I wish my mom would talk to me. Take up more space.

☾ ☾ ☾

We tell Mom we're going to study math, and we go upstairs to study magic. Nat and I find a spell that seems next to impossible, but we agree it's worth a try. We need something substantial, and we need it fast. I look at my calendar on the wall and am shaken by the red slashes, markings to remind me we've gone too many days without Jasmine. I refuse to go much longer.

Inez is still reading the same page she's been staring at for the last five minutes. I hold the book in front of her. "What do you think of this spell?"

She doesn't look up from the page. "Sure," she says.

"My auntie is coming to get her books back in a couple hours. We need to decide."

"I said it was fine."

Nat chuckles and waves at Inez like *Let her be*. But my mom calls up dinner's ready, and Inez doesn't budge. "You reading a Bible-length passage over there?" Nat teases.

Inez sucks her teeth and looks up at us. "Just go. I'll be right down."

☾ ☾ ☾

Late at night, I get out of bed to crack the window open and see Mom standing beside Papa's tree. I watch her there, body stiff and unmoving. While I wait, I notice small seeds lining my windowsill, tucked into the cracks. I'm not sure what kind they are, but they weren't there before. I look at Mom again. She turns around and looks at me too. Or not at me. My heart stammers as her eyes lock in on another part of the house—maybe another window, possibly something or someone else. Then the phone rings and startles me.

Mom's eyes bounce to my window, and I duck away to answer the call.

Auntie is on the line. "Did you rip a page from one of my books?"

I peek to check if Mom is still looking, and she is. "I gave them back to you in perfectly perfect condition earlier. Made sure not to fold any pages," I whisper.

"Next time, you can study them at my house," Auntie tells me before hanging up.

I rack my brain about Mom's behavior and the call all night. I hate when Auntie's disappointed in me, but I didn't take any pages.

When I force myself to sleep, I finally dream of Jasmine. She's running down a school hallway. I call for her, but she turns left and goes into the girl's bathroom. I see her feet under one of the stalls, and bang on the door. She unlocks it but looks right through me. Her eyes are not brown. They're not green. They're white. I take a step toward her, but she lunges and makes me hit my head on the sink mirror.

It cracks, and so does the dream.

I wake up gasping for air. I touch the back of my head, try to still the room, but I'm dizzy. That wasn't Jasmine. She wouldn't hurt me. I hurry to the wall, rip my calendar from it. Count too many days since she passed away. Remember Auntie said to trust her.

55

MILIANI

Papa's energy is already stronger in the yard. It's easy to feel every time the wind blows and I can smell him in it. I ask if he'll allow me to draw on some of his energy to get ready for the ritual, and each time, I feel a bit more power swelling inside me.

This morning, I touch the bark and close my eyes as the energy hits me in a wave. It crashes against the flat parts of me, fills the holes, makes my body heavy with feeling. It thrums in my fingertips, my heart, my feet. I breathe in and out, soak it in, thank Papa for giving me the gift of what lingers of his spirit, for leaving it right here for me. I open my eyes, and the grass is greener, sharper, the flowers bloom brighter, with a sweeter smell.

Jasmine would be proud. She'd lay out a bedsheet in the grass and fall asleep with her curls shiny and spread around her while the sun bakes her skin to a deeper brown. My ache for her grows. Suddenly it hurts, and I have to remind myself she'll be able to see the yard soon, touch the grass, feel the breeze. She can lie next to me if she wants to.

She can have all of this through Darleny's body.

I feel it rock my stomach like seasickness. Is something wrong with me for fantasizing about sharing intimate moments with Jasmine while she's in a body that's not her own? Will Jasmine be able to ask

Darleny for consent? *It'll be her body soon too*, I tell myself. But I shake off a shiver, try to stop picturing Darleny when all I want to see is Jas.

Mom comes outside and says something, but my throat is too thick to answer. I pick up the cup next to Papa's tree and drink the last sip of water. Her mouth falls open.

"I'm sorry," I say. "I got caught up talking to Papa, and I was thirsty."

She nods and rubs her face. "You should be in school already. I'll take you."

((((

The car ride is quiet; I forget Mom's even here. The sunlight through the windshield makes my skin golden. I can still feel Papa's energy on me. I concentrate on it. My fingers unfold slowly with Auntie's voice in my head, whispering, *Be like the leaves*, and then the light finds my palm. The humming starts in my ears and moves through my body. It heats me up as the light gets smaller and smaller. It rounds out until it's the size of a quarter, a circle on my skin. It burns and it feels so good. This is it. The first time I've been able to filter sunlight. I curl my fingers and capture it and my whole body vibrates with feeling. But Mom's voice cuts through. "Miliani?" My eyes snap up and the feeling leaves, and someone beeps and Mom swerves to avoid collision.

She pulls to the side of the road, breathing heavy, hands gripping the wheel. "What did you do?"

"Nothing, Mom. I was . . ."

She waves her hand at me. "Is that what my sister has been teaching you while you're off on your little adventures?"

Her sister. Not *your tita*, or *the dangerous one*, or *that child Lindy*. Her *sister*.

"What?"

"You think I don't know?" she says. "I told you I didn't want you around her. And though I knew you were going behind my back to spend time with her, I trusted you to make good decisions. Meditating and working with crystals is one thing. Having her teach you about herbs I understand, Miliani. But you know how I feel about that . . . ," she says. "That witchcraft."

She starts driving, and the rest of the way I feel the betrayal like we're still connected through an umbilical cord.

When she pulls in front of my school, she says, "You aren't to do magic with her anymore. Do you understand me?"

I nod, but her eyes are fixed on a point in front of her. I'm thankful they're not on me.

"Controlling nature can bring you to a dark place," she says. "It can take from you. You think you're controlling it, until it starts controlling you."

"But it can also bring good, Mom. You know that. Papa used to heal people."

She adjusts her mirror. "You aren't Papa. And if you want to become anything like him, you'll stay away from my sister and her magic. I've always allowed you to make your own choices, Miliani"—she finally looks at me—"but maybe I've been wrong."

When she drives away, the wind blows and a rush of power courses through my bones, billows as I breathe magic. I wish I could turn it off for a while.

◖ ◖ ◖

There is no spare-key situation at Auntie Lindy's. I ring her door-bell, throw rocks at her window, bang on the downstairs door. Her first-floor neighbor opens it and asks if everything's okay while I take the stairs two by two. Auntie doesn't answer the upstairs door, either, but the bobby pins in my hair make for an easy job. I'm not thinking of B&E, of how she might scold me, when I push open her door and let myself inside. My nerves spike as I pass by the empty rooms, worrying about why her car is outside if she's not here. I get to her special room and knock, but she doesn't answer. The blackout curtain is pulled, but the room is darker than it should be when I let myself in. I want to turn on the light but instead, call, "Auntie?"

When my vision adjusts, I find her. She's on the ground. I move to pull the curtain open, nervous she's hurt, but this startles her. She skids back with a blindfold over her eyes. She doesn't move it when she asks, "Miliani? What are you doing here?"

I am about to speak when I notice the canvas in front of her. It's not the only one. There are many laid out on the ground between Auntie and the bookshelves lining the walls. Some paintings have light brushstrokes. Some are deep and dark; others, colorful. The paintings that were against the far wall are turned, and I can see them now. Every painting in the room is of the same person. A young boy. It takes my breath. I drop to my knees beside Auntie and reach out to touch one of them, but she intercepts my hand and flings it away.

She takes down her blindfold, her eyes blinking rapidly, her breathing caught between her teeth. "Don't touch them."

She starts gathering her supplies, but there's too many canvases for me to study. The boy has soft black hair and a heavy bottom lip. He's not smiling. A chill tears through my skin. It's the boy from the picture in Papa's box. Lindy stands, puts the paintings one by one into a closet behind a tapestry I've never noticed.

"Miliani, did you break in?" I open my mouth to explain, but she snaps, "I'm not a child to worry over. You scared me."

☾ ☾ ☾

The night is cool. We sit on her stoop, and she eats walnuts to regain her strength. "I can't hear a thing when I'm in that state. It all goes to the darkness. Helps with concentration."

"The blindfold?"

"Yes." She throws a walnut into the bird feeder. "Don't do that again."

"I'm really sorry."

There's tension in her jaw. "I know. You're worried about your mom. Why?"

"She found out about the magic. She saw me work with the sun." Her tension relaxes, and she smiles bigger than I've ever seen her smile, but I'm still nervous. "What are we going to do?"

"Nothing."

"What does that mean?"

"Miliani, do you want me to teach you more? Do you want to still come here?"

"Of course."

"How did it feel? Controlling the light?"

My body tingles, thinking of it again. I run my fingers over the stone step. "Incredible."

She nods and looks up at the tree closest to us. The leaves are swaying from the wind. "So we keep doing what we've been doing. You're almost ready. Now we worry about widening the realms. Your mother knowing changes nothing."

"She said—"

"I'll deal with my sister."

Her tone is final. I switch directions. "Who was the boy in the paintings? I saw a picture of him in Papa's box too. Is he family?"

"You're asking far too many questions today, my dear niece." When I don't smile, she sighs. "You've been like this since you were a child, you know? Annoyingly curious. That's why you were Dad's favorite. He said your curiosity meant you had great promise."

I try to stop myself from smiling, and tilt my head to get a better view of her. "You're not going to tell me about the boy, are you?"

"You'll know soon, Miliani. Now, tell me what else is bothering you. You've found something."

When Auntie dips into my mind, it feels natural now, but I'm surprised she reached that far in because I'd forgotten myself. I open my backpack and pull out the jar of seeds. I tell her they were lining my window last night.

She brings the jar to her nose, then dumps the seeds into her palm. "Hmm . . . anise."

"They don't look like anise seeds."

"They're from the Philippines. They grow different there."

"What are they used for?"

She rips a dying daffodil out of a pot without cutting it, snaps it in half, and catches my eyes. "They're for keeping spirits out. Among other things."

And then it clicks. The strange questions Mom asks me, the random bouts of silence from the spirits in my house, the jar of lemon and herbs on the living room windowsill. Mom has been doing magic, too, trying to keep away the spirits. Maybe keeping Jasmine from me.

❮ ❮ ❮

The moon is out when I get home and find Mom in Papa's garden by the fence. She's planting seeds in fresh soil. She's still angry and she doesn't even look at me, but I don't want to look at her, either.

Inside, I unpack my things to make it look like I'm studying, but instead, I search. Knowing what she's done gives me clear eyes. Outside my door, I sweep more anise seeds away and mop the area with bleach. I find carvings on the side of my windowpane, symbols etched into the wood. These will take me time. I'll save them for tonight. Tucked between my mattress and box spring, there are leaves, feathers, herbs, a dead fly, and pine needles too. I flush it all down the toilet, and flush again to make sure everything's really gone. I wipe down my windowsill with vinegar. Take a chair and wipe down my door. All possible points of entry on the top floor get scrubbed. The smell's pungent, but I don't care.

From the window, I can see Mom throwing away the bags she used to lay soil. I run downstairs and sit at the table. She fixes us both plates of food. Today it's monggo beans and rice.

When she goes to bed, I grate down the wood with Papa's pocketknife to remove the etchings. My body needs sleep by the time I get done, but my mind won't rest without calling, "Hello? Jas? Anyone?"

An hour drags by as I wait. I'm tired. There are six blue candles left in my bag. I put them in a round jar on top of my nightstand, light every single one, then drift into sleep.

❮ ❮ ❮

My eyes open with a sudden start at the smell of wax burning down. I sit up, switch on the lamp on my nightstand. On reflex,

I reach out and touch the glass jar. It burns my fingertips, and I flinch forward, accidentally knocking it to the floor. The candle wax pours out, bleeds blue into the grooves. Someone laughs. Then I hear something like a snake hissing. Goose bumps rise on my flesh. "Hello?"

Hello.

"Who are you?"

Who are you?

The echo sounds like me, but a little deeper—playful almost. And definitely not Jasmine.

"Miliani," I say, and swallow. "What's your name?"

More laughter, cool air rushing by me. I bend to open the nightstand drawer and pull out the mirror Auntie gave me. I use it to reflect the light in the corner of the room, but something isn't right. I can feel the spirit's energy like it's rattling my own bones, but I don't know where it is. Suddenly, the lightest sensation brushes my back. I twist my body, use the mirror to look for the shadow on the wall behind my bed. But I hear a scratching sound above me and angle the mirror up. Over my head, on the ceiling, sits a small shadow, making a double out of my own.

I curl in on myself as the outline of the shadow takes on a clearer shape.

But as soon as it becomes more defined, it disappears.

My body is trembling. I trip over myself, tumble off the bed, try to tuck the mirror back in the drawer the way it was. I leave my room light on and creep down the hall to knock on Mom's door. I don't wait for her to answer because it feels like something is breathing against the back of my neck. When I push open her door, she sits up in bed. "What is it?"

"Can I please sleep in here tonight?"

"Why?"

"I don't want to be alone," I say. "I'm not feeling well." I can't tell her what I've done. The mess I might have made.

She watches me for a few seconds before helping me make a bed on the floor. The anger I felt earlier starts to fade, and in its place is a desire to be near her. She goes back to bed, and I scoot as close to her as I can get. Sleep doesn't find me until the birds start to sing. And even then, I can hear a low giggle while I dream.

56

INEZ

The second time we go to the beach, Mili is quiet the whole drive. She grips the wheel hard, and when she makes a turn, her hands tremble. We ask her if it's the spirits, but she insists she's fine. I think she doesn't want to give us another reason to be scared when she's finally learned some elemental magic and we're about to do a spell to try to bust open the realms.

At Conimicut, the sand is hard and damp under my feet, but the rain has stopped, leaving the sky a deep, deep blue color with only a slice of moon coming through the clouds. It feels good to be here—away from home, where I have to lie to Mami about why I'm not eating, and fight fatigue so she doesn't ask why I'm taking another nap. But then I feel the weight of the page from Lindy's spell book in my pocket. Heavy like a lie of omission, and thicker because it feels like it could be freedom.

Nat pretends to wave around a wand, teases, "It's so dark out here. The perfect night for casting a spell." Mili ignores her and lights a torch she set near a flat rock that's close to the water. But Natalie's words resonate, remind me that this night is the type of night the page in my pocket describes: dark, the moon a gibbous, by a body of water. And following the attainment of energy, which is what we're here for.

"Inez, you good?" Nat asks, pulling me back to the beach.

I'm not, but I nod and watch as Mili holds up the jar she's been playing with. We get closer to her, and I cringe. Nat says, "That's fucking huge. Those are chilling in your basement?"

Miliani turns the jar over in her hand and twists open the lid. The spider inside is dead. It's brown with long legs and a fat body. It looks as if hundreds of baby spiders are about to burst out of it. I find my stomach beneath my shirt, press till it's sore. There's only one growing inside me, only one baby I'll have to birth, but the thought bursts my nerves open like the axons are splitting. An actual baby. To raise, and take care of, even though I'm still learning how to take care of myself. My heart is thrumming in my ears when Miliani sets the spider down on the rock and Natalie complains she's going to itch all night. Mili proves the spider is harmless by poking at it with her finger. I mimic her by poking my stomach once more.

While we get ready for the spell, Natalie lights candles of so many colors they begin to melt a rainbow in my mind. Mili crushes herbs into a wooden bowl filled with seawater and a sprinkle of sand. The three of us take turns pricking one another's fingers with a sewing needle to hold over the spider's body until it's swimming in our blood.

Mili reminds us how serious this spell is, how necessary. If we pull this off, we should be close enough to anchor Jasmine to this world forever. If we pull this off, we might be able to do anything. Thinking possibilities pulls words from the page in my pocket and decodes them like hieroglyphics. Puts the outcome of the spell within reach, makes it real. Mili says we have to focus like we've never focused, but I'm already there. Locked in. For Jasmine. And for me.

We join hands, forming a triangle around the spider, and chant the spell again and again. Nothing happens at first, but Mili starts to chant louder and suddenly my eyes burn and everything around us becomes fuzzy. But only until my vision clears with a sharpness that makes me think I've experienced evolution. The dark around us lights up with night vision, and the hairs on the spider stand out against the thick of our blood. The smell of rosemary and sea salt is so intense it coats my tongue. My fingertips begin to buzz. Natalie fumbles over a few words, looking down at our hands, but Mili's voice rises loud enough to drown out the waves crashing against the shore. Against my chest, the obsidian pulses. Then a surge of static shocks us silent, and we separate, staring at our hands—until Miliani breathes in loudly and Natalie's eyes brighten in the dark. And the spider, it spreads its legs like a flower and begins to move.

I scoot back from the rock, my fingertips still thrumming. Natalie covers her mouth. "Oh my god. Are we all seeing this? Is it really . . . ?"

Mili leans forward, placing her hand in front of the spider. It climbs. Slowly stretching out over her skin. We watch as it makes its way to the middle of her palm and pauses there. "It is," she says, her words colored by tears in her throat. "It's alive."

"We're dreaming. I'm convinced we're dreaming," Natalie says.

"You can hold it," Mili offers. "Feel for yourself."

Natalie backs up. "No, thanks. You got that."

And Mili's laugh sounds more real than it has in weeks. I hope, I truly hope, this means we'll hear so much more of it soon, but her expression grows serious as she looks down at the spider and says, "We're really going to get Jasmine back."

It sounds like the first time she believes it with her whole heart.

I think it's the first time I truly believe it. We brought a spider back to life. We brought something back to life. I'm not sure how much of this was divine intervention and how much of it was us, but I can feel the power coursing through my body like it's bonding with atoms, swirling with the blood in my veins, coating my lungs with each breath.

Mili lays the spider back on the rock, and as it crawls over a crack, she pulls me and Natalie to her. We hug and scream, and Natalie's body shakes. And I laugh. I cry. We sit there watching the way our magic made a miracle—something that should be impossible, unreal, a fantasy, living here on earth after death. Evidence of our desire manifesting makes my own desires seem so close to being tangible I can feel it in the lightness of my limbs. But the feeling fades, and my thoughts are interrupted when the spider stops moving.

I let go of my friends and still the bones in my body, but I can't still time. Mili leans over the rock to watch the spider curl in on itself. My bones betray me as they start to move. My leg mimics the spider's, starting to twitch. Soon that stops too, and I choke on all the silence surrounding us. I find myself beside Mili, reaching out to touch the spider, softly, so softly, and still it withers down to nothing. Dust blending with the dark of the rock.

Like it had never lived at all.

I shake my head, again and again. But Mili puts a hand on my shoulder. "Don't worry," she says. "I knew this could happen. Auntie Lindy said most times necromancy spells are temporary, if they work at all. The one with Jasmine will be different. She'll have an anchor."

"Why didn't you tell us? And why don't we know what her anchor will be yet?" Nat asks, her voice wavering.

Mili's gaze flitters away from us. "Because my auntie's still try-ing to figure it out," she says. She bends to blow the dust from the rock, erasing the evidence of the spider's existence. "And I didn't tell you because it could've interrupted our intentions. It's purer to believe it was going to live."

Natalie nods, her eyes glossy with unshed tears. "So we still did it?"

"We still did."

She reaches for Mili and they hug, and they talk to each other, to the moon, and I think they talk to me. But their words blur and thin out, and all that's left is the sound of my breathing. I try to remind myself we made something incredible happen, but it doesn't stick. What does it mean that the spider didn't *stay* alive? What does it matter if it decomposed to dust and was carried off with the wind? I shift my body away from them, my hands flutter-ing like the beat of my heart as I reach into my pocket and hold the folded page up to my face. What if this was my only chance and now it's gone?

"Inez," Mili says, touching my back. I turn and look into her face. A smile spreads her cheeks wide, until it doesn't. She scoots closer to me, brows low and close. "What's wrong?"

"It's not going to work," I say, and hearing the words out loud makes me want to curl in on myself, shrivel like the spider. I see what my future might look like.

A life with a child. Under my mother's roof, while she helps me with night feedings after working sixteen hours a day to provide for all of us. Victor putting his video game away to hold the baby when anxiety racks my body. Aaron selling drugs to buy diapers. Papi only getting to see his grandchild through pictures in the mail.

All the times they're not able to be there for me, and I have to raise a child I didn't want. And my body—never belonging only to me again. Growing and changing for a life that will come before my own. My body forever at the will of anxiety, of pregnancy and postpregnancy, of a baby who will need my mind, my soul, to help it thrive and grow. And magic can't fix it.

Magic can't stop my body from making me a mom.

I sob, push my fingers into the sand, try to steady myself through the shakes.

Natalie's on my other side now, stroking my hair. "What's wrong? Talk to us."

"The spider was supposed to live," I whisper. "It was supposed to make us stronger."

Mili looks at Nat, then back at me. Her voice is careful, like she's talking to a child. "But it did work. Didn't you see? We brought something back from the dead. We're stronger. Can't you feel it?"

"But it didn't *stay* alive," I say, my voice rising some. "It's not enough."

"Jasmine's going to—" Mili starts, then stops short. She stares down at my hand and snatches the page. She reads for a few seconds, then her eyes pierce through me. "You're the one who took a page from my auntie's spell book?"

"I didn't tell you because I knew you'd look at me like you're looking at me now," I say.

Her mouth opens, then closes. She runs her hands over her face and passes Natalie the page. Nat gasps and leans to grasp my shoulders. "A spell to cause a miscarriage? What are you thinking?"

I shake my head, place my hands over my stomach, and say, "I don't want to keep it."

"Then let's go to the clinic," Nat says.

"I can't. I can't ask you guys for the money, and—" I cut myself off. I have reasons, but I don't know how to explain the rest to my friends in a way they'd understand. I wish I didn't have to explain; I wish they knew without me having to say that it's not as simple as going to a clinic. I wish Jasmine were here to tell it to them.

"But," Nat says, "we'll figure it out."

"Even if we do . . ." I pause. My voice cracks. I feel like I might splinter. "I can't."

"Why not? What are you not saying?" Mili's tone is sharp, but her eyes are softer now.

"I can't have an abortion in a clinic. Do you remember all of those protestors outside of it? The signs?" I chew my lip. "I do. Sometimes, I see them when I close my eyes."

Nat says there's nothing wrong with having an abortion, not to let *those people* get to me.

"You're right. There's not," I say. "But what happens if those people are like my people, huh? What happens then?" I dig my nails into my scalp. "What about my mom? What about my brother and my priest and all the people at my church? And what about my dad? What if the abortion record follows me and the immigration court uses it against us?"

Natalie's mouth slacks a little. She looks over to Mili. They can't understand. I don't know how to make them, but I try.

"I prayed," I say. "I asked God if I'd be forgiven if I went to the clinic, and got no answer. There was no sign. Then days later, I happened to find the page. Of all the books, hundreds of pages, it was in my hands." I point a shaky finger at Nat. "Not yours. Not Mili's. Mine. And there was my sign. And maybe, maybe the sign was from God, maybe it wasn't, but suddenly the page was in front of me and it felt like one. It feels like one."

Nat shifts and hugs herself. Mili looks at me like she's examining my insides. "You do realize you're talking about a sign in the form of a page with a spell that sounds like it could kill you, right?" she says. "And you thought we'd be down for it? You trust us with your life?"

"I do," I say. "Of course I do."

Mili sighs. She puts her hand on my knee, squeezes. "How much have you thought about this? You were just talking about keeping the pregnancy."

"I thought I didn't have a choice." My throat aches. I swallow. "And since then I've thought about it so much it feels like my brain is splitting, and I don't know much of anything, but I do know I don't want to be a mother. What if God was willing to show me another way so maybe I wouldn't have to be one? What if God is giving me a choice to use the same free will I use every time I do any other spell?"

Mili clenches her jaw. The fire from the torch makes her skin glow. After a moment, Natalie rubs my back. "That makes sense," she says, her voice reassuring, cooling my fire. "I can see why you'd feel that way. But what about Aaron?"

Remembering the excitement on Aaron's face and how hurt he might be makes me hurt, too, but Aaron already has siblings to take care of. So I tell Nat, "The baby is going to push his life in a bad direction. I know it. This feels like what's best for the both of us." I look down at myself. "But none of it matters. It won't work. I don't have any choices left."

I want to scream, but I don't. My body feels heavy, and I can't cry anymore. All I can do is turn to look past them into the ocean. We stay in silence so long I think I can fall asleep right here, stay until this night disappears. Natalie puts an arm around my shoulders. I can't even look at her. "Talk to me," she says.

"It hurts so much," I tell her.

She pulls me to her chest. "Shh."

"I don't want to have a baby."

Natalie tilts her head and looks me in the eyes. "I know," she says. "And I know it's not the same, but I remember feeling so helpless when my mom was in that coma. I had to do something, and I remember feeling like magic was my only option." She kisses me on the cheek and turns to look at Miliani. "Can it still work?"

Miliani doesn't hesitate. She nods grudgingly, and it's so hard to believe that I stare at her, willing her to say it out loud. She doesn't, but Nat says, "After all Inez has done for me. Gone through for us. Maybe we should try?"

Miliani stares up at the gibbous moon, wrapping her arms around herself. After what feels like a long time, she says, "If she's sure."

Natalie grabs my face with both of her hands, looks at me awhile, then stands up and helps me to my feet. I feel like I have whiplash. "You'll help me?" I say.

She leans her forehead against mine. "We said no matter what."

The tears come again. I glance at Mili, but she's looking down at the scar on her palm.

(((

We strip down to panties and bras. I take off the crystal necklace. Obsidian is used for protection, and I know I can't wear it when we try this. We walk into the water. Natalie jokes about never getting in again after this, and I'm not sure if I laugh out loud or just think I should laugh. Everything becomes a little blurry as we get waist-deep. We shiver. We grow quiet. I form a cup with my hand and sip some seawater. The salt thickens my throat and feels like sludge going down. This spell is different; there are no words to chant. I'm so cold I start to shake. Natalie and Miliani touch my stomach, and my nerves bubble there. But I'll only be under for sixty seconds. I've held my breath longer than that swimming in pools and playing at this same beach. I take a breath when they each place a hand on my shoulders. Miliani's eyes—soft with love I know is for me—are the last I see before I'm pushed under the water. At first, it's easy. I feel and focus with intention, and pray to God. I pray I won't need forgiveness after this. I pray that if I do, I'll be able to get it. I pray for strength so I won't panic and risk needing forgiveness for something that won't even work. But some seconds later, my body begins to go on alert.

My arms flail. I grasp one of their hands, try to peel them away, try to rise. They continue to hold me down, and my breasts ache and burn, and no matter how many times I blink, I see nothing but darkness in front of me. But then, I remember my baptism, and the trust I put in God, in a priest, and it helps me put my trust in my friends so I'm able to relax and concentrate on my whole body. Making it feel like mine again. Making it belong to me. And I start to see a faint glow around me. I feel weightless. I think I might float.

But suddenly, Natalie and Miliani yank me from the water. My body jerks. I'm dazed. I choke up what I swallowed. I reorient myself and see my friends in front of me. And I feel the same. Exactly the same heaviness I felt before we started. "What happened?" I say. "It was too soon."

They don't answer with their mouths; they answer with their eyes. I feel their fear before they push their bodies closer and bury me with it. My own fear rises as the glow around us grows brighter. I might not be breathing when I notice the dozens of clinging jellyfish surrounding us—their bioluminescent bodies swaying in the water and giving off a green light. We stiffen, try to clamp and cling to one another like barnacles. Bile rises in my throat. My pregnancy feels like a rock between us. I blink in and out. From this moment to the one before. Then it starts to rain.

It pours down on us, thunder and lightning crackling over our heads. I stumble back, and Mili grasps me, but the jellyfish spread their glowing tentacles and start to swim away, the green fading as they go. The water turns dark again, and so do the thoughts in my mind. It was wrong. It was all wrong. They pulled me too soon because nature said it was wrong. Maybe God. I feel nauseous. I feel tired. I feel pregnant. They pull me by my arms and lead me out of the water while rain makes ripples around us and lightning brightens the sky.

❨ ❨ ❨

On the ride back home, my clothes stick to my skin. Natalie sits beside me in the back seat, trying to talk to me, trying to comfort me, but then gives up and begins to flip through her camera. Her fear is still palpable. The jellyfish, the spell. I watch her body shake. Miliani drives slow. The rain is coming down so hard I wonder if she can see the road in front of her.

Halfway to Providence, the pain in my heart is too much to bear, and I can't help but say, "It didn't work. It didn't fucking work."

part three

☽ ☽ ☽

MANIPULATING THE SUN

Jasmine, you never taught me how to live without you.

57

INEZ

In this dream, Jasmine asks why I'm not wearing the necklace. We look in the car for it before it appears in front of us, hanging from the mirror, the black stone glinting and sparkling in the sun. "There it is," she says, taking it off the mirror and bringing it to her lips. She speaks to it under her breath. Puts a spell on it with me sitting there watching. She hands it to me, and I hold it close. "It'll help keep you safe. The baby too." She rubs my belly and says, "She's going to be a little witch. The first of our children. She'll be a badass."

"How do you know she'll be a witch?"

Jasmine laughs and leans over to kiss my cheek. "Everyone knows, silly."

But my stomach deflates before my eyes. I scream. "It's gone. The baby is gone."

"What are you talking about?" Jasmine says. "What baby?"

I touch my flattened stomach. "It was here, and now it's gone."

"Inez." Jasmine leans and looks at me close. "Wake up. There's no baby."

I shake my head again and again and sink into my seat. I sink so deep the car disappears from under me and I'm sinking into an ocean. Deeper. Deeper. The water burns my throat. I forget how to swim. I scream for Jasmine, and air bubbles climb while my body descends—so low I panic in pitch black, trying to see my fingers in front of me. Until a green light brightens the dark spaces. Clinging jellyfish spread their tentacles. I stop struggling. I give over to drowning to watch them draw in water and push it out. But then they force themselves forward, toward me.

Over the top of me, in between my legs, their jelly bodies slide over the bare skin of my arms, burning my flesh as they wrap and go, wrap and go. I feel the stings all at once and not at all. I squeeze my eyes shut against the pain, the numbness. The darkness behind my lids is green. I let the water take me. Until suddenly, I'm lifted up out of it and floating on my back. Jasmine's face looks like it's part of the moon as she stares down at me.

"It's time to wake up, Inez." She kisses my temple. "It's over. Wake up."

I'm on the floor when I do. My whole body aches. I roll, groan, search for sting marks on my skin with freezing fingers. And then I hear a whisper. *Inez. Sweet Inez.*

I scoot back on the rug, try to grab my bedsheets and stand. The voice isn't Jasmine's. *Inez*, it says, closer this time, but then the crystal warms under my nightgown, heating the cold parts of me, and the door to my room swings open.

Mami comes in and switches on my light. "Mija, did you fall off the bed?" She helps me up. She can tell it hurts. Her face contorts. "Oh. You're bleeding."

I touch my nightgown and my fingers come back wet. Mami talks in the background, something about pads and cleaning the stain on the carpet. She pushes me into the bathroom. "Your period's early, no? You said you had it two weeks ago." She opens the cabinet and gets me a jumbo-sized pad and two facecloths, then leaves to go get me a fresh change of clothes. But she's out there awhile. She must be cleaning blood from my carpet before the stain sets.

(((

The next morning, I'm in the bathroom when Mili knocks at the door. I know it's her before I peek through to make sure. When she's inside, I throw my arms around her.

"Thank you," I say. "There's so much blood."

We seem like the same height today, as if something inside me really did curl in on itself and wither away like the spider. She pulls back to wipe the tears from my face, and hers is wet with them too. I bleed through another pair of pants, and it gushes as I lean against her. I apologize over and over.

"Shh," she says. "Undress. Let's make you better." She runs the bath. The water is hot, but I sink right in. She kneels beside the tub and cleans my face with a rag.

"It hurts," I tell her. "It hurts so much."

She kisses my forehead and quiets me down as the water in the tub starts to turn pink.

"Close your eyes," Miliani says. "I'm here. Rest your eyes."

58

NATALIE

Before each bus stop, I know how many people will be getting on. Ma mixes up the words *tuition* and *intuition*. If I told her about how hard my intuition has been working since the spells on the beach, she'd say something like "That's tuition for ya. I always know when something bad is 'bout to happen before it does."

For me, if I think about Ray, he'll call. I know what Mr. Ortega is going to say before he opens his mouth. Even my vision is sharper, something that'd be beneficial if I could take pictures without worrying what they'll look like. Now, the ghosts feel like living, breathing beings. They stand behind me when I open closets. Their screams cut through my music. They play with my hair.

Inez's mom asks me to bring a bowl of soup up to her as soon as I get there. "But be careful. We don't know how contagious her stomach bug is."

I open Inez's door with soup in one hand, Kit Kats from the bodega in my pocket, love in my heart. I set the soup on her nightstand and sit beside her in bed. She leans her body against mine and groans. "How bad is it?"

"Feels like my stomach is trying to come through my back."

"I'm surprised your mom hasn't taken you to the hospital."

She reaches back to touch the top of the headboard. It's the fancy kind, with white wood and engravings in the corners. "Mami's try-ing home remedies first. She knows I hate hospitals."

"You've been sick three days now. She getting suspicious?"

"Maybe," Inez says. "But I'll be back in school tomorrow, whether I feel better or not."

Darleny's crystal catches my attention. I pick it up from the nightstand. "Why aren't you wearing this? Maybe it'll help."

She shakes her head. "I'm done with witchcraft for now."

"You don't mean that."

"I do. I'm scared, Nat. Can't even change my pad in the bath-room without the lights flickering. Mili's little protection jars don't do a good job protecting now. It's been so much worse since we . . ." Since the spider. Since we aborted the fetus. The latter still makes me feel uneasy. I see the darkness under her eyes when they flick toward me. "Feels like God is punishing me. Maybe it wasn't the right way to do it. I should've went to the clinic."

"He isn't. Don't think that way."

Inez pulls away from me, moves some fallen hair from her face.

"And what even is the right way?" I say. "How do we know?"

"I don't know, Nat, but maybe we shouldn't have started mess-ing with dark magic."

I tilt my head at her. "I'd hardly call waking my mom from a coma dark magic."

"No, not that. You know what I mean." She frowns. "Haven't you been scared?"

I have a feeling Inez is more scared of what the decision means for her than she is of ghosts, but I tell her, "Terrified. And I don't know what to do with myself lately. Photography felt like an extension of me before. Feel like I'm losing part of myself."

"You shouldn't have to," she says. "When Mili told us there'd be sacrifices, did you think it'd be the thing you love the most?"

"Of course not," I say. "But it won't be forever, right? We just have to do the anchoring. We're almost there."

Inez sighs. "You and Miliani might have to do it without me."

The shock hits me in the stomach. "But what about Jasmine?"

"I don't think Jas would want us suffering to bring her back from the dead. She wasn't the perfect Catholic, but she believed in God, she believed everything happens for a reason. What if we're hurting ourselves and defying her beliefs too?"

"But she didn't find space."

Inez gnaws at her lip. "I don't think I can do it anymore."

I'm surprised to hear this from her when she'd been pushing for us to open the realms. Even her tone shakes me up. "The magic . . . It did exactly what you wanted it to. It works."

"I know it works, and that's why I'm done."

"You'd be okay with letting Jas go?"

Inez closes her eyes. "I keep thinking we never got the chance to grieve. I keep wondering, what is too far? Do you think she'd even want to come back this way? Against her will? What if we stop her right as she decides to move on?"

I wonder what the three of us would look like without Jasmine forever. She always seemed like the tie between us. Maybe she still is. Maybe Mili won't be able to handle the pain. Will I be able to? How do I begin to breathe when I left a mess between us? I have no answers, nothing for Inez either, but she's looking at me.

"Do you regret it?" I say instead.

"I never wanted to be a mother."

"That's not what I asked."

She leans against me again. "I don't regret it."

☾ ☾ ☾

Harriet's on her porch, braiding hair, while I wait for Leanna on mine. There's always some neighbor's child sitting at Harriet's feet, begging for nicer cornrows than the ones she gave the last kid. The girl from four houses down sits on a pillow on the floor in front of Harriet. "Do you have to pull so hard, Mrs. Harriet?"

"Do you have to be so tender-headed?" Harriet takes a second to wipe the sweat from her forehead. It's muggy and moist today, the way it was before the rainstorm at the beach the other night. It feels like thunder and lightning coming. Talking to Inez has me paranoid, thinking God might strike me down for being a part of that spell, so when Harriet catches me looking and says, "Come here, Natalie," I don't refuse.

Being closer to Harriet might feel like I'm closer to God.

On her porch, I look down at her work. "The design is perfect."

The girl scrunches her nose at me. "When you getting yours done? You look rocked."

It's been a bit since my last wash, and I haven't bothered to put my hair up in a puff or refresh it with water and conditioner. It's big and round on my head, beautiful, but when the wind blows, it smells like my scalp needs tea-tree oil.

Harriet laughs. "Alisha, your mouth gets worse every year. You coming to church this weekend?"

"If Mama makes me."

"She would wanna."

The girl talks junk under her breath, and I interrupt before Harriet gets her. "That's a good one." I point down at the comic book in her lap. "You'll be surprised in the end."

She looks up at me, mouth open, cheeks higher. "You read?"

"Uh-huh," I tell her. "*Cloak and Dagger* is my favorite."

She smiles. "Mine too."

Harriet twists an elastic in place, eyeballs me. "You still upset?"

"I'm not sure," I say. "I know about Leanna. You should've treated her better."

"She could've come to me if she was in trouble. I was right here. But she loves her lifestyle, being out this neighborhood with her fancy things, and I can't love her decisions."

"I guess that's fair, but what if she didn't think she was in trouble?"

"Oh, child." Harriet chuckles. "I just hope you'll come to me if you ever are."

Leanna pulls up and beeps before I can respond. The little girl says, "Damn, that's a clean whip," and Harriet must have yanked her hair a tad tighter because she sucks in a sharp breath.

❨ ❨ ❨

At Butler, Leanna walks a few feet in front of me like we're strangers. We weren't close before, but at least we could be in the same space. I don't regret doing the truth spell, but I wish she'd talk to me. As we go, my eyes keep catching shadows creeping along the walls. Leanna turns her face toward them for a moment, and I swear she sees something, but she keeps moving.

In the visiting room, we see more color in Ma's cheeks than during the visit two days ago. She's eating better, socializing. She tells us about the cute security guard in her unit. Then her gaze bounces back and forth between us. "What's going on with you two?"

"Nothing, Ma," Leanna says. "Listen, they're talking about discharging you Friday."

"Don't 'Nothing' me, Leanna Leigh," Ma says. "You haven't cut a glance in your sister's direction since I walked in. I didn't die and come back to life for you two to act up."

"You didn't die, Ma."

"Sure did," Ma says.

Leanna gets up and fixes her shirt. "I'll see you in a few days, Ma."

She tells me she'll be waiting in the car, and when I'm sure she's gone, I ask Ma if she knew Leanna was a stripper. She says yes and it makes me fume. More secrets. Ma and Leanna keeping me in the dark, separately and together.

"She's a grown woman, Natalie. Don't be mad."

"She left when she was seventeen, Ma. That's hardly a woman. You'd let me strip?"

She shakes her head. "That's different, Natty. I couldn't tell that girl nothing at six, forget seventeen. And she lives a good life, helps take care of us. You should appreciate it."

"I do, but have you even asked how it makes her feel?"

"You're thinking way too hard about this, baby. It's why she didn't want you to know."

I suck on my top lip to keep from sulking. She reaches over and squeezes my thigh softly. "Natty, did you bring me more of that stuff? One more to get me through."

It doesn't seem like she needs the elixir now—she looks good after the last few—but I give it to her anyway. She downs it quick, and when she licks her lips, I feel queasy.

59

NATALIE

Broad Street is the place to be when the weather gets nice. Looking to buy some CDs? Three for ten on Broad. Need a haircut? The barbershops compete, one on every other block. The food trucks are out, and there are so many family-owned spots to eat there's no need to leave the area. And the drama is entertainment at its best. Toward the back of Central High and across from Burger King, you might see a shirtless man jumping on cars until the police come, if you're lucky.

Today, people are shooting dice outside the bodega. They ask me if I want to join in on a game, and I want to, but my shift's about to start. The bodega feels cool when I walk in, and even smells better. Ray sounds proud when he shows me the work he did. Says he got a bonus in his last check. I'm proud of him too, but receiving a last check means he won't be working here anymore, which means we won't be spending as much time together. Thinking about it makes me feel insecure, clingy, reminds me how I ended things last year without even trying. I don't want to make the same mistake. So I take a deep breath and ask him to show me his work again. To explain it better, in language I can actually understand. He pulls me to the corner where the cameras don't reach, kisses me. "I can buy us a nice dinner with my bonus."

"Aren't you officially done here?"

"I am. But that doesn't mean I can't stop in later with something fancy for my girl."

I duck my head, try to hide my smile under the cover of my fro. Hope it hides the nerves twisting my stomach, probably showing on my face, making my voice shake when I say, "What good is being your girl if you might get an itch and decide to move to Georgia in six months?"

There's a beat of silence before he tilts my chin. "Who knows what I'll want to do in six months, but right now I want to be here with you." He plants kisses on my cheeks, on my forehead, leans back to stare into my eyes. "That good with you, Williams?"

My heart beats fast. "Yeah," I say, and smile. "That's good."

I want to try, even if it means knowing sometimes things end and sometimes people leave, but trusting Ray with my heart anyway. "How about pinchos from a chimi truck?"

The sides of his eyes crinkle. "Really? That's fancy to you?"

"Chimis, and pastelitos on the side."

☾ ☾ ☾

Over the phone, Inez says she's still not feeling good enough for school, but she won't tell me how her heart feels. Instead, we talk about how we haven't picked out prom dresses. I could care less, but pretend to be excited to do it with Inez.

When we hang up, there's not much to distract me. Ma

should've been here two hours ago. Dev is at practice, and Leanna's working. There's nothing to do but wait by the kitchen window—with a chair, then without a chair, with lunch, then without lunch. No good can come from it, but I ache to touch my camera. I pass by pictures until I get through the shadows and see my friends again. My body relaxes, finding memories in their faces, but then the screen starts to flicker. Jasmine's face is the first to go before the screen fades to black. My fingers tremble as I try to turn the camera back on. I rush to plug it in, and the charge light glows red. My camera wasn't dying.

I recoil from the counter when a horn beeps, then walk to the window on weak legs. Ma is here. She gets out of a red Honda Civic. All tall and lanky, and wearing the clothes she wore when she went into rehab. I can't wait to hug her. I let my eyes wander the room. I can't wait to not be alone today.

When her driver pulls off, Ma glances in the direction of Harriet's porch and drops her bag to the ground. She takes a seat on a step and puts her face in her hands. Harriet isn't home today, so Ma thinks she has privacy, but I watch.

I think of Jas in the picture on my camera while I wait. I wonder if she's around now, growing angry because we're taking too long. I tell myself she wouldn't mess with my camera but how do I know for sure?

Ma gets up and walks down the steps, and I can't wait anymore. My feet move on their own, fast, down the three flights.

I open the downstairs door to beg her to stay, but she's standing in the doorway with a confused look on her face. "Where you heading, Natty?" she says.

60

MILIANI

It's been four days since Inez started bleeding, and she shows up at my doorstep, pale and shaking from a fever. "Told my mom I was going to the bodega." She drops her mom's car keys in my hand and leans against the porch rail. "Not sure if I'm going to die by her hand or from soaking through pads in under an hour."

"You're really going to joke right now?" I feel her head. "Why didn't you tell me you were still bleeding heavy?"

"Please take me to Lindy's," is all she says. I can tell by the way her lips are moving it's hard for her to speak. My stomach sinks. I haven't known how to tell Auntie we didn't just bring the spider back to life the night on the beach.

"I'm taking you to a hospital, Inez." She looks so sick I'm not sure how she made it here. I help her inside the car.

"No hospitals," she says, and lays her head on the dashboard. "They'll call my mom."

"Your life is more important right now."

"What if they can't help me? We did this with magic. What if we need magic to fix it?"

A consequence. There's always a consequence. Inez slumps back in her seat and closes her eyes. She doesn't open them again the whole ride.

◖ ◖ ◖

When we pull up, it seems like Auntie is already waiting on the stoop for us. She rushes down the stairs and opens the passenger door. "What the hell did you do?"

Upstairs, she tells Inez to lie on a cot in the living room and gives her a sheet to try to stop the shivering. "Keep her cool," she says, and hands me a wet rag. The sheet and the rag feel counterproductive, but I do what I'm told while Auntie goes to the kitchen and comes back with a jar. "We'll have to strip her down," she says.

I look at Inez, but she only nods. I help her do the rest.

Auntie takes a glob of the pasty ointment from the jar and hands it to me. We start rubbing Inez down in a rush. "Make sure to rub a thick layer over her feet and chest," Auntie says, working the ointment into Inez's arms.

"This smells like shit," Inez says. It does. It's musty and strong like rotten wood.

Auntie raises both brows. "The sickness could have taken your foul mouth too."

Inez tries to laugh but coughs instead. Auntie passes me a pillow to prop her head, and places her own hands below Inez's belly button. She pushes. Inez tenses up in pain, groans that it hurts, but Auntie keeps pushing. She pauses for a few seconds before pushing again. After a few more pushes, she lifts the sheet and checks Inez's pad.

The blood is still bright red, but now there's so much more of it.

Natalie rushes over after I call her and climbs into the cot beside Inez.

"You won't be able to stay in bed with her for long. We've got to keep her cool," Auntie says to Nat, then makes me follow her into the kitchen.

She has two plant pots on the table. The plants inside have been recently watered. They trickle to her kitchen floor. My breathing catches when I finally recognize them. They're the plants we potted during our first training. But now, they're bursting out of the pots. Auntie's vines are splayed out over the table. And my plant has lots of pretty purple flowers I've never seen before. Auntie plucks one and throws it into a pot on the stove. "Well, what are you waiting for?" she says. "Come help me with this."

I stir the pot full of coconut oil, watch it melt around the purple flower while she adds to it. There's an odd mixture of things going from her hand to the pot: a milky substance from a jar she keeps below the sink, cayenne pepper, lemon, lime, parsley, a whole garlic clove, brown liquid from a medicine bottle. This calms my nerves some. If Auntie Lindy can heal my wounds, she can heal Inez too. She turns up the burner on the stove and says, "The page from my book."

"I didn't know she had it. Not until after the spider spell."

"You should've told me before you went and did something this reckless. I could've told you it was a bad idea. And had I known how desperate she was, I would've given in and signed for her. I would've paid for it if I had to. Why didn't you come to me?"

"You said—"

"Miliani, do you understand the situation you put her in? The risk? This is inexcusable."

My lip starts to tremble. "We weren't even sure it would work."

"So you use your gifts for something you're not sure of? I told you stronger, not stupid."

"Yes, Auntie, but you said we'd have to make sacrifices."

"Tama na," Auntie hisses in Tagalog. "I thought you'd think of bloodletting, maybe sacrificing an animal, a plant, your privacy, your hair, Miliani, not your friend's unborn fetus."

My chest grows tight. I stir the mixture faster. "She needed us."

"Is that the only reason you did it? Or was a part of you hoping it would bust open the realms for the anchoring ritual too?"

I feel a burn in my chest before it hits my cheeks. "I wouldn't do it because of that. You didn't see how broken she was. I thought we could fix it."

She turns off the stove. "Well, you better hope I can fix the mess you've made in her. I'm giving it a few hours, and then I'm calling the ambulance and you're calling her mother."

(((

Auntie tilts Inez's head back and makes her drink the stove concoction lying down. It takes a long time. Natalie's concerned Inez will choke and keeps trying to lift her head, but Auntie pushes her hands away. When it's over, she forms a crystal grid with the largest clear quartz crystals I've ever seen. She lays them on the floor, and they surround Inez in the shape of a diamond. She draws lines with chalk to connect them.

The hours pass slowly, and Inez doesn't look any better. Her temperature is higher than ever, and she can barely keep her eyes open. She starts coughing. Auntie turns her on her side, and Inez throws up—a black tar color and texture. I start to cry and reach for her, but Auntie tells me to stay put. She peels back Inez's sheet, and Natalie inhales beside me.

A large pool of blood stains the white sheet under Inez. It's dark and thick. Auntie puts one hand on Inez's head and one on her sternum.

She bends low. I don't know if she's praying over Inez or fixing this with a spell. I don't know if I should even be breathing, but I say a silent prayer too. I haven't prayed in a while and I beg God to listen.

"It's too late," Auntie says, rising to her feet. "I should've already called an ambulance."

My world dips and spins and shakes when Auntie gets up and heads for the house phone and Natalie moves to pull Inez into her arms. My feet won't come off the ground. I watch Natalie stroking Inez's hair and begging her to wake up, and it looks like Jasmine's funeral all over again. As soon as I find the strength to move closer to the cot, I place my hands over her the way Auntie did and pray the medicine works before it's too late, but her pulse feels weaker. I beg her to take some of my energy. I tell her to take as much as she needs, but she's barely breathing. "Maybe it'll help you fight through this, Inez, Please, please take it."

It's too late. We are going to lose her too. But as I take my hands off her, she stirs a little. And when she groans, Natalie checks her pulse and chokes on tears to say, "It's stronger."

Auntie comes back into the room and tells the operator on the line she doesn't need an ambulance anymore. I sway on weak legs before dropping down beside Inez to touch her forehead. It feels cooler already, and the flush is starting to come back to her cheeks, and she's not dead. Her eyes flutter open, but Auntie tells her, "Sleep, dear Inez. Save your strength."

☾ ☾ ☾

A few hours later, we lay Inez across the back seat of her mom's car. Natalie tries to help her come up with excuses for the hours she's been missing while I say goodbye to Auntie.

"If you came a minute later . . ." She stops, rubs her nose. "You're aware she almost died?"

I don't know what to say, so I say nothing at all. I almost killed one of my best friends with magic. I should've refused. Auntie sighs. "You should keep your distance from me for a while." She dumps the remaining medicine she gave Inez into the flower garden near her stoop.

"What?" I follow her steps. "Auntie, I know I made a mistake, but I didn't mean to."

"Miliani, I'm not going to be responsible for decisions like these. You said you wanted to learn, but there's too much of your mother in you."

"What do you mean?"

"Forget it," she says. "But you need to keep away. Please."

"Auntie, I need you. Jasmine's been gone too long. She needs us. And we're close—I can feel it. Things are different now. We can hear the spirits. We can—"

She shakes her head and looks out into the street. "I need to gather my thoughts. Make sure I'm still doing the right thing here."

My throat feels tight. I don't want to cry again. "I'm sorry, Auntie."

She takes my chin suddenly, pulls me close. "Dad was right. You are special, Miliani," she says. "Too special."

She heads up her stoop and shuts the door behind her.

61

INEZ

My back doesn't hurt when I breathe now. I can roll over without pain. I cry in bed, hoping Mami doesn't hear me mourning parts of myself that are lost. I'm different now. I tell myself different isn't always better, except this time it is.

But the spirits won't let me sleep. They are outlines of dead bodies on my bedsheets. They like to tell me things, call me "silly," "stupid girl." They run cold fingers along my arm until I take another Benadryl, a sleeping pill, call Mili to chant a spell, pray when we hang up.

Daylight comes through my window before I can dream of Jasmine scolding me. *Why aren't you wearing the crystal?* She lays it flat on my chest. *I'm not going to be happy till you put it on.* Dream Me does as she says, and it makes Dream Jasmine smile like a suncatcher.

I wake up knowing it's already on my neck. Did Jasmine's spirit slip it on me while I slept? I'll never know, but this is the best I've felt in days; even the spirits shift and quiet to a dull hum in the background.

62

NATALIE

It's hard to shake this heavy heart. Inez tells me she's better and insists there's no reason to feel guilty, that the miscarriage spell was her decision, but it's hard to be here with Ray and not wonder if it's wrong after she almost died. Ray tangles his legs with mine as we watch videos he took last week for a wedding. Electrician work brings in enough money for the bills, but sometimes he'll pick up a videography job on the side. From a distance, he filmed the bride leaning in and planting a kiss on the groom's ear while everybody else was busy dancing. If I inch closer to him, I can kiss his ear like that. But he palms his face to look at me, and a tingling sensation crawls up my spine before a second pair of eyes peeks at me from under his arm. They're white; they don't blink. I startle, slide back on his bed until I bump into the headboard.

The white eyes disappear, but Ray's are wide.

"What's wrong?" He sits up and looks around the room. "Did you see something?"

Did I? Or was I looking for something that'll get us through this faster. After what happened with Inez, I'm anxious as hell to pull Jasmine from the other side and lock it up after her. But who knows what's going to happen. Mili's been panicking since Lindy shut her out days ago. She thinks we're out of time.

Ray grabs my hand when I think about leaving to check in with her. To get myself together. "Tell me."

I look at him good, feel the weight of reassurance in his touch. I could tell him—he'd listen—but what I like most about our relationship is how uncomplicated it is right now. I'd rather not risk tainting it with telling him I brought a spider back to life and damn near killed my friend and now I never feel safe. Not even as I lie here beside him. I'm not sure if he's safe around me anymore either. If anyone is.

"Okay, it's okay. You don't have to tell me." He brings my hand to his lips, kisses it. "I'm guessing it was my face that spooked you anyway."

I laugh. "You're irritating."

"I try," he says, then changes direction. "How's your mom?"

"She's okay," I hurry to say, but it's a lie.

This is the first time Ray and I have spent time together since Ma came home. I've been too nervous to leave her alone, since Dev senses how unhappy she is and hasn't wanted to be around her. She might've been on drugs before, but at least she seemed happy when she was home. Yesterday, she said, "I don't need a fucking babysitter, Natalie. Get your own life," and cried between sips of a coffee. Today, I decided to give her space. She could be resting right now, watching what she wants to watch instead of pretending to be interested in what we like, or maybe she's sniffing lines of cocaine on someone's sink. The withdrawals are hitting. The elixir must not be in her system anymore.

"Well, I hope she'll be okay," I say, and clear my throat. "Can you play the video again?"

He moves to rest his head against my shoulder. "This one is boring."

"You're seeing it from your adventurous eye. Not your creative eye. The way you move seamlessly through the moments, woof." The way I can look at it and not see shadows there, pay attention to it so I'm not searching his room for ghostly faces.

"Boring," Ray says.

I'm not sure why, but I ask, "Do you feel that way about me?"

Ray lifts his head, and his brows knit. "You're far from boring."

I look at his corkboard on the wall. There are pictures of him with friends on white sand beaches, snowboarding and mountain climbing, and so many different sunsets. "You do this dope stuff in front of the camera. There's nothing I do that's even a little cool besides capturing the moments." Except taking pictures of the dead and practicing necromancy, but both are more scary than cool.

"Pretty sure the time you swam in cold-ass water in the dark counts," he says. "Not everyone's interested in hanging off a mountain with a rope and some hooks. You can be fun in other ways. I like you just fine."

"Really?"

"Really." He reaches out to touch my fro. "But if you feel that way about yourself, maybe something in you is telling you to take risks. You wanna go mountain climbing?"

"Sounds like an easy way to fall to my death, or have a heart attack."

Ray props his head up with a pillow. "How about starting with something less extreme? Call out of work and go dancing? Eat sushi?"

"A little more extreme, and something that won't leave me broke. But, yes, I can try," I say. I will, I decide. But another day. Maybe. Right now, I want to kiss Ray. So I do.

(((

Back at home, I'm quick to call Inez first. She seems strange when she answers. She doesn't speak about her brush with death or tell me not to talk about ghosts when I let her know about the white eyes in Ray's room. "Just eyes? What about the rest of the face?" She laughs, then, "You should ask Mili. I'm still only seeing shadows, and not as much as before."

When we hang up, I realize she sounded strange because she seems happy. I don't know how to feel about it, but Inez isn't the only one who seems happy today. Ma talks to me about the counselors in the program, the other people who need support, the ones who grew up in Prov. She knows someone from middle school who has been three years clean thanks to CODAC.

She even does the dishes while I clean the countertops.

"You look good today," I say.

"Mmm. You know what might make me even better? The stuff you gave me in Butler."

My insides twist. "I don't think . . ."

She turns to me, grabs both my arms with wet hands. "Would you ask Miliani's mom?"

I look down at where she's got ahold of me. "No, Ma. I'm not going to ask again."

"Oh." She smacks her lips together and lets me go.

When she turns back to the sink, an uneasy feeling gets a grip on me. I wonder if her mood would've shifted to sweet if I told her I'd get more.

63

INEZ

The first thing Dr. Baker asks at my therapy appointment is how I'm feeling about losing the pregnancy, with a direct follow-up of wondering if I need to tell my mom. I say everything is fine. There's no need to involve Mami. The fetus is gone. I've imagined telling Dr. Baker about the things my friends and I do when no one else is around. I've pictured her with a placating smile, nodding like she understands, but when the details get deeper possibly sending me off to Butler. There's no way I can tell her about a magical miscarriage spell, or how suddenly I'm feeling like myself again. Like myself—with a caveat. A change I can't quite describe, one I have yet to figure out. But I feel mostly like me again.

She plays with her pen cap. "Inez . . ."

"I don't know what to say, Dr. Baker. Do I tell you I'm seriously wondering if I ever want to be a mother? Or that I don't feel like a monster for wishing a miscarriage on myself and for being glad it's over?"

Dr. Baker purses her lips. "Are those things true?"

"Yes." I grip the obsidian crystal. It's keeping me steady. I think it's keeping the spirits from hurting me the way one of Mili's mom's wards might.

"I'm relieved," I tell Dr. Baker. Mostly anyway. There's still the fact that Aaron doesn't know I'm not pregnant anymore. "I feel relieved. Does that make me a horrible person?"

"It makes you a person, Inez," she says. "Nothing more."

"So why does it feel like you're looking at me different? My friends are too."

"Because we're looking at you like someone who had something big happen to them. We care. You can talk about how relieved you are, or you don't have to talk about it at all."

"You don't think I'm a monster for not feeling like a monster?"

"It hasn't crossed my mind once."

Dr. Baker might feel differently if she knew I used magic for a miscarriage, but her answer alleviates some of the guilt I've felt wondering if I'm steadily failing God's tests.

64

NATALIE

The one person I'm not expecting to see when I get home from work is Uncle Robb. But here he is, sitting on my kitchen counter, throwing back a beer while Ma puffs on a cigarette. The room is thick with the smell and smoke. Ma usually doesn't let him in the house. *He's a thief, and a pig,* she says. And I feel like pulling her aside to ask what the hell he's doing here, but first ventilation is required.

When I open the window, Uncle Robb pinches my side. "Don't do that," I say, and look at Ma, but she didn't seem to notice. She has caked-up blue eyeshadow on her lids, and she's smearing pink lipstick on her lips. "Are you going somewhere, Ma?"

Uncle Robb jumps down from the counter and tosses his beer can in the trash. "We're going to celebrate her homecoming."

I move closer to her and soften my voice. "Ma, the nurses said it'd be best if you stay in."

Ma puckers her lips. "Fuck the nurses. They don't get to tell me what to do anymore."

"That's right." Uncle Robb staggers over his feet. "She's not a prisoner."

Ma stands and rubs my arm. "Mommy's a big girl, Natty. You

don't have to worry about the drugs. We're only going to say hi to some old friends."

"I promise to have her home before your pretty self goes to sleep tonight," Uncle Robb says, burping and banging on his chest.

I almost tell her I'll get more elixir, but it's too late to change her mind for the night. She leaves to her room to grab a jacket, and I get it together enough to start cleaning the cigarette butts from the table. Uncle Robb snickers from behind me. I ignore him.

But then my skin prickles the way it did in Ray's room, the familiar feeling that has my eyes darting around. I can't see anything. But I can feel something behind me. "You're really filling out, little Nat. Thought you'd be sickly skinny forever, but you look nice," Uncle Robb says, and suddenly I feel something ice-cold on my elbow. It cools my whole body right before I'm yanked backward. My arm skids across the table, along the cigarette ashes, and I bump right into another body.

"What the hell, girl?" Uncle Robb grunts. He is close, too close. I turn and watch him try to reach for me before he loses his balance and stumbles into the stove. I hope it hurt him good. "Fuck. You elbowed me in the stomach."

When I find my voice, I say, "That's what you get. What were you doing up behind me?" My skin is warm everywhere. I touch my elbow, feeling a numbness there while searching the room for the ghost and also moving to put more space between me and Uncle Robb.

"Why are you so stuck-up?" He groans and rubs his back.

Ma comes out, oblivious to the ghost touching me, to my discomfort over her creepy-ass brother trying to touch me too. She's happy to sling her arm around hurt Uncle Robb, then lean over to kiss my cheek. The smell of beer on her lips lingers on my face. "Your uncle's sleeping over. Your grandmother started her drama again."

"He's what?"

She looks between me and Robb, and for a second, something protective flashes in her eyes. For one moment, she seems like my mom. "Only for a night. Right, Robb?"

"That's all I need," Uncle Robb says, and winks at me. "See you later, girl."

❨ ❨ ❨

I pack my bag, with cigarette ash still graying my arms, then call Dev's friend's house to tell him I'm sleeping out and he should too. He doesn't bother to ask why, probably planned to already. I can call Ray or Mili, but the only person I want to talk to is Leanna. She doesn't sound too happy to hear my voice, but when I tell her about Uncle Robb, she says, "Be right there."

While I wait, I wonder if the spirit was Jas and she was warning me about Uncle Robb.

❨ ❨ ❨

Ava has a plate waiting for me, and Leanna sets the guest bed with fresh sheets, but they're heading out for the night. I don't ask if Ava is also a stripper and they're going to work. I just wish they weren't leaving me alone with spirits lurking.

A few hours later, I lie in the guest bed, playing with the chain around my neck. Ma's diamond ring still shines the way it used to, but the chain is dull. It's worn and needs to be cleaned, needs some loving, like Dev said about Ma. I can't believe she left with Uncle Robb, but she did ask me for the elixir.

A couple of summers ago, she came to my room and begged me to go to the beach with her. "Come on, Natty. We'll catch the really big quahogs." She could've asked Dev or Harriet, but she wanted me. She'd needed me, but I'd already bought a ticket to an art festival. She left before I came home from the festival and didn't come back for eight days. Eight days wondering if she would've been home had I gone with her to the beach instead.

But Jasmine came over every one of those days, forcing me to tell her eight good things about myself, eight good things I've done for other people, eight things I want in life. If she was here now, she'd tell me Ma is not my responsibility, she'd say, fuck the elixir, let's put on music. This is what I try to focus on before sleep: Jasmine and me dancing again, and even the ghosts lingering in Leanna's house, so I don't wonder what Ma's drug of choice is tonight.

(((

I wake in the middle of the night to pee, and see Leanna out on the balcony. She bends to lay her head against the ledge, and she stays there until I slide open the balcony door. It makes her flinch. "Damn, Nat. I could've fallen over."

"It looked like you wanted to," I say. "Why are you out here?"

She hugs herself. "I keep having these dreams about ghosts trying to crawl inside my body. There was this ugly little kid who ripped his head off his shoulders and handed it to me."

Leanna laughs, but I'm busy trying to calm my breathing, wondering if her nightmares are a consequence of a truth spell.

"Anyway, it's ridiculous," she says, and turns back to look out over the balcony.

"It's not ridiculous," I tell her. "Sounds scary as hell."

Bugs buzz around the lights that shine down into the neighbor's yard. Even though it's dark, I can see the Hula-Hoops left out on their grass next to a swing set, the tricycle parked beside the patio. We're quiet until Leanna says, "I like my job."

This catches me off guard. "You like guys touching all over your body? You don't even like men. What about how much you hate Uncle Robb?"

"He takes what he wants without permission. That's different. I have control. There are rules. And when people get out of line, they face consequences. Still don't like men, but no job is perfect." She shrugs, and we both smile. "Natalie, I'd never encourage any-one to try it, but if it wasn't for stripping, I have no idea where I'd be now."

"Maybe you would've ended up back home with me and Dev."

"What do you want to hear? That I'm sorry I never did?" She grips the balcony rail. "I had to learn to take care of myself." She takes a beat. "I'm sorry if it felt like I abandoned you, but I also refuse to be ashamed of myself. I've worked hard not to be."

My eyes sting hearing her apology. I hold the tears back so she can really hear me when I say, "I'm not ashamed of you." Her shoulders slack. "But I'm pissed you were sneaking around, lying, the way—" I cut myself off, look out into the neighbor's yard, imagine the kids doing cartwheels and playing fetch with their dog.

"The way Ma does," Leanna finishes, frowns. "I didn't realize."

"Did you think I wouldn't love you?" I say. "And do you know how much easier it would've been with Ma, with Dev, if we were in it together?"

"I tried. I—"

"Giving me money doesn't fix everything," I say. "It sucked for me and Dev. I'm the one who tried and it sucked for me."

Leanna pushes a thumb against her cheek, bites deep. "I thought I was doing the right thing at first, keeping it from you. And then, over time, the distance, it just . . ." She trails off, braces herself against the balcony ledge. I think of the distance between me and Jasmine, how much easier it was to let it grow. I stand next to Leanna. We look out at the sky. "Natalie, if I could go back and change that part, I would."

I let myself feel it all when we fall silent. Let it sink in, and hope her words patch up parts of me. "So you're okay?"

"I'm happy," she says. "Look who I found to love."

I think of Ava and her colorful hair and her cool taste in music and how much she loves my sister. "Maybe you both can go back to school together," I joke.

Leanna shakes her head, laughs. "When will you hear back from schools?" Then she must see it on me because her big eyes get real small. "Tell me you turned in your applications."

"I . . . I can't."

"But I gave you money to pay for them. What'd you do with the money?"

"I still have it. I'll give it back to you."

"I don't want the money," she says. "I want you to have a future. Don't you want one?"

"Of course," I say. "I'll work at the bodega full-time, then apply to art school as soon as Devin graduates. Plenty of people go to college late in life."

I say it the way I've practiced, but saying it to someone else feels harder.

Leanna is surprisingly gentle. "I respect people who do, but are you really going to put off your dreams because you think I can't take care of Devin? You're not his mother."

"And neither are you, but he still needs someone."

She sighs. "You know what I think? Deep down you're scared to leave because you think leaving makes you like me. But if you were like me, you'd decide the only way to change your life is to do something. I thought art school was that for you, but bet you get caught up with that boy you think I don't know you've been sexing and let your talent rot away."

Woof. The truth spell must still be kicking. "There goes the Leanna I know."

"The Leanna who loves you," she says, and we stay on the balcony awhile in silence.

65

MILIANI

Nat talks while crushing herbs in a bowl, but I can hardly hear her because I'm trying to imagine white eyes. I wonder if they looked like Jasmine's eyes in the dream I had a while ago. Maybe it's a sign that she's losing herself.

"Like the creepy kids in *Village of the Damned*," Nat says by way of explanation.

We're close. The vibration around us is rife with energy now. I feel like I can reach through a filmy layer and grab something from the other side. I could grab Jasmine, but not without Auntie telling me how.

Natalie shakes the vial I hand her. "Do you think this has anything addictive in it?"

I continue crushing herbs in one of Mom's rice bowls. "No, but magic itself can be addicting. You know that."

"Am I wrong for giving it to her?"

"You're doing whatever it takes to help her. Isn't that what magic is for? To help people?" I believe what I'm saying, but still feel pained by Auntie's words.

"But what if it hurts them more? Look at what we did to Inez."

"We didn't mean to do that, and she got what she wanted." I regret it right after I say it, but it's too late to take back.

Natalie jerks back in her chair. "At a cost. She almost died."

"You think I don't know that?" I push the bowl away and look at her, the anger rising inside me. The fear. "We messed up, and now we might've messed things up for Jasmine too."

"That's all you can think about, huh?" Nat studies me. "Have you checked in on Inez's mental state? Do you care about me not being able to practice photography or wonder how it feels being the one surrounded by ghosts while you're protected by wards?"

This strikes me in the chest and makes the anger die out, but pride still pricks at me. "Well, we didn't do all of this for nothing." I wave my hands at the vials. "Someone has to think about Jas. Seems like I'm the only one still thinking of her."

"That's not fair." Natalie stands up. "We've all been going through it for her. We're scared all the time, and you can't even tell us when it will end. What more can you ask for?"

"That you don't see the good in magic only when it's good for you," I say. "You think I'm selfish? You and Inez haven't had a problem using magic to fix your lives. The spirits will still be here even if we can't get to Jasmine."

"You're fucked-up," Natalie says.

"And so are you. Don't you want to fix things with Jas?"

The heat burns off us and makes the air in the room feel thick like a sauna. We stare, daring the other to say something else. Natalie sighs first. Takes a seat beside me.

"You said some shitty things, but so did I," she says. "We're going to get her back."

"I'm sorry." My eyes fill with tears. "I really do need her."

Nat pulls me to her, but my heart hopes my words haven't created space between us.

66

INEZ

For the first couple of days, I thought of what to say to Aaron. *The baby is gone. Can we go back to normal? Is any part of you relieved?* But too many days have gone without him popping up or calling, and I'm pissed. I go to his house to tell him off, but his mother answers the door. She makes the same face she did months ago when she walked in and started yelling at Aaron for having strangers in her house. But she didn't care that I was kissing her son on her furniture; she was mad I'd seen her walk in with a stash of weed to sell.

Now, she opens the door a crack. "Can I help you?"

"I'm looking for Aaron. He hasn't called me in a few days."

She sucks her teeth, says, "He's in jail. Don't come here no more," and slams the door.

☾ ☾ ☾

Instead of heading home, I go to the library. Aaron's mom is lying. She doesn't want me distracting him from running the streets to help pay her bills. But I type his name in the prison database, and there it is, right in front of my face. It doesn't say he was arrested for selling drugs—it says he was charged with armed robbery. He's being held without bail. This isn't selling drugs to survive; this is something else.

The vieja behind me is waiting on me to get up from the computer, and she's all grunts and moans. She strikes the bottom of my chair with her foot at the same time the realization strikes me. This is because of the spell. I used magic to make Aaron stop selling drugs. I did this. The consequence for interfering with his God-given free will made him turn around and do something far worse. The vieja kicks the chair again. She's lucky we're in a library. She's lucky Mami taught me to respect my elders because I want to scream.

((((

Back at home, I'm eager to take a seat beside Victor on the couch while he and Mami are reading passages. She doesn't ask why I'm late coming home, and I'm thankful because I feel too heartbroken to lie. I might tell her the man who knocked me up is in jail and has no idea we aren't having a baby anymore. I might tell her because of me messing with magic, I may have condemned him to a different fate than the one originally meant for him. Mami's pleased I want to study, and I'm happy to ignore my confusion over the Bible if it means I can be with her and Victor, feeling like a part of a thing we've all shared, close to the love of God, who helped get us through the pain of Papi being deported. And right now, I hope God will look into my soul and forgive me for not knowing exactly what I need to be forgiven for. But then Victor starts to read the first passage and Mami stops him and points at my chest. "What is that?"

My body stiffens. I forgot to tuck the necklace into my shirt before coming inside. Mami stands from the big couch to get closer. "Tell me before I rip it from your neck."

"It was Jasmine's," I rush to say. "Her sister wanted me to have something of hers."

Mami's nose flares. "But I've seen people wear those before. People who pray to gods that don't exist and worship the devil."

"You know Jasmine wasn't like that, Mami. She probably thought it was pretty."

Mami exhales and backs away from me. "You're right. She was a Catholic. God rest her soul." Mami sits and smooths the page of her Bible over. "But why would she own that?"

"It's just a rock, Mami. A pretty rock."

"It is cool-looking," Victor pipes in.

Mami cuts him a look. "I understand why you have it, but do you have to wear it?"

I take it off and put it in my pocket, but the warmth I felt from wearing it starts to dissipate. There's an uptick of energy around us in an instant. I close my eyes and open them. Try to focus on Mami, on Victor, on the Bible in my lap.

Mami nods. "Read the next passage, Inez."

67

NATALIE

Uncle Robb isn't around when I get home from Mili's. Ma's splayed out on the couch, one leg hanging off while she snores and drools on her pillow. I kneel down in front of her, examine her arms for new marks, check her nose, her breathing. Everything looks good. Her breath smells like alcohol and her hair like cigarettes, but she's home. My body feels heavy when I sit back on my butt and lay my face in my hands.

"Natty?" Ma's raspy voice comes. "Are you crying?"

I use my shirt to wipe my eyes and lay my forehead against the couch. "I'm tired."

She plays with my curls. "Where'd you go last night? I was worried."

I'm always worried, I want to say. "Leanna's. Didn't really want to stay here with Robb."

She stops playing with my hair. "I'd never let him get near you."

"You've never let him stay here before." I can't keep anger out of my voice. "Why now? What changed, Ma?"

"He knows I'd kill him if he ever tried anything. He wouldn't."

"I don't want him here anymore. If he is, I'm not."

She frowns. "If you don't want him here, baby, then that's that. I'll tell him to crash someplace else."

I want to be okay with her answer, nuzzle my head against her, hug her, but I can't. "I also don't think you should be going out. You didn't answer me. What changed?"

"You gotta trust me, Natty. I'm clean. You've helped with that, baby. If it wasn't for you and that stuff you've been giving me, I don't know where I'd be right now." She laughs. "Probably still in the hospital with the undercooked meat."

I look up at her. Maybe the elixir did this. Is the reason she let Uncle Robb into our world because it made her desperate? Did I do this? I seesaw, remembering how worried and helpless I felt last night. What if she does something worse than drink without the elixir?

She touches my face, and we're back in the hospital, she's in a coma, she's not okay. I run my thumb along the vial in my pocket, and my finger sparks with a charged feeling. Without the elixir, it might get worse than Ma hanging with Uncle Robb. She might not come home at all.

I take it out and hand it to her, and she smiles like she's won the lottery.

☾ ☾ ☾

There's little space on the Mount Pleasant bleachers with ten minutes until the game starts. I squeeze somewhere up front and watch the teams huddle to go over game plans while people in the crowd scream over one another and order food from the vendors. Devin looks at me, squinted-eyed. I know he's wondering where Ma is. But he doesn't have to wonder for long because I see her standing in the door behind him. She said she wasn't going to come, but she's here, staring at me, a side smile on her face. I wave her over with a hand, but she backs into the corridor. The people next to me promise to save my seat, and I'm on my feet to get her.

When I'm in the hall, I call out to Ma as she descends a staircase. She glances at me but keeps going down. My camera hangs from the strap around my neck. I hold it to my chest and run. I chase her down two flights and into the lower level. It's dim down here and smells earthy, like mildew, but to my left I see Ma way down the corridor. She's bending over a bubbler to sip water.

I'm out of breath when I call to her again. She doesn't hear me. I jog a little. Then slow as I pass empty classrooms. The dark spaces play tricks on my peripherals.

I whisper to her when I'm close enough. My heart starts to stammer; a chill crawls up the length of my spine. Two hours ago, she wouldn't even move from the couch . . . now she's here. And she's still sipping. With deep slurping sounds. I reach out to touch her, try to keep steady, but right before my fingertips find her shoulder, someone touches mine.

I turn around and swing, my fist colliding with Devin's chest.

He grabs both my wrists. "What the hell, Nat? That hurt." I turn out of his grasp, look for Ma, but she's not there. She wasn't here. It was never her. My head spins. My chest heaves. I shake some. Devin pulls me back to him. "What's wrong?"

I straighten out, flatten my fro with both hands. "Don't scare me like that."

"Called your name a couple times, elephant ears." He smiles. I don't. "What are you doing all the way down here? There are bubblers upstairs."

"I just . . . ," I start, and look around again, still on alert. The ghosts can look like us now, but I can't understand why they'd shift to look like Ma. Are they sending me signs? Jasmine would never do something this shady. She wouldn't use Ma's face, even if she were already changing on the other side. Then I remember Mili's words and wonder if Jas would mess with me because she's angry I haven't been doing enough to bring her back. Maybe she's been messing with me all this time. Dev interrupts my thoughts with an elbow nudge.

I push past the pain in my chest. "Dev, aren't you supposed to be on the court?"

"I am. Right now. But saw you run off and was making sure you were good."

"I'm good," I say. "I'm fine."

"Where's Ma?"

I try to picture her as I'd last seen her, and not the spirit wearing her face. "She was snoring and drooling," I say, and tell it to myself again. She's alive.

Dev shrugs, but my heart breaks for him. He tucks me under his arm. I feel safer there. "She hasn't made it to a game all season. Just happy you're here."

"Me too," I say. But when we make our way back down the corridor and up the staircase, I turn my head slightly, enough to see the spirit wearing Ma's skin, until it's not.

Until it resembles a young girl, waving a small hand at me and watching us leave.

68

MILIANI

Three-way calling was made for this: comforting Inez about Aaron, comforting Natalie about the spirit shape-shifting to look like her mom. Still, neither of them can comfort me. I can do elemental magic now, my friends helped open the realms, we can anchor Jas so I can see her again. But Auntie won't even speak to me.

After hanging up, I find Mom in the kitchen crouched by the birdcage, a curious look on her face as she reaches into the cage to touch Petey's head. "Why aren't you eating, boy?"

I glance outside the window at the thick clouds and dim sky. "Maybe it's the weather."

She shuts the cage. "Hmm. Could be."

When she leaves, Octavia puts her beak through the cage and lets me touch it. I whistle for her. "Not feeling that song? I hear that. I'm not feeling anything right now." She sticks her beak through the cage again, and I whistle another.

This one flows out on its own: the familiar melody the spirit in my room was humming, the one I've caught my mom singing again and again. Octavia backs away from me. She and Petey stop moving to stare at me. I whistle a bit more and Petey cocks his head before walking over to me slowly.

"You like this one?" I bend close to the cage. When I whistle again, he hisses and darts forward for my face. He misses my cheek with his beak by half an inch, but the shock makes me stumble back and bang my hip on the kitchen table. The pain radiates up my side as I move to throw the cloth over their cage.

☾ ☾ ☾

The only part of school that doesn't feel trivial is seeing Darleny. When she stands behind me at the bubbler, I close my eyes, pretend it's Jas, then she leans over to whisper, "Time's up."

Time's up. I shiver and turn. Words spill out of me before I can stop them. "I don't have Jasmine's necklace."

Her forehead tightens. "Who said it was hers? She gave it to me years ago."

"But I thought you weren't into witchcraft? Wasn't Jas a freak to you too?"

She hugs her books close. "Don't say I didn't try to be nice."

I start to panic when she walks off, but it's too late by the time I make my body move. I turn the hall and see her by Jayson's locker. She shrugs at me before leaving him standing there, and I take large steps to get to him. *Maybe I can make this go away. Maybe I can do—*

"Don't." He cuts off my thoughts, holds up his hand.

"Jay, talk to me." I reach for him, but he's quick to put distance between us.

He slings his backpack over his shoulder and slams his locker. "You had me out here looking like a fool, telling you I'll wait, and you were in love with someone else for years."

"Jayson. But . . . but it wasn't even like that."

"What was it like?"

What was it? I was in love with Jas. I still am. I open my mouth. Nothing comes out.

He gives me a dry laugh. "See you around, Miliani."

I take a breath. I can't cry. Not now.

((((

Natalie and Inez take one look at my face, then usher me to the girls' bathroom. Nat tells a freshman to scatter and leans on the sink. "Now we're never giving her the necklace."

Inez plays with the coils of the cage, watching the crystal rattle inside. "I was dreading not having it anyway."

"He's going to hate me forever," I say, and blink back tears. "Nothing is going right."

Natalie leans forward to rub my arm. "He'll hate you for a little bit, but not forever."

"We should do a spell to make him forgive you," Inez says.

They laugh, and I do too. A few tears slip from my eyes because of it. After Inez came to us with the news of Aaron, we all agreed spells to control other people are now on the back burner until we figure out how to do them right. Natalie wonders if the truth spell is doing damage to Leanna. She's also speculated about the elixir helping the spirits shape-shift into looking like her mom, and without Auntie I can't be sure she's wrong.

"I thought you were done with magic," I say to Inez.

"I've changed my mind." Inez looks at Natalie, then back at

me. "We've come too far. I need to help Jasmine." She touches the obsidian crystal. "Feels like she's been helping me."

I move to hug her. She's been feeling so heavy lately, I try to shoulder some of it, but I also want to soak up her conviction and feel like it's still possible to help Jas. "What if we can't do it without my auntie? What if it's already too late?"

"We've done so much without her already," Inez says. "We'll figure it out."

I nod my head, will the tears to stay away. "We need to. Before Jas changes. Before—"

"We will. Don't worry." She holds me closer, then leans back in my arms. "But we *told* you to tell Jayson first."

"You had to say it, didn't you?"

"I did, but I am sorry."

☾ ☾ ☾

The last twenty minutes of class, Mrs. Elanzo lets us do whatever we'd like. Jas would insist we bunk class to go downtown and check out the shoe stores, eat pizza slices, and avoid the cops. None of it mattered really, as long as we were somewhere together. As I remember, a horrible feeling washes over me for thinking of Jasmine when Jayson can hardly look at me. I'm so caught up, my emotions a mess of things, I don't hear the phone in the classroom ring or Mrs. Elanzo call out to me, but when she comes over and taps my desk to tell me I'm being dismissed, it feels like I manifested it.

Outside the main office, Auntie Lindy is waiting for me. She's wearing square glasses with dark-black lenses, a white T-shirt, and yellow Chuck Taylors. Her hair is tied up in a topknot, and she looks like she's late for fifth period.

She looks like she came to bring me the sun.

"The receptionist is a funny lady," she says. "A little strange, but her mind is wide-open. It was too easy to sign you out without being on your emergency card."

69

MILIANI

I'm anxious. Adrenaline makes my face hot. I blink, and we're in Auntie's car. I blink, and she's still here to save me.

"After listening to your dozen voicemails," she says, "I realized there isn't any more time to dwell over your foolishness." She shoots me a serious look and starts the engine. "The spirit looking like Natalie's mother is the sign we've been waiting for."

My heart beats like it's doing double laps. I can almost feel Jasmine's cheek pressed against my chest listening to it. "Are we really going to do this?"

"We are," she says. "But there are some tasks we need to get done for it first."

☾ ☾ ☾

We drive almost forty minutes to a farm in Wakefield to buy a dozen baby chicks. The whole road smells like fresh-cut grass, manure, and wet wood. On the ride back to Providence, she makes me hold the chicks in a box on my lap. She tells me we need them for the spell to test my elemental-magic abilities, and something stirs in my chest even after she says we won't have to kill a single one.

"Why don't you calm them?"

I look down at the chicks. They're cute, but they're all chirping and making noises and climbing on top of one another, and their little heads are bobbing up and down like they're trying to find out where they're heading. "But I don't know how," I say.

"Can't you feel it?" She takes her eyes off the road to glance at me. I imagine them round and wild under the dark of her glasses. I wonder if she's powerful enough to drive by sensing the vibrations in the road. "You're much stronger now after both spells on the beach. You must know."

I do know. I feel it all around me. The energy sparks in my limbs, my toes, shoots out of my fingertips and coats the spaces around me, but I don't know what to do with it.

"Calm them," she says.

Reaching into the box to stroke their feathers is a first instinct, but this doesn't quiet them. I cradle the box and center myself. And then, after a breath, I can almost see my skin glow. Warm energy pours out of me and into the box. The chirping gets quieter and slower until it stops all at once. The baby chicks are so still I have to reach out to make sure they're still alive.

"They're restful now, that's all," says Auntie. The elation is clear in her voice. She's happy for me. She knows how close I am to getting Jasmine back. I still feel guilty because we wouldn't be here without the spell that almost killed Inez, but my body pulses, the exhilaration coursing through me. It's flooding and flowing, and I don't want it to leave.

❨ ❨ ❨

Auntie parks in front of a small house on a dead-end street. I know it's a place I've been before, as a kid with Papa. I remember the blue shutters and the garden gnomes and hiding behind the lilac bush. I hold the box tight to me while we wait for the door. A man answers it, but I don't remember him. He's hefty, with oval glasses and a head of stark-white hair. He says something in Tagalog to Auntie, but he's talking fast and I can't make out any of the words. She takes the box from me and hands it to him. He looks inside. "Ay, come. Come."

From his kitchen window, I watch him bring the chicks to his backyard. He unlocks the door on a shed and closes it behind him. He comes out a few minutes later without the box.

"Zack will get them prepared while you and your friends get what we need for the ritual," Auntie says, snipping the stem of a plant on his table and pocketing it right before he walks in.

He hands us both sugarcane sticks to chew on, then gets close to me, not touching me but examining my face. "She does resemble him. Is she similar in spirit?"

"No. She's very different."

I back away from him. "What's going on here?"

He laughs. "I see what you mean already."

Auntie taps her fingers on a chair. "Do you have some of that cayenne paste you make?"

"For who?" Zack asks. "I don't have much left and another customer already asked."

"For my sister," she says, and then Zack doesn't ask another question, just goes into his cabinet and hands Auntie a brown paper bag.

"Say hello to your mother," he says to me.

❨ ❨ ❨

On the ride home, Auntie refuses to tell me why she got cayenne paste for Mom. And I have a feeling Zack was comparing me to the boy in the pictures, the same one in Auntie's paintings. I have a feeling she has compared me to him before too. She doesn't deny this but doesn't admit it either, so I say childish things: "You never tell me anything" and "It's not fair."

Auntie pulls right into my driveway and squeezes my shoulder. "You already know, Miliani. Think. Remember." Mom comes out of the house and stares at us before heading to the yard. Auntie hands me the paper bag. "Give this to my sister, tell her it's fresh. Tell her it's from Zack, and it will help protect her."

"Protect her from who?"

"Go."

☾ ☾ ☾

Mom wipes her hands on her shirt. Her fingernails are black from the soil. She has some smudged on her cheek too. I hold out the bag and tell her it's fresh. She reaches to grab it but hesitates. "Why don't you place it on the kitchen table for me?"

"What is it, Mom?"

"Medicine." She turns her back to me. "Now do as I asked."

Inside, I take my sneakers off at the door and put the bag on the table. Then I sit on the stairs and wait for Mom to come inside. When she does, she moves with heavy feet through the kitchen. She opens the bag slowly, takes out the paste. It looks like a brownie from here. She brings it up to her nose and smells it. I try to focus on my senses so I can smell it too. I think I smell chamomile and ginger and beetroot and rotten eggs. She sits at the table and brings the brown clump to her mouth to eat. Watching makes my stomach turn, but I stay until she finishes every last bit of it, then lays her forehead on the table—her hands resting flat in front of her like she's making an offering.

I climb the stairs, confused about what I'd watched, needing air from the window, my bed, maybe to throw up. But outside my door, something pierces the skin of my bare foot. I hiss and lean against the wall to see what it was. It hurts to pull out.

It's a white shell with little brown lines, and there are more on the floor. Two small piles of them, and I know exactly what they are. A lost memory comes back in an instant.

Papa, can we play the game? You know, the one with the little shells.

They're called cowrie shells, Miliani. And the game is sungka. But your mother said it's time to go inside and get ready for bed. Maybe tomorrow.

You said that last night, Papa. Just one game.

So Papa went into the shed and took out the sungka board. It was brown and old, the wood chipped in places. But it was beautiful. The round pits filled with shells were like little bowls of fruit. *In the Philippines, we played with seeds or stones sometimes*, Papa said, setting the board on the grass and motioning for me to sit across from him. *But cowrie shells work best.*

Why do we always play outside?

I told you, playing sungka inside is bad luck. Do you want our house to burn down?

No.

Okay, then. Set your side up, and no cheating.

The cowrie shells felt perfect in my hand. Easy to pick up and put down. I wasn't very good at the game, but Papa played three rounds with me and said I was improving. We were going to play another, but Mom walked outside and told me to go to bed.

The next day, when I asked for the sungka board, Papa said Mom had bought us a new board to play with. This one was mancala, and we could play it inside. It had shiny marbles that were pretty to look at and the wood was smooth, but I missed my bowls of fruit. I missed the sungka. When I told Papa this, he said, *We play the mancala, or we don't play at all.*

I haven't seen cowrie shells since, but here they are. The missing shells. Perfectly placed in circles like they'd fit into the pits. I almost call to Mom and ask her why they're here, but I know she didn't do this. I collect all the pieces and slip them into my pockets. They feel heavy there, like they hold the weight of a spirit. Like they might burn a hole through my pocket.

I heave, lean up against the wall to catch my breath, sickness washing over me in a double wave. I can't bear to bring them inside my room so I unload them in the pot full of lilies near Mom's. But then a whoosh of energy speeds by me, grazing my cheek, stinging and scratching my skin as it goes. I shudder. My face burns.

I look around, hug myself, check to make sure the cowrie shells are still in the pot of lilies. A gash in the wall behind the pot catches my eye. I reach out to touch it. Swear it wasn't there before. I walk backward until I reach my bedroom door.

Inside, I check my mirror and find a red line on my cheek.

The spirit almost cut open my skin, but why couldn't I see it? What does it mean being the conductor of the ritual if somehow Mom is still blocking me from seeing the spirits the way Nat can?

I realize right then she must be using the sungka as a ward. I think about getting the cowrie shells, wondering if the spirit hurt me because it was sending me a sign to keep them, but I don't know if I can handle the heaviness again tonight. I'll confirm with Auntie later.

I light a black candle, but it burns out again and again.

70

NATALIE

We come back from school to a home-cooked meal: baked mac and cheese, real mashed potatoes with the skin, and buffalo chicken wings. There's even banana bread spicing up the kitchen. Devin narrows his eyes when Ma claims she's showing us love. But I'm happy to be distracted with a family dinner instead of sitting in my room, worrying over going to the cemetery with Mili tomorrow for a "ritual task."

Leanna's coming over, and Devin is excited. He starts taking the board games out of the closet and gives the kitchen table an extra wipe-down, even though Leanna's going to do it again. When he heads out of the room to wash up, I set the table and watch Ma check the food. Every time she glances back at me, I remember the ghost slurping water, staring at me, wearing Ma's face so good it took me too long to tell.

She opens the tinfoil on the baked mac. "See all that cheese bubbling up the sides?"

My stomach hurts from hunger pain. "Stop teasing me. You know Leanna takes forever."

Ma laughs. "Baby, I need more of that liquid gold. Gotta keep this good energy up."

I step back. "I told you the last one was the last one."

Ma's face contorts into an ugly, confused look. "Thought it was from her garden. She ran out of garden or something?"

The elixir is supposedly more healing than controlling, but I don't want to take any chances. Lindy denies it, but I think the elixir is connecting Mom to the other side somehow, and if the ghosts can already face-snatch her, it might get worse. Besides, I'm not Ma's drug dealer.

"Please don't ask me again," I say. "You've got the power already inside of you, Ma."

She opens her mouth, but Leanna knocks on the door.

☾ ☾ ☾

My sister's always happy around Dev, but tonight she laughs at my jokes and even at Ma's too. She doesn't stare down at her watch or try to wash the dishes before everyone is done eating. She asks me if I've been working too hard.

"Oh, Luis is a softy," Ma cuts in. "He'd never work Nat hard a day in her life."

Dev sucks his teeth. "She comes home dripping with sweat, going up high on the ladder to stock those shelves. And she works wild hours."

I swallow my food. "I ask for those wild hours. It does get hot in there, though, but Mr. Ortega hired someone to fix the air-conditioning."

"You talking about the cute boy I saw in there the other day?" Ma says. "If he wasn't so young, I'd snatch him right up."

"Gross." Dev's lip curls. "Plus, that's Natalie's boyfriend."

I almost choke on my water. Leanna leans back in her chair and wipes her buffalo-sauced hands on a napkin. "He's your boyfriend now?"

"Yes," Devin cuts in, shoving a mouth full of mac in his mouth and swallowing. "He isn't the best-looking, but he's not half-bad a ball player. He used to shoot with the old folks at the Rec sometimes."

My cheeks are already hot as hell when Ma says, "Natty, you should've said something. We could've invited him for dinner. I could've had that boy for dessert."

I groan, and Leanna hisses. "Ma, you're foul."

"Thank God I'm done eating," Dev says, scrunching his nose. And we all laugh together for the first time in years.

71

MILIANI

It rains for the second day, and the universe is opening up to allow connections with the earth. When Papa was alive, we'd sit on the ground, let the dirt soak through our jeans, let the rainwater bathe us. By his tree this morning, I did just that.

Now, I sit on the porch and watch the storm give us a show of back-to-back lightning and thunder in the sky. Energy surges through my skin as I sit here, even more so when I hold my arm off the porch and let the rain hit it. Mom sits across from me, pretending to read a book, but bites at her lip while staring at her jittering leg. I prepare myself to ask her for the sungka board. Auntie needs to take off its wards. I start in my head, then stop again. I don't want to risk Mom trying to keep me from my friends, from her sister, or somehow sabotaging the anchoring ritual when we're so close to it, but I can't do it at all if Jasmine's spirit isn't visible to me.

When I open my mouth, a loud rumble of thunder interrupts me, then lightning strikes so close I think it hit Papa's tree. Ma gasps, and as if she's had a vision, she stands to shut the screen door that swung open. But she's too late. The birds are squawking, and one of them comes outside. "Octavia," she cries. "Come here, girl."

But Octavia flies off the porch, flapping her little wet wings, and disappears into the rain. I close the house door so Petey doesn't get out too, and follow Mom off the porch. We search for Octavia in the trees in the yard, in the bushes up the street, in the sky. We scream her name over and over. I whistle as loud as I can, with two fingers the way Papa taught me.

Finally, Octavia whistles back.

We follow her songs, walking through our neighbors' yards without their permission. I climb trees to call out to her with the lightning still striking close. It feels like Octavia is whistling from somewhere up in the clouds, leading us in circles. Mom tells me to get the car keys, and we drive around for a while before she drops me home to wait in case Octavia comes back. "She'll find her way," she says.

I'm drenched, and Octavia isn't singing anymore. The wind picks up, and the sky is darker than it was. Mom pulls up an hour later, and I'm standing beneath Papa's tree. She won't look at me or talk to me. I follow her into the house, and neither of us bother to take off our shoes. We track mud across the carpet, over hardwood, making a mess on the tile kitchen floor.

Ma looks into the cage and takes a small breath. Petey isn't in it. But I find him perched on the TV stand in the living room. He pecks at me when I try to pick him up. Mom tells me to move out of the way and extends her hand to him, but he doesn't respond. A loud cry escapes from her, making Petey flinch. I use two hands to grab him and put him in his cage.

Back in the living room, I try to console Mom, but I'm scared she'll recoil at my touch. "Did you leave the cage open?" she asks.

"No, I was with you the whole time."

Her eyes dart around the room. "I made sure it was locked."

"You always do."

"I always do," she repeats, sending shivers through me. "It wasn't me. It wasn't you. It had to be . . ."

"Had to be who, Mom?"

She shakes her head, peels off her jacket, and pushes her wet hair out of her face. "She'll come home. She'll pick up on my scent and come home."

I try to keep from crying. My skin is cold. My heart hurts. "I'll fix us some tea."

"No. Call me if you hear her whistle. I'm going to get dry, then wait on the porch."

72

NATALIE

Lightness never lasts in my family. Leanna gets a call from Ma's sponsor, and none of us say a word on the ride to CODAC. The center is colorful and has big round chairs and soft rugs, and photographs on the wall of people who made it through the program.

Ma's mentor, Veronica, has a huge dimpled smile, even for bad news. "You've violated the conditions of your Butler discharge. You're supposed—"

"I remember what I signed," Ma says.

"You've missed every day this week."

"I've been busy, and it's hot in this place. Going home chafed every session, right under my boobs. Do you like sweaty boobs, Veronica? That's acceptable at the beach, but not here."

Veronica's smile comes down a notch. "We've turned on the air conditioner. I assure you it'll be cool from now on." She types some things on her computer while I try to stop my mind from running to the possible places Ma has been this week, since she hasn't been here. "If you violate again, I'll have to report it to the hospital."

Ma nods and stands. "Noted. Let's go, girls."

"Wait. You'll need to take a drug test." Veronica tries to hand

Ma a pee cup. "Get as much urine in there as you can, and you can be on your way."

Ma doesn't take it. "Today's not testing day."

"You missed the last one, so we have to be sure there isn't anything to worry about."

"You said you didn't do any drugs," Leanna pipes in. "So why are you worried, Ma?"

Ma snaps her head in Leanna's direction. "Who even told your ass to be here?"

Veronica clears her throat, puts the cap back on her Sharpie. "Donna, in this building we use kind language. If you're not feeling like yourself, you can see Mrs. Jen for some counseling."

"Just gimme the damn cup."

((((

Ma smokes a cigarette in my sister's car without permission. But Leanna looks straight ahead, doesn't even bother to roll down every window or cuss under her breath. We're all thinking of Ma's failed test and how she'll need an immediate reevaluation from Butler.

Ma tells Leanna not to come inside when she tries to park in front of our house.

Leanna grips the steering wheel so tight her knuckles turn pink. "So now that you've been caught slipping, I need permission to come in? We should talk about it."

"Not today," Ma says, and gets out. "Don't you gotta go make some dirty money?"

This cuts Leanna deep. I can see it on her face. My eyes water. It cuts me up too.

I get out of the car. "You serious, Ma? You're really going to talk to her like that?"

"Shut up," she tells me. "I'll be here for Leanna's lectures in the morning."

My sister speeds off, and Ma waves me away with a hand. She pulls out another cigarette and puffs on it hard. Harriet's looking over at us from her porch but doesn't say a thing.

73

MILIANI

Mom doesn't respond when I tell her I'm heading out. She just leans over the porch and looks up at the sky. There's an ache in my chest, leaving her like this, but we have orders from Auntie, and Jas needs me.

Natalie's no better. When we meet at the cemetery, her eyes are bloodshot, even in the dark. I hug her, stroke her hair until she stops crying about her mom's failed drug test. I promise her she did the right thing by not giving her mom more of the elixir, but I wish Inez was here. She begged off, saying she couldn't get away from her mom, but she's probably still sad about Aaron or spooked about what we have to do now. At least Nat came.

This is the first time I've seen Jasmine's grave since the funeral. Some people die in old age, ready and ripened for death, and even though it's still sad, their family leaves a warm energy to linger. That's not what I feel standing over Jasmine's headstone. I'm stricken with her family's grief. It's chaotic and unwelcoming, inhospitable. I drop to my knees on the grass, close to the dirt of her grave. Natalie puts her hand on my shoulder. "Get the shovels," I say. "Please."

The cemetery doesn't have much cover from the streets, and cops frequent Broad at these hours like they're trying to meet their ticket quota for the month. There's only one good tree, but the clouds are hiding the moonlight and we don't have to dig deep.

"What if we catch a felony?" says Nat.

"You can go if you want to. I'm doing this."

I have no time for Nat's nerves, not when we're within days of the ritual. I push myself to my feet. My legs wobble and my arms are weak, but I begin to dig. Natalie digs too.

We go until there's a hole deep enough that the soil isn't tainted by people or animals. Auntie says this soil is special, containing bits of life still on Jasmine's body when she was buried. We need to collect what remains for the ritual. We put it in mason jars, packing the soil good and tight. I think if we keep digging we can get to the casket. But Jasmine's body would be decomposing, rotting, no longer warm the way it was at her wake.

Suddenly, I'm glad we didn't have to dig too deep.

Natalie stands, offers me a hand. "Let's cover this hole before someone calls the cops."

When we're done, we sit in the dirt and catch our breath. I take Darleny's crystal from around my neck and stare at it. It was a fight to get it from Inez. She thinks Jasmine gave it to her, seems scared to be without it, but Auntie said I should wear it while digging for the soil because it might soak up some energy too. As hard as I'm trying, I feel nothing with it on.

Finally, I give it to Natalie. "Anything?"

She closes her eyes, says, "Wow. Oh, damn."

"What's it like?"

"Like I'm floating."

I tell myself it's okay if I don't feel anything as long as one of

us does, but a sting of jealousy pierces my heart until Natalie grabs
my hand and I almost feel like I'm floating too.

☾ ☾ ☾

Natalie comes with me to Auntie's, who doesn't complain about it
and sings while we help her pack the cemetery dirt into a kava plant.
These plants are often used for large-level healing of the body and
to promote good health. We work in complete quiet, using our fingers to make sure the grave dirt is mixed in perfectly with the soil
housing the plant. It takes a while because the soil is dry and rough
and we can't soak it while we work. When we're done and Auntie seems satisfied, we recite a spell in Tagalog I don't understand.
Moments like this, I feel a gap, distance. Mom, Auntie, and Uncle
Jonathan were all born in the US, but they had longer with Papa.
They had one another.

Natalie's not thrilled either. "I should know what kind of
magic I'm doing," but Auntie still doesn't bother to explain.

She washes her hands in the kitchen sink. "When it's time, you
have to burn the plant over the hill," she says to us. "If the leaves
turn blue and float off into the city, they'll find her spirit and she'll
materialize in the mirror I gave you, Miliani."

Natalie asks questions like *What shade of blue? Will her spirit come
to us in a haze? What will it smell like?*

Auntie sighs. "I forgot how annoying teenagers are. Don't you
want to be surprised?"

Nat rolls her eyes, then scratches her chin. "Can I at least use
your bathroom?"

Auntie smiles and says of course, but as soon as Natalie leaves the room, her smile fades. "Mili, after Jasmine materializes, you only have an hour to get the twin and do the spell."

I look over my shoulder to make sure Natalie is still gone. "I really hate this. Keeping secrets. The fact that we have to link them together."

She leans her hip against the counter, stares at me. "We're doing this again? Don't you want her back?"

"More than anything," I say. Heat creeps up my neck at the sad look on Auntie's face. Maybe she thinks I'm making the wrong decision. Maybe she doesn't want me to be devastated if it doesn't work. Maybe something else. I don't ask. I can't think about it.

She straightens out, looks away. "Were you able to get something else from the twin?"

I shake my head. "Are you sure the hair isn't enough?"

"Bridging the gap between them will be easier with blood or some bodily fluid."

"I wish you'd told me sooner," I say. "Darleny hardly lets me near her now."

One corner of her mouth curves. "You could kiss her. It'll be practice."

"Don't tease me." My cheeks might burn off my face. Who knows if Darleny will allow Jasmine to kiss me. If Jas will even want that. If I'll still want it. "I'll figure it out."

"Quickly. You haven't even retrieved the sungka board."

My voice catches. "Mom's bird is missing, and she hardly talks to me. Can't you do it?"

Auntie's brown eyes are deep and unsettling under this yellow light. "Us Rivera women always do whatever it takes."

Natalie comes back in the room and clears her throat. I don't know how much she heard, but Auntie doesn't look worried. Nat touches the pot and asks, "Do we burn the whole plant?"

"Even the bulb." Auntie sighs. She grew this kava herself. It's spent years in her garden.

"Thank you," I tell her. "I'm sorry we're using it up."

"You can't be sorry when you burn it. That'll take from the spell. Never feel sorry when you do any spell." Her gaze is intense. "Do you both understand?"

I nod quickly, and Natalie says, "Yes, ma'am."

74

INEZ

Natalie opens her backpack during lunch and gives me goodies from the bodega: sour gummy worms, Big League Chew, hot fries, and a bottle of orange Fanta. She hates that I drink so much soda, but she bought my favorite anyway. This is the love I need right now. We lick hot-fry sauce off our fingers and talk about Aaron while we wait for Mili.

I might not be able to see him until he's released. Whenever that will be. His sentence is still pending, and he hasn't tried to call me. If I'm able to visit him one day, will immigration court find out? I try to push down the shame of wanting to visit him in jail, finally tell him I'm no longer pregnant, make sure he's okay after what he did.

"Armed robbery, though?" Natalie says, and makes the shame bubble up all over again.

"Some people do awful shit when they're desperate," I say. "I blame his mother. Always making him feel like he has to be a provider when he's only a kid." I don't notice what I'm saying and who I'm saying it to until she stops licking her fingers. "Nat, I'm sorry."

"No, it's true," she says. "Sometimes kids who grow up like us don't have many choices. But, Inez, there's no excuse for what he did. And I know the spell we did had consequences, but I'm pretty sure we didn't force him to do anything. He still had a choice."

Nat's probably right. I've been trying to forgive myself for interfering. Aaron could've stopped and struggled, but he chose something else. "Thought you said no judging," I say to her.

"I'm making sure you see this for what it is." Natalie flicks my forehead with her cheesy finger. "I don't want to see my best friend wasting her life trying to save someone else."

"Are you practicing what you preach?"

Nat tells me she's going to try, and then we stuff our mouths with gummy worms so we can freak Miliani out when she sits down. But she's boring. "Don't choke on them," she says, and goes straight to talking about this weekend's spell.

The most important spell we'll probably ever do. I wouldn't mind if it's the last.

"Let me get this straight," I say. "If the leaves turn blue and float away and Jas appears in the mirror, that means we caught her?"

"Uh-huh."

"Then we attach her spirit to the earth and she'll be able to walk around? Live some kind of ghostly half-life?"

"Yes," Miliani says, but she doesn't look me in the eye.

I shoot Nat a look. We know she's hiding something but she's hard to talk to. I don't know if she hears us when we say we're scared of the spirits; she just wants to know if they're corporeal.

"So no blood sacrifice or conjuring other spirits to help us?"

Miliani sighs at my sarcasm. "That's it."

"Bullshit," I say, and her eyes widen. "You're keeping something from us."

"I'm not."

Natalie crosses her arms. "I heard you and Lindy whispering yesterday. There's definitely something shady going on."

She blows out a breath, lays her head back against the locker. "I have to get the sungka board from my mom," she says. "I won't be able to see Jasmine if I don't."

I exchange a frown with Natalie. "That's what has you so stressed? We'll flip the whole house if we have to."

She tells us she's been doing that, and there's nothing left but to ask her mom for it. Me and Nat nod in understanding, and I feel her pain. I'd never be able to ask Mami, either.

"What are you going to tell her?"

Mili groans. "Whatever it takes."

"You'll get it somehow," Nat says, "but I've been wondering, when we do get Jas back, what are you expecting from it?"

Mili's eyebrows knit together. "What . . . What do you mean?"

"We're worried about you, Mili," I say. "We don't know if you've come to terms with the fact that Jas will still be a spirit. You're prepared for that? It's not like you can be together."

Mili ducks her head. "I'm more prepared than you know."

I don't believe her for a second but let her reach for my soda can. She'll be sad when she's able to talk to Jasmine but still has to live life without her. I'll be sad when I have to do the same with Aaron. I ignore the tightening in my chest, take my soda from Mili, and complain she drank more than half. Nat says we're rotting our bodies from the inside. I joke we're always so close to death these days it doesn't matter. They say I'm sick, but they laugh.

Sometimes, when we have these kinds of conversations, I

wonder what it would be like to be one of those seventeen-year-old girls on TV. The ones who worry about their hair and have fights over the cutest boy in school, and roller-skate at the rink on weekends. What kinds of conversations would we be having then?

75

MILIANI

Inez keeps watch when I stop at Darleny's locker and turn the combination lock. Jas would prank Darleny sometimes: leave fake spiders and draw on Darleny's notebooks and steal her gym sneakers. I'd stand there laughing and watching and learning the combination. Never knowing I'd need it for anything. I don't have to lie much to Inez. I tell her it'll be useful if I have something of Darleny's—a living blood connection—in order to anchor Jasmine during the spell. When the lock falls open, I dig through Darleny's gym bag, take out a used tank top that's still damp with sweat, and her water bottle. Put both in my backpack.

"Hurry," Inez whispers, but I spot Darleny's brown journal on the locker shelf and something in me screams to reach for it. I flip it open, and Inez hisses. "What are you doing?"

A lot of pages are blank, but some have scattered thoughts, soccer plays, bits and pieces of started poems, and there are a few pages addressed to Jasmine. I start with the last one.

Jasmine,

I'm sorry I wasn't a better sister to you when you were here. I'm sorry for the things I said. I understand why you were looking for Miliani, but I was jealous. You were my only friend, but with her around it felt like I'd always come second. That's dramatic, right? I knew if I told you, you'd say something to me like we met before meeting Mili, we come first forever. But you changed when you started messing with Miliani, and I was scared you and I were growing too different. Tell me how to fix us. How do I fix us now? Jas, all that corny stuff they say about twins is true. I can hardly make it through fifth period without thinking of you. It's so hard to not see you there, sitting in the next row, writing those stupid spells in your notebook instead of paying attention. I've been sneaking out, sitting on the bench under the tree in the schoolyard. You remember how we used to sit there during lunch freshman year? Gossiping and joking and trading food. I don't know how I'll get through the rest of my life without you. Jasmine, you never taught me how to live . . .

I can keep reading, but this invasion of privacy is beginning to feel like too much to bear. I contain my tears, lock them inside, while I slide her journal back in its place, locking her feelings away too. I can't have a heavy heart when it's time to bring Jasmine back. Can't ever be sorry when doing a spell. And Darleny said it herself: She doesn't know how she'll get through her life without Jasmine. She'll forgive me when she realizes she doesn't have to learn to live without her sister.

"Why were you snooping through her journal?" Inez asks as we walk down the hall.

I shrug. "I couldn't help it."

Inez snorts. "You wanted to see if she's sorry for telling Jayson, huh?"

I laugh nervously. "She's not."

"You're wrong for invading her privacy," Inez says. "That's crossing the line."

"I'm wrong for a lot of things," I say.

☾ ☾ ☾

But after school, I catch up to Jayson. He pops off one of his head-phones to tell me to go away. I tell him we should talk about it, and he says we shouldn't talk about anything ever again before he gets in his car and drives away. I want to fix things with him, but there's no time. I have to let him go like I let Isobel go.

76

INEZ

At home, I'm not surprised to find Mami in the kitchen talking to Papi on the phone because she sent me for a calling card yesterday. But I am surprised she's smiling and twirling the phone cord with her finger. She looks happy and distracted; she's not even dressed for church. I'm hoping she'll forget altogether, but she glances at the clock, says, "Coño," and passes Victor the phone before hurrying upstairs. Victor lowers his voice when he goes on about his newest video game. I steal the phone from him.

Papi tells me Mami's going to visit this summer. She's been saving money for tickets and didn't say anything to either of us. The revelation makes me feel warm. I can't wait for my parents to be together again. They deserve it.

"I know you're going to be an adult soon, but I hope you'll come so I can hug you while you're still my baby."

I start crying so hard. The culmination of years without him—and mostly the past few months—while I've grown, while I've struggled, swells in my spirit. I wish he was here to hug me right now. I want to feel his love before the ritual.

Papi sounds confused at first, but then begins crying too.

"I'll always be your baby, Papi. I can't wait to see you."

77

MILIANI

The picnic table Mom and I sit at was handcrafted by Papa years ago. His tree is flourishing with the sweetest pears I've ever tasted. I don't bother washing them; Papa will take care of us without worry or fuss. We eat pears and sit in the yard in silence. Mom is even more quiet now that Octavia is gone. Last night, I caught her asleep under Papa's tree. She mumbles about sanding down the picnic table because of splinters but runs her hand along it like she's welcoming them. I tell her I'll handle it. I swallow and put down my pear core.

"Mom, I need to use the sungka." She stops eating and stares at me. "And I need you to trust me with it."

"Trust you?" Wrinkles form on her forehead. "You've done nothing lately to earn trust. I don't know what your tita is telling you, but you don't need that board and neither does she."

She stands and starts to walk away. It's so easy for her to leave me.

"What are you scared of?" I call out. "Who is the spirit you're keeping from me?"

She turns sharply, fire in her eyes, but then walks toward the garden, kneels near the planted tomatoes, and begins to dig. I come up from behind her, insistent and tired of her ignoring me.

"Is it a family member? Please speak to me." She stops digging, sticks her hands into the dirt and unearths the sungka sack. She heads to the table and pulls out the board. The cowrie shells come tumbling out too. The wind whispers things between us as she looks at me.

When I'm close, she asks, "Do you remember how to play?" I nod. "Set the board."

I hesitate before picking up the shells, but they don't burn anymore. She watches as I distribute them into the pits, says, "You could've hidden them in the pot a little better."

"I wasn't trying to hide them," I say. "I didn't know what to do with them."

"What happened when you played with Natalie?" she asks.

"The spirit was humming the song you've been singing."

She purses her lips. "And who do you think this spirit you speak of is?"

"I don't know," I say. "I thought it was Auntie's child."

Mom's brows jump high. "Lindy's too selfish to have children."

"So . . ."

"So you can go first," she says, and straightens her back. The sun gleams against her golden skin, bounces off the thick white streak in her hair. It looks like she's shimmering.

She wipes her hands on her shirt, but her fingernails are caked with dirt. Little pieces of it shed off and color the shells, blend into the pits as we play. Playing sungka with her is tricky because the rules are already a little different than mancala, and *her* rules are way different than the rules I was taught. But she's patient with me. She beats me in five games, and the sun is starting to set when she tells me to set the board again. There's something different in her eyes.

She usually looks away when I catch her staring, but now she looks at all of me: my face, my hands, my mouth when I speak. "I want you to blow on them before your first move," she says.

I do as she asked, and then the cowrie shells warm my palm. When I drop them in the bowl, she takes in a deep breath. This game is slow, careful. Mom watches my moves very closely. Mom lets me win. "Why'd you do that?" I say.

She picks up a shell. "You'll find happiness in your lifetime, my child. You'll age well." Her voice trembles with the next prediction: "God will grant you a very long life."

I am stunned by her words. "You can see that?"

She nods, brings her dirty fingers to her mouth, bites at the nails. I watch her. I don't speak. She starts to cry. "He's back. You've been doing dark magic, and you let him in."

"Who, Mom?" I reach over to take her hand. She slides it back slowly; her fingertips scrape against the picnic table. My voice grows a little higher. "Who is it?"

"Your brother."

The earth stops spinning. Everything stills. I can't breathe.

Auntie argues with the studies that say adults can't remember anything before the age of three. *That's false. We can go back, deep, and find memories from way earlier, if we try hard enough.* And I've been practicing, doing memory tricks, meditating on it, but I don't remember having a brother. Yet Mom says I was five when he died.

"He was eleven. Very thin. Small dark eyes." She collects the cowrie shells from the bowls. "Your Papa taught him how to fish using a net. He had so much energy. We were constantly moving, playing, hiking. You were small, but he'd try to show you how to use a knife. How to throw it. He'd use the trees as target practice. Never missing. He never missed."

I touch my cheek. Feel the whoosh of energy, the sting like it's fresh. I remember the gash in the wall and shudder before finding my voice. "Why don't I remember him?"

"My sister and I thought it would be easier if we helped you forget."

"Easier for me? Or easier for you?"

"Don't you dare speak to me that way." The creases in her forehead deepen. She lifts her chin at me and, with a flat tone, says, "I'm sure you've done worse messing with magic."

"I'm sorry, Mom." I shrink in my seat. "What happened to him?"

She looks like she's done sharing with me, but she isn't. "The sungka told me he would die years before he actually did. But even with knowing, being cautious, praying every day, I . . . I couldn't stop it." She swallows hard. "After he died, I used it to communicate with him."

She tells me my brother had so much promise when it came to magic, but he tripped down the stairs and lost his life. Just like that. She could feel his restless spirit, so anxious. She couldn't accept that her son would never find space; she knew wandering spirits are often the unhappiest. The angriest. When she and Auntie Lindy called upon him with the sungka, he was confused, he was scared. They kept calling to him to let him know he wasn't alone, that it was okay for him to move forward.

"But that kind of communication," she says, running her fingers along the sungka board, "gets addicting. He wanted to keep communicating with me directly, and I wanted the same. And each time we invited him more into our realm, the imbalance got bigger." She looks toward the sky, hugs herself. "Eventually, I was close enough to be able to physically feel him. Why wouldn't I want to keep it that way? I couldn't think of a reason. So I used a spell to bind him to me," she says. "So he can be with me"—her voice tilts into something like fear—"forever."

For a second, I think about the anchoring spell for Jasmine and wonder if it's the same one she used for my brother. "So why don't you seem happy about it?"

"He means well. He does," she says. "But he's sick. He's changed, and . . ." She stops, something catching her attention and making her slow-turn toward the empty spot beside her.

"Mom?" I say. "Is he here?"

She doesn't tell me. She shakes it off and starts to struggle to put the sungka board back in the sack.

"I'll do it," I say, shattering for a second. I ache to comfort her, ache for her to comfort me. But she nods and leaves for the house.

After putting away the sungka, I can't bring myself to go after her. The air feels stale now, as if the truth drained the potency right out of Papa's magic. I had a brother. A living, breathing sibling, who used to play and train, who studied magic. Someone I lost. Someone who would have altered my existence if he had survived. I think of all I've missed: having someone to lean on, to fight with, someone to love. I think of Mom getting sick, knowing now why we moved in with Papa years ago and how much more of her I might have had if things were different. How much happier we all could have been.

For a moment, I can picture it: A boy a few years older than me, helping me season the tapa while Mom fries it. The three of us in the kitchen, laughing and joking, listening to music. Mom smiling at us. Telling us she loves us. Mom kissing me on top of my head. But then the loss of him, of her, of pieces of me, hits all at once. Sprinkles of memories come back to me, but I can't tell if they are real or things I want to see.

I'll never know him. I'll never know who any of us would've been.

78

MILIANI

By the time I drag myself into the house, Mom is already busy. She's using a toothbrush to wipe lemon and herbs into the windowsills. "We need to put the wards back in place. Give me your grandfather's knife. The one you took from his room. I need it for the etchings."

How did she know? How do they always know? I take the knife from my pocket, run my thumb along the sun-and-moon symbol, hate to hand it to her, hope she'll give it back.

"Why do you want to keep him out?"

"I have to." Mom works etchings into the windowpanes. She's going so fast I'm scared she'll nick skin and won't bother to stop. "Get the anise seeds down from the top left cabinet."

"We can't close the realms, Mom. Not yet."

"I don't know what you're messing with, Miliani. But there could be extreme consequences for creating imbalances. Get me the anise. Now."

I head to the kitchen, and instead of looking in the cabinet, I call Auntie.

She picks up on the first ring. "You know," she says.

☽ ☾ ☽

I'm spreading anise seeds around the living room when Auntie comes in without knocking. Mom doesn't look at her. She lights a stick of sage.

Auntie walks over and snatches it from Mom's hand. "There's a different way."

"Your way is what made this mess in the first place."

"No," Auntie says, pointing a finger toward Mom's chest. "It was you who pushed it too far, and when you couldn't handle it, you pushed me and Dad and Jonathan away too."

"You were doing it wrong." Mom hurries to get the words out; they nearly run together. My body starts to tremble. I've wanted so bad for Mom to be open with me, to speak about magic, but not like this. "Every time you tried to sever the connection, your magic brought him closer. And after our father died, it seemed like you wouldn't leave me alone."

Auntie looks startled. "Leave you alone to do what? To create this barrier around yourself?" She gestures to the room. Her voice wavers when she says, "You gave up on magic too soon. You gave up on me." She looks at me fleetingly. I hold my breath. "Even your daughter has suffered because you didn't want to work hard enough to make it right."

Mom's nostrils flare, and I think she might launch herself at Auntie. But she looks at me and her bottom lip juts out. She hugs herself. "You don't have kids, Lindy, and you don't know what it feels like losing one, being haunted by one."

"You're right. I don't." Auntie takes one of Mom's hands in hers. This is when Mom's supposed to pull away from the touch, the way she does with me when I try. She doesn't. "But if you let me help, we can fix this without you giving up magic forever."

My heart thrums hard at the look on Mom's face when she asks how. It's thrumming harder when Auntie tells her she knows how to strip the connection. The right way.

Mom glances at me, then back at her sister. "Miliani shouldn't be here."

"We need her," Auntie says, not bothering to look my way. "She's strong. She's made the realms thin enough. We can do it now."

I feel Auntie's words like I'm coming through a bad dream. The stark deprivation of air right before realizing you're awake. I take a step back.

Mom pulls away from Auntie too. "Because you've been goading her."

"I have," Auntie admits, and it steals the rest of my oxygen. "For us."

Mom takes a good look at me and says, "Tell me what we have to do."

I can't listen to anything else. My head spins as I force my feet to move. I make it to Papa's tree and hope he'll hold me up. I have a brother. I *had* a brother. He died, and he's haunting my house, he's haunting my mom. And Auntie Lindy betrayed me.

My mind filters through memories of her. How interested in me she was the night of Jasmine's funeral, how quick she was to say she'd help. I dissect each memory until all that's left is lies. The training, the pushing for us to get stronger, all the talks about bringing Jasmine back.

Jasmine. An image of her walking a thin ledge in downtown

Providence breaks through. Me, telling her she's going to fall. Her, never listening, always wild. *No, I'll float*, she said.

If Auntie lied about why she's helping me, can we even bring Jas back? Does that mean I'll never see her again? I lose focus on my surroundings, then blink, but it's still a blur. I turn so my back is against Papa's tree, slide down until I feel earth beneath me.

☾ ☾ ☾

Light is long gone from the sky when the front door opens and Auntie walks over to tell me more lies. She reaches up to pinch one of the tree branches. I don't try to keep the tears away or try to block her from my mind. She should see and feel what she's done.

"The training, feeling a . . . bond with you, none of that was fabricated, Miliani."

"A bond founded on lies is no bond at all. You broke whatever we had," I say. "It might have been real for you, but it's not to me. Not anymore."

Her eyes widen, but she shifts them to look up at the sky. The moon hovers over us. The moon mocks me. Jasmine might not get a chance to see it again.

"Very well," Auntie says. "I knew you'd be upset. I'll accept that. It's worth it."

I feel a twinge of pain in my heart. I wasn't expecting to lose what was growing between us, but how can I trust her now? "Was anything for Jasmine real?"

"You can see with your mother the way the spell works," she says. "It's very real. But if you're asking my intentions, my focus was on helping our family."

"So *I'm* not your family?" I whisper. "You used me."

"Yes, Miliani. And I'm sorry you're hurt. But I don't regret it."

"This whole time." I start to sob. I hate it. I don't want to cry. "My friends went through with all of this . . ."

"They should be grateful. They're stronger, too, thanks to you." There's no remorse when Auntie says, "I'd do it again. It'll help heal your mother. We can be a family again. There's so much more you can learn if we're a family again."

My heart holds the word *family* close, but the rest of me remains hard when I ask why she wasn't honest from the beginning. She moves closer, squats down so we're at eye level.

"We need at least three people to complete the spell to sever the connection." She's too close. I try to look away, but she's got a lock on me. "We needed someone strong, fresh in magic, that shares our blood ties. Dad was sick by the time we tried. We couldn't use him for the spell even if we'd had the heart to. But he'll be helping us from the other side now. Your uncle Jonathan's heart was never into magic," she says. "Then you showed up at my doorstep, passionate about saving your friend, willing to widen the realms, and there it was. Someone whose heart would be in it. I didn't have to coerce you to get stronger for the spell to work."

"But—"

"You were already filled with wanting. I needed you to concentrate on that so your journey was centered. Had you known about your mother, you might've thought differently about bringing your friend back. And that grief? That grief may have taken you too long to work through. After seeing you in my home, my flesh and blood, so close I could reach out and touch you"—she almost does now but drops her hand back at her side—"I couldn't risk it. I couldn't wait any longer to be with you and my sister again."

I try to ignore the pull I feel to alleviate the tension between us. "I don't feel differently about Jasmine. I need her," I say. "What if we still want to do the anchoring? Would it work?"

"Yes," she says. "But dead things change in death. She hasn't been gone as long as your brother was, but she still might not be the girl you were in love with. It's a gamble."

Suddenly, it's easier to breathe. "But she'd be with me."

"The choice is yours, Miliani, and maybe I'd make the same one if I were you." She stands. "I need you to help me tonight."

"Why should I help you with anything?"

"Because it's for your mother." This strikes me, peels away another layer of my defense, but I'm not sold until she says, "And if you help with the severing spell, there's no doubt you'll be ready to channel the moon for the anchoring."

I swallow, ask, "What about Darleny? Will she end up like Mom?"

"It's possible, but they're identical twins. Their spirits are already intertwined. Darleny should be able to handle it better."

I can't tell if she's lying, but I have no other choice. I ask what she wants from me, and she says the mirror for seeing spirits needs to be charged with my energy for the severing spell.

"The energy will linger for your anchoring. We both win."

"It isn't a game," I say. "And I have something else to do."

"You're going to your friends."

"Stop it. You're not allowed in my head anymore."

"You're strong, but not that strong." She smirks, reaches into her pocket, and hands me the mirror. It gives me the same sinking feeling in my stomach as it did the night I saw the spirit in it. My brother's spirit. I keep it covered and tight to my chest. "Take this with you. Have your friends help you charge it."

"How did you get this? You went into my room?"

She turns and walks toward my house, calling over her shoulder, "Just get it done."

79

INEZ

Mili is a blur. She is the background to the stars over our heads. She doesn't register as a person to my mind until she says, "Can one of you say something?"

Nat and I are sitting on the steps of my porch with Mili standing below it on the sidewalk. Mami keeps parting the blinds to peek at us through the window. There's solace in the fact that she couldn't hear Mili explain the only way to bring Jasmine back is to put her spirit inside Darleny's body. Mili shuffles from side to side and sighs. I'm trying to remember breathing techniques, but Nat might not be breathing at all.

I squeeze the porch rail, trying to ground myself in my senses like Dr. Baker has told me to. Maybe the metal will absorb some of the shock. I'm surprised none of us are crying, but we're tired. I'm so tired.

Natalie dusts the pebbles off the step. "This is . . . I don't even know what it is."

I stand, pace the porch, tilt my head so Mami knows I see her. She shuts the blinds. I chance a glance at Mili, watch her lip quiver, and know it must've been hard to tell us this after she struggled with telling us about her dead brother, her mother haunted by him, and Lindy's real motives. But I don't want to see her shame, to share in any part of it. I think she should be the only one to feel it. She asks if we hate her, and I don't know how we got here. We've strayed so far from people who didn't have valid reasons to ask questions like this.

Natalie tugs at her hair, blows air from her chest. "You took away our choice, Mili."

"I asked if you'd be all in no matter what," Mili says.

"But you let us believe we were doing something good here. Something right."

"Not leaving Jasmine to wander on the other side is right. She wouldn't leave any of us."

"How do we know that?" Nat asks. "You think Jasmine was so perfect, but she wasn't, Mili. She was just a person. She hurt me sometimes. She hurt you too."

Mili's shoulders slump. She starts to cry.

"I'm sorry," Nat says, "but none of us have any idea what Jas would've done."

"I know," Mili says. "I know her."

"Well, maybe you don't know the rest of us," I say, standing up to pace the porch. "We don't even know the long-term effects of what we did to Nat's mom. To Aaron. I nearly died."

Mili has no fight left in her. She covers her face with her hands and sobs.

"Nat and I made those choices," I say, "but we might not have if we knew Jasmine would come back in someone else's body."

"That's exactly why I couldn't tell you," Mili says.

"But do you see how unfair that is?" I ask. "I was fine with letting things happen. I understood life happens. And now . . ."

Mili looks at me then, sets her jaw. "Now you can fix your life. The way you both have been doing. I'm sorry and I don't want you to hate me, but I have to fix my life too."

"I don't hate you," Nat tells her. "But you could've told us."

"Could I really?" she asks. "Would we be this close to anchoring Jas if I did? Would we have done any of the stuff we've been able to do? You both admitted you might've done things differently, and that wasn't an option. Not for me or for Jas."

I snort. I can't help it. "You're so mad at Lindy, yet you sound just like her."

The words must cut because she takes a few steps back. One more and she'll stumble into the street. She claims she's nothing like Lindy, stops, shakes her head. Now, I do feel her shame. Right in the crevices of my own soul. She tells us she's sorry, but she can't lose Jasmine. She says it over and over, and offers to do the spell alone.

"We seem to be at this crossroad a lot lately," Nat says. "What if it kills Darleny?"

"It won't kill her." Mili's eyes snap up. "I'm not a monster. You think I'm a monster?"

Nat and I don't respond. Mili bows her head. She looks like she might crumble. The crystal vibrates fast against my chest. I bring it to my lips, place small kisses on the cage. "I didn't sign up for this," I say. "But I made a promise. We all did."

"I don't think I can get down with this, though," Nat says.

"It might not kill Darleny, but we know what it did to your mom."

Mili's body shudders. She opens her mouth to speak, to defend her decision, but she says, "You're right. I can't make any promises for what it'll mean for Darleny, but I'm hoping she'll be happy to have Jasmine with her. I need to do this. I'm going to."

Nat gets up and walks down the street, stays there alone for a while, leaning against a fence. The silence between me and Mili is suffocating. I can't breathe until Natalie comes back and asks if it'll be painful when the spell hits Darleny.

Mili says it won't be, and now there's something so soft in her eyes. It gathers in me, forms a ball in my throat.

"And I won't lie to either of you again," she says.

"The whole truth?" Natalie asks.

"I promise."

We let the wind speak, the screeching of beetles, the faint sounds of Mami's music kicking on inside the house. Mili opens her backpack and takes something out of it.

"Can I ask a favor? Auntie says we need to charge this to help my mom. We'll need it for Jasmine too."

No one moves for a few minutes. No one says yes or no, but then I stand and they follow me to the side of my house. Out of sight and away from the windows. We each hold two fingers to the mirror and charge it under the moon. Natalie can't look at either of us, but she doesn't quit.

I try to recharge my heart, but it's exhausted. I miss Jasmine, but she feels close still. It feels like she has a hand on my chest and she's saying, *Steady. Be steady, Inez. We'll always be together, no matter what it looks like. Be strong. Mili needs you this time.*

My eyes burn with tears, thinking of Mili's hands over me the day I almost lost my life at Lindy's. I stare at her, but she's staring up at the moon. She closes her eyes, and I swear her entire body glows with light.

80

MILIANI

The night air feels dead, stale to match something inside of my heart. I walk up my street and see Auntie sitting on the trunk of her car. I take the mirror from my bag to give to her.

She inhales. "It's humming. You did good. Tell your friends they did good." I try to go inside, needing to get away, needing to be alone, but she says, "Your mom did the anchoring spell alone before I could stop her."

My heart drops. I'll be doing the same spell, but I'll do it better, I'll have my friends. My mind filters through images of Darleny, switches to memories of Mom, distant and crazed. Then my friends saying, *We made a promise*, but looking at me like I'm a monster.

"Your mother has been suffering for many years. Your brother's spirit was constantly changing; it conflicted with her body." She runs her hand along her car trunk. "She was scared he'd hurt you through her. She fought off thoughts of hurting you."

I cover my mouth, close my eyes. Auntie jumps down from the car and pulls my hands from my face. "Look at me. Those blackouts she had? She was trying to keep him away from you." She pauses. "Long enough to figure out how to drown out his spirit. But she would've let him take control, Miliani. She would do anything for that boy. Anything except leave you."

Tears spill down my face and land on Auntie's wrist. She doesn't move, doesn't flinch. My throat is tight and her skin is warm on mine and suddenly the sweet taste of the breeze hits me too. "She wanted to strip their connection for me?"

Auntie pulls away and takes a few steps backward. "She realized the needs of the living outweigh the needs of the dead. She made a choice. She chose you."

I swat at my tears, my heart aching to hear her say it again, but instead she tells me that without a severing spell, Mom had to put up the wards to live a seminormal life, cleanse herself every single day, and stop practicing magic. Their spirits are still entwined, bound in this realm, but without her body ripe for it, my brother lingers in the spaces Mom inhabits. She can feel him wandering the house, watching, locked inside and locked out, too, but without direct interaction and magic, his presence is weaker. The work she has done for years didn't break the connection, but it helped mute it.

"She must be so tired," I say.

Auntie frowns. "Go inside and sleep. You'll need energy for tomorrow."

81

NATALIE

It's late when I get home after charging the mirror, but sleep seems like a secondary need for my body now. The first: trying to digest the secret Mili kept from us. Wishing she told us sooner. Wishing she didn't tell us at all. I'll be part of a spell that might cost some of my soul, but I wonder how I'd feel if it was me and my sister, or me and my brother. I'm not sure if it makes it better knowing I'd give up a piece of me for them. We've crossed lines and blurred boundaries, but the price has to be steeper for using Darleny's body without her consent. Maybe afterward, the ghosts will be able to jump through my camera lens and eat my face off. Or maybe Lindy can close up the realms once Jasmine is safe on this side, and it'll finally be over.

I feel the familiar sensation in my body too late. The water in the trapping-spell jar we made at the beach begins to bubble in the corner of my room. I watch it swirl until it rises. The hair on my neck rises with it.

When it stops, my heart still beats fast. I move to get up from bed, but suddenly the jar bursts open. The glass breaks into pieces, shards flying everywhere. I scream and scoot back on my bed, shielding my face, but then a cold puff of breath tickles my ear and whispers, *Go*.

My door creaks open to reveal a dim light warming the hall-way. I should know better than act like a movie and follow spirits, especially after chasing the one who wore Ma's face, but I walk over the glass carefully and creep my way to the kitchen. There are no spirits there. Only Ma, digging inside the cabinet where I stashed the money Leanna gave me for school applications. She must've caught me checking for it one day because that's the cabinet for collecting cobwebs.

"Ma, what are you doing?" My voice trembles. "Didn't you hear me scream?"

She's dressed in a leopard skirt and a pink top with frills on the sleeves. She has a large purse on her shoulder and long black boots on her feet, even though it's probably 70 degrees tonight, even though she's supposed to be in bed sleeping. The envelope is in her hand when she comes down from the counter. "I'm going to visit some friends. Have a bad dream, Natty?"

I can't even look at her. "Visiting friends with my money?"

"I'll pay you back when my SSI check kicks in."

I make myself strong, my face as hard as possible, even though it feels like the whole of me is about to break. "Just go, Ma. Take it all and go."

She shoves the envelope in her pocket and leans to kiss me, but I turn my head. She chews on her lip, nods. "Okay, baby," she says. "I'll see you soon."

Devin is standing behind me when I shut the door on Ma. "You let her leave?"

"She was going to leave no matter what I did."

He shakes his head. "You know exactly what she's going to do with all that cash."

When he goes to his room, I lean against the counter for support, to breathe steadier breaths. Dev comes out a few minutes later to tell me Ma stole his Game Boy too.

I run to check my room, careful not to step on broken glass. My camera and my laptop are still in my backpack, and relief almost has me choking up. But she swept clear my jewelry box, leaving nothing behind but a worn-down silver bracelet. She took the watch Leanna gave me one year for Christmas and some necklaces she'll find out are real good fakes. But she'll pawn the chain with the diamond ring she gave me. I'll never see it again. I shouldn't have taken it off.

☾ ☾ ☾

I clean up the broken glass with bare hands. My eyes burn watching the sun rise through the blinds. Right now, Mili is trying to save her mom, but not even magic can save mine.

82

MILIANI

"This one is perfect for the severing," Auntie says when she brings the baby chick. "Zack says it's calmer than the rest." I have to ask again if she's going to kill it because she's a liar. She doesn't make promises because she doesn't believe in them. I have to take her word for what it's worth, which is shit lately. Mom is sitting by Papa's tree on the grass. Right where Auntie needs her. "We'll do the spell here. Dad's energy will act as a bridge to the spirit realm."

Mom reaches for the baby chick, and it stops squirming in her arms. "An animal, really?"

"That's part of what we were missing last time."

Mom puts the chick down and lets it run around. "Will we need the sungka?"

"I've found a less tricky way to communicate with him," Auntie says. I know she's talking about painting before she pulls a palette from her duffel bag. She hands me candles and makes me set them deep in the dirt under Papa's tree, then explains how we have to use the energy from the elements to enhance the spell, during which she and I will hold mirrors so we can find my brother in them.

Once we both do, we'll have to flip the mirrors toward Mom, who will handle the rest.

The sun is beating down on the grass. I imagine the neighbors looking over our fence and calling the police. "We're able to do it now?" I say. "Don't we have to wait for the moon?"

"It's a sun spell. We use night to connect with spirits, and day to break it," Auntie says. I think about all of those afternoons in her backyard, training to control sunlight. Betrayal sparks fresh, but I listen when she says, "Now stop asking questions so we can start."

Mom gets in the center of the circle of candles with the baby chick. Her hair flows loose; the streak falls forward and covers part of her face. She grips the chick, and it chirps to be let loose, until she whispers something and it calms down in her hands.

Auntie and I sit outside the circle on opposite ends, and we light the candles. I know they won't blow out unless Auntie does it herself. She has a mirror almost identical to the one she gave me, except the jagged lines run in the opposite direction. They are two pieces of a whole. She tells me to unwrap mine. My hands tremble, thinking of all the times I've used this mirror. In it now, I can see my reflection and the blue of the sky and Papa's pears and the grass.

It looks like a normal mirror until I can't stop looking at it.

"Don't stare too long," Mom warns. "Not yet."

Auntie picks up her paint palette and holds it out to Mom, who tucks the chick between her thighs before using Papa's engraved knife to slit her own palm. She then holds her hand out, past the fire and over the palette. Her blood drips with a slow trickle. Auntie slits hers next and does the same. When it's my turn, I'm embarrassed for flinching, but they hardly notice. Auntie uses a twig to mix our blood together, then digs her fingers into the ground right below Papa's tree and puts some of the dirt into the palette. She pulls out a familiar bottle with a black lid. It's the bottle I got from the botanica weeks ago. The liquid looks even more luminescent now; it reminds me of the jellyfish the night on the beach. Auntie pours it in and chants something low before she places the blindfold over her eyes.

"Lift your pant legs," she tells Mom, and leans over the circle of fire to paint symbols with our blood onto both of Mom's ankles. The symbols are intricate and go all around, forming cuffs. Auntie takes a few shallow-sounding breaths. I wonder if using her power this way hurts her. I worry that the fire is burning her skin, but her body is steady, even though her voice wavers. "I can see him so clearly now," she says, and starts to paint symbols on Mom's wrists. These ones are thicker than the ankle ones and look like a bunch of interconnected vines. When she's done, she removes the blindfold—the trap for her falling tears—and stares at Mom. But Mom looks no different. She's still stroking the chick's head, with our blood coating her skin like artwork. If the neighbors see this, they'll sell their house and move away.

The entire spell is in Tagalog. Maybe Auntie is speaking directly to my brother. Maybe he was taught what I wasn't. Or maybe she's calling on spirit guides to help. She looks at me. "Stop thinking those thoughts and use your mirror now. Focus on what you need to see."

When I touch my mirror, a surge of Inez and Natalie's energy runs through me. My body quakes until it metabolizes. I smile because it feels like they're here. In the mirror, I look for what I need to see. I look for Jasmine. I picture her standing by the fence, smiling at me, telling me she's waiting.

But it's my brother who materializes behind me, so close my heart stammers like it'll shift and collide with my sternum and rip right through my chest. I almost drop the mirror.

Auntie screams, "Stay in place. Focus."

I stare into it and see my brother reaching for my hair. A rush of cool air makes lines of goosebumps cut across my flesh. My body burns with knowing as he reaches through the mirror and touches me. His small fingers tug on pieces of my hair. His eyebrows go high, and he laughs and pinches my cheek hard. It stings, but I can hear Auntie telling me to focus. My brother doesn't look dead. He looks like a child. A child with my same eyes and my same hair and my same smile. For a few seconds, my mind clouds over and all I want is to hug him close. But then color drains from his dark eyes until they're small balls of burning sun.

It hurts to look at him.

"Keep your eyes open, Miliani," Auntie says.

Then he digs his nails into my scalp. The pain sears through me. I scream.

"Tama na," Mom yells.

I crane my neck—his nails still deep—to see Auntie hold up her mirror. She calls out to him. He lets me go, and looks toward the sky.

Auntie says, "Now, Miliani," and we flip the mirrors in Mom's direction. I crane my neck to look in Auntie's mirror, to see the way my brother is looking at Mom, smiling at her, his eyes turning brown and filling with so much love for her.

Mom turns her head to glance back and forth between my

mirror and Auntie's. She chokes on a cry when she closes her eyes, and then my brother seems to look through her and catch his own reflection in my mirror. His face falls. He stays like that for one second, two seconds, so long I almost forget what we're doing. Until Mom holds the baby chick in the air and Auntie starts to chant. I repeat what she says over and over. And we each lift a hand until we catch a piece of the sun.

The heat courses through my body; it burns until it doesn't. My brother disappears, and the chick chirps and chirps. It sounds like there is pain piercing through its body while Mom's convulses. Papa's tree starts to shimmer, but I blink back tears and the magic is gone.

Mom clutches the baby chick to her chest. "Put him back," she screams. She cries. She gets on her knees and begs. "I changed my mind, Lindy. Put him back. Please. Please."

Auntie blows out the candles on her side and crawls over to Mom. "Shh, big sister. Relax. It's all right."

Mom uses one hand to push Auntie away, still holding the chick with the other. "No. Light the candles. Please. I was wrong. I can't lose him again. I can't. Put him back."

"You're only feeling this way right now," Auntie says. "The hole will fill again. It will get better with time."

Mom sobs so hard I feel it rack my bones. "I did my job," she says. "I raised my daughter. Please, Lindy. I'll do better. He needs me. I need him, Lindy. Please. He's just a boy."

Auntie moves slow to take the baby chick from Mom's grasp and place it on the floor. The chick is twitching as it starts to move. Mom tries to reach for it, but Auntie grabs her hands and says, "He was a boy. He's not one anymore. He hasn't been for a long time, big sister."

Mom fights and begs, and howls so loud I wonder if we made a mistake, until Auntie locks eyes with her. "It's over now. Shh. You're free. You need to let him be free too." She says this in that soft, hypnotic voice I now know is magic. Mom's tears are steady and she whimpers some, but she grows quiet and still. She lets Auntie pull her in, hug her close. And when Auntie starts singing softly, a song in Tagalog I suddenly remember Papa singing to me when I was a child, I realize it's the same song Mom and my brother were singing. Everything comes back to its beginnings.

I'm shaking when I drop the mirror in the grass. My head is still sore. It's pounding, and I'm scared to touch it because I know there's bits of blood, bits of me missing.

Mom's shoulders relax. Auntie pulls back enough to take the bowl of water and salt she mixed up and use it to wash the blood off Mom's ankles, her wrists.

She kisses the cut on Mom's palm and cleans it too.

The chick chirps again. I take a deep breath and reach out for it. The energy is unmistakable. It isn't just a baby chick anymore. My brother's spirit found space, but I wish it wasn't like this.

"It had to be done, Miliani." Auntie spares a glance at me while Mom rocks and hums Papa's song to herself. "When it dies of natural causes, the energy of your brother's spirit will freely settle in the place it dies. I just have to make sure it's far from here."

I stroke the chick's fur. It twitches under my touch. "So he'll suffer until then?"

"It was the only way."

Pain crawls through my bones, over my soul, and the only solace comes when I crawl over to Mom and reach for her hand. She stops rocking and humming to look at me, and she doesn't pull away. She laces our fingers and holds me too.

83

MILIANI

Auntie kneels beside the couch where Mom's resting. "Take some time to heal," she tells her sister, "but I'll be waiting. We can go to the Philippines. Meet more of Dad's family. Get Miliani's passport and finally show her how beautiful it is there. We can all learn new things."

The energy in our house is already changing. It feels like something has lifted from this space. There are invisible walls coming down around us. It is open.

"Thank you for everything, Lindy." Mom reaches up and strokes Auntie's jaw. "But I don't know if I'll ever practice again."

Auntie pulls back, leaving Mom's hand suspended in air. "You're feeling unwell. That's all. It'll get better soon."

"You're right," Mom says. "But I know the hole inside of me won't be filled by magic."

Auntie is quiet for a long time before she stands up and leaves without a word.

I follow her to the car and watch her fumble with her keys. My cool, smooth Auntie Lindy, who's always careful and calculated, fumbling with her keys.

"Miliani, I don't want to hear your thoughts. Go take care of your mother. Her body will go through an adjustment period."

I'm still sore in my spirit over what's happened. From Inez and the miscarriage spell that almost cost her life, to Natalie's mom becoming addicted to the magic I provided, to Mom being haunted by her own son and suffering because I began practicing spiritual magic around her. So much has happened in a short time. My body feels the weeks like they are years.

I'm still sore over Auntie's lies, but I think of how much she missed her sister. My mind circles over how much Darleny misses her sister too. All the thoughts weigh me down and confuse me but make the thought of losing Auntie too much to handle. I wrap my arms around her from behind. She tenses but doesn't pull away. She still has me.

She places her hands over mine. I can hear the tears strangle her voice. "If you knew all I have done in my lifetime. If you knew . . ." Her words trail off as she seems to remember things I've never seen, feel pain I've never felt. "You're more than I deserve, kid."

I kiss her on the cheek, but she pulls away from me.

"You'll have to do the anchoring spell tonight," she says. "The realms can't be open like this for long. It'll cause too much chaos. I'll give you until dawn before I close them."

My chest tightens. "But—"

"The severing spell has made you even stronger," she says, and turns to cup my face. "Listen to yourself. Move smart. If you want to do the anchoring spell, it has to be done now."

She gets in her car, and I watch her drive away.

C (C

Mom groans on the couch. She sweats and throws up in a bucket. Her body burns like she has the flu. Auntie said she'd go through changes, but I worry after watching Inez bleeding out on Auntie's cot. Mom lets me lay a cool rag on her forehead and closes her eyes at my touch.

My body is a conductor. It's a silver cage; it's copper wire. I am breathing out gold.

Mom stops shaking from chills when I clasp her arm.

"I have to go," I say. "But I'll be back." I'll have her when I do. I'll have Jasmine too.

"Be careful," she says through clattering teeth, shaking as soon as I move away from her.

84

INEZ

We walk through Uni Park and up the worn stone path. Mili swears she didn't know we'd have to do the ritual tonight, but I'm not even mad. If we're going to do this, I'd rather do it now. The moon is at its apex when we reach the top of the hill with the kava plant. Lindy said because Uni Hill is the highest point in Providence, it's naturally going to soak more of the moon's energy at night, which will help with the ritual. I try to imagine how pretty it'll be when the kava leaves burn blue and float off into Prov to collect Jas's spirit. I do it because thinking of anything else feels awful, and feeling awful seems to be the general mood among us right now.

Natalie's been biting her nails, picking at the skin around them, and giving half-hearted smiles, and Mili has hardly looked at us. Maybe it's guilt. Probably it's a whole lot of nerves worrying over it not working. But my mind jumps back to years ago in the cemetery. Knowing we'd never bring Miliani's grandpa back from the dead and trying anyway. This time, with a different spell—and after all we've been able to pull off—I know it can work.

I turn to Mili and say, "We'll deal with guilt and any other bad shit after we're able to talk with our best friend again, okay?"

Mili looks at me sharply. Her lips are tight, but she slowly nods.

I turn to Nat. "Okay?"

"Okay," Nat says. "After."

"Watch Jasmine swoop right in and make things better for Darleny too," I tell them. I'm also telling myself one more time, after countless times the past two days. The moon is a bright quarter over our heads, giving off a yellow glow and lighting some of the dark spaces between the trees surrounding us. "Are we ready?"

Mili turns to stare off at the path, and Nat tilts her head. "Still worried about your mom?" Natalie says.

"She looked so awful." Mili frowns. "I left her."

I set the kava plant on a flat rock. "She'll be okay," I say, but it's a half-empty promise. We only have Lindy's word.

"Yeah." Mili gives me a tight smile. "Yeah. And so will Jasmine." She bends down to shuffle through her backpack, pulling out the mirror wrapped in its cloth and setting it near the kava plant. She goes through her bag again. Carefully at first, but soon her searching becomes frantic, and when she doesn't find what she was looking for, she stands and kicks her backpack.

"Where's the lighter?" She pats the front pockets of her jeans. Her back ones. She looks at us suspiciously. "I had it. Where the hell is it?"

Natalie takes a step with an outstretched hand. "You told me to hold it."

"Oh," Mili says, taking it. "I'm sorry. I'm sorry."

"It's okay, Mili. We're all nervous," I tell her.

Mili shakes her head and walks over to the rock. "I'm not nervous. I'm ready," she says, and looks at us once to make sure we're ready too. We're as ready as we can be. "Okay." She flicks the lighter and extends her hand to the plant.

Then she hesitates. From where I stand, even though it's dark, I can see her bottom lip poke out. She begins to cry. "If I didn't leave Jasmine's house that night, she wouldn't have gone out looking for me. She wouldn't have been on the road while I was at this very spot. She'd be alive."

"Mili," Natalie says, moving close to touch her arm. "Don't talk like that. You can't blame yourself. It wasn't your fault."

I imagined what it would be like when Miliani finally decided to grieve, but I never imagined it would be like this. Here. Now. She grasps the lighter and hugs herself, sobbing. "It *is* my fault. We wouldn't be standing here right now if it wasn't for me."

"Come on," says Nat, rubbing her arm. "Don't do this to yourself. You can't."

"I don't deserve your pity. I've been so damn selfish." Mili says the words like it's the first time she's realized it. She shakes her head. Shakes Nat off. "We can't go through with this."

I'm too tired to hold my tongue. "Are you serious? After everything we've done to get here? After everything we've sacrificed? Pull yourself together and burn the plant. You don't get to feel guilty. Not right now. We deserve this. Jasmine deserves this."

"I don't deserve anything." Mili holds herself.

"Why are you talking like that?" I say. "We know the truth now. We're with you on this."

"I'm a horrible person," she says. "I'm a monster for wanting this after I've seen what it did to my mom. What if that happens to Darleny? I told you I'd tell the whole truth, and I'm going to. My mom . . ." Her voice cracks. "My mom has been sick for years. And today, I left her like that to come here. I left her alone, when she needs me. I'm so selfish. But I just . . . I wanted to hold Jas again, you know?"

Natalie steps closer. "We know. We know. It's okay."

"No. It's not." Mili clears her throat. "If either of you would've seen the way this has hurt my mom . . . Darleny doesn't deserve it."

"But you said it wouldn't be the same," Natalie offers.

"I said that. Auntie Lindy said that. But I can't trust her or myself. I can't promise it won't be bad for Darleny." She pauses, head down. "I've been hurting everyone. Even the both of you. I didn't know. I didn't know I was putting the dead before the living."

Mili drops the lighter to the ground, and her knees go with it. "She's dead. Jasmine is dead." And she cries hard now. The kind of crying that starts in your chest and comes out from some deep part of you. I can't stop my own tears, seeing her this way. She held me in the bathroom not long ago, and I want to hold her too. I want to do more than that. I want to take the pain.

But Natalie kneels down beside her first. She hugs Mili from behind. "You're not a monster," she says over and over, but Miliani doesn't stop crying.

I think of Mili's reassuring eyes the day on the beach before she helped push me down into dark water. I run a finger over my left palm, the skin slightly serrated, the scar lying on top of another scar. A promise on top of another promise. Suddenly, there's only one thing I can do.

"Fuck this," I say. "We made a pact. We said no matter what." Natalie shifts, and Mili's eyes lock with mine. I pick up the lighter from the ground. "If you're a monster, so am I."

Before I can worry about what God will think, I set the plant on fire.

"Inez," Miliani screams. "What did you do?"

She pulls free from Natalie and scrambles to her feet to try to get to the plant, but it's already too far gone. When she bends near the rock, wide-eyed and pulling at her hair, the pain claws its way up my throat. The smell of burning fills my nose while the plant starts to flake off. It's so hard to breathe. Maybe God will punish me by killing me right here.

Mili lifts the mirror from the rock and holds it up into the air, her fingers shaking as she breathes hard.

The leaves burn quick, but they don't turn blue. They don't fly away in the wind. Nothing magical happens.

Miliani clings to the mirror, waiting to see Jasmine's spirit materialize inside of it. Her hand is unsteady, and Natalie and I get behind her for support. The mirror stills, and Mili gasps as she looks deep into it and sees herself, then me and Natalie staring back at her. Her face contorts from confusion to pain. I feel my face mimic hers as she drops her arm to her side. She squeezes the mirror so hard it cuts into her flesh.

Natalie and I catch her body before it falls. We hold her while she screams, crying Jasmine's name until she can't cry anymore.

And we all watch as the kava plant burns down to nothing in front of us.

85

MILIANI

I am a beacon. My body calls to blue jays, makes cicadas spring from the earth to be close. It makes the grass grow toward me and the wind whisper against my skin. But it won't bring Jasmine's spirit to me. I am on the Hill, searching Providence for signs, and feel the vibrations of her footsteps. My body is a magnet, but she'd find me even if it wasn't.

"Why are you up here alone? You should grieve with your friends," Auntie says.

I am tired, too drained to hide truths. She knows that being with them means accepting we'll never be with Jasmine again. I don't have to say it. She drops down beside me on the grass. We're shoulder to shoulder, and it aches bad and it aches good to be this close to someone right now.

Auntie tells me she had an inkling Jas had already found space when she couldn't feel any residue of her spirit in the grave soil.

It doesn't hurt enough looking up at the sun. "I wish I had known. You should have—"

She tilts her head to catch my attention. "Had I told you she might've found space, would you have listened and moved on?"

"I might have."

"You wouldn't have." She digs her fingernails into the dirt below. "But now you will."

(☾ (

Mom tells me Papa's room is as much mine as any other room in the house from now on. I consider calling Natalie and Inez to ask if they'd go through boxes with me, but I'm not ready to face them. For them to hug me and tell me I still have them. So I comb through his closet myself, search like there's secret passageways to different dimensions, but only find a pack of lint rollers and a tapestry from the Philippines. It's burgundy and yellow, and on the third night I lay it out on Papa's floor and fall asleep. Jasmine doesn't come to me in my dreams. I wake while it's still dark, with a blanket over me and a pillow under my head, and go back to sleep thinking of Mom's face.

(☾ (

In the morning, we eat nothing but garlic rice because we're tired of eggs. Mom's energy is shifting, same as our house; it's lighter and open. She looks into my face more and plays with Petey a lot. She insists that I help her cook.

"Mom, how do you know where a person found space after they died?"

She looks up at me. "Is this about Jasmine?"

Hearing Mom say her name with such softness makes it feel like she's never even said it before. It also makes my face warm.

"She found space," I say, "but I wish I knew where so I could visit her sometimes. The way we get to sit with Papa."

"Hmm. It's hard to know," Mom says, forming a ball of rice with her hand. "You'd have to search places she loved, objects she found important. You'd feel it if you found it, but some people search forever and never find their loved ones. Her spirit could've gone off into the ocean, and then you'd never know because of the way the moon pulls it."

My stomach sinks. "What should I do now? Let her go?"

She puts the rice ball down, examines me. "I hope you can, very soon, but I can't tell you what to do. There is no right or wrong way to go about these things, but I think you should know sometimes a person's spirit is resting closer to you than you think. Maybe you weren't looking hard enough before."

Right after she says it, the doorbell rings. She goes to answer it while I sit with her words, but then I hear her cry out from the living room. Someone is talking and I don't recognize the voice. I rush to get to her, but freeze in the doorway. Our neighbor from up the street has a cage in his hand, and he's telling Mom he found Octavia hiding out in the tree behind his shed.

She turns to look at me and, for a second, my heart is her heart. We feel the impossibility, then the knowing, then the joy like we are one.

86

NATALIE

Three days after we fail to bring Jasmine back, I find myself on Harriet's porch, sitting on my butt while she braids my hair. *Buncha naps*, she repeats, but never stops braiding. I need to be near someone who loves me right now, but when silence sets, I get hit with knowing Jas is truly gone, and feeling like Mili might be gone too. Even Inez is distant. She's probably battling guilt, or maybe she's just devastated. But I worry they're pushing me away unintentionally because I don't deserve to grieve the same as them.

I'm happy Harriet can't let the silence rock long. "Your mama has a good heart, but there's nothing you can do for her anymore."

I grit my teeth to help dull the pain of Harriet's tugging fingers, of her words, and feel a lump in my throat. "Doesn't God teach us not to give up on people?"

"He also teaches us to know when it's time to leave things in his hands, baby."

"Is that what you're doing with Leanna? Because it feels like you could've tried harder before you gave up on her. Maybe you can show her you still love her."

"She knows I still love her." Harriet raises her voice. "I've prayed on that enough."

"She doesn't know. Praying isn't going to fix this one," I say, and Harriet sucks her teeth and pulls my hair tight. "Ouch. You're going to rip out my edges."

She loosens her grip. "Maybe I'll get some holy water for her."

"Harriet."

"I'll consider talking to her, but if she rolls those big bug eyes, I'm snatching her hair harder than this. And it won't be pretty."

"That's fair."

I blow out a breath. "Do you think my mom's going to die?"

She stops braiding and rests her hands on my head. "We're all going to die."

"I know," I say. "But I'm worried about her."

"I'm worried 'bout her, too, but all we can do now is pray."

My eyes well up. "Can we, please? Right now?"

I want to believe there's a path forward for me. Life might not make much sense now, but there's space somewhere for me, and I'm going to find it.

"Of course. You can read from my Bible while I braid." She hands it to me and tells me what page to flip to. I smooth the pages like I've seen her do countless times.

While we pray out loud for Ma, I pray on the inside too. I hope with all my heart I'll be able to grieve alongside Inez and Mili, or accept it if they feel that particular space doesn't belong to me.

(((

Leanna and I sit in the living room, looking through old pictures in the albums Ma keeps under the coffee table. There's so many of us. Brown-skinned babies with ice-cream cones, jumping rope, and blowing bubbles. There are Polaroid pictures too. They're all of feet. Mostly mine. I had no idea Ma kept these.

"I was jealous Ma bought you that camera," Leanna says. "We went to a pawnshop one day. She pawned half her jewelry to get enough money for your birthday. You were always her favorite."

"That's not true."

Leanna rolls her eyes and picks up one of the Polaroids. "Guess she saw something in you from the beginning. It's the best thing she's ever done for any of us. These, though, this pack of film, was just a waste of her money. Look at those crusty feet."

I lean over to look. "Pretty sure those are your crusty feet."

"Definitely," she says. And then, "Ma was never going to go back to the facility. You know that, right?"

"Yeah," I say. "I know."

❨ ❨ ❨

When my sister leaves, I sit by my bedroom window and take out a vial of elixir. I know Ma isn't coming back this time. She has enough cash to sustain her habit for a while if she's smart. I lift the vial to my mouth and take a sip. It tastes like cilantro and beans in some kind of bitter soup. I wait an hour, two hours. I feel nothing. Maybe there's no reason for me to feel anything because I don't have an addiction, or maybe it works like manifestation and if you think you need to be healed, then you'll be healed. I lift the screen on my window, picture Jas beside me with a hand on my knee as I dump the vial out. *Be brave*, she says, and I swear I hear the elixir splatter against the concrete three stories down.

When I turn to look for Jas, she's already gone, but the cordless phone on my bed rings.

"I miss you." Inez's voice is low on the line. "And I think we need to talk."

87

MILIANI

I'm scared to face my friends. It's almost been a week since we watched the kava plant burn together. How can I say being with them now might feel like I'm betraying Jasmine? But worse than seeing them in school is knowing I'll see Darleny wearing a face that'll haunt me until I graduate. I don't want her to look at me. I don't want her to ever speak to me again.

I find my friends by the lockers, and they crush me in a hug and go on about how worried they were. Nat stopped by yesterday, but my mom said I was resting. I wasn't, but I don't tell them that. Inez says, "We're happy you came," and my stomach sinks because I'm not happy.

Nat plays with the power switch on her camera. "We're here if you wanna talk about it."

I lie and say we will, then, "Inez, where's the necklace? I need to give it back to Darleny. I don't want her looking for other ways to ruin my life." Nat shoots Inez a look and bites her lip.

The bell rings, and Inez says, "That's part of the reason we've been calling so much. We've been talking." She stops, exhales. "What if Jasmine found space in the crystal?"

I narrow my eyes, laugh a little. "What?"

Students pass by us to get to class, and it feels like the whole world is shuffling by.

Inez lowers her voice. "The dreams, Mili, they seem so real. And it always feels like she's with me, protecting me from the spirits, when I have it on. Is that what it feels like when you're next to your Papa's tree?"

I feel a twinge in my chest. Heat bubbles through my body. "It is, but why would she reach out to tell you to wear the crystal and not me?"

Natalie interjects. "She didn't reach out to me either. But I guess I'm the last person she'd want to have it." Then quickly, "Mili, maybe she didn't want to keep you stuck."

A sting of guilt goes through me, remembering the things I said to Nat about her needing to make things right with Jas. Now, she never can. "That's not true. If some of her energy is in the crystal, she let you feel her; she wanted you to float too."

She smiles a little, then moves closer. Nat and I have mastered the dance of easing each other's pain. "Now that you know she's found space, maybe it'll feel different."

The room hasn't stopped spinning; my fingers flutter around my backpack strap. I've been around the crystal this whole time and felt nothing at all. "I can try. Inez, where is it?"

Inez sighs, reaches into her pocket, and pulls the crystal from it. Her hand is shaking as she holds it. "I don't want to let it go," she says. "But I think Jas protected me from spirits when I was pregnant and while I was weak after the spell on the beach. She can rest now." She kisses the cage, tears in her eyes. "We don't have to give it back to Darleny, regardless, you know?"

"We should," I say. "You know that."

Inez nods and hands it over. Nat looks from her to me. "Maybe we can come over tonight. Help you try to figure it out."

Inez looks hopeful, but I shake my head. "Think I need to be alone with it."

I can see the hurt flash on their faces, but I appreciate it when Natalie reaches out to tug my hair. "Would be like Jasmine to find space in a kind of crystal she didn't even like, just to make a point." They think this is funny, but I still feel pained by the theory.

Then Inez asks, "Do you think she went in there to be close to her sister? To protect her?"

My eyes start to sting. Darleny *was* wearing it the night of the accident. Her journal entry flashes in my mind, her writing about having to spend the rest of her life without her twin. Maybe Jas found her own way of telling Darleny she wouldn't have to.

88

INEZ

"Do you believe in God, Dr. Baker?"

She sits back on her blue suede chair and smooths out the fabric of the arm. "The logical way to do this would be to bounce the question back. Ask if you're struggling with your belief because this is your therapy session and not mine," she says. "But, yes. I think there's something or someone up there watching us."

I wish I could tell Dr. Baker about Jasmine finding space and how I keep wondering if that means part of her is in the crystal and part is in heaven, too, but I ask, "Does your job make you feel that way more or less?" She bites on the cap of her pen. "Don't worry. It's confidential."

She laughs. "That's a tough one because both. But I'd say most times, I leave here believing a little less. The things I've seen and heard . . ." She takes a deep breath. "Are you believing in God a little less these days?"

"You said you wouldn't do the logical thing," I say.

"I implied I'd answer the question first. Now it's your turn."

"I still believe in God," I tell her, fixing my eyes on the wallpaper behind her. "But sometimes, I hope God isn't the same God my mom believes in."

"Why is that?"

"Maybe it would make God a little more like the rest of us."

"Imperfect?"

"Really fucked but trying," I say, and shrug. "And a little more forgiving too."

"That would be nice," Dr. Baker says, tilting her head at me, waiting awhile before shifting to jot some notes down in her book. The session is usually over when she does this, but she never rushes me out. I stay for an extra minute, wondering how I would've felt about myself if the leaves of the plant did turn blue and float away.

I touch my neck where the crystal should be and hope it didn't hurt Mili too much to hear me say I still felt close to Jas when she doesn't feel her at all. Maybe she'll be able to feel something now. I want that for her, but it's still hard knowing I won't anymore. When will it be okay to not feel her comfort close again? Even if God is exactly as I was raised to know, I pray there's still a place for me in heaven next to Jasmine when I die.

☾ ☾ ☾

Mami and I are on our hands and knees polishing the living room floor, like they've probably got Aaron doing in prison. The phone rings, and my heart races. Maybe it's him. But Victor is on his feet already because he was dusting the blinds, so he goes to answer it. A few seconds later, he peeks his head in and tells me it's Mili. I fight off disappointment that it's not Aaron because I've been waiting to hear from Mili since I gave her the crystal yesterday.

Victor hands me the phone when I'm in the kitchen. "I'll go help Mami with the floor," he says.

"Finally," I say into the phone. "I've been worried. You know I hate to worry."

"I'm sorry, babe. I know," Aaron says. "I'm so sorry."

This isn't a dream. It's real. Aaron is on the line, and I need to contain myself because Mami is in the next room. His voice breaks as he talks to me. He's a horrible person, he tells me. He loves me. His little brothers. If he could change it, he would. I ask how long we have. He says a few minutes. But it only takes Mami one to come tell me to hang up and get back to cleaning. Aaron hears her and his intake of breath sounds weighted with tears.

I touch my neck, forget the crystal is no longer with me. But I stand strong, chin high, and tell Mami, "I'll be there soon. This call is important," like Jasmine would tell me to.

For a second, Mami looks like she'll snatch the phone out of my hand and beat me with it. But then she goes back to the living room.

I'm unable to hold my tears any longer. "Are you still there?"

"I'm still here, babe."

"I miss you," I tell him. "I miss you so much."

"I miss you too. I'm sorry. I was scared you'd hate me."

My stomach clenches. "I don't, but I hope you know how wrong it was."

"I'm so ashamed," he says, and I let the silence hang between us even though seconds are leaving us. He should be ashamed. But that doesn't stop me from loving him or wanting to believe him when he says, "I'll be better when they let me out. I promise."

"I really hope so." I lean up against the wall, wanting to tell him about the baby but knowing I can't risk saying it with Mami probably trying to listen in.

Then he asks, "How's our baby?"

"Gone. I lost it."

"Oh God, Inez. I should be there. You shouldn't be alone. Are you okay?"

"I am," I say, because it's true. "Even better now. I was so worried about you."

Aaron tells me he can't talk much longer. "Will we be okay after what I did, Inez?"

I know how loaded that question is. He's not just asking if I can forgive him or trust that it was a bad mistake, he's also asking if I can be with him because I'm supposed to sponsor Papi. Aaron doesn't even know I have no idea when that will be now. I bite my lip and play with the telephone cord, not ready to answer his question—for him or for me.

"I don't know. But I really do love you."

"I really do love you too," he says, voice lighter, before the line goes dead.

I'm so thankful for the little time we had. I'm not even upset we didn't get to say goodbye. I remind myself to thank Victor later, and go help him and Mami with the floors.

89

NATALIE

It's Devin's last game of the season. He's in the locker room, sitting on the bench with his face in his hands. I know he's crying because Ma isn't here. I rub his back. I tell him his team is waiting. He says, "I don't care. Fuck this game."

"Hey, hey. It's okay to cry, but don't you dare give up on what you love. You're the one that taught me life keeps moving even when you feel like it's gotta stay still. Ma's not here, but I am. You hear me?" I mush his face between my hands. "Don't let her take this from you."

He moves out of my grasp. Sobs bend his back for a bit. He sucks in a breath. Turns to face me. "I love you, Natty."

Hearing him call me what Ma does makes me cry too, but I wrap my arms around him and bring him close. "And I love you, Dev. Always." He usually seems so big next to me, but right now he's my baby brother. "How long do you need?"

"A few minutes," he says. "Just a few."

I kiss his head. "I'll be waiting for you in the bleachers with my camera, so play a good game or I'll catch you slipping."

He laughs, wipes his nose with his jersey. "Sisters are annoying."

❨ ❨ ❨

When I get to the bleachers, Leanna's there with her purse on the seat she saved me. She has on a shirt with Dev's number on the front. I make fun of her some, but it makes me proud to have her here. Dev comes out, and his team huddles around him. I bet they're comforting him in their own way. The court buzzer goes off, and he looks back at us and he smiles big.

❨ ❨ ❨

After Leanna takes us out to celebrate Dev's big win, she sits at our kitchen table and sorts the house bills. I take deep breaths while standing in front of her, reminding myself of the talk I had with Ray about taking risks. She looks up when I pull letters out of my bag and lay them down in front of her. She picks all six of them up, but after reading the first one, she gasps so hard tears spring into my eyes.

"Oh my God, Natalie," she says, spreading them over the table. "These are all acceptances?" I don't answer. She looks up at me. "How'd you pay for apps?"

"Worked extra hours at the bodega," I say. "And some schools waived the fees with proof of low income."

She bites the side of her cheek for a moment. "Why didn't you tell me you applied?"

"I didn't think it would matter," I say, "but I want to go to art school. Tell me how we can make this happen. Tell me if it's possible."

Leanna puts down the letters and gets up from the table to hug me. She cries and I cry, and the hug feels like I've needed it all my life. "You're going to art school, Natalie. You don't have to worry about a thing."

❲ ❲ ❲

The plan is to move Dev in with Leanna as soon as summer hits. Harriet offered her spare bedroom for whenever he needs to be closer to school for early games. Dev doesn't complain about the move, tells everyone his big sis is going to RISD, even though I haven't decided on a school yet. Mr. Ortega hands me a bonus check to help me pay for freshman year's books. It feels like everyone's making sacrifices for me. It's so heavy and scary I want to change my mind. Decline my acceptances to take pictures in my bedroom with the blue carpet and the wooden walls and the window that looks out at Harriet's porch.

❲ ❲ ❲

Newport Bridge looks different when you're not in a car. Ray lets me hold his hand real tight as we glance over the edge. Down, down, down into the water. The wind blows and takes my air supply with it. I wish my friends were here with me. I wish they could see me doing something wild. I let go of Ray to hold the railing. "Okay, this isn't so bad."

"We could've started with a smaller bridge," he says.

"No. I got this."

Ray pulls out the harnesses we need to climb. "You sure? Maybe we should go get some ice cream and tacos."

"This now, that later?"

His beautiful smile shines brighter for me way up here.

I look up at the bridge while he's tying the harness around me, and it feels like it's miles into the sky. My breath gets caught in my throat, and I shake my head. "You know what, let's go get those tacos. I won't be able to attend art school if I'm dead."

He laughs and pulls me in for a kiss. "You're perfect," he tells me. "And I think I'm in love with you."

90

MILIANI

I'm camped in Papa's room, holding the crystal. Now that the balance has shifted back to a more normal equilibrium and Mom's etchings aren't in this room, it feels more magical than it has since before Papa died. If Jasmine is going to show me something, I figure it will happen here.

But nothing does.

My body is starting to adapt to the stiffness of Papa's floorboards when Mom walks in and says, "Come on. Let's go outside."

❨ ❨ ❨

There's a cool breeze, but I wrap Papa's tapestry around my shoulders and kneel beside her. She says a prayer in Tagalog, and we sit with him while the sky grows dark. "I took his space for granted," she says, "but in my mind, I talked with my father every day. Especially on the hard ones." She turns to me. "Just because you don't feel her spirit, doesn't mean she's not in heaven listening."

Mom's right. And maybe Jasmine intended for it to be this way. Maybe she didn't want me to find her space because she knew I'd be consumed with the energy and never let go. I close my eyes and talk to her. I want to say nice things, but I tell her how pissed I am. I tell her she should've never come looking for me. I needed space, but not this much space. Not forever. I tell her she ruined us. I tell her she left me. I tell her I'll never forgive her. I shudder from the pain. I sob. And then . . . then I tell her I love her, it'll be always, and her love, the way she loved, was enough for me. That I'm so sorry for leaving her feeling like it wasn't.

Memories of her and me move through my mind, spread through me and fill me up, and when I open my wet eyes, Mom's still right beside me. She stands, and I follow. She wraps her arm around me, points out a few stars in the sky, then leads me inside.

(((

Mom brings down blankets and pillows from the bedrooms because I told her I didn't want to sleep upstairs. She sits with me on the big couch. I watch her when she's deep into *Valentine* (probably trying to figure out why I find it any good, and not flinching at the parts I find terrifying). She's really here, laughing freely during chase scenes, smiling and rolling her eyes, reaching out to squeeze my hand when I don't speak for a while. Midsqueeze, a knock comes at the door, but she doesn't let go to answer it. She laces our fingers, fills me with so much warmth I feel my tears form.

But when the knock comes a second time, she leaves me sitting here wiping my face with the sleeve of my hoodie and wondering if there's a chance Auntie's at the door.

But instead, Inez yells, "Surprise, bitch," and she and Nat launch themselves at me.

They splay me out on the couch. Give me too many sloppy kisses.

We are a meld of hair and limbs and warm bodies.

I groan under the weight of them. "What are you doing here?"

"Your mom called." Inez lays her head against my outstretched arm. "Let us love you."

My heart stings; my eyes sting too. "It's going to be so hard to let her go," I say.

Inez touches the crystal as it dangles on my neck. "We know."

"But you're not alone," Natalie says, cupping my cheeks with her hands.

I nod, and then I cry. They cry too. We press our faces together. We talk. We laugh. I peek out from under Natalie's arm to see Mom heading up the stairs with a cup of tea. She turns when she feels my gaze. *Thank you*, I mouth. She smiles, and then she goes.

☾ ☾ ☾

We spend the night watching slasher flicks. *Scream 2* ends as the birds start to chirp outside the window, with my birds following from the kitchen. It's been a good night. So good I suddenly feel guilty Jas is not here. She'll never be here to share one of these nights with us again. But I think she'd want us to be happy. She'd want *me* to be happy. I tell my friends we should do the water ritual, and Nat heads to the kitchen for a bowl of water.

When we settle, I hold the bowl in my hands first and look inside. "Nat, I see you as an extremely successful photographer, but not too bougie for your friends. Jas will be proud to see it." I pause while she cries. "And you'll have too much great sex and go skydiving and snorkeling."

She shoves me and takes the bowl while we're all laughing. She looks into the water. "Inez, you'll find some damn joy that's yours to keep, which might mean finding a new church too." Inez smiles and nods. "And you'll give me back the sweater you borrowed last year."

"Shut up. It's my favorite sweater," Inez says, snatching the bowl so some water spills over the side. "Miliani, I see you discovering new species and even new magic. I see you beaming with light. Happiness all over you. Healing and free with us right at your side."

I choke on my cries. They both reach out to hold me. We listen to Petey and Octavia's sweet songs.

I wipe my tears and pick up the bowl again.

"And Jasmine," I say. "Our dearest Jas. I see you at peace, energy glowing and wild, wherever you are. Maybe taking peeks at us to make sure we're living a little recklessly." I inhale, exhale deep, try not to tremble. "When you do, you'll feel how much we all love you, and you'll know we will be thinking of you every single day, until we meet in the afterlife."

"We'll miss you," Natalie adds. "So, so much."

"Always," Inez says.

I twirl the water with a finger. For a moment, my entire body vibrates with feeling.

91

MILIANI

According to Inez, Senior Ditch Day isn't Senior Ditch Day because teachers are here. "It's a field trip," she says, playing with the grass near her feet. The three of us are sitting side by side with our knees up and pressed together.

"At least they didn't make us sit with them," says Nat.

Inez twists her body and shields her eyes from the sun while she looks at our teachers. They're all posted up on the large landing of the cement staircase that overlooks the park.

"Only because they're observing us from up there like we're in a fishbowl."

I laugh because it's true, but I'm happy we're here. Freshman year, we cleaned broken glass and picked up trash in this park as a school. Afterward, we planted some purple flowers. Being here in our last week of high school feels full circle. Besides, India Point Park in Providence is acres of green grass and old trees with roots that hold a long history here. Two rivers converge and create a beautiful view of the waterfront. People jog the paved walkway, and others sit in lawn chairs to soak up the sun. It's quiet, and peaceful.

Until the students from our school start yelling and acting wild.

A few feet away, Darleny, Jayson, and their friends set up a volleyball net, and Darleny catches me staring while she's unloading her bag. The obsidian dangles from her neck. She touches it and offers me something like a smile.

Inez crosses her legs and touches her own neck for a second. "Still think we should've kept it."

"Don't start," Natalie says.

There's a twinge in my chest. I wet my lips. "It belongs to Darleny."

Inez groans but doesn't disagree. I watch the way it glistens like a black diamond in the sun while Darleny chases her friends around. As she laughs, smiles, looks happy, the way Jasmine would want her to. It's where it should be. At least for now.

I think of taking Papa's tapestry out of my bag and laying on the grass with it, but I'm not ready to rest. Instead, I run my hand over Natalie's braids as she snaps pictures of some kids from our class trying to climb a tree.

"Let's do something," I say.

Inez makes a humming sound then, "Truth or dare? Double dare you to stick your bare foot in the river, Nat."

"You're playing this game all by yourself," Nat says, scrunching up her nose.

"After everything we've been through, you're still scared of the water?"

"We have no idea what's living in these murky Rhode Island waters. Especially now."

I watch as a small brown spider moves through the blades of

grass beneath our legs. My friends don't know it's there, and if I don't tell them they'll be better off. So will the spider.

While they go back and forth, I imagine Jasmine forcing us to our feet and vetoing our boring plans with ones of her own. I stand, the backs of my thighs prickling from the grass, and reach for the two of them.

"Let's go find a spot where we can use magic to mess with the teachers," I say.

They smile and take my hands, and we move toward the sun.

AUTHOR'S NOTE

Thinking back to writing this book while working overtime as a CNA, doing physically exhausting work, while praying the state wouldn't take my food stamps. I'd earned just enough to press against their income limit, but without the stamps, I wouldn't be able to afford to feed my family well. And I was depressed then. Sad as hell feeling like I lost the chance to chase my dream after accepting an offer from Michener Center for Writers—only to rescind my acceptance. It felt like an impossible journey after looking at the reality of what it meant to move across the country for an MFA as a single mom with two kids. I'd have no other financial or social support to ensure we'd be all right. So there I was, up until three in the morning writing this book, praying my children would forgive me for all the hours I typed away at the computer. But I didn't just do it for me, I did it for them too. They love art. They make it every day. Art is in them the way it was in me at their age, but I grew up the way a lot of people in my community probably did: below the poverty line, with the notion that if I didn't go into medicine—get a job that paid—I'd never be able to feed myself. Art wasn't for me back then. So, this book isn't just for myself, for my children; if anything here resonates, it is for *you* too. I poured my entire soul into it. The characters are fictional, but they are familiar to me.

They are people from fractured households with no generational wealth or trust funds to fall back on, having to grow up fast because the world will come for them, people from marginalized groups who feel something bittersweet each time they see someone like them on the cover of a book. I want these people, my people, to read about magic and find themselves in the pages.

Dear reader, I see you. Thank you for taking the time to see me too.

ACKNOWLEDGMENTS

Before any other human, I have to thank my mother, Angelique, for pouring love into me when I needed some to pour into this story. Thank you for teaching me to be strong. How to laugh with my whole soul and build relationships with my whole heart. I love you so much, Momma. Your baby, forever.

To my babies, my moon and sun. I'm not sure when I'll want you to read this book, but when this page finds you, please know that I wouldn't be an author if it wasn't for looking at the two of you and realizing I needed to follow my heart. To show you that you can follow yours too. Thank you for hugging me while my back ached from long days at the computer, kissing me and telling me your own stories to get me through. There will never be anyone or anything I love more. My'ah and Jada, you chase my dark away.

To Antonio, blood isn't the only way to be family. Thanks for being a proud father, the best grandfather, and someone we can depend on. We really love you!

To Nilson Abreu, you are a superhero whenever I need you to be and I'll love you forever for it. We make the best team for our kids. And when they are happy, we are better for it.

To my brothers Los, Jadin, and Troy for being so supportive and brainstorming with me tirelessly. Thank you for being my first friends and for giving me this love of sibling stories. I feel about you all the way Nat feels about Dev. Forever. You mean the world to me.

Thank you to my amazing nana Dolores who helped raise me, my dad Alex, my vovo Armanda, mother-in-law Juana Abreu, my aunties and titis, uncles, cousins, all six of my brothers, everyone in my ridiculously big family for the wild memories: good and bad, I come from them. They made me the person that wrote this story.

Jose Rivera. Dear Papa, thank you for walking me around Providence, teaching me to fish and garden and telling me stories. My childhood was filled with so much good that is in this book. Back then, I looked at you like you were magic and it is in everything that I do now. Mahal Kita. Your *full moon*, forever.

To my best friends of nineteen wild years: Kathy Reyes, my cousin Shy Lopez, and Jenny Ramirez. Those Kennedy Plaza walks were some of the best walks of my life. Mili, Inez, Nat, and Jas wouldn't be the girls they are without you. I wouldn't be the woman I have become. You are all my family. My squad. My four-some, and all the other corny things we've called our four-person friendship over the years. I love you bitches.

To Dania De La Cruz, who made her way to the afterlife early. Grief is hard and I learned it young. I think about you all the time. I love you. Till we meet again.

To Carlos Cruz Sr. and my auntie Debbie Collier. If I close my eyes and concentrate, I can almost hear you both telling the world you're proud of me. Thank you for pure love and for my life. Rest peacefully.

To Em North, my writing soulmate and friend, who has read this book three times!! There is no one who seems to get what I'm trying to say more than you do and I'll never forget it. I love you!

To emily m. danforth. Hi, friend. Thank you for seeing something in me years ago, for telling me publishing is a place I belong too. For writing with me, talking horror, and all the laughter.

Shirlene Obuobi, my little writing sis. Thank you for your love of *Deep*, for reminding me to be brave (especially when that imposter syndrome hits), and loving me through my madness the way I love you. "Prepare for trouble, make it double."

To Isha Abreu, ug, you've been so solid through this journey. I guess I love you a little bit and appreciate you a lot.

To my auntie Lolita Villanueva, Karla Alba, Kyle Kirrin, Kelly Cardenas, uncle Jose Rivera Jr., auntie Yolanda Rodrigo, Cris Rivera, Beryl Fisher, Belle Ellrich and other booksellers and bloggers, and anyone else who played a part in reading bits of this book, helping me with it, or hyping it up. Thank you all so very much. You're incredible and appreciated.

To my amazing agent, Jess Regel, who seems to know what my anxious brain is spiraling about before I even say it. Thank you for finding *DIP* a home & being on my team. You're a badass!

Thank you to my editor, Mark Podesta, for coming through to make *DIP* a better book. Your happy is infectious! To Tiff Liao for seeing something in this story, for teaching me so much, and for editing with love. To Christian Trimmer, Aurora Parlagreco, Cienna Smith, Alexei Esikoff, Ally Demeter, Cindy Kay, Gaby Salpeter, Brittany Pearlman, the editing and production team and everyone at Holt who helped bring this book into the world.

Thank you to Carrie Shipers. This book was only a baby, and I was feeling defeated by perfectionism when you said, "Fifty beautiful pages will only ever be fifty beautiful pages if you don't keep putting down words." It was probably one of the most important things I'll ever hear.

Special thanks to the incredibly talented authors who read and blurbed my book in its early stages: Kylie Lee Baker, Vanessa Len, Lyndall Clipstone, Romina Garber, Racquel Marie, Melissa Albert, Kalynn Bayron, Lillie Lainoff, Ryan Douglass, and Goldy Moldavsky.

Philip M Johnston. There will never be enough words. You know how I feel about you, the sun, and the existence of *Deep*. Thank you for mirroring me and connecting me with the parts of myself I avoided until I needed to write this book (and all the ones to come). *Always. All ways.*

Thank you to my younger self, for not giving up. Look at what we created. Look at our book baby. I'm so damn proud of you. My eyes are burning with tears as I type this. Please keep pushing through the hard times. It'll be worth it.

Most importantly, to God for all of this, and for loving me anyway.